The Power of Love

by

Ronny Whitman

Love is two hearts connected as one, a soul-to-soul

bond, gifted by God

Dedication

To those who encouraged and supported me in writing my first novel, especially Jonee, Thea, and Linda. Including Marteen, who I will never forget.

Introduction

This story, although based on actual places and historical names, everything in this story is fiction, of my own creation after visiting Dunham Massey Castle in 2013.

I wanted to show a different outlook of the times, that what if – the possibility, that a few felt the power of the universe – the spiritual connection of souls and land.

Prologue

It was weeks since Baroness Massey gave birth to her daughter she named Grace, and only a few weeks prior, Lady Davenport gave birth to her son and heir she named Robert.

With their firstborn, Baron Massey and Lord Davenport decided to form an unbreakable agreement to secure their place in northern England by marrying Robert and Grace after their seventeenth year of life, thus, merging both houses making them one. By doing this, it would increase their wealth and power within the lands of Cheshire and Manchester.

Baron Massey walked into his daughter's nursery, *my daughter*, he thought with disappointment. Yes, he wanted his firstborn to be a son, but when he looked at his daughter, all thoughts of a son disappeared. *His daughter, his Grace*, he thought, looking at his daughter. To see her takes his breath away, and for Baron Massey to feel this way about a daughter, surprised him, but a wonderful surprise.

To think of his daughter marrying Lord Davenport's son, *that scoundrel*, he thought, moving to stand in front of the window next to his daughter's cradle, and peering out the window to the forest beyond, *and he would be the one to have a son*, this thought fueled his growing anger. He looked down and found his hands curled into fists at the idea of wanting his firstborn to be a son, and it disturbed him more than he knew. A son would have solved their problems since his son would have been the one to marry Lord Davenport's daughter. Through their marriage, his son would become lord of Cheshire and Manchester after Lord Davenport's life ended.

This contract would have been in my favor, not his, he thought, shaking his head, *no, I cannot believe such a thing*. He turned back to look at his daughter asleep in her cradle, *nay, look at her, my beautiful daughter, how can I think of wanting a son?*

Grace lets out a cry, and he moved quickly to her cradle and when he looked down, she was asleep again.

He smiled, "My God, look at you, just the thought of this child…my daughter," sighing, "Brings me…" *You soften my heart*, he thought. "…My daughter, I love you with all my heart," he said, staring at his daughter with amazement, how this baby has weakened him, "And I am not an easy man to be weakened, but you, my daughter, you can easily bring me to my knees."

Grace's eyes fluttered as she tried to open them, and when she did, they were staring directly at him, and her mouth curved into a small grin at the corner of her mouth.

Baron Massey smiled, *ah, she knows her father,* he thought with a warm heart. With this, he knew he was done for; there was nothing his daughter could do that would anger him. There was nothing she would ask; he could never refuse. She had him, and he could not be more pleased.

Then, a terrible thought entered his mind —

Oh God, I look at this child, my daughter whom I love with all my heart.

"This baby lying here in her bed, why did I make such an agreement," shaking his head, feeling distressed, "And yet, how can I not? To make such a deal, with a man like Lord Davenport, for what? To rectify what our family lost all those years ago —"

Baron Massey turned away from his daughter unable to look at her and returned to the window, and he looked out and allowed his mind to recall the tale his father told him about his great, great uncle —

"My father's father felt his great uncle had so easily given up Dunham Massey Castle to a Booth when his daughter married into that family, after failing to bear an heir." Baron Massey turned back to his daughter, "Nay, this has to happen. I pray to you, God, you will protect my daughter from not only myself but from suffering the pain of an unloving marriage as Lord and Lady Davenport do," he said, then looked down at his daughter asleep in her cradle, he smiled and softly rubbed her tummy.

"When my Grace at age ten meets Robert, her future husband, she will take the time we give her to know the boy he will be, then the man he will become."

At this, Baron Massey's thoughts turned back a few days ago when he signed the contract with Lord Davenport regarding Grace and Robert's future after the priest performed their preliminary marriage that sealed the agreement.

***

They were alone with their daughter before the priest was to perform Robert and Grace's pre-marriage when Baron Massey voiced his doubts. "My love, our daughter is the answer to our prayers, and her marriage to Robert will return Dunham Massey to its rightful owner," Baroness Massey said, putting her hand softly on her husband's face with a soft caress, "To you my love, a Massey."

Baron Massey turned and kissed the palm of his wife's hand and said, "You are right my love," he looked at his wife's lovely face, her soft, smooth milky skin with high cheekbones and a slightly pointing chin, he smiled, *she hates this beautiful pointing chin.* Then looking at her eyes, they were large blue round eyes; at times, you could see a hint of green. "If we had a son…" he started to say, then closed his eyes feeling ashamed to what he was about to say.

Baroness Massey interrupted her husband, "Yes, my love, a son would have been a great blessing, but a daughter is double the blessing. She will give birth to a son, and with this son, he will be given ownership of Dunham Massey, thus keeping it with a Massey line. Yes, part of him will be a Davenport, but he will have all the power that comes with being a Davenport."

"Yes, my love, you are right," he said, then took his wife in his arms and kissed her.

It was decided, one month after Robert and Grace's birth, when the agreement was made, and the preliminary wedding was to be performed by a Catholic priest, and both parties were each other's witness with the priest being the witness over them all. Once both parties signed the agreement, there was no going back, and if any reason either party decided to break this agreement, then the one at fault would forfeit all their lands, wealth, and titles and be banished from the lands, never to return unless upon death. If either one refused, they would immediately be put to death; thus, an agreement no one dared break, and so the agreement said:

I, Baron John Hamon Massey the Second, on this twentieth day, in the fourth month of 1518, along with Lord John Davenport, agree to the merger of both houses. Through the marriage of Lord John Davenport's son, Robert John Davenport, to my daughter Grace Rachel Marie Massey in their seventeenth year of life, where at that time they will marry, bringing both families together merging them as one. In doing so, both will gain power, wealth, status, and land. To secure this agreement, in ensuring this agreement cannot be broken, a preliminary wedding is performed by a priest, Father Peter of the Catholic Roman Church of Cheshire, to one, Robert John Davenport, and to one, Grace Rachel Marie Massey, until the day they will marry in the house of God, therefore, binding and sealing this agreement.

In this agreement, Lord John Davenport will assist Baron John Hamon Massey the Second in regaining their ancestry home, Dunham Massey Castle, from the Booth family, to whom now occupy this castle. After a determined time, Dunham Massey Castle will be passed to the Davenport's family through a future descendant marriage.

If, for any reason, this marriage does not take place, regardless of reasons, the two parties in question proving to be at fault will forfeit their rights and relinquish their power, title, wealth, and land and will be banished from the land or face immediate death.

In signing this agreement, both parties agree to secrecy in maintaining their silence to the contents and reasons behind forming this agreement.

Baron John Hamon Massey the Second
Baroness Elizabeth Marie Massey
Lord John Davenport
Lady Mary Davenport
Father Peter of the Catholic Roman Church

***

Returning from his memory when the agreement was forged, Baron Massey looked down at his daughter and returned to his conversation he was having with God.

"I pray Robert and Grace will find the love and happiness her mother and I are blessed to have, and not one of obligation as Lord and Lady Davenport have. No matter how wrong I feel this is, it must be done, and this merger will unite us and make us stronger, thus allowing us the power to regain Dunham Massey from the Booths. To live on the land in this small manor," once again his anger swelled, "This is an insult to the Massey name," he yelled!

Grace started to cry, Baron Massey quickly softened his voice, "Ah child, I am sorry," he said as he picked up his daughter and gently put her over his shoulder, he began to bounce her while patting her on the back in his attempt to soothe her, "Shhhh my little one. I am sorry to upset you," he sighed, feeling ashamed that he allowed his anger to upset his daughter.

***

At Bramhall Manor, Lady Davenport was in the sitting room, holding her son while looking at his sleeping face. Every time she saw her son, she was amazed at the miracle given to her, someone for her to love, and someone who will love her in return.

Lord and Lady Davenport's marriage was arranged as most noble families were, but unlike Baron and Baroness Massey, she did not find love with her husband, nor he with her. Yes, she believed time would change that. Still, after a year of marriage, especially after given birth to their son and heir – which usually brought couples together, finally find love – this was not the case for Lord Davenport. He did not show her any affection, and the closest he's come to show happiness, possibly caring, was when he saw his son – his heir after she gave birth, fulfilling her duty as a wife, so long as their son survived and did his duty. To know this about her husband brook her heart, and when she thought about Baron and Baroness Massey, one of the lucky few arranged marriages to find love. When you look at them, there was no questioning how much in love they were.

So why can I not have love? Yes, he is a hard man, but I believe deep inside lies a soft man, a man I can love and a man who can love me, she thought with sadness.

Lady Davenport's eyes began to water, and a tear rolled down her face falling on her son's cheek. At the feel of her wet tears, her son opened his eyes and looked at her, and she quickly wiped away her tears, then looked at her son's big beautiful brown eyes as they stared up at her. She smiled, filled with so much love for this small child, her son.

"One day, my son, you will marry, and when you do, I pray you will find the love I did not find with your father. The thought of you marrying without finding love is too much for me to bear. I do not want you to live an unloved marriage as I do," she placed her hand on his cheek, "That you my love," she bent down and kissed her son on the forehead, "Will be all the love I shall ever need if I never find love with your father."

Lady Davenport heard a noise, and when she looked to see who it was, she saw her husband standing in the doorway, "My husband, come and look upon your son," she said with a smile.

In a harsh deep voice, "Do not turn our son into a girl," he said, walking over to his wife sitting in the rocking chair, "My son," placing his hand on his forehead, "Will grow to be a strong man like his father, as he will be Lord of this land one day."

"My husband, he will be the finest and strongest son in the land; after all, you are his father," she said, looking up at her husband, and was startled at what she saw – emotion, possibly even love in his eyes. Then as quickly as she saw this, it was gone, and she wondered, *was it possible he can love*, looking down at her son, *and it will be because of you, my son.*

"Take good care of my son. I must go out and make my rounds. As magistrate, I must ensure order is kept. On my way, I am going to stop and see Baron Massey."

"Please congratulate him and Baroness Massey on the birth of their daughter for me."

Lord Davenport growls, then he said, "I shall do as you request; I want to lay eyes on this daughter myself. I also need to work out the final details of Robert and Grace's betrothal with Baron Massey," he said, turning as he leaves the room.

Sighing, *I do not think he can ever love*, she thought with disappointment. She looked at her son, and all sadness disappeared, "You are enough for me, my love."

***

Baron Massey felt torn with his decision in signing the agreement with Lord Davenport, but his worry and anger may be for nothing if Grace and Robert did not live to become betrothed. *No, I cannot think of such a thing*, he thought. His heart hurts at the thought of losing his daughter; he's grown to love very much. He would kill any man who would harm her. Baron Massey felt his daughter was asleep again, and he placed her back in her cradle. *Oh, my precious child, what have I done*, he thought.

A part of him wanted to save his daughter from such a fate, but the other part – he knew must be done, "If not this little girl, it will be another."

Baron Massey has not shared his thoughts or feelings with his wife, he dares not, since she wanted this merger more than he did. This merger could return his ancestral estate, thus, the return of their status and power within the land to what it once was.

At the time of their marriage, Baroness Massey only agreed to marry him when he promised to fight to regain Dunham Massey – for a Massey to be Lord of Cheshire once again. For him to do this, he must align himself with the most feared and powerful man in the land, Lord Davenport.

Watching his daughter, he again prayed, "God, please protect my daughter and her future," leaning down to kiss his daughter on the forehead.

Baron Massey was unaware his wife was standing outside the nursery door listening to him talk to their daughter – expressing his love for her. For Baroness Massey to hear her husband speak of the love he has for their daughter, she smiled, feeling great joy of their incredible miracle —

Baron Massey walked over to the window and whispered, "God, why did I sign such an agreement?"

— until she heard her husband talk about regretting the signing of the agreement – when she heard this, she began to fear and worry, so she decided to make her presence known and put a stop to her husband's foolish talk. But then, something she heard stopped her —

With Baroness Massey's sharp hearing, she heard her husband question the signing of the agreement and begins to fear he wanted to back out of the agreement, an agreement she knew they could not back out of, she must make herself known. Baroness Massey attempted to enter the room to remind her husband of the terms of their agreement with Lord Davenport and why it must be honored, when she heard his next words.

"How can I not?"

When she heard this, she relaxed, then decided to leave her husband alone with their daughter.

Baron Massey's thoughts turned to his father's portrait hanging in the great room and remembered the stories his father told him about their famous relative, Hamon de Massey, in the way he gained Dunham Massey Castle.

***

As swords clashed, Masci and his men yelled, "Attack! Attack! Attack the Normans! Kill – Kill them all!"

And they did, they slaughtered every one of them, not leaving one alive to tell the tale. Once the slaughter – the blood bath was over, Masci and his men looked at the scene, admiring the carnage before them.

To see the carnage, Masci felt it was a lifetime before they defeated the Normans than the mere minutes it took. He turned away and started for their camp for much-needed rest when he heard horses approaching, in what sounded to be hundreds of horses riding fast in their direction. Unsure who it was, Masci and his men prepared themselves for another battle, but when the riders came into view, he saw the English flag with King William's coat of arms and was amazed to see the king himself leading his knights and soldiers. Masci turned to his men and immediately gave the order to stand down.

He lowered his sword and placed it back in the sheath and said, "Wait here, I'll ride out to meet the king."

Masci's men bowed and stepped aside. Then he noticed from his side one of his men was approaching bringing him his horse. Without delay, Masci grabbed the reigns and mounts on his horse, and he rode out to meet the king.

As King William, his knights, and soldiers were riding to join the fight they saw only moments ago from a nearby hillside, were amazed to see the carnage that lay before them, with bodies everywhere, leaving nothing for his knights and soldiers to fight. Then they heard a horse riding towards them, King William's knights quickly formed a shield to protect their king from harm, and when the man came into view, King William recognized him as the Frenchman Hamon de Masci and ordered his men to step aside.

Masci noticed the royal knight's position themselves in front of King William, so he slowed his approach and pulled his horse to a stop, not wanting King William's knights to think he was the enemy and kill him. As he was about to announce who he was, he noticed the knight's move away from the king, and Masci took this as a good sign; he kicked his horse and continued to move slowly not wanting to come across threatening just in case he was wrong.

Once he was a few feet from the king, he called out, "Your Grace," pulling his horse to a stop then bowed at the waist, waiting for the king to address him.

King William acknowledges Masci, "You…are you not the Frenchman Hamon de Masci?" King William asked.

"I am, Your Grace."

"Monsieur Masci, rise and come forward so I may look upon the face of the man responsible for this carnage," he said, waving his hand to encompass the slaughter behind Masci.

Hamon de Masci straightened before urging his horse to continue, stopping directly in front of the king, and when he looked at the king, he saw a sinister smile and said, "Yes, Your Grace, I did."

"Well, Monsieur Masci, you and your men slaughtered those filthy Normans, and it seems you did not leave one for my men," King William said in jest as he waved his arms to encompass his men behind him.

His men roared in disappointment.

Masci smiled, bowing to the king, "I am sorry Your Grace, my men were anxious to destroy these," turning back to look at the carnage, "Filthy Normans that were plaguing your lands," he said, spitting on the ground, then turned back to the king, "My men are strong and fierce, it was not a worthy battle, as it was over as quickly as it started. My men are willing to fight to the death, and we take no prisoners," Masci said with pride.

"Monsieur Masci, you and your men have done England proud. This battle at Beakhamstead is the final battle to end the war, thanks to you and your men, the war is won."

The king's knights and soldiers raised their arms and roared, cheering Masci and his men on their success in beating the Normans.

Masci turned to look at his men who were eagerly waiting for his return and raised his sword, and he waved it in the air letting his men know all was well. When his men saw this, they cheered in triumph.

Masci felt proud, he puffed out his chest, and sat even taller on his horse, then turned back to the king, "Your Grace, we only did what was expected of us."

"Monsieur Masci, remove the remains of these Norman scum, so their blood does not continue to spoil English soil, then take your men and rest. At the end of the fourth night, come to London, where a large celebration will be taking place, and there you will claim your reward."

Masci bowed at the waist and smiled, "As you wish Your Grace."

Without another word, King William, along with his knights and soldiers, turned their horse and began their long journey back to London.

When Masci returned to his men, he relayed the good news, another roar of cheers erupted, along with pats on the back.

"We will drink well this night and rest until the fourth night when we will head to London," he announced, and another round of cheers erupted.

***

When Masci and his men arrived at the king's castle in London, they received a hero's welcome and were treated like royalty. Masci's men were given bed chambers in the knight's quarters, while Masci was given a bed chamber in the royal wing of the castle, for he knew this was a great honor.

After changing into his best clothes, Masci headed down to the celebration. When he entered the grand ballroom full of people laughing and dancing, he noticed a precise path leading directly to the king, who was sitting on his throne at the end of the room.

The grand ballroom was an enormous room, with marble columns wrapped in greenery and white roses. The ceiling was also draped with greenery along with white and gold silk, and on each end of the room were long tables with a stuffed peacock in the center surrounded by an assortment of food ranging from, English, French, Spanish, and Italian, to satisfy the guest from these lands.

Upon entering the ballroom, the merriment and conversation came to a halt, and everyone turned and looked at him.

King William looked to see why the room abruptly went silent and saw it was his honored guest, Hamon de Masci, he smiled and raised his glass, "Ah, Monsieur Massey, come forward and stand before your king."

Masci nodded and preceded towards the king with everyone watching him, but not only watching him, they were also examining him, the women with lust in their eyes and the men, some with respect and others with suspicion. *Have they not seen a French warrior before?* Masci thought.

At first, this made him uncomfortable; he was not a man to draw attention to himself unless it was in battle or a good fight – he smiled a little. In this ballroom, to have so many eyes on him made him feel uncomfortable, but he must endure, so he put his shoulders back, puffed out his chest, and straighten to his full height of six feet four. At this, he heard the women say "Awww…" and whispered, "What a powerful warrior," as they giggled to each other.

He smiled, feeling proud and increased his stride; within moments he was standing in front of the king, Masci bowed waiting for his king to address him.

"Monsieur Massey, rise and look upon your king."

Masci rose as his king commanded, and when he did, he saw King William smiling at him.

King William looked at his people who gathered in front of him and raised his arms and said, "Behold, Monsieur Massey from Normandy France, who comes from a powerful and honorable noble family, Viscount William de la Fete of the Bellamy family. Monsieur Massey, along with his men, wiped out the remaining Normans at Berkhamsted, thus ending the war."

As the people applauded and cheered, Masci looked around to the people surrounding him. He saw the women looking at him with lust in their eyes, while the men – some he saw earlier that looked at him with suspicion, were cheering and praising him. This was when he first noticed his men for the first time.

King William put up his hand to hush his people, then waved for Masci's men to move forward before he addressed the good people of England.

"Now," directing his arm to Masci, "Monsieur Massey will say a few words."

When Masci heard this, he was not happy with the idea, but there was nothing for him to do, he could not say no to the king.

"The defeat at Berkhamsted could not have been possible without my men," Masci said, looking at each one of his men who had formed a circle around him. Masci's men consisted of Frenchmen, Englishmen, Irishmen, Scotsmen, and a few Spaniards.

"It was their bravery and strength that allowed me to accomplish such a defeat."

Masci's men yelled, "Nay, it was your leadership that allowed us to plough through those Norman bastards," spitting on the ground in disgust.

At this, the people cheered and yelled, "here-here!"

King William raised his hand to hush the people, and the room immediately went silent, waiting for their king to address them.

"Monsieur Massey, from this day forth, you shall be known as Baron Massey of Cheshire. With this title comes with numerous lands within the county of Cheshire, and with these lands, you will receive castles and manors, among them, including Chester Castle and Dunham Castle."

King William announced then handed Baron Masci his title and the deeds to the lands, castles, and manors.

Masci reached out and took the documents, and when he did, the people of England cheered and applauded to the new Baron of Cheshire.

With his title and deeds, Masci bowed to his king, then turned and took his leave, feeling on top of the world. After receiving congratulations and pats on the back from his men, he moved away, and when he was somewhat alone, he unrolled the document holding his title. When Masci did, he noticed an error; his surname was no longer Masci, it was changed to Massey – Baron Hamon de Massey of Cheshire. Baron Massey turned to look at the king, and when he did, he saw the king watching him with a sinister smile.

Ah, he did this on purpose, thus why he said my name wrong when he announced my new title, Masci thought. Masci – Massey shrugged his shoulders as the spelling of his name did not matter.

A few moments later, he felt the hairs on the back of his neck stand up, and when he turned around, he saw a broad bearded warrior of a man watching him.

After Baron Massey received his new title and land, Lord Davenport watched the man of honor, curious about the new Baron. He also received the title of lordship with lands, including Whelthrough, Henbury, and Woodford, in his role in helping defeat the Normans. If he was correct, his land borders Baron Massey's land in Cheshire, and decided it would be smart to befriend a man who held such prestige, honor, and power.

When he saw Baron Massey turn to face him, he approached the man, "Massey," he called, walking over to the man.

With a slight nod, Baron Massey acknowledged the man approaching him, "To who do I have the honor of addressing," he asked.

Bowing to the new Baron, Lord Davenport said, "I am Lord Orme de Davenport of Manchester."

Returning the bow, he said, "Ah, an Englishman with a French name," Baron Massey said in jest.

Lord Davenport smiled and said, "Yes, Baron Massey, my family originated from France, but we have been in England for many generations now, and I am afraid where we are from is lost to me now. My family comes from Morton, Cheshire, the place you just received from the king," he said with a little cynicism. "And you, My Lord, from your name and accent, you are a Frenchman?"

Baron Massey smiled, "Yes, I am from Normandy France, are you familiar with the place?"

"Yes, a little," he said, changing the subject, "Baron Massey, I hope you think right of me, I would like us to become allies. It seems our lands border each other, and with our friendship, we can become powerful allies, allowing us to rule over northern England."

Baron Massey smiled, *ah yes, our friendship can be a grand alliance*, he thought, then said, "Yes, I see your meaning, and I think it to be an excellent idea, I accept your friendship."

Baron Massey puts out his arm, and Lord Davenport grabbed it in a warrior hold sealing their newfound friendship, and when they saw a server passing by, they grabbed a drink and said, "Let us drink to our new friendship," Lord Davenport said, raising his glass in the air.

Baron Massey also raised his glass, "To friendship," and then they drank. He then said, "Lord Davenport — " Well, he attempted to speak but Baron Massey stopped him.

Lord Davenport put his hand up to stop Baron Massey, "Please, call me Orme, since we are to be friends and allies."

Baron Massey nodded in agreement.

Lord Davenport asked, "Baron Massey, are you married?"

Baron Massey smiled, "Call me, Hamon, please."

Lord Davenport nodded in agreement.

"No, but I think the king," looking to where the king was sitting, "Has ideas for me to marry a lady of his choosing, an English Lady," Baron Massey said, raising his eyebrows with a sinister smile.

Lord Davenport laughed, "Ah, yes, I think he wishes the same for me, but I am already betrothed to a fine English lady, and once I have settled my lands, we will marry."

"I see," he said, smiling. "Well, for me, it will depend on the lady the king introduces me to, as I prefer a French woman. Now, there is nothing wrong with English women, but…" with his sinister smile and in a whisper, "French women are very passionate women, no," he said with a wink.

Lord Davenport laughed and slapped Baron Massey on the back, then they both laughed together.

After both men gained control of themselves, Baron Massey continued, "So yes, I would prefer a French woman, but if the king can provide me with the right woman…" Massey winked again, raising his eyebrows, "Then I will gladly marry her."

Again, both men laughed and patted each other on the back, then grabbed another drink from a passing tray, celebrating their titles, lands, and friendship.

***

Baron Massey was heading out of London with his men feeling enormously proud of what he and his men had accomplished. This was what he wished for when he left France for England to join the fight against the Normans. Now he rides, ready to begin his new duty as the new Baron of Cheshire.

Once Baron Massey arrived in Cheshire, he took ownership of his lands, castles, manors, and homesteads. Massey gave his highest-ranking men the larger manors and castles, and his other men were allowed to pick from what was left, unless otherwise arranged by Baron Massey.

Baron Massey had no issues in evicting those who were already on his land, his men, however, chose to keep the tenants to work the land, and if their homes were in good condition, the tenants were instructed to move to another location on the land and build a new home.

For himself, Baron Massey took possession of Dunham Castle, then later renamed it, Dunham Massey Castle. Lord Davenport and Baron Massey, along with their families remained friends for several generations, until a misunderstanding in the sharing of their lands destroyed their friendship, to one of severe hatred.

***

The reason for this, even to this day, is lost, Baron Massey thought as he returned to the present. *My father could never tell me what caused the rift between our two families; it was something never discussed. Forbidden.*

"From what Lord Davenport told me, he too did not know the reason for the end of their friendship." He looked down at his daughter, "What could have happened? Did I make a mistake," he shook his head, "Nay, this must be done, it was my father's last wish on his death bed for me to regain Dunham Massey from the Booths," he said looking at his daughter, "My daughter, I am sorry, I pray you and Robert will find love as your mother and I did."

Baron Massey kissed his daughter on the forehead, then he turned and walked out of the room.

Chapter One

It was the beginning of summer in 1526, ten years after the agreement between Lord Davenport and Baron Massey was forged. Grace turned out to be a beautiful and proper young lady, always doing what was required and expected of her. She was a quiet and timid girl, although soft spoken, she spoke with absolute and elegant decorum, a very accomplished young lady in reading, writing, and playing the piano. Grace showed promise in becoming the perfect future bride for Robert Davenport, Lord and Lady Davenport's son.

Grace was lucky to have a sister born a year after her, and they formed a close sisterly bond – a perfect friendship two sisters had.

Elizabeth Anne Massey was born on the fifteenth day, in the twelfth month of 1519. Unlike her sister Grace, due to the Massey French bloodline, Elizabeth was born with beautiful, lightly tanned skin and large almond shaped golden-brown eyes, who proved to be nothing like her sister.

As Grace was quiet and timid, Elizabeth was the opposite; she was loud and outgoing; unlike a girl of nobility should be. She was her own individual that by no means listened to anyone, doing what she enjoyed, in this, she drove her father and mother mad. To no one's understanding, Elizabeth had grown to love the outdoors and spent most of her time roaming the vast estate and surrounding forest of Dunham Massey. At an early age, it was discovered Elizabeth had great talent, not in enjoying a musical instrument or having the rational of voice but the power to draw, developing nature with essentially extraordinary lifelike scenes – capturing the accurate essence of nature. Elizabeth could easily lose track of time for hours as she sat outdoors, drawing the various trees, flowers, and at times, the small animals of the forest. It was astounding in the way she brought them to life.

Although her family knew of her artistic gifts, they knew not to exaggerate it as Elizabeth preferred solitude versus attention. They learned this when her family brought a famous artist Albrecht Dürer to Dunham Massey to determine her skills as an artist, and if he found potential, he was to guide her in becoming one of the greatest woman artists of their time.

Baron and Baroness Massey met Albrecht Dürer on their visit to Italy. They enjoyed the man and his art, hence, offered him an open invitation to visit them at Dunham Massey when he was next in England.

When Albrecht Dürer met with Elizabeth, she was shy and seemed uncomfortable with him in her presence. So, he decided, before he agreed to teach Elizabeth, he needed to see her talent. When he asked Elizabeth to draw something for him, he saw no great talent, just a girl who drew as any girl would draw; flowers, vases, nothing special. Herr Dürer told Baron and Baroness Massey this, but they insisted Elizabeth has excellent talent and asked him to be patient and give her a chance to know him, and then, they were sure he would see what they already knew. Against his better judgment, he agreed to continue guiding Elizabeth.

The time Herr Dürer spent with Elizabeth, he became aware of her quiet nature, how she only performed when she was alone. He only learned this when Elizabeth failed to show up at their arranged meeting time. When he sought her out, he learned from her sister that Elizabeth was in the forest drawing. So, Herr Dürer went in search of Elizabeth and found her only a short distance away from the manor, just inside the forest tree line. He quietly approached where Elizabeth was sitting cross legged on the ground, drawing the forest trees and flowers around her. He watched from a distance, and what he saw shocked him, her drawing was exquisite. The details of the trees, flowers, and forest floor were perfection. Elizabeth was bringing the forest to life on paper. There was no doubt, Elizabeth indeed had a great talent.

After he watched for a short time, Herr Dürer made his presence known. "Ahem," clearing his throat.

Elizabeth was startled when she heard the noise and dropped her pad and chalk, then turned to see who was behind her. "Herr Dürer, you frighten me."

"Forgive me, My Lady," he said, bowing to her.

She picked up her pad and chalk. "There is nothing to forgive; you just startled me. What brings you here," she asked?

Herr Dürer raised an eye at her question. "My Lady, it is you that brings me here when you failed to show up at our arranged meeting time."

Elizabeth gathered her pad and chalk and put them in her pouch, then stood and brushed off the dirt from her gown.

"Oh, Herr Dürer, I am sorry. I came out this morning and lost track of time. Do you wish to meet now?"

"My Lady, may I see your drawing please?"

Elizabeth hesitated, but then pulled out her pad and handed it to Herr Dürer.

Herr Dürer took the pad from her, and when he looked at her drawings, he was astounded. There were several pages of drawing ranging from trees, flowers, rabbits, birds, and wolves. They were truly magnificent. So lifelike, her talent nearly matched his own.

"Elizabeth, you have great talent. Why did you not draw like this during our time together?"

Elizabeth felt embarrassed, and she said, "I do not know. I guess…I find it difficult to draw when I am being watched. It is easier when I am alone."

Herr Dürer was still admiring her talent, and without looking at her, he said, "I understand My Lady. I have known other artists who feel as you do. I will talk to your mother and father and let them know they should not pressure you to perform in front of people; you will choose when you are ready."

Elizabeth smiled, "Thank you, Herr Dürer, I am very grateful."

Albrecht Dürer found a kinship in Elizabeth. She reminded him of the boy he once was when he started drawing. He decided he always wanted to remember Elizabeth as she was, so he asked Elizabeth if she would allow him to paint a portrait of her and was pleased when she agreed. Her painting was one of innocence, a child giving thanks with her hair hanging down over her shoulders.

Later that evening, after dinner, Herr Dürer informed Baron and Baroness Massey what he learned about Elizabeth's talent and encouraged them to let her be, and they are not to mention her artwork; her talent was best left alone. To allow her to come out when she was ready.

***

Although Elizabeth and Grace were so different, they were the best of friends. They loved each other very much and spent most of their time together, which caused their mother and father to worry that Elizabeth's wild behavior would rub off on Grace. To their delight, Grace remained the beautiful, quiet, and respectable young lady they wished her to be.

Baroness Massey had given up hope of ever bearing an heir, until five years after giving birth to Elizabeth, she gave birth to a son and heir, who Baron Massey named John Hamon Massey the Third, in remembrance of their heroic ancestor's Hamon de Massey, as he was named.

John was born during the summer on the twentieth day, in the sixth month of 1524. He was a big and healthy boy with dark brown hair, round dark brown eyes, and like his sister Elizabeth, he had lightly tanned skin. He was the son that any father would be proud to have, a perfect likeness to his father. Baron and Baroness Massey were the happiest and proudest parents to have finally given birth to a son and heir.

John was no timid boy; he grew to be a wild, boisterous and an outgoing child just like his sister Elizabeth. However, with John being the only son and heir to the Massey fortune, there was nothing he could do wrong. John did what he liked; a spoiled boy getting anything and everything he wanted. Although Grace and Elizabeth loved and adored their little brother, he proved to be a great annoyance during the times they help to care for him, although, even with this, they love their brother very much.

***

When the time came to introduce Robert and Grace to each other and reveal only a portion of the agreement, Baron Massey sent for Grace to come to his study.

Grace was in her chamber, reading her book when there was a knock at the door.

"Enter," she called.

When the door opened, it was her handmaid, she curtsied and said, "My Lady, your father requires your presence in his study immediately."

Still reading her book and without looking up Grace replied, "I will go as soon as I finish this page."

As the maid was straightening Grace's room she said, "Nay child, your father needs you now."

Grace rolled her eyes and marked her page, and without delay, she headed to her father's study. On her way there, she wondered what was so important for her father to summon her with such urgency.

From the moment Grace was born, Baron Massey took a special interest in his daughter. It was not because of her intended marriage to Lord Davenport's son, no, there was something different, a special bond with his daughter, one he could not explain. When Elizabeth was born, he thought the bond he had with Grace would be the same, but it was not, and no one was more surprised than himself. Grace was his world, even after his wife bore him a son and heir. There was nothing he would not do for his daughter Grace.

When Grace arrived at the entrance to her father's study, she found the door was open and her father sitting behind his desk with her mother by his side. Her father's desk sits in front of the window facing the door, it was not a large window, but it was big enough for the daylight to fill the room with its light. Baron Massey's desk was a thick and solid desk made from the strongest cherry oak in France; it was created precisely to fit his needs. The front paneling has square molding, and somewhere, only known to her father, was a secret compartment. Although her father's study was a small room comparable to their cottage, for her father, it fit his needs, and even with its small space, it appeared to be spacious and comfortable.

To see her father and mother together, she wondered, *what could it be that requires both mother and father?*

When Grace entered her father's study, she immediately looked to the portrait of their ancestor who acquired Dunham Massey, Hamon de Massey, as she has always done. It hangs on the right wall, just above the bookshelves with an assortment of English books, along with books from France and Italy. To the left of the room was an oval French rug, and resting on the rug was a dark red two-seat chair with two large wooden chairs covered in French royal blue fabric. It was odd though; the chairs were usually situated in front of her father's desk, *no matter*, she thought. To her surprise, sitting on the chairs was a man and a woman she did not recognize, and on the two-seat chair was a boy about her age.

"Father, you wanted to see me," Grace asked?

When Baron Massey saw his daughter, he smiled, then stood and walked around his desk to greet his daughter. He took her hand and said, "Ah, my dear, yes, come in and meet Lord and Lady Davenport, along with their son and heir Lord Robert Davenport."

Grace greeted Lord and Lady Davenport and their son with a curtsey, "I am pleased to meet you," Grace said.

Grace did not understand who those people were, or why she was required to be there, and was curious as to why these people were in her father's study and not in the drawing room where her mother and father usually received their guests.

Elizabeth shrugged her shoulders; the matter was no concern of hers. And then, she felt it was odd; *Father does not like having so many people in his study*, she thought. He considered this his own private space, and the only time her father had people in his study was when he was doing business. Then it dawned on her, *of course, these people are leaving, otherwise, why would he summon me to his study.*

As Baron Massey guided his daughter to where the Davenport's were sitting, she noticed the table in front of the two-seat chair; there was a tray full of pastries and fruits with an open bottle of wine.

Lord and Lady Davenport with their son, stood when Grace approached, they bowed and curtsied as she did to them.

"My dear, please have a seat next to Lord Robert," Baron Massey said as he guided his daughter to the seat next to Robert. "Your mother and I, along with Lord and Lady Davenport, have something to speak to you about that involve yours and Robert's future."

Grace took her seat and looked at Robert and he at her. Grace became suspicious of the reason she was sitting on the chair next to Robert that was made for two. Then Grace looked at her father with a raised eyebrow in question; then, she turned back to look at Robert.

Robert was a thin boy with dark hair and brown eyes, and he seemed to be as suspicious as she was. It was clear, they both had questions about the reasons they were there and to what future her father was referring to.

"Both of you have reached your tenth year of life, and the time has come to inform you of the agreement Lord Davenport, and I forged at the time of your birth, an alliance forged between both our families that you," Baron Massey said, motioning his hand to his daughter, "My dear daughter, you will marry Robert Davenport."

Grace and Robert looked at each other with surprise, as this was the first, they heard of this.

Baron Massey turned to look at Robert, "When you turn seventeen, you will marry, merging both our families together as one. In doing so, it will strengthen our wealth and power within the land, and Lord Davenport has graciously agreed to assist me in regaining Dunham Massey Castle from the Booths."

Baron Massey looked at Lord Davenport, who nodded in agreement, then he continued, "We agreed when you," looking at Grace and Robert, "Turn ten, we would bring our families together to allow you and Robert to meet and be given time to get to know one another. This will begin in seven days hence and will continue until after your seventeenth year of life when you will marry. We decided to rotate between Bramhall Manor and Dunham Massey," he said, turning to his daughter, "We want this for you, to allow you a chance to get to know each other before you marry, an opportunity neither one of us had before we married. We want you to grow to like each other, and hope, with this time given to you, you will come to love each other.

As you know, your mother and I did not have such an opportunity. Still, after time, your mother and I grew to love each other very much," Baron Massey said. He turned to look at his wife and smiled. "Unlike Lord and Lady Davenport," he said, turning to look at Lord and Lady Davenport, feeling a bit of sadness for their situation.

To hear Baron Massey's words, Lady Davenport adverted her eyes; she does not want Baron Massey to see how much his words hurt her. She felt great sorrow in not finding the love Baron and Baroness Massey had.

"We hope with the time given, you will form a bond with each other, and if this goes well, you will find love before you marry. What we offer you is rare, something not normally done. So, my dear daughter," he takes her hand, "And Robert," taking his hand, "Take this time we give you," then places Robert's hand on top of Grace's, "And get to know each other. Build a friendship, a bond, and if all goes well, you will grow to love each other," Baron Massey said, looking at Grace with love, "As your mother and I did."

Baron Massey looked at his wife, "Your mother and I did not know each other, nor did we like each other. In time, I won your mother over, and we came to love each other very much," he turned back to Grace and Robert, "As I am sure you and Robert will," he said, then turned to Lord Davenport, "Our first gathering will be at Lord Davenport's estate at Bramhall Manor in Manchester, and the following seven days will be here at Dunham Massey Castle. I have already made arrangements with Lord Booth to utilize Dunham Massey Castle when the Davenports are here," Baron Massey said.

He left his daughter with Robert and moves to stand next to his wife. Baron Massey took his wife's hand in his and looked at her, and she at him, both filled with love and happiness. He did this to remind his daughter that an arranged marriage can find love and happiness. Then Baron and Baroness Massey turned to Lord and Lady Davenport, and without words, acknowledged the beginning of a magnificent merger.

Baron and Baroness Massey, along with Lord and Lady Davenport, turned their attention back to Grace and Robert. At this, Grace and Robert looked at each other, then back to their mother and father and nodded in understanding.

For Lady Davenport to see Baron Massey take his wife's hand in his and look at her with so much love, saddened her heart. To see this was a reminder that she and Lord Davenport never came to love each other.

Lady Davenport turned to look at her husband, *if he were to look at me as Baron Massey looks at his wife, and she at him, no one could doubt how much in love they are,* Lady Davenport thought, softly sighing.

In the years during Lord and Lady Davenport's marriage, and after giving birth to their children, neither one of them had grown to love each other. Lady Davenport desperately wanted to love her husband, and for him to love her, but he had proven to be too hard of a man. Instead of love, they came to an understanding; she would do her duty as his wife and as Lady Davenport, by giving him his heir.

She turned to look at her son, and prayed, *I pray Robert will find love with Grace, I never found with my husband,* she thought, then returned her attention to the matter at hand as Baron Massey was saying —

"Now, let us toast to our newfound happiness and soon to be family," he said, and everyone raised their glasses in the air then drank to their future.

After the celebrations were over, Grace was given leave to return to her chambers, and on her way back, she thought about what just happened, as she felt frustrated and upset.

I am only ten. How am I to be expected to do what they ask of me? Why has this been put upon me and not Elizabeth? Then, the little voice in her head said, *you know why? You are the firstborn and the eldest daughter.* At this thought, Grace rolled her eyes.

When Grace arrived at her chamber and opened the door, she found Elizabeth sitting on her bed, waiting anxiously for her return.

When Elizabeth went to Grace's chamber to visit her sister, Grace's maid told her she was summoned by their father, and Elizabeth has been desperately waiting for Grace to return, wanting to learn what happened.

"Grace, finally," Elizabeth said, exacerbated, "Come, my dear sister," patting the bed next to her, "Sit next to me and tell me why father summoned you."

At first, Grace only smiled at Elizabeth, and then after a few moments, she walked over and sat next to her sister and told her what happened.

Elizabeth was stunned, "Oh...Grace, how do you feel about this?" she said with sadness.

"Elizabeth, what am I to do? Everything was arranged when Robert and I were born," shaking her head, "No, there is nothing I can do. I am trapped," she said, flabbergasted.

Grace was disturbed at the idea of being betrothed to another at her young age. She looked down at her hands that were resting on her lap, wondering how she was going to get out of what her mother and father were expecting of her.

Seeing the concern on her sister's face, Elizabeth said, "No, I suppose there is nothing you can do." Then with sudden excitement, as she bounced up and down on the bed she said in a loud voice, practically yelling at her sister, she asked, "Tell me! What is Robert like? Is he handsome," grabbing her sister's hand as she smiled?

Grace looked at Elizabeth, annoyed on how excited Elizabeth was about her situation, "Elizabeth! Be serious! This is not something to be happy about!" exhaling, she said in a firm, loud voice.

When Elizabeth heard how angry Grace was, she immediately changed her tone to a more serious one and put her hand on Grace's arm, "I am sorry, Grace," she said, but then with curiosity, "Tell me, sister, what does this Robert look like? He cannot be that bad."

Grace allowed herself to relax a little, then said in a calmer voice, "Very well. I cannot say if he is a handsome boy, but he does have a nice, friendly, and kind face with dark brown hair and brown eyes. He is a bit taller than me, and he is very thin. I guess you can say he is a fine-looking boy, as you will soon find out," Grace said with a smile.

Elizabeth looked at Grace, surprised at her sudden change in attitude, and asked, "What…what do you mean, Grace?"

Grace laughed, having pulled one over on her sister. "Well, my dear sister, father, and Lord Davenport wants Robert and I to spend time together, so they arranged for us to get to know each other in hopes we will form a bond and or even love," she said, cringing at the thought.

There was no way she was ready for this, nor did she believe she would ever be.

"We are to spend time on the sixth and seventh day of the week, and our first gathering will be at Bramhall Manor in seven days hence, which is the beginning of many others to come. We will switch time between Bramhall Manor and Dunham Massey Castle. Father has already arranged this with Lord Booth."

Elizabeth was excited to hear this, more so than Grace was. "Oh, Grace, how wonderful! I cannot wait to meet your betrothed, your future husband," Elizabeth said with mockery, giving Grace a light smack on her leg. "I will be sure to give you my opinion of this Robert Davenport, this boy who is to marry my sister," she said, laughing.

Grace rubbed her leg and looked at her sister, annoyed with her excitement. Although she was annoyed, she could never be angry with her sister. Elizabeth was her best friend, and she would always love her.

With Elizabeth, I know I can get through this. I am sure she will find ways to make me laugh at my situation, she thought.

Chapter Two

Lady Davenport had the manor in an uproar preparing for the Massey's first official visit – everything had to be perfect.

After giving birth to Robert, Lord and Lady Davenport were blessed with three more children; two additional sons and a daughter. Their second son Edward was born on the twenty-fifth day, in the seventh month of 1519 with slightly tanned skin that he received from his father's French bloodline, and had dark brown hair and large brown eyes.

Early on, it showed Edward's body had a natural growth of muscles; it was clear he would grow into a handsome young man. Some even said he was the spitting image of his father, not only in looks but in comportment as well.

With Edward's young age, he already attracted the girls within the land and the daughters of the servants.

Edward and Robert were so different; Robert was a kind and gentle boy, where Edward was wicked and cruel, always causing mischief when he could, driving his nursemaid's mad.

Two years following Edward's birth, Lord and Lady Davenport welcomed their third child, a daughter, who they named Rachel Louise Davenport. She was born on the first day, in the first month, of 1521 with fair skin, curly blond hair, and sky-blue eyes, she was a real beauty.

Early in her young life, Rachel showed to be an extraordinarily brilliant and talented young lady, and for those who had the pleasure of hearing her, said Grace had the voice of an angel.

Rachel loved music and played the piano and the harpsichord magnificently, and when she was not making music, Rachel loved to read but had little interest in art. It seemed there was nothing Rachel couldn't do, a daughter, any mother and father were proud to have.

Two years after Rachel's birth, Lady Davenport gave birth to her final child, another son, who they named Daniel. He was born on the fifth day, of the second month, in 1523, Daniel, much like his sister, was born with fair skin, curly blond hair, and large, beautiful hazel eyes.

Although Lady Davenport loved all her children the same, Daniel was her baby and her favorite, he was adored by everyone. He was nothing like his brothers; he was not wild, nor was he timid. He enjoyed whatever his brothers enjoyed and followed them like a lost puppy. Although Robert did not mind, Edward would always voice his irritation to Daniel; with this, it made Robert his protector.

***

When the day came for their family's first gathering at Bramhall Manor, everyone was excited except for Grace. For her, it was too soon.

When their carriage arrived at the outer edge of Bramhall Manor Estate, Elizabeth was amazed at how enormous the Davenport estate was. There were trees as far as the eyes could see in every direction she looked.

Bramhall Manor was in the center of a grand estate, with only one road in or out, covered with vast oak trees with several boughs stretched across the road forming a tunnel. Once they passed the row of oak trees, they came to a large opening covered with grass and patches of flowers of all types and colors, with a small pond in the distance.

"Oh, how grand their estate is," Elizabeth said with astonishment.

Elizabeth looked from window to window, trying to take in as much as she could before their carriage reached the manor.

"There is so much to explore," she said in awe. "Just think," turning her attention back to Grace, "One day you will be Lady of all this," Elizabeth said, opening her arms wide to encompass the vast estate.

Elizabeth was extremely impressed with Bramhall Manor and was itching to explore everything she could.

For Grace, though, all she could do was stare at her sister with irritation.

For Baron and Baroness Massey, they looked at each other and smiled as they felt blessed and pleased with the arrangement they formed with Lord Davenport.

Baron Massey was determined to make this work, and finally, after all these years, regain Dunham Massey and return it to its rightful place.

Owned by a Massey, as it was always meant to be, he thought.

Baron Massey felt incredibly pleased with himself, excited with what the future held for him. He reached for his wife and pulled her into his arms and kissed her long and hard.

However, their kissing was not welcomed by their children.

"Father, please? You should not do such things in front of your children," Elizabeth said with disgust.

John snickered, finding it amusing.

When Baron Massey ended his kiss with his beautiful wife, he looked over at Elizabeth and smiled.

Elizabeth rolled her eyes and returned her attention to the beautiful landscape.

Grace, however, did not seem to notice; she was too busy staring out the window as they approached her doom, Bramhall Manor, wishing she were back home.

Elizabeth turned to her sister, "Grace, I hope the Davenports will allow me to explore their estate and the forest surrounding it."

To listen to her sister carry on, annoyed Grace. She never understood Elizabeth's love for the outdoors, and she made her feelings known.

"You and your love for the outdoors…honestly Elizabeth, enough is enough! How can you not find the outdoors disgusting," winkling her nose in disgust, "It is full of those filthy crawly and horrid creatures!"

Elizabeth turned to her sister and laughed at Grace's irritation.

When the Massey's carriage arrived at the manor and came to a stop, they were relieved to be able to finally abscond from the carriage after riding half the day on a long and bumpy road – their bottoms were sore and were pleased their journey was finally over.

Anxious to leave the carriage, but they waited patiently, and when the carriage doors were opened, they gracefully stepped out of the carriage.

Baron Massey, as the head and master of the family, stepped out first, followed by his wife, then Grace, Elizabeth, and finally, little John. However, little John refused to leave and held up in the corner of the seat, which irritated Elizabeth.

No matter how hard she pulled on his hand, he refused to move.

When Baron Massey saw the difficulty Elizabeth was having with John, he decided to intervene.

In a loud and firm voice, "John, do as your sister ask, and step out of the carriage now."

With reluctance, John did as his father said.

With everyone finally out of the carriage, they were greeted by a tall thin and plain looking man of about forty.

"Welcome, My Lord," he said as he bowed, then stepped back into the manor, where he stood next to a large oval French table in the center of the foyer.

Standing at his side was a short, stout grey-haired older woman, who at the wave of the older man's hand, together approached the Massey's.

As the old man approached Baron Massey, he bowed and said, "Welcome Baron and Baroness Massey, Mistress Grace, Mistress Elizabeth, and Master John. I am George. Please allow me to take your cloaks and gloves."

Baron and Baroness Massey, Grace, Elizabeth, and John handed George their cloaks and gloves.

"Lord and Lady Davenport are waiting for you in the great room," he said, waving to the old woman, "This is Mave, she will show you the way." He bowed again, then stepped away.

Mave curtsied and said, "Follow me, My Lord and My Lady."

As the Massey's walked towards the great room, they were impressed by the size of the home and the portraits that were hanging on the walls of families from the past.

"It's the room straight ahead," Mave said, motioning to the girl standing at the side just behind her. "This is Mary, one of the housemaids."

Mary approached Baroness Massey with her head down and curtsied.

"Mary will provide for you, My Lady, Lady Grace, and Lady Elizabeth with anything you need during your stay at Bramhall Manor."

Mary nodded in agreement and curtsied again.

Baroness Massey looked at the girl, who was a small thin think of about thirteen, she looked like such a frail child.

"Thank you, Mave, we did bring our lady maids with us, Mary may assist them."

"Of course, My Lady," Mave said, as she motioned for Mary to go out to the carriage and assist the ladies' maids.

Upon Baron and Baroness Massey entering the great room, Lord and Lady Davenport, along with their children, were standing waiting to greet them.

"Welcome," said Lord Davenport, "Allow me to introduce you to my wife Lady Davenport," she curtsied, "Our firstborn son and heir, Lord Robert," he bowed, "Our second-born son, Master Edward," who snickered as he bowed, and Lord Davenport gave him a stern look. "Our lovely daughter, Lady Rachel," she curtsied, "And finally, our youngest son, Master Daniel," he said with humor.

Daniel smiled with amusement as he bowed to his father's jest.

The Massey's bowed and curtsied as they were introduced to the Davenports. In turn, Baron Massey introduced his family.

"Thank you, Lord Davenport, we are honored and delighted to be here," he said, then turned to introduce his family.

"Please allow me to introduce you to my wife Baroness Massey, our first-born daughter, Lady Grace, our second daughter, Mistress Elizabeth, and finally," he smiled, filled with joy, "Our one and only son, Lord John Hamon Massey the Third, " he said with pride as he puffed out his chest, in finally producing an heir.

Turning to Grace, Lord Davenport said, "Grace, please take your place next to Robert," then he looked at Robert, "Robert, take your betrothed outdoors," he said as he turned back to Baron Massey.

Lady Davenport smiled as she watched Robert and Grace, then turned and said to Baron and Baroness Massey, "We had our staff prepare a wonderful outdoor lunch for Robert and Grace, as it is such a wonderful day."

"Robert, once you finished lunch, show Grace around the estate," said Lord Davenport. "This is your time to become acquainted with one another. Take advantage of this time together and use it wisely."

Robert placed Grace's arm in the crook of his and said, "Yes, father," as he guided Grace to the French doors at the end of the room that leads to a vast and beautiful garden with a view of one of the many ponds on the estate.

Grace was feeling nervous, so she pulled Robert's arm to stop him before they reached the doors.

"Robert," she said, looking back at her sister, "Will you mind if my sister Elizabeth joins us?"

Grace could not do this without the support of her

sister, not to mention, she needs Elizabeth to put her plan in motion.

Robert looked back at Elizabeth and motioned for her to join them.

Just as Elizabeth was about to move to join her sister and Robert, she hesitated, not sure if it was proper, so she looked at her mother and father seeking their permission.

Baron Massey looked at Elizabeth and then at Grace; it was clear Grace was afraid and he knew how close she was with Elizabeth. Baron Massey turned back to Elizabeth and nodded, giving her permission to join Grace and Robert.

Grace looked at her father and smiled with gratitude, relieved that Elizabeth was by her side, and together they walked out the French doors.

When Elizabeth stepped outdoors, she gasped; it was breathtaking, with the large full trees, bushes, and flowers of all colors; she was admiring everything as she followed Robert to the picnic area, which was only a few paces from the small pond. In the pond were lily leaves, a few large rocks at the edges, and white geese swimming in the pond.

Perfect, Elizabeth thought.

As they approached the large blanket that was practically covered with a vast amount of food, Elizabeth and Grace, with wide eyes, gasped at the amount of food there was. There was enough food to feed the whole kingdom.

"Lord Robert —"

Robert interrupted Grace, "Grace, we are betrothed. Please call me Robert."

Grace smiled, "As you wish, my lor…Robert."

Grace returned her attention to the array of food, "It will be impossible for us to eat all this food, Robert."

Robert laughed, "No, of course not, but it looks impressive, does it not?"

Grace and Elizabeth laughed, "Yes, very," they said in unison.

"Mother was unsure what you would enjoy, so she had the cook prepare a little of everything."

At the edge of the blanket that was not covered by food, Robert assisted Grace down on the blanket facing the pond and then reached for Elizabeth. When he reached for Elizabeth's hand, as soon as their hands touched, there was a sting, as if they were scorched by fire, so they quickly pulled their hands away and looked at each other with perplexity at what happened. Not knowing or understanding what it was. After a few moments, they laughed and broke the awkwardness.

Then with care, Robert reached for Elizabeth's hand again, and when they touched with no sting, he gently eased Elizabeth down next to Grace, then took his place on her other side.

Bramhall Manor was indeed a vast estate. You could see land and forest in all directions, as far as the eye could see. It was stunning, and Elizabeth was enraptured at everything she was seeing. Compared to Dunham Massey, Bramhall Manor was far more beautiful, and she could not believe the splendor of such an estate as it was.

Looking to the right of the pond, were rows and rows of flowers of all types and colors, and flanking the flowers, were tall and thick full trees, with bushes throughout. However, on the left, and beyond the flowers, trees, and bushes, lined a vast forest, that was so thick you could not see anything beyond the first row of trees from where they were sitting.

Elizabeth turned and whispered to Grace, "Look at this place, Grace? You cannot deny the beauty lying before you, even with your disgust for the outdoors," Elizabeth said this last comment with a small snicker.

Grace looked at Elizabeth and smiled, unable to deny what her sister said – she was right; this place was a true beauty. Grace twisted to look at her surroundings, and there were grass and trees as far as the eyes could see, with the pond only a hundred paces from where they were sitting, along with the flowers. Grace could not deny it, Elizabeth was right, it was indeed beautiful.

Elizabeth again whispered to Grace, "Robert is very handsome, Grace. You should be happy."

Grace turned and looked at Elizabeth with irritation, but ignored what she said, instead, Grace turned and focused on the amount of food lying behind her.

The food ranged from chicken, grapes, apples, ham, and a variety of bread and cheeses, with an assortment of pastries and pies. There was also a variety of drinks with wine, water, and milk.

Standing and turning back to the food spread before them, Robert said, "My ladies, please help yourself to what you wish," then he began grabbing food, filling up his plate with enough food to feed all three of them and the servants too, who were standing by to assist them if needed.

Grace and Elizabeth looked at each other, then burst out laughing.

"Robert, by what means are you so thin if you eat like that," Elizabeth said.

Robert smiled and shrugged his shoulders, "I know naught. I know I can eat as much as I desire and still look as I do," he said, looking back at the food, "Are you not hungry? As you see, there is plenty."

Grace and Elizabeth looked at each other, then back at Robert as they raised their eyes to the servants.

Robert understood and waved for the servants to assist Grace and Elizabeth. "Tell the servants what you like, and they will prepare a plate for you."

Grace and Elizabeth did just that, and once they had their food and drink, they could not help but watch Robert eat and laughed as they shook their heads.

As the three enjoyed their meal, they talked about trivial things to become more acquainted with one another. After all, once Robert and Grace are married, they will be family.

After everyone had their fill of food, Robert asked, "Grace, what do you like to do? Do you draw, play a musical instrument…?"

Grace smiled, "I love to read, it is my passion out of all others, but I do enjoy playing the piano. Drawing though…I cannot claim to be as good as Elizabeth, but I do try," she said, turning to look at Elizabeth, then laughed.

With surprise, Robert asked, "Reading?"

Robert was surprised and yet – *fascinating*, he thought.

"I am amazed Baron Massey taught you how to read," Robert said, then saw the irritation on Grace's face, so he quickly moved to correct his words of criticism. "Forgive me, Grace, I meant no disrespect. My father also permitted Rachel to learn to read and write after my mother convinced him how it would benefit her to learn to read and write. I am merely surprised, as you are aware, females in any class are not generally taught to read and wright."

Then, to show interest in her love for reading, with excitement, he asked, "What kind of books do you like to read?"

With pleasure, Grace answered, "Oh my, I would say anything with adventure, are the ones I enjoy the most. I allow the story to develop me, so I can become part of the story…the adventure. I want to be able to travel and see the world," Grace said.

Well, I did, she thought feeling disappointed.

Grace looked down at her hands resting in her lap and noticed she was twisting her napkin, as she did when she was nervous or revealing more than she should.

Grace took a deep breath, and once releasing it, she looked up at Robert, who was watching her closely. She took control of herself and said, "Well, a girl can dream, can she not?"

No one could know her true feelings, her true desires, in her wanting to travel and see the world, nor did she have any interest in ever being married.

I must find a way to get out of this, she thought.

Robert saw Grace tense as if she revealed more than she should. So not to cause her any more distress, he said, "How fascinating!" Robert was truly intrigued and went on to say, "I would never believe 'a girl'," he said to ease the tension in Grace, "Could enjoy the need for adventure." However, it did not have the effect he wanted.

Grace and Elizabeth gave Robert a questionable eye when they heard 'a girl'.

When Robert saw the look on Grace and Elizabeth's face, he knew he was in trouble, so he put his hands up in surrender. In an attempt to save himself, he quickly went on to say, "I love to read as well and would like to seek adventure, to go out and prove I am the best swordsman England has ever seen. I wish to one day join the king's army and become a great knight and fight for our country."

Robert stood up without realizing it and started sword fighting with an invisible opponent. When Robert realized what he was doing, he quickly stopped and slowly turned to look at Grace and Elizabeth, only to see the surprised look on their faces, so he suddenly fell to the ground laughing, as if his actions were intended for humor.

As Grace and Elizabeth watched Robert, Elizabeth could not help but notice Robert's moves and was in awe.

When Robert looked at them and fell to the ground laughing, after a moment, they too joined him in laughter. They laughed so hard that they fell on their backs with their eyes closed as tears started to form.

When Robert, Grace, and Elizabeth finally gained control of themselves, they went back to a semblance of decorum.

Robert turned to Elizabeth and smiled, "So…you are the artist?"

Before Elizabeth could answer, he proceeded to ask her the same questions he asked Grace.

After, Elizabeth began to answer his questions, "Yes, I do love to draw," she said with a broad smile on her face and proceeded to answer his other questions as well. "Well, I cannot say I am an excellent reader, nor do I care to read unless I am forced," she said as she turned to Grace. They looked at each other for a moment before they burst out laughing then spurted out, "Which I am forced a great deal," she said, still laughing.

Once she composed herself, she went on to say, "Musical instruments, well…no - no, I do not care to play, that is Grace's talent. Although to please mother and father, I do try to play the harp, but very badly," she said with a small hint of disappointment.

Robert and Grace laughed when they saw the disappointed look on Elizabeth's face.

When Elizabeth saw them laughing, at first, she was upset, but then she thought, *I can imagine how I must have looked, and they are right to be laughing at me, as I would have laughed at them*, and so she joined in the laughter.

With Robert, Grace, and Elizabeth seeming to be getting along very well, Grace began to wonder, *maybe I have prejudged Robert.* But then, as she continued to watch and listen to Elizabeth and Robert, she further thought, *how strange*…looking closely, there seemed to be something between Robert and Elizabeth, what it was, she did not know, but…there was something there, she was sure of it. *Could it be interest…could they be interested in each other? Humm*, she thought, and decided this was something she would need to ponder more when she was alone.

With seriousness, Elizabeth said, "What I do enjoy…no, love…is spending time outdoors exploring all there is to see," looking around at the beauty surrounding her. "At times, I will find a place in the forest to sit and draw any and everything I see around me, trying to capture the beauty nature has to offer."

At hearing this, Robert perked with interest and said

with shortness of breath, "Fascinating. Never did I believe I would find another with the same love and passion for spending time outdoors as I do."

Elizabeth looked at Robert with suspicion, wondering if he were mocking her, how could he know of the love and passion she felt for the outdoors from her words alone. Then, there seemed to be more in his expression, then mere words.

Robert did not miss the suspicious look on Elizabeth's face and knew he had to explain himself.

"I can tell…"

Elizabeth turned with surprise and thought *how can he know what I am thinking.*

Robert smiled and continued, "…Though you did not show it, it was in the sound of your voice. The faraway look in your eyes, as if you were returning to the place which you love. Only another person who genuinely loves the outdoors can see this. I spend hours of my time exploring this vast estate," he said, opening his arms to encompass the estate around him, "And the forest beyond."

Elizabeth looked at Robert, amazed at the accuracy of his words, and she could hear the truth in them.

"Fascinating," she said in a whisper, repeating Robert's words. Then they both laughed.

Irritated at Robert and Elizabeth's interest in the outdoors, however, as Grace watched Robert and Elizabeth, she thought, *how can one love the outdoors…disgusting.*

Then, further observations of Robert and Elizabeth, what she believed was there before, had become clear to her.

There was something between Robert and Elizabeth, and a way to free me from this agreement, she thought.

"I have to tell you though, I am no artist," Robert said. "If you like, when we are done with our meal, we can walk the grounds."

Elizabeth's eyes lit up and smiled widely.

Robert saw her joy and excitement, and this pleased him more than he knew.

For Elizabeth, this offer, with the idea of exploring such a vast estate stole her breath away. Elizabeth looked at Grace, and what she saw she didn't care for, in how unhappy she was at the idea.

Grace was looking at her hands resting in her lap, when she felt her sister's eyes on her. She looked up, there it was, that look…please, please, please, with pleading in her eyes. Grace rolled her eyes. That look always overtook her sensibilities every time.

Elizabeth watched her sister, praying she would not say no. That, for once, Grace would put aside her dislike for the outdoors and agree to walk the grounds.

For Grace to see that look in Elizabeth's eyes, how could she say no? And so, Grace reluctantly agreed, but not for the reasons Elizabeth believed, but for her own selfish reasons. However, she decided to make Elizabeth stew for a little while longer.

"Grace, please, will you bear the venture? After all, this will be your land one day once you and Robert are married," Elizabeth said, using her sister's future against her, that one day she will be Lady of Bramhall Manor.

Looking at her sister with irritation, Grace knew what her sister was doing, then, how can she deny her.

Sighing in resignation, "Very well, if I must," she said in that snooty irritated voice of hers.

Hearing the irritation in Grace's voice – one Elizabeth was familiar with, she smiled, Elizabeth knew this was difficult for her sister to agree, and if she spoke further – well, it was best to keep her mouth closed, not wanting to take the chance her sister will change her mind.

Robert stood up, then helped Grace and Elizabeth up. Arm and arm, Robert slowly guided them down to the pond, to allow them time to take in the beauty that Bramhall estate had to offer.

Robert told Grace and Elizabeth the story of how his family came to have the estate after the war against the Normans.

Although Elizabeth heard Robert speaking, she was oblivious to his words. She was in awe at the magnificence surrounding of Bramhall Estate; it was grander and more beautiful then compared to where they were sitting, especially in the way Robert was showing them, taking in every inch of the splendor the estate had to offer.

Robert loved watching Elizabeth; in the way she took in everything of what he was showing them. For Grace, though, not so much, she seemed to be uncomfortable, fussing the whole time they were walking.

Maybe she will warm up once she sees my mother's garden, Robert thought, and started in the direction of his mother's favorite place, her garden.

After arriving at his mother's garden, Robert motioned with his hands, "This is my mother's garden," Robert said with pride.

Elizabeth was captivated by everything she saw, but Robert's mother's garden was the best she has seen yet, with the array of flowers as far as the eye could see.

"Beautiful," Elizabeth said as she stepped away from Robert, and moved in a complete circle, taking in everything she was seeing.

Robert smiled at Elizabeth's reaction, then he put out his arm for Elizabeth to take. When she placed her arm in his, he continued their walk and proceeded to show them his mother's garden.

"Lady Davenport designed it herself," he said. "From my understanding, she took a great deal of time and care in designing this garden."

Robert released his hold on Grace and Elizabeth, then stepped away to walk over to a section of lilies of different colors, he opened his arms as if he were presenting a fine gift – his mother's garden. Robert was immensely proud of his mother's gift she bestowed on this land, and to be able to share it with his betrothed and her sister, and with Elizabeth being a kindred spirit, for her to love the outdoors as much as he did was a wonderful surprise.

"From my understanding, my mother went through a great deal in selecting the various flowers you see here," he said, pointing to the different flowers. "She selected flowers from all around the world, and what you see here is what survived the journey."

Elizabeth looked around at the varieties of colors: yellow, blue, red, and purple, and inhaled the exquisite aroma, then whispered, "Beautiful."

When Robert heard Elizabeth say 'beautiful', he looked at her and smiled. As he watched Elizabeth, it amazed him how she did not only see the beauty; she felt it as well. To observe this gave him great joy, in the mere way she expressed herself.

She truly does love the outdoors. To watch her, it cannot be rebuffed, Robert thought.

"How beautiful," Elizabeth said again, this time louder for everyone to hear. "Lady Davenport did an amazing job with the wonderful array of colors…the smells…are incredible. I believe I can very easily spend hours, if not days in this magnificent garden."

Robert smiled at hearing Elizabeth's words, they filled him with immense joy and pride for his mother.

Robert loved his mother very much, more than he could ever express.

"I believe you can draw some incredible pictures too?"

Elizabeth looked at Robert and smiled, "Yes, I believe I can."

Grace was watching Robert and Elizabeth intently, and it excited her. Grace was delighted for her sister, because at that moment, she was correct in what she saw earlier, there was something between Robert and Elizabeth, and she planned to encourage it as much as possible.

However, with Robert and Elizabeth enjoying themselves, she was growing weary. She had her fill of the outdoors and decided it was time for her to return to the manor and use this opportunity to put her plan in motion, by persuading Robert and Elizabeth to continue their walk without her.

Grace, unladylike, yawned loud enough to capture Robert and Elizabeth's attention.

"Robert, I wish to return to the manor?"

Elizabeth quickly turned to Grace with disappointment; it was visibly written all over her face, she was not ready for their adventure – their tour to be over, as there was still so much more to be seen.

Grace kept a stern face, trying not to smile at her sister's distress. No, she was not proud of taking joy over Elizabeth's disappointed look, but it had to be done.

"Robert, will you please be so kind as to walk me back to the manor?" Then she turned to Elizabeth and said, "Elizabeth, will you help me? Will you continue the tour of the estate with Robert alone, and when you are done, will you give me a full report of your adventure?"

Shocked, Elizabeth asked, "Grace, are you sure? If you need to return, we will return together," she said as she turned to Robert.

Robert nodded in agreement, "Yes, of course. Grace, we will return together," he said, as he began to walk towards the manor.

Not moving, Elizabeth said, "Or, we can sit here and rest a bit before we continue."

"Yes, that sounds like a wonderful idea, I can have one of the servants bring a blanket, and we could —"

Grace interrupted Robert and said, "Robert, you are very kind, but I have no interest in exploring the outdoors," she pointed her finger at Robert and Elizabeth, "You and Elizabeth will be better off without me."

Elizabeth looked at Grace. She was concerned for her

sister, as it was supposed to be Grace and Robert's time together, not her and Robert. She must convince Grace to remain unless she was still insistent on returning to the manor, then they will go together. It was not proper for her to spend time with Robert without Grace, then, at the same time, she wanted desperately to continue to see the rest of the estate.

"Grace, we will return together, I can explore the Davenport estate another time."

Grace smiled at her sister, "Elizabeth, I will be fine. You know very well if I took this," she motioned with her arms to encompass the vast land and forest still to explore, "Away from you, you will be poor company on the way home."

Elizabeth looked at Grace, stunned at the suggestion, but at seeing how Grace was eyeing her, pleading with her, she slowly conceded and agreed that Grace was right.

"Are you sure, Grace? I hate to leave you alone."

"My dear sister," taking Elizabeth's hands in hers, "I am no withering flower. I will be fine, and I will not be alone. There will be mother and father, little John, and the Davenport's. So, you see, my dear sister, I shall be fine."

Elizabeth felt defeated and looked at Robert for help. "Robert, what do you think? Should we return Grace to the manor, and once she is safely inside, return to continue our tour?"

Robert watched and listened carefully to Elizabeth's and Grace's conversation. He agreed with Elizabeth; he was concerned with the idea of Grace returning to the manor alone and wondered what his father would think? This outing was intended to be their time together, not his time with Elizabeth, although the idea of spending time with another who was the same as he – this made Robert feel guilty. He needed to spend time with Grace, not Elizabeth. But, before he surrendered to the idea, he needed to be sure this is what Grace wanted.

Robert asked, "Grace, are you sure this is what you want?"

Grace smiled, even though she was becoming irritated at their perpetuating concern and their endless questions.

Grace released her breath she was holding and said, "Yes. Now let us return if the two of you want to return before night falls. If this happens…"

She stopped, then tried again, again playing on Elizabeth's love for the outdoors.

"…Elizabeth, you know if you return before you are ready, you will pace up and down our chamber all night, and I will not be able to sleep."

Elizabeth raised an eye at her sister.

However, this did not deter Grace, and she went on to say, "Do not look at me like that, you know I am right."

As Elizabeth listened to her sister, she could not deny what she said, so, in resignation, Elizabeth nodded in agreement, and they began their walk back to the manor. Once Grace was safely inside, Robert and Elizabeth returned to where they left off at his mother's garden.

Chapter Three

When Baron Massey saw Grace returning alone, he was not pleased, then, displeasure turned to concern, as he started to wonder if something had happened to Robert and Elizabeth, for this would be the only reason that would explain Grace returning without Robert.

Baron Massey looked around to be sure he did not miss Elizabeth returning earlier, but he did not see her and wondered, *where is Elizabeth?*

Without delay, Baron Massey moved with haste to speak with Grace and learn why she returned without Robert and Elizabeth.

"Grace…"

When Grace heard that oh so familiar voice, she knew what her father wanted, knowing there was no avoiding it, Grace turned to her father to face his questions. Grace put on her best smile, but then when she looked at her father, he was not angry, instead, he was concerned and worried.

"Why are you here?" Baron Massey demanded.

Baron Massey looked behind Grace to the French doors, hoping he would see Robert and Elizabeth walkthrough the doors any moment, but he did not, and proceeded to question his daughter.

"Where is Robert and your sister Grace? What happened?" Baron Massey asked, without giving Grace time to respond. He was too angry at this point. "What went wrong?" he asked, wondering where Elizabeth and Robert were.

Grace knew when she walked through those French doors there would be questions. *How am I going to explain returning without Robert to father?* she thought, but then when she saw the concern on her father's face and how angry he was, Grace did not look forward to explaining her reasons to him.

Grace touched her father's hand to calm him, then said in her sweet and soft voice, "Father, I am only tired. You know how much I hate the outdoors and how much Elizabeth loves it. I asked Robert to return me to the manor so he could continue to show Elizabeth the estate."

At hearing this, Baron Massey exploded with anger, not caring who heard him.

This sudden outburst caused Grace to flinch, not once has she seen her father so angry, and to see her father's disapproval, she felt ashamed.

"Grace, it is you!" he yelled, pointing his finger at her. "Not Elizabeth, it is you who is to spend time with Robert! This is your time together…to become acquainted," he said in a calmer voice.

Grace stood there and listened to her father, knowing there was nothing she could say or do that would help her. However, she was her father's favorite, and she knew how to ease her father's anger.

Then he realized what Grace was doing. "To pull your sister into this…this is very bad of you, Grace."

"Father?" she said gently, moving her hand to her father's arm, "I understand, but it is only for a short time."

Grace looked at her father with those fluttering eyes, a look she knows weakens his demeanor.

"Father," she said warily, "When Robert returns, I will devote the remainder of the evening and morrow to him." Grace leaned into her father and whispered, "I promise father."

Grace looked at her father with pleading in her eyes as she fluttered her eyes, a look her father could not resist.

Baron Massey released his breath he had been holding, knowing the look Grace gave him was his undoing.

This child has me wrapped around her finger, he thought as he smiled.

He reluctantly gave in, knowing he had a soft heart when it came to Grace, she could convince him of anything.

"Very well Grace, for now, I will release you from your obligation, but my daughter, it is for tonight only," he said, giving Grace a stern look. "You must find ways to spend time with Robert. You," he pointed at Grace, "Not your sister. Is that clear?"

Grace felt relieved. She smiled and nodded in agreement. It never failed, Grace knew her father had a soft heart when it came to her, and she extorted this whenever she had the opportunity. She could practically convince her father to do anything for her.

"Thank you, father. I will. I promise," Grace said with delight. Then, with quick haste, she made for her bedchamber to read her book, one filled with adventure and mayhem.

***

Robert and Elizabeth returned to his mother's garden and spent a few more moments admiring the various flowers before they moved on.

Robert guided Elizabeth around the estate, and made a complete circle, then returned to where they started from. However, Robert found he desperately wanted to take Elizabeth further, beyond the forest trees, to his favorite place in the woods. A place he has never shared with anyone.

So why her? he thought.

Aloud, he said, "Elizabeth, I understand…due to propriety, we should remain in view of the manor," he turned to look in the direction of the manor then asked, "Are you willing to be a little adventurous by following me to a place beyond the forest line?"

Elizabeth looked at Robert and wondered what he meant. She glanced back at the manor – yes, they should stay in sight of the manor, then she turned to the forest, did she have the courage? Her curiosity got the best of her.

Elizabeth asked, "What do you have in mind?"

Depending on what it was, and if it was worth it, she would willingly risk impropriety.

Robert looked at Elizabeth and smiled, "Do you trust me?"

Elizabeth hesitated, "Hum, I do not know you well enough to say I trust you," she said with a smile.

Although Elizabeth didn't know what Robert intended, her curiosity was too great, and she did her best to hide the excitement creeping up in her. Unfortunately, her eyes already betrayed her.

Robert did not miss the excitement in Elizabeth's eyes, he smiled and said, "I think you trust me enough, even after our short time together," and without further words, Robert pulled on Elizabeth's hand to guide her to the edge of the forest.

Nervous, Elizabeth hesitated, firmly planting her feet to the ground.

Robert did not force Elizabeth, as he saw she was hesitant, but waited patiently for her to choose to follow him. If Elizabeth decides to return to the manor, he would be disappointed, but he would understand.

Elizabeth knew Robert was patiently waiting, she again turned back to the manor, and then to the forest directly ahead of her, it was decided, her curiosity overtook any impropriety, and she allowed Robert to guide her into the woods.

Robert led Elizabeth to the edge of the forest trees, then he turned to ascertain if she was still willing to go beyond the forest tree line. He wanted to give her a chance to change her mind. Robert saw her excitement, but her hesitation as well. He could not deny her reluctance; after all, it was close to dark, and they would need to return soon. Robert was willing to go against any impropriety with his need to show Elizabeth his special place, he dared not delay another day.

"Are you…will you go with me into the forest? I

understand the unknown can be frightening," he said, turning back to look at the forest, "There is nothing to fear, it is my forest, and I know it well."

Robert pulled on Elizabeth's hand, encouraging her to follow him into the forest.

Elizabeth watched Robert closely as he spoke; she could hear the truth in his voice. She looked again from where they came, and then to the forest before her, and it was decided, her curiosity got the best of her, she was not going to turn back. Elizabeth nodded, with that confirmation, Robert guided her into the forest.

Within moments, Robert and Elizabeth were standing beside what seemed to be a group of colossal trees. As Robert guided Elizabeth around the trees, she noticed it was not just a group of trees, but it seemed to be a great circle. When Robert steered Elizabeth to the far side of the trees, he reached through and pulled back the thick branches, revealing a small hidden entrance.

When Elizabeth entered, she was astounded with what she saw; it was nothing she expected, it was beautiful. In the center was a surprisingly spacious, clear of debris, with a large rock seated in the center. Next to the rock was a small well-used fire pit. Elizabeth felt veneration and she had to see every inch of this place. With care, Elizabeth slowly moved in a small circle, and was amazed by how she could not see the forest beyond the tight fitted trees. If Elizabeth had not seen it for herself, she would never have believed this place existed, and thought, *this is a perfect hideaway.*

With wonder, Elizabeth asked, "Robert, how is this possible? Did your family create this…your ancestors? This cannot be natural."

Robert shrugged his shoulders, "I do not know. I agree it must have been created by someone. By whom, I cannot say. I dare not ask my father, as I do not want anyone to know of this place. Since I discovered it, it has become my secret place I can come and be alone."

"Robert…and…and you chose to share this," she opened her arm to encompass the open space, "Your secret place with me." With astonishment and yet with confusion, Elizabeth asked, "Why?"

Elizabeth was honored that Robert chose her to visit his favorite place —

But why? It should have been Grace he chose not me, she thought, after all, they hardly knew each other.

Robert again shrugged his shoulders, "I do not know, only…it felt right," Robert said, then nonchalantly he asked, "Do you like it?"

Robert stood there anxiously waiting for Elizabeth's answer, although he asked the question as if her answer was unimportant, somehow it was, it mattered a great deal to him.

Elizabeth was astounded, how could she not like it, she thought the place was incredible.

Elizabeth turned to look at the large rock seated in the center; it seemed to have a flat surface.

Marvelous, a place where we can sit down, she thought.

Elizabeth turned to Robert and asked, "Robert, did you place this rock here?"

Robert shook his head and said, "No, it was already here when I found this place."

Robert walked over and gathered twigs and wood he kept near the fire pit, then built a fire, and sat down on the ground and gestured for Elizabeth to join him.

When she did not move, he said, "Come Elizabeth, sit and enjoy the warm fire, there is a chill in the air. We will enjoy the warm fire until you…we are ready to return to the manor. Unless…" he hesitated, does he dare ask. *Will she want to return,* he thought?

Warily he asked Elizabeth, "Unless you would rather return to the manor now?" praying she will say no, but patiently waited as Robert thought, *please, please say no.*

No! Elizabeth yelled silently in her head. Then she thought, *he is right. There is a chill in the air.* She suddenly shivered.

Elizabeth finally said, "No, how can I leave such a wonderful place, but…"

"But what?"

Elizabeth turned her attention to the rock, "Robert, do you mind if we sit on the rock? If I sit on the ground, my gown will become soiled…if mother and fa —"

Robert cut Elizabeth off. No more needed to be said. Robert stood and walked over to the rock, then gestured for Elizabeth to join him.

For a few long moments, Robert and Elizabeth sat in silence, taking everything in. Then, suddenly Robert stood up, turned, and reached for Elizabeth to take his hand, it was time for them to return to the manor before darkness was upon them, or was there another reason, as he suddenly felt what they were doing was wrong.

Robert turned to look at Elizabeth, although he felt what they did was wrong, he also felt excited, knowing there was someone else who loved the outdoors as much as himself.

Elizabeth was saddened that Robert wanted to leave so soon. She reluctantly slipped her hand in his and allowed him to help her off the rock. Once they were standing face to face, Elizabeth looked up into Robert's big brown eyes and asked, "Robert, what is wrong? Why must we leave when we have just arrived?"

"I am sorry, Elizabeth. Night is upon us, and we must return to the manor before daylight turns to night, and father sends his guards to find us."

Disappointed, Elizabeth nodded in agreement and allowed Robert to lead her out of the forest. However, Robert and Elizabeth were taking their time to walk back to the manor when Elizabeth had this sudden need to tell Robert how much she enjoyed their time together.

"Robert, thank you for this day. It was wonderful. Your family's estate is magnificent," Elizabeth said, looking around to the beauty that surrounded her. "There is a great deal here to see and explore."

Elizabeth looked back in the direction from which they came and said, "Thank you, Robert, this meant a great deal to me, for you to trust me with your secret place," she said, taking another look around, unable to get enough of the estate.

Robert looked down at Elizabeth and smiled, amazed to find one as he, who loves the outdoors as much as he did.

"Elizabeth, on your next visit, and if Grace does not mind, I would love to show you the other side of our estate, and if you are willing, I will take you further into the forest," Robert said with a smile.

With excitement Elizabeth said, "Oh Robert, I would love that very much! Thank you!"

Then she realized, "Oh, please…please allow me to do the same when you visit Dunham Massey."

"Of course, whenever you wish, so long as Grace does not mind." Then he suddenly realized, "Elizabeth, it seems you and your sister are close, but I must ask…" Robert hesitated, but he had no choice, he had to ask. This was his secret, one he chose to share with Elizabeth, and only Elizabeth. "Elizabeth, I must ask you —"

Elizabeth cut Robert off, "You do not want me to tell Grace."

Robert let out his breath and allowed himself to relax. "Yes. Do you mind?"

Elizabeth laughed, "No, of course not. Robert, you can trust me," she said, putting her hand on his arm.

When Elizabeth rested her hand on Robert's arm, there was a strange feeling that crept in the center of his chest, to his heart, and what it was he did not know.

Elizabeth saw the look of confusion and concern on Robert's face, and realized her error, so she quickly pulled her hand away and said, "Oh, I am sorry, do forgive me?"

Robert shook his head and said, "No, it is all right," although he was still concerned with what he was feeling and wondered, *what could this mean?* He gave himself a quick shake and pushed the thought out of his mind.

Elizabeth still saw the concern on Robert's face and went to reassure him, "You trusted me with a great secret, one I will not betray by telling my sister. You can trust me."

Not wanting to betray his thoughts, Robert eased his mind as they continued their walk to the manor.

When they arrived at the French doors, Elizabeth stopped Robert before they entered, not wanting their time to end. There was something special about Robert, and what it was she did not know. What she did know, was she never wanted it to end.

"Robert wait…please, before we go in, I want to thank you again for showing me your family's estate and trusting me with your secret place."

Robert laughed. He knew what she was doing. He felt the same way. He too did not want their time together to end but decided to say nothing.

Elizabeth went on to say, "I look forward to showing you around Dunham Massey when you visit. There, you too will find a vast estate full of trees as far as the eye can see, along with many different ponds and lakes. It…well," Elizabeth looked down at her hands, unaware she was twisting the front of her gown due to her nerves. After a few moments she said, "I have never had anyone I could share…what I love so much…the outdoors with." Then, with sadness, she said, "Though it is not as vast as your family estate."

"Elizabeth, I know what you say and believe…nay, we shall become great friends," Robert said and smiled with a sudden warmth in his heart. "And no matter the size of Dunham Estate, I am sure I will love it."

Elizabeth smiled and said, "Yes, Robert, I do believe

we shall be the best of friends."

Robert opened the door to the great room and stood aside, allowing Elizabeth to enter. Once they were inside, everyone turned to look at them, and Robert did not miss the questionable look they received. To their relief, no one spoke; instead, everyone proceeded to the dining room.

As they entered the dining room, Elizabeth was amazed on how enormous the room was, with a hearth befitting such a room, and above the hearth hung the Davenport's coat of arms, a man with a robe around his neck. Directly in front was a large, long French cherry wood table capable of seating twenty guests.

Lady Davenport arranged the seating to be boy girl boy girl, and Robert had the pleasure of being seated between Elizabeth and Grace, one to be his wife, and the other, a new friend and eventually, his sister.

The table was decorated beautifully. There were four tall silver candle sticks that held seven candles each, accompanied by Lady Davenport exquisite flower arrangements situated across the table.

Once everyone settled into their assigned seating, a line of servants entered the room carrying trays filled with sumptuous food, starting with Lord Davenport at the head of the table.

The first course was a bowl of pea soup, followed by the second course of roasted pheasant, accompanied with potatoes and carrots, then after, there were three more courses along with an assortment of different bread, cheeses, grapes, and berries. To wash it all down, they had a choice of wine, water, and milk, and for dessert, they were served marzipan.

After dinner was completed, everyone was directed back to the great room so they could be entertained by Grace and Rachel playing a duet, with Grace playing the piano. At the same time, Rachel sang a lovely song, "Pastime with Good Company".

Robert sat on a long bench with a tall back made of dark cherry wood, with dark velvet red cushions capable of seating three comfortably.

Robert sat on one end of the bench, and Elizabeth sat on the other end, leaving the middle opened for Grace when she was done entertaining them.

Robert watched and listened to Grace play while his sister sang. He loved to hear his sister sing, and it never ceased to amaze him how beautiful her voice was.

God bestowed a magnificent gift, in giving Rachel the voice of angels, Robert thought.

Robert also admired Grace's talent in playing the piano, how her fingers moved smoothly and gracefully across the keys, as her head swayed back and forth to the sound of the music. Both ladies were extraordinarily talented and amalgamated well.

Robert thought, *how my betrothed is as gifted as Rachel.* At this thought, Robert smiled.

While Grace and Rachel performed, Edward, Daniel and John were sitting at one of the large round tables situated in the far corner of the room playing cards.

While enjoying their daughter's musical gifts, Lord and Lady Davenport, along with Baron and Baroness Massey, talked about how Robert and Grace's first meeting went.

"They appear to be getting along well," said Lady Davenport.

"Yes, I agree, they do seem to like each other, which is very important," said Baroness Massey.

"Look at Robert, in the way he's watching Grace, he does seem to like her," said Lord Davenport, looking at his wife.

"Like is a good start, but I want them to form feelings for each other," said Lady Davenport, as she watched her son intently.

Lady Davenport turned to look at her husband, as she thought of their life together and her arranged marriage.

She once believed that one day they would find love, but unfortunately, it never happened. Instead, they came to an understanding, and accepted her status and responsibilities in marrying a man of Lord Davenport's character, power, and reputation.

Lady Davenport turned to look at her son, and then at Grace, and thought, *I pray they find love, that his father and I never did.* This thought caused Lady Davenport's heart to ache with sadness, which surprised her after so much time had passed.

For many years after Lady Davenport married Lord Davenport, she held hope in her heart that one day John would finally see her, a woman he could love. To her dismay, as the years passed, that hope turned to acceptance of a loveless marriage, accepting her life the way it was, dedicating it to be a good and honorable wife and mother to a husband of Lord Davenport's stature.

Lady Davenport was confused and wondered, *why now? Could it be because of the way Baron and Baroness Massey feels about each other, in the way they show affection for one another?* For Lady Davenport, this had to be the reason why. What else could it have been?

Lady Davenport turned back to her son and prayed. *My Lord, I beseech thee, to bless my son Robert, for he will have the love with Grace I do not have with his father.*

***

Grace was relieved to be home and with Elizabeth by her side. As they walked into Grace's chamber, it was a good size room, not large, nor too small. Grace's bed was situated in the center of the room – a cherry wood canopy bed covered with pink silk floral drapes and matching bed coverings. Her window was located to the left of the door and it too was covered in the same pink silk as her bed.

The bed was so high off the floor, that Grace had to use small steps to reach the mattress. Once Grace was settled on her bed, she sighed at the fill of her soft and comfortable mattress that was made from the most delicate goose feathers.

On the wall, to the right of the door was a beautiful cherry wood dressing table and mirror, with a cream floral pink pitcher and a matching washbasin that rested on a side table. Sitting on top of her dresser was a French silver set hairbrush and comb, along with a matching mirror Grace's mother purchased from France on one of her many visits.

Sitting at the foot of Grace's bed was a solid French cherry wood trunk with eloquent French design. Inside, Grace kept her most precious items, of course, at the age of ten it was limited to the books she loved to read, which she read more than once, and a brooch her mother gave her that once belonged to her grandmother. It was a tradition going several generations back for the mother to give the brooch to the first-born daughter on her tenth birthday.

It was a beautiful star shape brooch intertwined with silver and gold with mini diamonds at the tip, with the most exquisite deep red ruby situated in the center. It was a beautiful piece Grace was proud to have.

On the walls were eloquent silver candle holders, and behind her bed was a set of wardrobes that were placed back-to-back, one held her gowns while the other held her cloaks and gloves. Her favorite cloak was made of dyed blue rabbit fur and matching stained leather gloves to match her sky-blue eyes.

Grace and Elizabeth talked about how their first visit went at Bramhall Manor, and Elizabeth wondered if Grace liked Robert. After all, they were to be married, at the same time, for some reason that she could not explain, Elizabeth did not want Grace to like him.

Although Elizabeth had not lived her life, being only nine years old, beside her sister, she never felt a connection as she did with Robert. Grace was not only her sister, but her best friend, someone she could talk to about anything and loved her sister very much, but Robert, he was similar to her, and she thought, *we are the same.*

Elizabeth needed to know what her sister thought of Robert and asked, "Grace, what do you think about Robert?"

"Oh, Elizabeth, I do not know...Robert is a good boy, but...honestly, I have no interest in spending time with him...he bores me," Grace said looking up at Elizabeth with hope in her eyes, that Elizabeth will help her by taking her place in spending time with Robert.

For Grace, the thought of spending time with Robert was unbearable, and she believed it was a ridiculous arrangement made by her mother and father, and believed Robert and Elizabeth were a better match.

Elizabeth felt somewhat relieved from her sister's words, but at the same time, she was surprised and ashamed. This was her sister's betrothed, how could Grace say or feel such a thing, and why did this please her. This confused Elizabeth. Grace's description was nothing to what she saw of Robert. To Elizabeth, Robert was an exceptional young man. He was kind and caring, funny, and generous.

No, Grace could not be right, Elizabeth thought.

"Grace, you cannot mean what you say? I found Robert to be congenial. When he showed me around his family estate, he was warm and kind, not at all boring. I believe you did not spend enough time with him, and when you do, you will agree with what I say."

At first, Grace was surprised and angered with Elizabeth's opinion of Robert, until she realized —

Wait, this is good news...she likes him, Grace thought, as a small smile curled the side of her mouth, but not big enough for Elizabeth to notice.

Grace slid off her bed and walked over to Elizabeth, who was standing by the window. What she was about to do, would shock her sister, but it had to be done.

As Grace stood in front of Elizabeth, she said in an angry voice, "Well then, you should be the one to marry him."

Grace folded her arms and looked directly into her sister's shocked eyes. When she saw Elizabeth's expression, she had to turn away, so Elizabeth did not see the smile she was fighting to control. Elizabeth had to believe her anger was real.

A shocked Elizabeth said, "Grace, for what reason do you speak so?"

Elizabeth could not believe her sister's reaction to Robert, and it disturbed her to see Grace so angry, but not only anger, there was pain in her eyes as well.

What is she thinking? Robert is wonderful…how can she not see that? Elizabeth thought. This confused Elizabeth. *How can she not see what I see in Robert?*

After Grace gained control of her emotions, she turned back to Elizabeth and pouted. At that moment, Grace was extremely pleased with herself. When Grace saw Elizabeth's perplexed face, she could not help but burst out laughing.

"Oh, Elizabeth…" laughing uncontrollably, "I am sorry. I did not mean to be so harsh," Grace said, still laughing.

After Grace gained control of herself, she then said, "Forgive me, Elizabeth, you know how I become when I am tired," she said trying to explain away her hysterical laughing, not wanting to give away her actual reasons for laughing. "I am laughing at the situation father put me in. Elizabeth, I am too young to be thinking of such things right now," Grace confessed.

Grace then looked at Elizabeth with her most demure look and asked, "Forgive me, Elizabeth," she said as she fluttered her eyes.

Elizabeth, unable to control herself at Grace fluttering her eyes, she burst out laughing and reached for Grace's hand, "Grace, you are wicked. Of course, I forgive you.

You are my sister, and I love you," Elizabeth said, then Grace and Elizabeth hugged.

"Oh, Elizabeth, thank you."

"Grace you may not care for Robert…I have to admit…I am very fond of him," Elizabeth said, stepping out of their embrace, as she was unable to look at Grace. Then softly, Elizabeth said, "For Robert to be interested in the outdoors as much as myself… if you do not object Grace, I want to be able to form a friendship with Robert? To be able to spend time with someone who loves the outdoors as much as I do is…well, I do not know the right words…" Elizabeth looked up searching for the right words…then, "He is wonderful, exciting…okay, I found two words," Elizabeth said with a broad smile.

Grace looked at Elizabeth, feeling happy and relieved.

"Elizabeth, you are more than welcome to spend as much time with Robert as you like. I feel…if I can spend the least amount of time with Robert, it will be for the better."

Grace's words concerned Elizabeth, Robert was her betrothed, someone she was to marry, who she will spend the rest of her life with.

Grace must like Robert, Elizabeth thought.

Elizabeth needed to understand what was going on with her sister and understand why she felt the way she did.

In a soft voice, Elizabeth asked, "Look at me, Grace?" Elizabeth took Grace's hands in hers, "Why do you feel this way after spending so little time with Robert? Did something happen during your time with him, something I do not know about? Grace you are to marry Robert, for you to feel this way so soon…worries me. Please, Grace, help me understand why you have no desire to spend time with Robert, who will one day be your husband. Grace," Elizabeth took Grace's hand. "It will not matter if you like him or not, and the last thing I want is for my sister to be unhappy," Elizabeth said.

Elizabeth watched her sister's face and what she saw she did not like. The look was of hatred at the idea of marrying Robert, and this confused Elizabeth. She did not understand her sister's behavior and knew she had to say something, hoping she could change the way her sister felt.

"Yes, right now you may not care for Robert, but with your time together…once you know him better, I am sure your feelings will change."

Grace knew she could not try to convince Elizabeth otherwise; she never kept anything from her, so the only thing she could do was to admit the truth to her sister.

"No, Elizabeth, I do not care for Robert," Grace said, looking down at her hands, she was twisting the front of her gown. "It is not just Robert…Elizabeth, I have no interest or desire for any boy right now, and the thought of spending time with someone…disturbs me…outside of you of course," Grace said glancing up to look at Elizabeth, as she simpered, "Of someone who I know nothing of, nor do I care to. I did not choose this. It has been thrust upon me against my will. I am a girl of ten, how am I to think of such things right now?"

Grace saw the concern on Elizabeth's face and knew she had to say something that will ease her sister's concerns.

Sighing, "Elizabeth," taking her sister's hands, "I will do what is asked of me, and when the time comes, I will marry Robert Davenport whether I want to or not."

As Elizabeth listened to her sister, her words did not ease her concerns, but she believed in time, Grace's feelings for Robert will change by the time they are to marry.

Her feelings for Robert will change once she knows him better, I am sure of it, Elizabeth thought.

"My dear sister, I know you feel this way now," she said pulling Grace's hands to her chest. "In time, and before you marry, your feelings for Robert will change.

Both of you will grow to love one another."

Grace knew there was nothing else she could say that would help, so she decided it was best to let it go – for now.

"Elizabeth, maybe you are right," Grace said, then hugged her sister. "You will help me, won't you?"

Elizabeth felt pleased with her sister's answer, "Of course, you only need to ask. I will be there for you, Grace. There is no need for you to do this alone," Elizabeth said, returning her sister's hug. "I love you, Grace."

"I love you too Elizabeth and thank you."

Once Elizabeth and Grace broke their embrace, they stood there for a few moments looking at each other before realizing how ridiculous their conversation was, and at the same time, they burst out laughing.

***

A short time after Elizabeth left Grace's chamber, Grace laid in bed unable to sleep, as she stared at the top of her bed thinking of her future, the one that was thrust upon her.

How can I honor my mother and father in this? Yes, I am young, too young to worry about such things. Yet, here I am being forced to endure…to spend time with a boy I care nothing for, nor do I feel it will change as Elizabeth believes it will.

Right now, the only thing I care for is to read my books. I love reading…to immerse myself in the stories. The adventure…that is what I want…I want adventure, to be able to see what the world has to offer. Instead, I am forced to endure this, in what is to come, a marriage I want nothing to do with. I wish there was a way out. Why not allow Elizabeth to marry Robert? They seem to be a better match then we are.

At this thought, Grace sat up in her bed, "Perfect. This is a great idea," she whispered.

Then Grace returned to her thoughts, *no, mother and father will never allow it. Not to mention the agreement they spoke of.*

"Oh, what am I thinking?" Grace said aloud, throwing one of her pillows at the foot of her bed. "I am ill-fated," she whispered, falling back on her bed.

Grace turned her thoughts to God and began to pray, *My Lord, if there is anything you can do to help me escape my fate, please do so.*

At this last thought, Grace crawled under her covers and curled up on her side, allowing herself to succumb to sleep.

Chapter Four

The following morning Grace woke up still worried about the fate tossed upon her and desperately needed to speak with her sister. So, without delay, Grace threw back her covers and grabbed her robe, putting it on as she quietly stepped into the hall and made her way to Elizabeth's chambers.

Elizabeth's chambers were a mirror image to Grace's, but instead of pink floral silk drapes, Elizabeth's window and her bed were covered with solid dark red silk. Elizabeth's furniture was like Grace's, but instead of the pink floral basin and pitcher, Elizabeth's was white with red roses. She also had a trunk at the end of her bed that held her drawings and drawing pads along with chalks. Elizabeth also had a pair of ruby teardrop earrings that were given to her by her mother, who received them from her grandmother. The earrings were not an heirloom like Grace's brooch, but a gift given to her grandmother from her grandfather on their wedding day.

After entering Elizabeth's chambers, Grace approached Elizabeth, who was still asleep. She gently shook her as she whispered, "Elizabeth, wake up. I need to speak with you."

When Elizabeth woke up, and after the fog dissipated, she saw Grace's worried face and immediately sprang up, and wondered what caused Grace to be upset.

"What is it, Grace? What is wrong?" she said, grabbing Grace's arm.

"I am sorry to wake you, but I must speak with you. I am frightened and need your help," Grace said in a shaky voice.

Feeling even more concerned, Elizabeth asked, "What's the matter, Grace? What do you fear?" Elizabeth took Grace's hand and pulled her to sit on the bed next to her.

Grace did as Elizabeth wanted, and she sat on the bed

and said, "Elizabeth, I cannot do this. I cannot spend time with Robert. I do not like him!" Grace said with anger, firmed in her decision. "We have nothing in common!" she yelled.

Elizabeth squeezed her hand, "Grace, lower your voice, we do not want to wake the house."

Grace nodded than took a deep breath, and once she let it out, she continued, "All he wants to do…" rolling her eyes as she glanced up "…is spend time outdoors," Grace said crossing her arms, "You know how much I hate the outdoors, Elizabeth. How can I do what mother and father have asked of me?"

Grace allowed herself to relax, moving her hands, resting them on her lap, and with sadness, she looked at Elizabeth and said, "Help me, sister," then with desperation she grabbed Elizabeth's hands and said, "Help me, Elizabeth? Tell me what to do?"

Hearing Grace's words confused Elizabeth; she did not understand why she felt as she did. "Grace," she started to say then stopped herself, as a sudden feeling of fear came over her, one she didn't understand.

Elizabeth became upset and pushed Grace aside, then jumped out of bed. She grabbed her robe and put it on as she walked across the cold floor to the window on the other side, with the need to feel the crisp morning air on her face, knowing it would calm her.

Elizabeth removed the latch and opened the shutters, securing them to the wall, then pushed open the window and leaned out, allowing the crisp cold air to caress her face in a soft embrace. Elizabeth closed her eyes and inhaled the fresh cold air, holding it for a few moments before releasing it in a slow exhale.

When Elizabeth opened her eyes, she sought the forest that lies beyond the thick mist, once the faint outline of the forest was in view, it calmed her even more. After a few moments, from the corner of her eye, Elizabeth caught the rising sun as it woke from its slumber.

When Elizabeth gained control of her unexpected feeling of fear, she turned back to look at Grace, who was sitting on her bed, watching her intently. Elizabeth reached out her hand, wanting Grace to join her.

For a moment, Grace hesitated, then gently rose, and slowly walked to Elizabeth, not understanding why Elizabeth jumped out of bed.

Once Grace was standing in front of Elizabeth, she took Grace's hands and said, "Grace," looking at her sister with love, "Where is this coming from? How can you decide after such a short time with Robert…for you to feel this way about him?"

Grace tensed, fearing Elizabeth could see right through her deception.

Elizabeth did not miss Grace's sudden fear, and with concern she said, "Grace, I love you," rubbing the top of her sister's hands. "You are my sister, and I will help you no matter what. Before I do, you must help me understand why you feel this way about Robert after so little time?"

As Grace watched Elizabeth, she saw the love her sister had for her; it gave her the strength she needed to explain her fears to her. Grace took a deep breath and began to explain, hoping it will be one Elizabeth will believe.

"Elizabeth…" she started to say, then stopped and looked down at the floor, now unsure of her words.

Elizabeth wanted to push Grace, but when she saw how difficult it was for her, she decided not to press, and allow Grace to find her words.

When Grace was ready, she looked at Elizabeth and tried again. "I…" again she started to say, but still struggled with the right words.

Grace turned away from Elizabeth, realizing it was too difficult to look at her while attempting to lie to her. Then Grace thought, *will Elizabeth help me if she knows the truth?* Grace sighed and thought *no, she would not.*

Elizabeth will want me to do what is right, to honor mother's and father's wish for me to marry Robert.

Grace took a deep breath, and when she let it out, she proceeded to tell Elizabeth her plan – the lie she concocted.

"Elizabeth, I am young…mother and father, along with Lord and Lady Davenport have forced this upon me…betrothed to a man I do not care for. My feelings in this will not waiver, even if I were to spend time with Robert," Grace said, then looked at Elizabeth.

Grace saw the concern on Elizabeth's face and grabbed her hands, giving them a squeeze of reassurance, "If I must," Grace closed her eyes, "I will do what is required of me. For now, I do not want to worry or think of it," she said, squeezing her hands again and proceeded to ask Elizabeth what she needed from her. "I pray…will you help me, sister?"

Elizabeth watched and listened to Grace carefully and had many questions but held her tongue, encouraging her to continue.

"Grace, please continue. You may ask me what you will?" she said as she guided Grace back to the bed to sit down.

After they were seated, Grace looked at Elizabeth and said, "I want to ask you…" but found she could not. Instead, she looked down at their adjoined hands before continuing. "I am unsure of your feelings —"

She will understand, you know this. She loves you and she will help you, Grace thought.

"Elizabeth…will you please…I need…" nervous, Grace's voice cracked filled with mixed emotions as tears welled up in her eyes.

Elizabeth saw that Grace was upset and pulled her into a tight hug. With Grace's hands in hers, she rested them on her lap and said, "Grace, I do not understand your feelings, since you know Robert so little."

Grace began to believe speaking to Elizabeth was a

mistake and started to pull away, but Elizabeth did not yield and held on strong to her hands.

"Grace, you know I will do anything to help you," she said, smiling, "What do you wish me to do?"

At hearing the sincerity in Elizabeth's voice, Grace allowed herself to relax, and felt relieved. Grace looked up and smiled at Elizabeth as she started to say, "Well —"

When Elizabeth saw the way Grace smiled, she knew she had been misled, and realized she might have made a grave mistake and thought, *Grace, what are you up to, and what did I agree to do?*

"What I am thinking…" she stood up and began to pace in front of Elizabeth as she explained her plan. "My plan…I put a great deal of thought into this —"

Hm-hm, I am sure you did, Elizabeth thought as she watched her sister with a wary eye, knowing she had been deceived.

"— and I believe it will work with your help," Grace said as she stopped in front of Elizabeth to gauge her reaction and her response. "As you know, I am required to spend a few hours with Robert during our visits and…" Grace stood in front of Elizabeth and looked directly in her eyes... "Will you…will you take my place…" Grace saw the shocked look on Elizabeth's face, and before she could say a word, Grace quickly went on. "Elizabeth, you know you are a better choice than I am. Now, I know what you are thinking —"

Elizabeth's eyes widened as her mouth dropped open and thought, *I am sure you do. She cannot be serious.*

"— you and Robert love the outdoors," Grace went on to say. When Grace saw Elizabeth's shocked expression, and before she could say a word, Grace quickly went on, "I know what you are thinking?"

Elizabeth sat tall as she thought, *I bet you do.* Just as Elizabeth was about to stand up to yell at her sister, Grace stopped her.

"Please Elizabeth, I know you are upset, but hear my reasons."

Reluctantly, Elizabeth sat back down and crossed her arms, then gave Grace a look for her to continue, and listen to what she had to say.

"You and Robert have much in common with your love for the outdoors," Grace said as she watched Elizabeth intently, clearly seeing her annoyance. Grace quickly went on to say, "You said it yourself, 'To have someone love the outdoors as much as I do'. How can you resist this opportunity that I am giving you?"

Elizabeth was becoming angry, and when she heard her sister's last words, she rolled her eyes. *Grace has me there, and she knows it,* Elizabeth thought.

Her anger was starting to subside to humor. She quickly turned away from Grace, not wanting her to see the smile she was fighting to hide, knowing there was a ring of truth in her words.

Elizabeth liked Robert, she could not deny that, but she did not understand how this plan of Grace's was going to work, and how could they get away with deceiving their families. Then there was a sudden fear that came over her, at the realization she wanted this more than she was willing to admit. Then, she felt a sudden flutter in her stomach, *what could this mean,* she thought.

After this shocking realization, Elizabeth took a moment to gather herself before turning back to answer Grace's question.

"Grace, how am I expected to spend time with Robert, when you are the one who is to spend time with him? You know I am unable to take your place. You remember how upset father was when you returned to the manor alone on our first night. How do you plan on explaining this to mother and father?"

Grace did not miss the smile Elizabeth was trying to conceal, and it pleased her to know she was right, but was careful not to let on, and proceeded to explain her plan to Elizabeth.

"I will ask father…I will tell him if I am to please Robert…I will ask him to allow you to accompany me during my outings with Robert until I become comfortable spending time with him outdoors. Doing this will please father, because he will believe I am making every effort to make Robert happy, with me becoming interested in something he loves, even though I hate it so," Grace said, smiling with satisfaction that her plan will work.

"Grace, father knows you hate the outdoors. It disgusts you. How do you expect father to believe your sudden interest in the outdoors? Even if it is to please Robert."

"Yes, Elizabeth, I do. Father will believe that I am trying to know Robert by indulging in the thing he loves, by spending time outdoors." Grace smiled; she felt satisfied and confident with her explanation.

Elizabeth looked at her sister with a smile and shook her head. *As absurd as this sounds, it may work,* she thought.

"Very well Grace, we will try…if mother and father find out you will be 'forced'…" emphasizing the word to bring it to her sister's attention, because if they are caught, Grace will have no choice but to spend time with Robert. This next attempt, Elizabeth hoped it would change Grace's mind. "To spend time with Robert alone," hoping this will make her sister see reason. For if they were discovered, Grace would be on her own.

Grace did not miss what her sister tried to do. Yes, there was a chance their mother and father could find out, but Grace was sure they would not. And when Elizabeth's and Robert's friendship grew to more than friends… Robert and Elizabeth and especially Grace would work harder to keep their plan a secret.

"Elizabeth, I do not believe it will come to that. If it does, I will address the situation when it arises."

Elizabeth looked at Grace; there were times she did not understand her sister, it did not matter, she loved her sister and would do anything for her, even if she had her own selfish reasons. Although she was helping Grace, she believed this arrangement would benefit her more, however, if their deception were discovered… *no! It will not come to that,* she thought.

Firm with her decision Elizabeth said, "Alright Grace," sighing, "What do you have in mind? I know you already have a plan," Elizabeth said, with a raised eyebrow.

Ecstatic that Elizabeth agreed to help her, filled Grace with joy, and she burst out with a small scream and hugged Elizabeth. When Elizabeth didn't return the hug, she looked at Elizabeth and saw her irritation and reigned in her excitement.

"Forgive me, Elizabeth," Grace said, then turned and sat on the bed. Elizabeth followed suit as Grace began to tell Elizabeth her plan. "We will leave the manor together, and once we are out of sight; I will sneak back to the cottage and go through the servant's entrance and up to my chamber when we are home. When we are at Bramhall Manor...we need to talk to Robert about this first, but there, I will go through the servant's entrance and stay in the chamber we share. We will set a time to meet at the same place we part, then together return to the manor to re-join the rest of the family."

Elizabeth listened to Grace closely as she explained her plan, but doubted her plan would work. She believed after a few visits their deception would be discovered. However, for her sister, and even for herself, she would agree to go along with Grace's plan – *for now, she* thought.

"Grace, we will try, but if we are discovered, do you promise to make an effort to spend time with Robert?"

When Grace heard the words 'promise', for a moment, she hesitated as she watched Elizabeth, keeping her face clear from expression, not wanting to give herself away.

Elizabeth knows me too well, she thought. Looking at her sister, she further thought, *once I promise, she knows I will keep it, and once I do this, I will be forced to spend time with Robert if we are discovered. 'If', that is the question. No, we will not be discovered, this I am sure of. My plan will work.*

Grace then recalled seeing a spark of excitement from Elizabeth, and with this, Grace knew she had her.

Wait, is there more…do I see a glimmer of hope there as well, she thought.

Satisfied in what she saw, Grace said, "Very well, Elizabeth, I promise." Hoping she will not have to honor her promise.

While Elizabeth waited for Grace's answer, she allowed her thoughts to wander —

At the idea of spending time with another that loves the outdoors as I do is incredible. It feels me with great joy. This thought concerned Elizabeth, so she quickly cleared her mind and did her best to control – to hide her excitement from her sister.

Grace smiled, although she did not show it, she did not miss Elizabeth's attempt to conceal her excitement and decided to confront her on it.

Grace placed her hand on Elizabeth's arm and said, "Sister, you cannot hide your excitement from me in wanting to spend time with Robert."

Elizabeth closed her eyes, knowing her sister saw right through her.

Grace put her hand on Elizabeth's shoulder and said, "It's alright sister, I want this for you."

With her eyes still closed, Elizabeth slouched forward, unable to deny what Grace said, she knew her too well. Elizabeth could not deny it; this plan was as much for her as it was for Grace. However, she still questioned this plan of Grace's.

Can I do this? Is it possible? Can our families be so

deceived? she thought.

Elizabeth loved her sister very much, there was nothing she would not do for her – *but this? Can I do this…go against our families?* she thought. Then she thought, *yes, yes, I can.*

The thought of Elizabeth having someone else share her love for the outdoors was too much of a temptation to turn away from. If they were discovered though, it would not go well, and she wondered if it was worth the risk.

Elizabeth smiled and thought, *it is,* and so it was decided to let Grace know. "Alright, Grace, I will do this for you."

Ecstatic, Grace bounced up and down on the bed, then grabbed Elizabeth and pulled her into a strong embrace and said with delight, "This is for the two of us Elizabeth. Thank you, thank you, my sister. I love you very much."

At Grace's excitement, this concerned Elizabeth, and she said, "Grace, I need to know what will you do when the time comes for you and Robert to marry? Can you marry a man you do not know or want nothing to do with? Mother and father, along with Lord and Lady Davenport, are giving you and Robert this time to become acquainted with one another. To build a friendship, a bond, with the possibility of love."

Grace smiled at her sister; she had a plan for that as well. "My dear sister, there, you will also be of great help. The times you are with Robert, you will share those times with me. Through you, I will know of him, and when mother and father ask me of my time with Robert, I will answer with the truth."

Elizabeth rolled her eyes and thought, *she is clever.*

Elizabeth knew Grace was their father's favorite, and there was nothing he would not do for Grace, and whenever she could, she took advantage of it, with their father never being the wiser. Elizabeth was not surprised that Grace planned for every possible scenario.

Elizabeth shook her head; Grace never ceased to amaze her at the power she had over their father. "Grace, you cannot mean what you say?"

"Yes, I do sister."

Grace saw her sister waiver, and quickly grabbed Elizabeth's hand and said, "Please Elizabeth, you must do this for me," Grace pleaded, concerned that Elizabeth would change her mind.

Instead, Elizabeth nodded in agreement as she said, "Very well, Grace. I will help you."

Elated, Grace said, "Thank you, Elizabeth, you will not regret your decision." Then Grace gave Elizabeth another hug.

When Grace left Elizabeth, she felt exhilarated, but was too engrossed in her thoughts – her plan, one, she believed would save her from an unwanted marriage, that she did not notice Jane, Elizabeth's maid, greet her with a curtsy and a good marrow as they passed in the hall.

*I am proud to have Elizabeth as my sister. Without her help, my plan will not work. If I am forced to marry Robert…*shaking her head…*no, I cannot think of such a thing, my plan will work. It must work. Robert and I are a poor choice, and I have no desire to marry. Ever. Elizabeth though… she and Robert are an excellent match. It was evident in their short time together. With their time alone…* she smiled, *and their shared love for the outdoors, I pray they will form a strong bond…love, one that will force mother and father, along with Lord and Lady Davenport, to allow Robert and Elizabeth to marry. They are a better choice than I.*

When Grace entered her chambers, she found her maid Mary waiting for her with a fire burning in the hearth, making the room warm and cozy. However, she was not ready to dress and wanted to be alone.

"Good morrow Mary."

Mary curtsied and said, "Good morrow My Lady."

"Mary, I will not require your assistance in washing and dressing. I will wash and dress myself."

"As you wish My Lady," Mary said as she curtsied and left Grace's chambers, closing the door behind her.

Once Grace was alone, she said in a whisper, "Yes, this will work."

Grace removed her robe and walked over to the basin and pitcher. She took the pitcher and poured the warm water Mary had already prepared into the basin. She grabbed the cloth and soap that was resting on the table next to the basin, and once the cloth was sufficiently wet, she rubbed the bar of soap until it was well slathered and began washing herself as she sought God's help.

God, I beseeched thee to help me. We both know Robert and Elizabeth are a better choice than I. It hurts my heart to keep this from Elizabeth, but it is best, at least for now.

Feeling pleased with herself, Grace began to hum.

***

Grace's love for books came from her father, reading to her when she was a baby. The first book Grace read on her own was a book of poems, Petit Livre d'Amour, and later without her father being aware, Grace started reading books on adventure, and in reading these books of adventure Grace realized she too wanted adventure. However, as a woman, she would never have that experience. Knowing this; Grace at times found herself wishing she had been born a boy, for as a man she could travel and have the adventurous life Grace craved.

When Grace discovered books on adventure that included romance, she started fantasizing about a heroine who would sweep her off her feet and carry her away from her life as it was. And to her surprise, some of these fantasies included Robert as the romantic heroine and her as the lady in distress. However, as quickly as these fantasies entered her mind, she quickly squashed them. She did not like Robert, and it sickened her to think of him in such away. To Grace, Robert was no heroine, but a villain – an obligation forced upon her by her mother and father.

During the times the families spent together while the children played outdoors, they would try to entice Robert, Grace and Elizabeth to join them in their playful games, by chasing each other through the vast gardens. Other times they tried to persuade Robert, Grace, and Elizabeth to play hide and seek, but neither of them would have it, not wanting to be bothered with these childish games. Instead, Robert and Elizabeth would sit under a tree near the manor, talking as they watched their siblings play, while Grace, only a few feet away, laid on her stomach reading her book.

When the families were indoors, Grace and Rachel took turns playing the harp,

while Elizabeth played the piano, and at times Rachel would join her in a duet.

Chapter Five

<u>Spring of 1532</u>

Now fourteen, Robert and Grace, in three years, would be married. So far, Grace's plan has worked perfectly. However, after four years and with no sign Robert and Elizabeth were falling in love, she began to worry.

In the four years Robert and Elizabeth spent together, Grace was surprised they were still friends, and friendship was not good enough for her.

I cannot force them to fall in love, but shouldn't they have fallen in love after all this time, Grace thought, feeling frustrated. *I am running out of time! If Robert and Elizabeth do not fall in love soon and before we are forced to marry —*

Then it hit her, and she realized what might be holding Elizabeth back —

It's Elizabeth's love for me…I'm sure it's what's holding her back and keeping her from moving forward with Robert. Yes, this must be the reason. So, how am I to correct this? Grace thought.

***

For Robert and Elizabeth, these past four years have allowed their friendship to grow into a special bond, with their time together between Bramhall Manor and Dunham Massey's estate has been the greatest joy either of them could have hoped for.

One morning as Robert and Elizabeth were walking in the forest at Dunham Massey, they took in the beauty of the newly bloomed trees and wildflowers, along with yellow narcissus pseudonarcissus, Purple Orchis muscular, and creeping on the forest floor, the green Mercurialis. On this particular morning, Robert and Elizabeth were surprised to come across a small family of wolves since they became extinct in the early 1500s.

"Robert," Elizabeth whispered, "Where did a family of wolves come from?" Elizabeth asked with surprise.

"It's a mystery to me. Maybe someone brought them from Scotland, and somehow, they ended up in Dunham forest," Robert said.

Fascinated, Robert and Elizabeth carefully, so as not to disturb or frighten the wolves, cautiously and with little noise, walked over and stood behind a tree a few feet away from the wolves. There, they watched and admired the mother's interaction with her pups in the way she cared for them; cleaning their coats with her tongue, and how she used her nose to push them together, and when one tried to escape, the mother wolf quickly snatched it up with her teeth and placed it back with the others.

When Robert and Elizabeth saw this, Elizabeth let out a small laugh, then realizing what she'd done, she quickly covered her mouth with her hand, hoping the wolf didn't hear her, but it was too late. The mother wolf had already heard the noise and swiftly went to protect her pups as her ears perked up, trying to ascertain what threat was lying out there, and when she found nothing, she relaxed.

Robert smiled at this act, and then they quietly moved away from the mother and her pups.

***

When the weather warmed, Robert and Elizabeth spent time fishing and swimming at one of the many ponds and lakes on their family estates. One day, while at Bramhall Manor, Robert was swimming at one of the many ponds on the estate, while Elizabeth lounged on the blanket several feet away, observing the trees swaying in the soft breeze without disturbing the birds sitting on the branches. Some flapped their wings while others were preening their feathers, then turned her attention to the forest floor and admired the flowers spurting from the ground.

When Elizabeth's attention turned to Robert, it was just in time to see him stepping out of the pond. She was about to move her eyes away but found she could not, and found herself staring at Robert with fascination and was surprised by her body's reaction. In the way it warmed in an unfamiliar manner, with desire. She felt desire – sexuality, and this surprised Elizabeth. She found herself watching Robert in a way she hadn't before, noticing how much he had changed. He was no longer the skinny boy she once knew, but the man he was becoming.

As Elizabeth watched Robert, she noticed his strong chiseled face and jawline; she smiled. It was the first time she noticed the uneven hair patches on his face, causing her to snicker.

He's handsome, she thought. Elizabeth sighed. *How did I not see this before? How attractive he has become.*

Elizabeth no longer saw the skinny boy she once knew, but the man he was becoming.

She continued her perusal of his face a little longer before moving on to his neck and broad shoulders, then down to his strong arms — *They are strong,* she thought, as she imagined those arms wrapped tightly around her body, holding her tight. This feeling surprised Elizabeth, but found she could not stop, and continued her perusal of Robert's body, moving down to his taut stomach, she sighed again — *his body is beautiful,* she thought, as she unknowingly licked her lips.

Elizabeth was shocked by her body's reaction, how alive it became, with feelings, she was unfamiliar with, and it scared her, but found she was unable to look away. She needed to watch him, wanting to admire his magnificent body. *He is beautiful.*

Elizabeth swallowed the lump in her throat as her thoughts were consumed with desire for Robert, a wanting she was unfamiliar with. Then, she felt ashamed, angry, and suddenly she felt jealous of her sister, and this feeling shocked her, so she quickly turned away from Robert. This was her sister's betrothed, and she had no right to her feelings.

Still, she found the lure of what she was feeling too strong to resist. Elizabeth turned back to Robert as he was walking towards her. She noticed the water dripping, sliding slowly down his body as if it were caressing every inch of him. Elizabeth shivered, as her body warmed with desire and excitement.

Elizabeth watched Robert in an unblinking stare until he was almost upon her. Realizing what she was doing, she quickly snapped out of it, and right before he reached her.

This is impossible, she thought.

Elizabeth didn't understand what was happening since these feelings were so new to her, nor did she know what they meant. It didn't matter, because Robert belonged to her sister.

As Robert walked towards Elizabeth, he noticed her unblinking stare, and he became concerned and worried that something was wrong.

Is she unwell? he thought.

Once Robert was standing in front of Elizabeth, he asked, "Elizabeth, are you unwell?"

Elizabeth's face turned red at Robert's question. She felt embarrassed that he caught her staring at him.

Elizabeth swallowed the lump in her throat and said in a shaky voice, "Yes, of course, I am well." Unable to look at Robert, she went on to ask, "Why do you inquire?"

Elizabeth was afraid Robert knew what she was thinking and thought, *oh God, please tell me he does not know,* and then realizing, *this is ridiculous, of course not, don't be foolish.*

Robert reached down and grabbed the cloth sitting at the edge of the blanket to wipe away the water from his body.

"I am pleased to hear you are well. When I was walking over, you had this strange look on your face."

As Elizabeth watched Robert dress, she felt the heat in

her body once again rising, and she needed a moment to gather herself before she answered him.

"Oh, forgive me, my mind was far away, thinking of nothing in particular."

After Robert finished drying off, he dressed and then reached for Elizabeth's hand, "Come, let us take a walk in the forest."

Elizabeth took Robert's hand, "Yes, a wonderful idea," she said with a stutter, praying he didn't notice.

Once Elizabeth was standing next to Robert, she felt uneasy being so close to him, and wondered if he noticed. She slowly raised her head to look at him, and she was relieved to see it didn't appear he did. But, at the same time, she felt a little disappointed.

Elizabeth wondered if she wanted Robert to notice. *No, of course not,* she thought.

Elizabeth turned away from Robert to pick up the blanket. She rolled it up and tucked it under her arm as they prepared to leave.

Robert took the blanket from Elizabeth, and with his other hand, he guided her by the elbow further into the forest. As he did, he glanced at her, and for the first time, he noticed something different about her, but he didn't know what it was.

She is behaving incongruously, and unlike herself, he thought.

Robert recalled how Elizabeth was looking at him as he walked towards her, and the way she watched him as he wiped the water off his body. *Odd,* he thought. *Wait, did I see Elizabeth's face turn red when I was dressing?* If this was true, he didn't understand why. *It's strange; my dressing has never bothered her before…there was no awkwardness,* he thought, and this bothered him.

When he turned to ask Elizabeth, he stopped; she appeared nervous, and just as he was about to inquire, Elizabeth spoke first.

"Robert, I love the forest in the spring. It's so beautiful."

Robert looked at Elizabeth and thought, *you're beautiful.* This thought surprised him, but he shook it off and said, "Yes, it is."

Once Robert and Elizabeth were deep in the forest, her concerns about what she felt for Robert disappeared, and instead, she allowed the forest to embrace her.

Elizabeth stepped away from him and said, "Robert, listen to the sound of the wind blowing through the trees. The way it rustles the leaves, along with the sound of the birds singing and whistling. It's creating a beautiful sonic."

Elizabeth pointed at the flowers that were beginning to bloom, "Look at the flowers bursting from the forest floor," Elizabeth said, closing her eyes as she inhaled the beautiful aroma of the yellow corn marigold and purple orchis mascula. "Ahhh, beautiful," she whispered, then turned back to look at Robert. "They are alive and vibrant, as their aromas are enticing," she said, meeting Robert's eyes, "Do you not agree?" she asked with a smile.

What a beautiful smile, Robert thought. He was mesmerized by Elizabeth as he listened and watched her, in the way she was basking in the beauty of the forest, when suddenly, something unexpected happened – desire; he was feeling desire for Elizabeth.

Elizabeth stretched out her arms and closed her eyes, then tilted her head back and began spinning in a small circle.

When Robert saw this, he shivered as if he were hit by a cool breeze when the air was still. He shook his head, unable to believe what he was about to admit – *no, it's her…the sight of Elizabeth,* he thought as his desire for her increased.

After a short time, the light breeze turned into a strong wind, and for Elizabeth, it felt as if she was being wrapped in a warm and loving embrace.

"Robert, do you hear it?" she asked as she came to an abrupt halt. "Do you hear them?" seeing the confusion on Robert's face, she went on to explain. "The wonderful music the birds are making?"

As Robert watched Elizabeth, he was captivated by what she was doing, how it seemed she could feel and see something he could not.

"They are singing a chorus of songs," she said.

The way Elizabeth felt, she believed it was a wonderful gift nature had to offer, a true gift from God. Before Robert, she was alone in her love for the outdoors, but alone no longer.

Robert admired the way Elizabeth reacted to the forest around her, how alive she seemed to feel, and in the way, it enhanced her already vibrant life. How she found beauty in everything and everyone around her, and it took his breath away.

Robert understood how Elizabeth felt because he felt it too. Maybe not in the way she did, but it was there all the same. If he were to describe it, it was as if they were in their own little world, with the birds performing a concert just for them, in a celebration of life.

Robert felt a tightness in his chest, and when he placed his hand over his heart, he felt it racing, and instinctively he started rubbing his chest in a soft and circular motion as if he could rub it away, but to no avail.

What is this I'm feeling? he thought. This sensation worried Robert, but he continued to watch Elizabeth as he thought, *she is beautiful. How did I not see this before? With her thick long beautiful wavy hair, in the way it flows down, and ending at the lower part of her back.* This caused Robert to smile.

He found himself wanting to touch her hair, to feel it against his cheek, wanting to smell it – Robert froze. He jerked his head up, with heat rising in his face, as Elizabeth turned to look at him, radiating with joy.

Breathtaking, he thought, *and those eyes…beautiful, how did I not notice them before? Those beautiful brown eyes.* Robert shuddered at this thought, which confused him, and he needed to clear his thoughts of Elizabeth.

As Elizabeth watched Robert, she noticed his strange behavior and wondered what was wrong.

"Robert, are you well?" she asked, and then, "Are you cold? Do you wish to return to the manor?" she asked with concern. She wasn't ready to leave, but if he needed to, she wouldn't hesitate.

At first, Robert heard nothing Elizabeth was saying as his thoughts were elsewhere. *My love for the outdoors…*pausing in his thoughts as he watched Elizabeth, *I do not see or feel it in the way she does.*

Robert looked around the forest. He wanted to, to try and see the forest the way Elizabeth did, but instead, his eyes kept returning to her, and the sight of Elizabeth caused his heart to skip a beat. He was so focused on her that he didn't hear her speaking to him, and he knew at that moment, he could no longer deny it; something was happening to him. Something he did not understand, nor was he prepared to admit. The way his heartfelt, in what he was feeling…

When Robert finally found his voice, he said, "Eliz…" but choked on her name. He took a deep breath and tried again. "Elizabeth, to watch you…I wish I could see the forest as you do."

To Elizabeth's delight, Robert's words filled her with joy. She smiled and said, "You can," reaching her hand out to Robert, "Take my hand and close your eyes."

Robert moved closer to Elizabeth as he placed his hand in hers, then closed his eyes as she requested.

"With your eyes closed, it will allow you to see the forest the way I do…with your body."

After all these years, how did I not see how Elizabeth reacted when she's in the forest. Did she hide it from me because she was afraid of my retort? Robert thought.

Although what Elizabeth asked confused Robert, he trusted her implicitly.

"Now, breathe in and smell the forest around us."

Robert inhaled and took in the different fragrances that surrounded him, and it was intoxicating.

"Open your ears to the many sounds that surround us. The birds singing. The wolves howling in the distance. The sound of the wind blowing through the trees, and the rattling of the leaves swaying with the creak of the branches."

Robert nodded in understanding and tried to feel the forest as she did.

"The wind…as it flows around us. Don't just feel the wind. Feel it as if it were a blanket wrapping itself around you in a warm and loving embrace."

Robert found this amusing and smiled. He did not understand how the wind could wrap him in a loving embrace. But then, something started to happen, something that surprised him. He could feel it, and it felt as if he were being wrapped in a type of warmth – it did feel like love. As if the forest was coming alive, becoming a part of him. *Astonishing,* he thought.

Robert didn't understand what was happening to him, and he wondered if this was how Elizabeth always felt.

"Elizabeth, is this how you feel…as if the forest is a part of you?"

Elizabeth smiled, "Yes, Robert, it is…it is exactly how I feel…as if the forest is a part of me. I could not have expressed it better myself."

Robert was amazed by what he was feeling; it was as if he had a connection with the forest, one that penetrated deep into his soul. Also, there was something else – a stronger, a more powerful connection, one he did not understand, nor could he explain.

Robert's eyes snapped open, and then he looked

directly at Elizabeth. *It's her...Elizabeth.*

As Elizabeth watched Robert, her heart jumped. She felt something, a bond – *It's him...Robert. Is it possible...can Robert...will he ever see me differently...more than a friend,* she thought?

Robert and Elizabeth were two souls connected to the land and the life that surrounded them, in a connection they would never understand in life but in death.

With his newfound feelings of the forest, Robert suddenly felt the need to see more, so he convinced Elizabeth to go deeper, further than they ever had before into the forest. It was not hard since she was just as eager to see more of the forest as he was. This was something she would never have done when she was alone.

It was not long when they came upon a place that stood out, different from the rest of the forest. There were tall, thick trees, with branches fully bloomed with large thick leaves, unlike the rest of the forest. This fascinated Robert and Elizabeth since the rest of the forest was just starting to bloom.

Astonished with what he saw, Robert asked, "Elizabeth, have you seen this before?"

Elizabeth too, was mesmerized by what she was seeing and shook her head, "No. Never."

Robert and Elizabeth walked around the circle of trees and found that the trees were formed in a tight circle with no end in sight. Mystified, Robert and Elizabeth looked to find a break in the trees, wanting to see what was on the other side.

Just as Robert and Elizabeth were about to give up, Robert found a small opening on the north side of the trees. After showing Elizabeth, he pulled back the branches to allow her to enter without obstruction, then followed her through.

Upon entering, there was a powerful wind with a strong resistance as if something didn't want them there. But then, as quickly as the wind appeared, it disappeared as if they passed some type of test. Once they were finally on the other side, they found a large open space with a small lake.

Astonishing, Robert and Elizabeth thought in unison.

This place was unlike anything they've ever seen before. It felt like a place of great power – a magical place.

Once Elizabeth was on the other side, she was mesmerized by what she saw and was struck by a powerful force she didn't understand. At first, it scared her, then it calmed her, filling her with love, a welcoming from an unknown presence. What it was, she did not know. Then, Elizabeth felt a sense of knowing, a familiarity, a connection she could not understand.

It is peaceful here with a feeling I cannot explain, Elizabeth thought.

Elizabeth felt a prickle sensation on her arm, and when she looked down, the hairs on her arm were sticking up. *Strange,* she thought.

As Elizabeth looked around, she could not understand how the trees in this place were in full bloom when it was the start of spring, and everything outside was just beginning to bloom. When she looked at the lake, it also had dark green grass with yellow flowers spurting in small patches surrounding a semi-round lake.

As she stared at the lake, there was this need to go closer, as if it were calling to her, and without realizing it, she slowly started moving towards the lake, and just as she was almost upon it, she was filled with love.

Love? Why do I feel love? she thought with confusion. And then aloud, "I am loved," she whispered.

Elizabeth did not understand why she felt such love, but found herself wanting to embrace it. So, she closed her eyes as she did when she wanted to feel the land around her, and when she did, something seemed to touch her on the arm, and this startled Elizabeth, causing her to snap open her eyes, half expecting to find Robert by her side, but he wasn't, nor was anyone else around her.

Strange. There is nothing, nothing here, she thought, rubbing her arms. *It felt…as if someone touched me.* This confused Elizabeth, and then shortly after, she felt as if someone wrapped her in a warm blanket.

What does this mean, and why is this happening? she thought.

Suddenly, Elizabeth felt this need to be closer to the lake, so she carefully began to walk towards the lake until she was at the very edge of the water. Once she was standing there, what she was feeling earlier, intensify by tenfold.

Elizabeth's heart started beating faster, and when she placed her hand on her chest… *I can feel my heart beating…my chest tightening,* she thought.

Elizabeth looked at the lake and wondered, *is it possible…no, this cannot be…I feel as if the lake is pulling on my heart,* she thought, looking down at her chest, "my heart?" she whispered.

Elizabeth knew what was happening was impossible, and yet, she could not deny what she was feeling. Then, she was astonished when she heard words enter her mind that was not her own – *It is a great and powerful love you are feeling.*

These words surprised Elizabeth, and she didn't understand where they came from, nor did she believe they were her own. Suddenly, Elizabeth was engulfed with fear, as if she were being watched, and when she spun around, there was only Robert, who was standing a great distance away and was looking in the opposite direction. But then, as quickly as she felt the fear, it dissipated and was replaced with love. A love that calmed her, as if it wanted to reassure Elizabeth, she was safe.

Although Elizabeth felt calm, she still felt as if she was being watched. She looked around to be sure no one else was about, and when she found no one, she wondered if someone was on the other side of the trees, so Elizabeth listened, but the only thing she heard was the beating of her own heart.

You are being welcomed. This place is filled with love. A powerful love meant for you. There it was again, the voice in her mind.

After hearing this, only one thing could explain what was happening —

It must be angels. God's angels are filling me…embracing me with their love…God's love, she thought.

Elizabeth smiled, then looked to where Robert was and wondered, *does Robert feel what I am feeling?* Elizabeth needed to know, so she went to find out.

When Robert entered the place that was concealed – protected by a circle of trees, he was amazed at what he saw. The lake was a small lake surrounded by tall green grass with a large boulder at the end, and he felt something strange and unfamiliar —

No, not unfamiliar, it feels like love, a strong and powerful love, he thought.

Robert could not understand how one place could feel like love. It made no sense to him, and it was beyond his understanding.

Why do I feel this way? Robert thought, then started to move towards the other end of the lake, opposite from where Elizabeth was standing, though he took a moment to watch her. *She looks happy,* he thought, and this made Robert smile, then he continued his path to the lake.

Once he was standing by the lake, Robert looked up at the sky. It was a beautiful clear blue day with patches of clouds. It gave him comfort with a sense of peace, making him feel safe, with a feeling of being home.

Why do I fill so much love here? Why do I feel at home? How is this possible? Robert thought.

This love Robert felt was unfamiliar to him. It was

unlike the love he felt for his mother or her for him, and, on some level, his father's.

But this place, Robert thought, as he looked around, wanting to understand how he could feel such a powerful love that nearly brought him to his knees and tears to his eyes. Robert closed his eyes to prevent the tears from falling, then turned to look at Elizabeth, hoping she didn't see him, and when it was clear she didn't, he turned back to the lake.

Why is this place different from any other I know? he thought.

Once Elizabeth was near, she called out, "Robert, this place is wonderful. Do you feel how different it is?"

Robert turned to look at Elizabeth at hearing his name, "Yes, this is a wonderful place. A place like no other. Feel? What do you mean?" he said, not wanting to admit the truth, especially if she wasn't feeling the same way.

"This place is special, a magical place," she said, turning back to where she was standing. "There is a power here I do not understand. It feels…it feels like pure love, a love that pierces deep into the heart."

Elizabeth was surprised at the words that came out of her mouth, as they were not her own, but found she could not stop.

Elizabeth turned back to Robert, and found him watching her intensely. "It feels as if someone is calling out to us. Welcoming us. Do you naught feel it?"

Robert was amazed by this place. What she said was true. He felt it as well, and he needed to confess it to Elizabeth.

"Yes, Elizabeth, I do. It feels like love, a strong and powerful love, but there's more, what it is, I do not know." He looked around then said, "This place is for us, and we were meant to find it."

Elizabeth smiled. It filled her with joy to hear Robert's words. *Yes, love, we both feel the love,* she thought.

"Yes, Robert, you are right. This place is for us. A place we can come to be together."

Robert and Elizabeth found themselves caught up in the magic of this place, and together, they thought, *our place…why did I say that?* they wondered. Elizabeth and Robert continued to have thoughts in unison. *It feels right that this is to be our place,* they thought.

After these thoughts, Robert and Elizabeth turned to face each other and looked directly into each other's eyes, as they thought in unison, *it's fate,* a word they were unaccustomed with.

Robert turned to re-examine their surroundings, then he asked, "Elizabeth, do you feel it? It feels…this is to be our place. I cannot explain my words or why I feel this way…only, it feels right."

Elizabeth was surprised that Robert said the exact words she was thinking and said, "Yes, Robert, I was thinking those same words. This is our place."

After Elizabeth said the words, she felt this sudden desperation of other words that needed to be said.

Elizabeth touched Robert's arm and said, "We are to come to this place when we are together…" *Why?* Elizabeth wondered, but pushed the thought aside and continued, "Do you feel it as well?" she asked.

Robert was surprised by Elizabeth's words, and yet, he believed as she did.

Robert did not understand what was happening, but Elizabeth was right; they must return to this place when they are together.

"Yes, Elizabeth, I do," taking her hands in his, then he said, "This place is where we are to come during our time at Dunham Massey."

Robert turned back to the lake and opened his arms wide to encompass their surroundings as he said, "This is to be our lake. Our place."

There was something happening between Robert and

Elizabeth beyond what they believed or understood, but it did not matter; for Robert and Elizabeth, it felt right.

Robert and Elizabeth remained at the lake for a while longer, sitting near the large oak tree with a branch stretched out towards the lake, and waited until the sun was about to set before they finally began their return to the manor.

Thus, the beginning of the change in their relationship.

***

While Robert and Elizabeth were together, Grace would wonder how they were getting along – were they becoming more than friends? Were they falling in love? These questions made her anxious and desperate to speak to Elizabeth as soon as she returned.

Grace and Elizabeth's previous conversations gave her hope that her plan was working, but she wondered if they were falling in love. Not knowing the answer and knowing she could not ask Elizabeth directly, Grace tried to find her answer in the way she looked, in her body language, but to her dismay, Elizabeth revealed nothing that helped her. So, each and every day, Grace prayed that Robert and Elizabeth were becoming close and were falling in love, and once the truth was revealed, Robert and Elizabeth would fight to be the ones to marry, thus freeing her from the obligation that was tossed upon her.

Chapter Six

<u>**Spring of 1533**</u>

It has been a year since Robert and Elizabeth found their magical lake, where they have spent most of their time together while at Dunham Massey. Although they were in denial in not wanting to acknowledge their feelings for each other, this new year will change in a way neither of them was prepared for.

With the amount of time that Robert and Elizabeth spent together, they would often discuss the agreement between their families and Robert and Grace's upcoming wedding. A wedding that will merge their families together, and in doing so, will increase their power and wealth within the land. For Elizabeth, this subject started to become a contentious one.

Robert's and Elizabeth's favorite place was the large tree with the branch extended towards the lake. They wanted to be close to the lake, with the way it made them feel loved.

Elizabeth was leaning back against the tree with her legs outstretched as she was pulling at the grass, while staring at the lake, when suddenly she felt dread and fear, and it was something that needed to be said.

"Robert, I feel…I am afraid our friendship…our time together will end once you and Grace are married." There, it was said. This was something Elizabeth had been worrying about since the day they found this lake, and now that it was said she wondered how Robert felt.

Elizabeth turned to Robert, who was staring at her with a surprise look on his face. She took a deep breath and continued with what she needed to say.

"Robert, in two years, you and Grace will marry and I…I need…I need to know how you feel about this?" Elizabeth knew speaking so was a significant risk, but she needed to tell him and prayed Robert felt the same way.

Robert was lying on his side with his legs stretched out resting on his elbow, and when he heard what Elizabeth said, his heart began to race. Her question surprised him, and he found he didn't know what to say. He has not put much thought into this, marrying Grace was his duty, it didn't matter how he felt, as heir, he would do what was required of him. He will marry Grace.

When Elizabeth finished, Robert said nonchalantly, "Elizabeth, there is nothing to talk about, I shall do what is asked of me. What else can I do? It is my duty."

Elizabeth was surprised at Robert's uncaring words, and at the same time, she was a little disappointed. How can he not think of it? she thought. For Elizabeth, she had thought of nothing else since that first day they found the lake.

At first, Elizabeth tried to fight what she was feeling for Robert, but the more time they spent together at the lake, had only strengthened her feelings for him. Yes, she knew it was impossible, Robert could never be hers, and she believed she had accepted that, but now, she wanted to be the one to make Robert happy, and not only as his friend. She knew this was not possible, so she decided if it were not to be her, she would help Robert find happiness with her sister, and for her sister to find happiness with Robert. It would not be easy, especially since Grace refused to spend any time with him. *With the way Grace loathes Robert, I worry about their happiness.* So, Elizabeth decides to find a way to change that.

Elizabeth looked at Robert with sadness. She has feelings for him, feelings she cannot act on, and ones, he does not seem to share. So, she would do it, she would help him find love with her sister, and her sister to find love with him. She wanted them to be happy and thought, *but how, when they spend little time together.*

There was no avoiding the subject, and she needed to

know. "Robert, would you not prefer to marry someone you love?"

Robert did not understand the reason for Elizabeth's question, but at the same time, her question disturbed him. But he pushed it aside and went on to answer her question.

"What you speak of is foolishness," he said motioning his hand to brush away her words. "No one marries for love Elizabeth, you know this. It is a contract between two families, a merger to increase wealth and power."

Elizabeth was disappointed, she hoped Robert felt as she did. So, she took a deep breath, and when she let it out, she said, "Robert, what you say is true, however, I cannot say I agree with you. When I marry, I pray I will marry for love." *I wish it could be you,* she thought.

Robert's heart sank when he heard 'when I marry,' and he did not understand why he felt that way, or did he? Brushing if off he said, "Elizabeth, nothing will make me happier if you marry for love. For me, it will not be so," he said without emotion.

Robert had to turn away from Elizabeth, he didn't want her to see how much this disturbed him, and of feelings he didn't understand, with feelings of regret and sorrow, knowing he will marry a woman he does not love, nor does he know. To his surprise, he found himself wishing he were marrying Elizabeth instead of Grace. Acknowledging this, he understood – *this must be the reason my heartfelt as it did,* he thought.

Before this moment, Robert never thought about love, especially after Grace presented her plan for Elizabeth to spend time with him than her, not until now. And now, he found himself wanting to be the man Elizabeth loved and married, and wondered what he was going to do?

Elizabeth saw a change in Robert, and it concerned her, so she reached out and placed her hand on Robert's arm, "Robert, what is wrong?" she asked as she tried to make eye contact with him, but he fought her, and turned further away so she could not see his face. However, this did not sway Elizabeth, and again she asked, "Robert, please tell me what is wrong?" When he still refused, she began to worry, so she pulled on Robert's arm to force him to look at her.

Robert heard the worry in Elizabeth's voice and was unsure what to say that would ease her mind, but he knew he had to say something, what it was, he did not know?

Robert took a deep breath, and when he released it, he attempted to tell Elizabeth what he was feeling. "Elizabeth," he started to say with a stutter. "I…I only wish…I wish…" Robert stopped, what was he going to say, that he wanted to marry her. If he did, what would she think, and if Robert spoke of how he felt, would it change everything between them. *It may be best if I do not tell her what I am thinking or feeling,* he thought.

Elizabeth watched Robert and saw how he was struggling with his words, and she didn't understand why, but decided not to push him and waited until he was ready to tell her.

As Elizabeth watched Robert, she noticed how he started picking at the grass and this caused her to smile. It was unavoidable.

Robert knew Elizabeth was watching him, as she waited for him to talk to her. He sat up and took a deep breath, and once he let it out, he said, "I…I wish I could marry…" Robert stopped, he turned to look at Elizabeth, as he wanted her to see his eyes when he spoke the truth, and when he did, he saw the look of worry on her face.

The way Robert looked at her, she knew he saw the worry on her face, so to ease his concerns, she smiled and nudged him with her shoulder, urging him to continue.

When Robert saw Elizabeth smile, it gave him the courage to continue. He returned the smile and said, "I wish…I wish I were marrying you." There, it was done, he said what he needed to say, and he watched Elizabeth's eyes, wondering what she was thinking and what she would do. Will she mock him. Laugh at him. Then suddenly he was engulfed with fear, afraid of what she would do or say, so Robert turned away, afraid he would see the laughter in her eyes.

When Elizabeth heard Robert's words, she was overjoyed. She cared and had feelings for him, but she never thought or believed they could be together, let alone marry. So, it was a surprise when he told her he wished it were her he was marrying.

In a soft and gentle voice, she said, "Robert," reaching up to place her fingers under his chin, she pulled him towards her, urging him to look at her, but Robert resisted. However, Elizabeth refused to give up so quickly, so, with both hands, she grabbed both sides of his face and forced him to look at her.

Although Robert tried to fight Elizabeth, not wanting her to see his pain, especially if she didn't feel the same way.

In a whisper, Elizabeth said, "Robert, will you not look at me please?"

When Robert heard the compassion in Elizabeth's voice, he turned to face her, and she smiled, "Robert, I know what you are saying, I..." she stopped, suddenly feeling shy… "I feel the same as you do." When the words were said, it surprised her since it was not something she considered. Elizabeth looked down, staring at her hands as they were resting in her lap.

Robert sighed with relief, and smiled as he was filled with happiness and said, "I want you to be the one I love and marry. There's times Elizabeth…I wish the arrangement were with you instead of Grace."

Elizabeth smiled, causing her eyes to sparkle with happiness. "Oh, Robert, I wish that too."

Robert smiled. He was filled with happiness and relieved to hear her words and decided to tell Elizabeth what he was thinking.

"Elizabeth, how can I marry Grace when I feel nothing for her, nor does she desire to be with me. I spend more time with you than with your sister. Grace has refused to spend any time with me since the first day at Bramhall Manor. You…you I can easily grow to love. There is already a closeness between us, a friendship like no other, and it brings me sadness to know our friendship will end once I marry Grace."

Although Robert and Elizabeth admitted their feelings for each other, they knew these feelings could not be pursued. Elizabeth decided she would be the strong one to put her feelings aside and help Robert and Grace find their way to each other. Elizabeth knew their friendship would never change, and in two years, they will be brother and sister.

"Robert, you and Grace still have time to get to know each other, and with my help, you and Grace will grow to like each other, and possibly love, before the time comes for you to marry. If not before, I am sure your feelings will change after you are married. Grace is a good person, and I know once she allows herself to get to know you, she will like you, and possibly come to care for you as I have," Elizabeth said with a smile, confident in her words.

Robert tried to keep a straight face, because he didn't want Elizabeth to know how much her words hurt him.

Friends! Robert yelled in his head. Elizabeth's words surprised him, and he wondered, *how can she still want to be friends after declaring her feelings for me?* These thoughts angered Robert, with a wave of anger he never felt before, and it surprised him.

Robert took a moment to gather his thoughts, then pulled back his anger as he thought, *is Elizabeth's feelings for me…are they not as strong as mine are for her.*

In a harsh voice, one he did not intend, "Elizabeth, you may believe your words, I cannot!" he yelled, then immediately regretted speaking to her so harshly, and didn't miss how she flinched at his cruel words.

Shocked by Robert's reaction, Elizabeth turned away from him and looked out towards the lake, feeling hurt by his words.

Robert said in a softer voice, "I do not feel I can ever love Grace, and I do not think she will ever love me. You, though…you," Robert placed two fingers under Elizabeth's chin to force her to look at him. He tilted her head up, so she would see the truth in his eyes. "I know I can come to love…" *I feel I already do,* he thought, but he was not prepared to speak these words aloud. Not yet, so he decided to do as Elizabeth said. Robert took Elizabeth's hands in his and said, "For you, Elizabeth, I will try."

Elizabeth was surprised by his words, but she could not allow them to affect her. He was to marry her sister, and she will help them find each other.

Although he wanted to love Elizabeth, he knew it was impossible. He must find a way to like Grace and love her if it were possible. Satisfied, Robert stood and smiled as he reached down to help Elizabeth up.

Elizabeth graciously put her hand in his and returned the smile.

"Come, it is getting late, we must return," Robert said, and they left the lake quietly together.

***

Elizabeth went to talk to Grace, she needed to convince her to start spending time with Robert. It was time, and Grace needed to find a way to like him, and before they were married.

Grace tried to object, but Elizabeth explained, "If you do not allow yourself to know Robert, you will never grow to like him or love him." Then, without further words, Elizabeth left Grace's chamber.

It is time Grace face her responsibility. It was best to make it clear and leave before she could object and try to change my mind, Elizabeth thought.

When Grace heard this, she panicked, feeling her plan was becoming unraveled, but she was careful not to show that Elizabeth's words affected her – scared her. Then, when Elizabeth left after telling her she needed to start spending time with Robert, Grace noticed how distant Elizabeth had been, and it seemed as if she'd been avoiding her, since the last time she was with Robert, she didn't go directly to speak with Grace after they retired for the night, when she usually did to provide her with the information she needed. It was only after Grace pressed Elizabeth, did she finally visit her and provide her with what she needed.

There is more going on with Elizabeth and Robert then she is telling me. Grace smiled, *hum, maybe my plan is working,* Grace thought, and she was more determined than before to keep their current arrangement. *I will find a way to convince Elizabeth. I will. I must.*

***

Spring was coming to an end as summer was closely approaching, and Grace lived as if there was no care in the world after convincing Elizabeth to continue their arrangement, and with reluctance Elizabeth agreed. And so, Elizabeth and Robert spent the rest of spring trying to forget about what happened and what the future held once Robert and Grace were married.

***

It was the first day of summer when Elizabeth went to see Grace, to provide her with an update of her time with Robert, as she had been unsuccessful in convincing Grace to spend time with him, but she knew this had to change.

Elizabeth stood hesitating at Grace's chamber door, but after a few moments, she knocked and waited for Grace to grant her entrance.

"Come," Grace said.

Elizabeth entered her chamber and as she did, she asked, "Grace, do you wish to speak this evening of my time with Robert, or would you prefer I return in the morning?” Elizabeth asked with the lack of emotion or strength.

In truth, she didn't want to talk to Grace, but knew there was no avoiding it either. Grace had become suspicious when she resisted telling her about the times she spent with Robert. So, she will again relay her time with Robert, but Elizabeth must persuade Grace to start spending time with him.

Grace snapped her head up and quickly put down her book. She patted the place next to her on the bed as she said, “Come sister, sit beside me and tell me of your day with Robert.”

Elizabeth gave Grace a semblance of a smile, then sat next to her on the bed but avoided Grace's question. Instead, she asked one of her own, “Grace, how was your day?”

“I had a wonderful day sister, and you?” Grace said, putting the question back on Elizabeth.

“Grace, the time I spend with Robert has been wonderful. It has allowed our friendship to grow stronger than it ever was.”

Grace smiled. She felt pleased with herself and thought, *maybe there was more there than friendship as Elizabeth claimed.*

“Robert is worried that once you are married, we will not be allowed to be friends.”

Grace tried to speak, but Elizabeth put her hand up, stopping her.

“I told Robert this is not so, that you would allow us to continue being friends once you are married. I hope I was not wrong in my words to him,” Elizabeth said.

Grace stiffened when she heard the word 'married,' but then pushed it away, so Elizabeth didn't see how much it bothered her.

Then Grace decided to play her hand, “I know, you can

marry Robert instead of me," she said with a laugh, trying to play off her feelings and her fears.

Elizabeth ignored Grace's attempt at humor and in a serious tone said, "Grace, I know you do not mean what you say," feeling concerned for her sister, Elizabeth asked, "Do you not feel anything for Robert?"

In a tone lacking emotional attachment, Grace said, "No, nothing. I have no care for him or any husband." And then out of nowhere, and in an angrier tone than she intended, "I am angry that this has been forced upon me! What right did our families have to decide our fate before we were of age to decide for ourselves? They should have waited and allowed us to choose!" Grace yelled.

Grace's ideals of life as a woman were naive, and she allowed her books to give her a false sense of freedom as a woman, and her father did not help her buy spoiling her as he did, by always giving her what she wanted. A father chose the fate for their daughters, and for nobility, it was done at infancy without ever having a say. You could not say no.

"Grace, it is how it is done. Grace," Elizabeth said, feeling worried, "You must learn to like Robert and care for him, he is to be your husband." Suddenly feeling emotional, "The thought of him being with someone who does not care for him or love him..." Elizabeth stopped herself, afraid she was revealing more than she intended, of her true feelings for Robert. Elizabeth took a moment to gather herself before she said, "Even if the woman is my sister."

Grace did not miss the concern and sadness in Elizabeth's voice, which told her there was a great deal more happening than what she said.

Grace laid her hand on Elizabeth's arm and softly said, "Elizabeth, do you love Robert?" as she thought, *please say yes.*

If it was true, it meant her plan was working, and

knowing this, Grace wanted to jump up and down with joy, but instead she held her excitement.

Elizabeth felt perturbed at the idea of her being in love with Robert, and she was determined to correct this.

"Grace do not be absurd!" she said harsher than she intended. So, Elizabeth took a moment to gain control of her feelings and said in a softer voice, "Of course I do not love Robert. We are only friends. He is to be your husband Grace," she said, then turned away from Grace, afraid her words stirred something in her, she was too scared to admit.

In what Grace said, Elizabeth began to question if this was true. *Do I love Robert? Is it possible? No, this cannot be. It is preposterous. We are only friends and nothing more,* she thought, attempting to reassure herself.

Grace was not fooled by Elizabeth's words and tried to get Elizabeth to admit it.

"Elizabeth, take care, I feel there is more there than you are willing to admit. Elizabeth, we can see if they will change my name to yours, so you will be allowed to marry Robert," Grace said as she thought, *please, please, please, say yes. If she does, then I will be free.*

Grace felt excited knowing her plan was working, because she felt there was no doubt Elizabeth had feelings for Robert, ones she was not prepared to admit. Not yet.

God, let this be. If what I believe is true, then I will be free from this betrothal. God, please help Elizabeth and me, as Robert is the better choice for her, she thought.

Elizabeth was shocked at her sister's implications and said, "Grace, how can you ask that of me? No, I do not want to marry Robert. We are only friends. He is to marry you." Then to throw the attention back to Grace, she said, "You cannot keep avoiding Robert, Grace."

Grace decided it was best not to push so she said, "You are right Elizabeth, I am sorry. Let us not talk about this anymore," then she hugged her sister. "Now return to your chamber and get some sleep and we will talk of this morrow."

Elizabeth left Grace's chambers more confused than when she entered, not realizing she failed to do what she originally went to see Grace for. For Grace however, she was beaming with joy at the thought of Elizabeth and Robert's relationship may be turning into more than friends.

***

Later that evening, as Elizabeth was lying on her bed staring at the top of her bed, she replayed her conversation with Grace. Grace's words gave her a great deal to think about, but she had to remember her feelings didn't matter. It was Grace she must think about, not herself.

Robert is hers, not mine, she thought.

Elizabeth decided, whatever her feelings for Robert were, she had to put them aside for the love of her sister and their friendship. Their friendship was more important than any friction caused by their families, if they were to explore the feelings they talked about.

Chapter Seven

<u>**Winter of 1533**</u>

Since winter arrived, Robert and Elizabeth were forced to meet in the early morning hours before the rest of the house were awake. It had to be this way, since Grace absolutely refused to venture outdoors in the cold snow, no matter how much Elizabeth and Robert tried to convince her. The benefit from this, it forced Grace to spend time with Robert, as there was no other place for her to hide without raising questions, unlike during the warmer months. For Elizabeth, it made her laugh. However, in the evenings, while they were in their chambers at Bramhall Manor, Grace did not hide how much she hated the situation.

For Elizabeth, winter was her favorite time of the year. When she woke up in the mornings, she would rush to her window and was wildly excited to see the freshly fallen snow covering the ground and the trees, and it was breathtaking.

Elizabeth was to meet Robert at the place they designated their lake, which was prearranged with Grace's help. Elizabeth turned from the window and walked over to her wardrobe where she pulled out her favorite gown, the golden one with white French lace and a v-neckline. The gown was made of strong French silk that flowed loosely down to her feet.

After putting on her gown, Elizabeth stood in front of her long mirror and thought, *beautiful,* with the way her dark brown hair fell right across her shoulder, and how her gown radiated off her golden skin, creating a light – an aura around her. It was as if a ray of lights had shined down, engulfing her in a bubble of pure beauty.

Once Elizabeth was satisfied with how she looked, she turned to her wardrobe that held her cloaks and pulled out her favorite one, which was made of thick white rabbit fur and the matching leather gloves.

Elizabeth returned to the mirror to give herself one final look. Once she was satisfied, she turned and walked out the door and quietly made her way down the hall and down the stairs. Once she was outdoors and standing in the snow, Elizabeth took a moment to embrace the cold morning air before she began her walk to the lake.

As she started her walk, she was surprised to feel fluttering in her stomach with the feeling of excitement, knowing she would see Robert. This excitement has grown recently, as she anxiously waited for the weekend to arrive so she can be with Robert.

Elizabeth loved the cold and took her time walking to the lake, enjoying the beauty winter had to offer, in the way the snow sparkled in the sunlight, for her, it felt right, perfect, and beautiful. Elizabeth spent a great deal of her time outdoors, while everyone else remained indoors, staying near the warm fire.

As Elizabeth approached the lake, she was mesmerized by how the lake transformed into a magical winter wonderland, in the way the tree branches were filled with snow, as icicles were hanging down glistening against the water surface below.

***

Elizabeth saw Robert standing at the edge of the lake with his back towards her. She smiled. It gave her the perfect opportunity, so she quietly and slowly approached Robert, so he would not hear her. When she was close enough, she bent down and gathered a handful of snow in her hands and formed a small snowball. She pulled her arm back, and with all her strength she threw the snowball as hard as she could and hit Robert square in the back.

Robert felt something hit him in the back, and when he spun around and saw Elizabeth laughing at him, he instantly rushed towards her, but then stopped abruptly, and bent down to gather snow in his hands to form a snowball. When he straightened, he looked at Elizabeth and gave her a sinister smile.

Elizabeth's eyes widen when she saw Robert gathering snow in his hands, and when she saw the look in his eyes, she knew she was in trouble. So, she gathered her gown and prepared to run as she yelled, "Robert, don't you dare!"

When Elizabeth saw Robert's smile widen, she knew she was in trouble. After all, she did start it, so she began to run.

With Robert grinning wide said, "Would I not," and without further words, he quickly tossed the snowball missing Elizabeth's head by mere inches. The look on Elizabeth's face was priceless. With the shock and horror she displayed as the snowball flew passed her head, caused Robert to burst out laughing. He laughed so hard he fell to his knees as he held his stomach.

Elizabeth was mad at Robert for almost hitting her in the head. No, she was furious, and walked towards him with her hands on her hips. "Robert! You almost hit me in the head! You fool!" she yelled.

Still laughing, Robert looked up at Elizabeth, "You…" he tried to say, but was barely able to speak, "You are lucky..." laughing… "I…" laughing… "Missed…" more laughing… "If I wanted..." laughing… "To hit you..." laughing… "I would have…" laughing. Robert was laughing so hard he could no longer speak, causing an ache in his side.

Robert's actions infuriated Elizabeth, so she reached down to form another snowball, but before she could, Robert grabbed her from behind and pulled her down to the ground, then straddled her as he held her arms down.

Elizabeth struggled to get out of Roberts firm grip, but he was too strong.

Robert was still laughing, and through his laughter he said, "If you stop struggling, I will let you go. Remember, this was you're doing."

Elizabeth did as Robert said and stopped struggling, then stared at him for a few moments before bursting out laughing herself.

"You are right Robert. It was an excellent shot."

Surprised by Elizabeth's remark, Robert stopped laughing as his mouth dropped open. After a moment he said, "Oh truly, you think so...hum?" he said with a smirk.

"Yes..." laughing… "Yes, I do. I hit you in the center of your back," Elizabeth said, still laughing.

Suddenly, Robert was hit with the desire to kiss Elizabeth. He stopped smiling, and before he changed his mind, he kissed her long and hard.

Elizabeth was stunned when Robert kissed her, a kiss that quickly, to her surprise, turned to desire, with a wanting she didn't know she had.

When Robert kissed Elizabeth, he was overwhelmed with a passion he didn't know existed, and once he started, he didn't want to stop, but grudgingly, he lifted his head and looked into Elizabeth's eyes, and what he saw, first was the same desire he felt, then it quickly turned to one of shock and fear.

The passion Elizabeth felt when Robert kissed her, terrified her, and when Robert broke their kiss, all she could do was stare at him, feeling confused at what happened.

Seeing the way Elizabeth was looking at him, Robert said, "You didn't expect me to kiss you, did you?" he smiled with satisfaction.

Not knowing what to say or do, all Elizabeth could do was stare at Robert, and was shocked when her desire for him returned, realizing she wanted more.

Robert did not miss the change in Elizabeth, and before she could change her mind, he kissed her again. This time, this time he kissed her slowly and with all the passion he had, stirring something within him that he did not understand, nor at that moment, did he care.

While Robert was kissing Elizabeth, she forgot everything around her for a short time, but when her mind cleared, she was appalled with what she was doing, and immediately stopped kissing Robert, and placed her hands on his chest trying to push him off her.

Robert did not miss the change in Elizabeth, and when she started pushing at his chest wanting him to stop, he quickly rolled off her and lied on his back trying to catch his breath before he stood up. When he did, he reached down to help Elizabeth to her feet.

After Robert rolled off Elizabeth, she could not look at him, and when he offered her his help, she refused and turned away. "Robert, what were you thinking?" she said brushing the snow from her gown.

Elizabeth was nervous and scared, so before she said another word, she took a few deep breaths, then let them out slowly, as she tried to gain control of her emotions. She needed to understand what happened.

Robert watched Elizabeth, and with the way she was acting, he was afraid – afraid he made a grave mistake, and afraid this mistake would cost him their friendship. He had to make her understand, to see it was not just him, but it was the two of them.

"Elizabeth, you cannot question what happened. You wanted this as much as I did. We kissed, it is not wrong," he said as he reached for Elizabeth with the need to comfort her.

Elizabeth was frustrated with Robert, and stepped away when he reached for her, then yelled, "Robert, stop! How can you say that! This is wrong! You are to marry Grace!"

Elizabeth wondered what she was thinking when she allowed Robert to kiss her. Yes, she was angry with him, but forced herself to calm down, because she too was to blame, if not more so. She wanted Robert to kiss her, this, she could not deny.

Robert lowered his head in shame and said, "Elizabeth, I am sorry. You are right."

Robert carefully reached for Elizabeth's hand, and when she didn't pull away, he said, "Elizabeth, can you deny there is something between us. Something more than friendship?"

Robert's heart started to race; he could not deny what he was feeling. He looked at Elizabeth and wanted desperately to pull her back into his arms. He wanted to kiss her again but held back as he knew it was wrong.

Elizabeth was so nervous and scared, in knowing what she had to do. In a shaky voice, she said, "Robert, no I cannot, but what I feel does not matter. You are to marry Grace, my sister." Then, in a harsher voice, one she didn't intend, "We cannot do this!" she said, turning away from him —

Can I do this? she thought. *Is it possible?* Elizabeth shook her head at this thought, then slowly turned back to look at Robert. She could not deny what she was feeling, but acting on those feelings, knowing Robert was to marry her sister, was wrong. Then suddenly, Elizabeth was hit with an overwhelming amount of sadness, sadness at what she knew must be done.

"Robert," she said, looking down at the snow, unable to look at him, "We…" she started to say, but found she needed to take a deep breath, and after she let it out, she continued, "We…just for a time, we need to stay away from each other. Maybe after time has passed, we will come to realize what we did today…what our feelings might be is a mistake…they are not real," Elizabeth said, swallowing the lump in her throat, at the same time fighting back tears. "We are two people who share the same interest in our love for the outdoors, who came to care for each other," she said, with her heart pounding in her chest, as her stomach was twisting in knots.

What Robert and Elizabeth did was wrong, and

Elizabeth wondered how she allowed it to happen? Yes, she had feelings for Robert, and he for her – *no, this is dangerous,* she thought.

The love Elizabeth had for her sister, and the honor she had for her mother and father, this alone should have prevented what she and Robert did. But it did not, so maybe distance will.

Robert's heart dropped, and it ached – he was stunned by what Elizabeth said and was speechless. The only thing he could do was stare at her in utter shock.

When Robert finally found his voice, he said, "I don't believe what you say is true. Nor do I think you believe it as well."

She cannot believe what she is saying. Look, she cannot even look at me. She is hurting as much as I am. This she cannot hide. I do not believe there is truth in what she said, he thought, then Robert shook his head, *no, she is right.*

He cannot deny what Elizabeth said, not after that kiss, it would be impossible for them to continue as they were. But can he do this? Can she?

"Elizabeth," Robert started to say but his voice cracked, as he was filled with sadness, but he knew the words needed to be said. Robert took a deep breath, and after he let it out, he said, "What you say is not wrong…" he paused, he needed another moment before he finally said, "Do you believe it will work, because I do not?"

If Elizabeth had any doubts about Robert's feelings for her, she no longer. It was evident by the tone of his voice and the look in his eyes that his feelings were real. To know this, caused the ache in her heart to grow to a torturous pain.

Unable to look at Robert, she said, "I do not know. I know what we did was wrong, and for our friendship…we can no longer continue. For us to part…the time we spend apart will let us know if what we feel is real."

Elizabeth did not want their friendship to end, nor their

time together, but after what happened, how could they continue as they did. They could not.

Elizabeth felt lost; it was as if she was losing her best friend, the person who shared the love of the outdoors with. She made eye contact with Robert and said, "Robert, our friendship means more to me than you know…" Elizabeth turned away for a moment. She needed to gain control of her emotions before she continued.

When she was ready, she turned back, "The love I have for my sister means more to me than our friendship. I cannot do this to her. You have to understand that?" Elizabeth said, motioning her finger from herself to Robert. "Robert, we cannot do this to Grace. It is not right. I know she does not want this betrothal, but what we did is an unforgivable betrayal."

Robert looked down; he felt ashamed because he knew Elizabeth was right; there was no denying it. Unsure what to say or do, he began kicking at the snow with his foot, he did not want their time to end, but Elizabeth was right, what she said had to be done.

"For you, Elizabeth, I will agree to this."

Robert took a moment to gather his emotions before he looked at Elizabeth, and when he did, he looked directly in her eyes and said, "For the love you have for your sister, I will try."

Elizabeth nodded in understanding.

For Robert and Elizabeth, this was the hardest thing they had to do in their young lives, but after stepping over the lines of impropriety, it had to be done. So, together they left the lake, and once they were at the edge of the forest, they turned and went their separate ways.

***

As Elizabeth walked back to the manor, tears were streaming down her face as her heart was breaking, as her mind searched to understand what happened.

How did I let this happen? I am a horrible sister…an

*awful friend. It is my fault this has happened. I knew my feelings for Robert had changed since that day at the pond, and then when we found the lake. My feelings for him…*shaking her head not wanting to recall those feelings again from that day, but they would not leave her mind. *In the way I looked at him…how much I wanted him, but I knew it could not…can never be. This kiss should never have happened. I should have walked away when I realized my feelings for him were becoming more than friendship. But no, I did not. It was my need to have someone who loves the outdoors as much as I do, something I was not prepared to give up. It was too much to turn my back on. I was foolish to believe I am strong enough to continue this friendship. What am I to do now? What do I tell Grace? We can no longer continue this deception. Grace has no choice but to spend time with Robert. What do I say? How do I tell her? How do I convince her? Do I tell her what happened? I must. She is my sister. The one I can talk to about anything. When did that change?*

Elizabeth was rambling, she was so lost and confused, and before she knew it, she was at the cottage and headed up to Grace's chambers unsure what she was going to say.

***

Robert was walking in a daze, feeling numb and wasn't paying attention to his surroundings, as he was lost in his thoughts, reliving what happened —

That kiss, he thought, touching his lips with his fingers. *How did this happen? When did it change?*

Robert recalled that early spring day at the pond, then later in the woods.

That day when Elizabeth was watching me…I believed she looked ill? Was there more there than what I thought?

Robert allowed his mind to return to that day, to that moment he and Elizabeth were walking in the woods after his swim in the pond, in the way she looked at him. He didn't think much of it at the time, but now, as he recalled that day, there was more.

Was it desire? Did she desire me? The look she gave me was different, and with the way she seemed nervous around me, instead of the spirited brazen girl she usually was. For me, when I saw her in the forest, that was when I saw her for the first time. How unfamiliar feelings stirred in me, ones I should not have felt for, for one I call friend. I shook off that day as a moment of weakness and nothing more, but after this morning, when I saw Elizabeth in that gown, with her hair hanging over her shoulders...Robert smiled, her smile...she was beautiful. How could I not have kissed her? My desire to kiss her was too strong to resist.

At this, Robert knew their time apart would be the toughest days of his life, but it must be done. Elizabeth was right; time apart will help them realize what they were feeling was not real, and then they could return as they were, as friends.

Robert entered Dunham Manor, ignoring everyone and everything around him. He went directly to his chamber where he needed to be alone to think about what happened.

***

When Elizabeth arrived at Grace's chamber's, her door was ajar, so she pushed open the door and entered. Elizabeth saw Grace stretched out on her bed reading her book, and she desperately wanted to tell Grace what happened, but was scared.

Maybe she can help me understand what is happening, and together we can find a way to prevent dishonoring our families, Elizabeth thought.

The problem with this, Elizabeth was not aware of Grace's true plan; this was precisely what she hoped would happen. Telling her this will not induce Grace's help, but instead, it would give Grace exactly what she needed to push them together.

Elizabeth took a deep breath, and after she released it, she entered Grace's room. "Grace, I must speak with you?"

she said, in a soft voice that was almost a whisper.

Without looking up from her book, Grace put up her finger and said, "A moment, I need to finish this first."

When Grace finished, she closed her book and rested it in her lap, then looked up and smiled at Elizabeth. "Okay, I am done," she said, but noticed there was something wrong. Instead of asking what was bothering her, Grace instead asked, "How did your morning go with Robert?"

The way Grace was looking at her, Elizabeth feared she knew the reason for her visit, and didn't answer her sister right away as she thought, *how can she?*

While Grace waited for Elizabeth to respond, it was clear she was in distressed. There was something wrong – "Elizabeth, what's the matter?"

Elizabeth's shoulder slumped as she walked over to Grace's bed and sat down. "Oh, Grace…everything has gone wrong. This arrangement was a mistake. I should never have been the one to spend time with Robert, and I should never have allowed you to talk me into it," Elizabeth said as she took a deep breath and when she released it, she continued, "What am I going to do?" she asked, as she fought back her tears.

"Elizabeth, what happened to make you feel this way?" Grace asked, touching Elizabeth softly on the cheek. When she saw the tears, "Why the tears?" she asked.

Unable to maintain control of her feelings, "Grace…oh God Grace…Robert…" she started to say but stopped. In a firmer and calmer voice, she said, "It is your fault!" she yelled as her anguish turned to anger. "You forced me! You, who felt too good to spend time with Robert! You forced me, your sister, to cover for you! Why? So, you can do what you love the most, read! How is that fair? It is all your fault! You should never have asked me to spend time with Robert!" Elizabeth yelled, and she could no longer hold back her emotions, she broke down and wept.

Elizabeth was so angry with her sister for putting her in

this position, and at herself and Robert for allowing Grace to talk her into spending time with him, by using Robert and her interest in the outdoors to persuade her. She was mad at her mother and father and the Davenports for putting Grace and Robert in this position. So, lashing out at her sister seemed to be the best way to release the pain and anger she was feeling.

Grace was surprised by Elizabeth's sudden outburst with the anger she expressed. She didn't understand why or where this was coming from. Then it hit her, and she smiled inside, because if she were right, it would be the most fantastic news. But as Grace watched Elizabeth, how could she be so happy, when her sister was in so much pain. Although she believed what had Elizabeth so upset, she had to be sure.

Gently Grace asked, "Elizabeth, I see you are upset. Please sister, calm yourself and tell me what happened, that's caused you such distress?"

Elizabeth took a moment to calm herself before she answered Grace. Without looking at her, she began to tell Grace what happened and the truth of her feelings for Robert.

"Grace, Robert and I were having fun throwing snowballs at each other until Robert kissed me."

Grace's eyes widened, and she wanted to jump off her bed and twirl in a circle at Elizabeth's admission, but instead, she fought to maintain control and said, "He kissed you. Did you return the kiss?" she asked.

At Grace's question, Elizabeth's face warmed as it turned red, and she was unable to look at Grace when she answered her, "Yes, and…I think I am falling in love with him," she said.

Elizabeth stared at her hands as she twisted the front of her gown, and after a few moments, she slowly raised her head to look at her sister.

Grace was overjoyed with Elizabeth's declaration. Her

plan worked perfectly, better than she hoped. She had to be careful though, she could not show her happiness, not when her sister was so upset.

Gently and with care, Grace attempted to help Elizabeth see, there was no reason for her to be upset or ashamed. Instead, she wanted Elizabeth to know she was happy for her.

"Elizabeth, do you not see, this is wonderful news. Your feelings for Robert will free me and allow you to marry Robert." Okay, maybe she wasn't so subtle.

Elizabeth was shocked by Grace's words and looked at her with disbelief.

Elizabeth turned to Grace, "What!" she yelled. She was angry; this was not the response she hoped for. "What are you saying, Grace? How can you be so happy about this? I told you I think I am in love with Robert —

Grace had to control her need to smile as she thought, *ah, now she's in love, instead of falling in love.*

"— your betrothed! And you act like it is the best news you ever heard!"

It is, Grace thought.

"Elizabeth, do you not see? If you are in love with Robert and he is in love with you, then you can be the one to marry him. You are a better choice than I am. You know this is true."

"Grace, I do not understand you," Elizabeth said, looking at her sister as if she was a stranger. *What is she thinking?* Elizabeth thought.

"How can you believe this?" Elizabeth asked. She was stunned by her sister's reaction and yet – *is it possible? Am I in love with Robert? Can we marry?* At this thought, Elizabeth felt a little hope and decided to hear what her sister had to say.

Grace smiled as she thought, *yes, I am right…this is working.*

Grace straightened her back and composed herself,

"Elizabeth, I do not see why mother and father will not allow you to marry Robert, if you and he are in love."

"Grace, mother and father, not to mention Lord and Lady Davenport will never allow it. You and Robert are to marry. That is the agreement is it not."

"Elizabeth, I do not see how it matters what Massey Robert marries, so long it is a Massey? How difficult will it be for them to change my name to yours on the agreement. I do not see the problem. Do you?"

"Grace, do you even know what the agreement says? Can you honestly say it can be changed?"

"No, I have not been shown the agreement, but if it is to merge our families, I do not see why it matters if it is you or me. How difficult can it be to make a small insignificant change?"

"Well, if you think it can be done so easily, then you should go down and ask father and see what he has to say?" Elizabeth demanded.

Elizabeth does not believe their father will agree; however, Grace has been able to suede their father to obtaining what she wants in the past, so it may be possible she can do it again and get their father to agree. Elizabeth smiled, as her hope increased a little.

Determine to prove to Elizabeth the agreement can be changed, Grace said, "Fine, I will," then turned her head as she stuck her nose in the air. Grace stood and marched out the door going directly to her father's study.

***

When Grace arrived at her father's study door, she was pleased to see it was open, which meant he would receive her. Grace smiled, even if the door were closed, he would still receive her. She was his favorite, after all.

She peeked in and saw her father sitting behind his desk with his head down hard at work. Although his door was open, she wondered if this was the right time to bother him? *I must ask the question,* she thought, and then, *of course he will see me,* she thought as her smile widened.

Grace took a deep breath, and after releasing it, she proceeded to enter her father's study, knocking on the open door as she entered.

Baron Massey raised his head when he heard the knock on his door, and when he saw it was Grace, he smiled, he was always pleased to see his daughter. He placed his quill down and waved for Grace to enter and said, "Come in child."

"Good evening father, I see you are busy. May I have a moment of your time? There is something I wish to ask you?"

There's nothing he wouldn't do for Grace, "Of course Grace. How may I be of service?" he asked, leaning back in his chair.

"Father, I was wondering what would happen if I did not want to marry Robert?"

Grace did not miss how her father's soft demeanor changed to a stern one, but he did not interrupt her and waited for her to continue. It did cause Grace to hesitate, but her will was strong and proceeded to ask her father what she needed to know.

Swallowing the lump in her throat, "What if there was another?" she asked.

Baron Massey's anger grew with Grace's inquiry, but he pushed it down, not wanting her to see how angry her question made him. So, he forced himself to calm down before answering her.

"Grace, it is impossible. The agreement forged with Lord Davenport cannot, for any reason be broken. Not without severe consequences. Grace, by marrying Robert, you will do your family proud," he said before returning to his work. "Now leave, I have much work to do." But then he looked up feeling guilty at his harsh response, "I am sorry Grace. If it was anything else…good evening," and nothing further was said.

With that said, Grace left her father's study feeling disappointed, as she slowly made her way back to her chamber with her head down.

When Grace arrived at her chamber and entered, she saw Elizabeth sitting on her bed, anxiously awaiting her return.

When Elizabeth saw Grace enter her chamber, she jumped off the bed without waiting, "Well Grace? What did father say?"

With sadness and disappointment, Grace said, "Elizabeth, you were right. There is nothing we can do."

Elizabeth was surprised to hear Grace's answer; if anyone could sway their father, it was Grace. To know this saddened her. When Grace left, she had hope, and now, that hope is no more. Knowing this, she knew what she had to do – she could no longer spend time with Robert, and it was time for Grace to take her responsibility seriously.

"Grace, you need to start spending time with Robert. I can no longer."

Without further words, Grace nodded in understanding; she knew she was defeated.

Chapter Eight

When the Massey's visited Bramhall Manor, Grace and Robert came to a mutual agreement; Robert will spend the morning and evenings indoors with Grace, and she will spend the afternoons with Robert outdoors.

For Elizabeth, she began to spend time with Robert's sister Rachel, either sewing, playing a musical instrument, and at times, drawing. This was difficult for Elizabeth, since she usually did her drawings outdoors, where she could be alone. When she could not venture outdoors, she would draw in the privacy of her bedchamber.

Other times when she was alone, she wandered around the outdoors, and on occasion, she would see Robert with Grace near his mother's garden. These times brought an ache to her heart, since she wished it were her instead of Grace, and immediately felt ashamed because she knew it was wrong.

When the families were together, Robert and Elizabeth did everything to avoid making eye contact, and only spoke when necessary. To both of their relief, no one seemed to notice anything was wrong, as most of their focus was on Grace and Robert, in preparing for their upcoming wedding.

For Robert and Elizabeth, they were in their own misery, missing the time they've spent together and the times they spent at their lake. And Grace was forced to spend time with a boy she had no interest in. She too, was in her own little misery. Grace believed her time was better spent reading her books, indulging in the adventures and the fantasy world she created for herself.

After a few weeks of spending time with Grace, Robert became concerned about his future with her. If he had doubts before, he no longer. If he married Grace, neither of them would be happy, as they have nothing in common.

Robert felt he could no longer continue their deception and decided to let her know.

Robert and Grace were standing at the French doors about to go out, when he whispered to Grace, "Grace, I can no longer do this. I am miserable, and I know you are as well," he said, opening the door for Grace.

Grace was relieved to hear Robert's confession. "I am pleased to hear this. I too, am unhappy with this arrangement and feel our time is best spent elsewhere. Yours with Elizabeth and mine reading my books. I wish we can return to the way things were."

Once outdoors, Robert took Grace's hand and led her to the lake only a short distance from the manor, so they would not be overheard.

With Robert and Grace standing at the lake, he turned to face her, "Grace, neither one of us are happy with our situation. For myself, I do not know how long I can endure this deception."

Grace was pleased to hear Robert's confession. "I am pleased to hear this, and I cannot agree more. This time we've spent together have not been fair to either one of us. It is unfair for our families to force this upon us…our betrothal. We should be allowed to choose who we are to marry?"

"You know the answer, Grace. It is not how things are done for a family of our status, and a noble marriage is prearranged at the time of our birth, a merger of status and power. I do not agree with it anymore then you do, but we have no say in the matter."

"Robert, is there nothing you can do? Can you talk to your father and see if he will allow you to see the agreement? I am sure as his heir you have a right to see it and maybe…" Grace stopped, unsure if she should ask what she desperately wanted to ask.

If he will allow you and Elizabeth to marry instead of me, she thought.

"Robert, if you can see and read the agreement, maybe you can find something that will allow Lord Davenport and my father to change the agreement, allowing you to marry Elizabeth."

Grace knew this was a significant risk, knowing he might not find anything in the agreement, and even if he did, their father's may not agree to change it.

But if Robert can convince his father…with the power he holds, he may agree to the change, Grace thought.

Robert had thought about asking his father to see the agreement, but to hear Grace say what he's thought about himself —

"I do not know Grace. I have thought about asking father," Robert shook his head, "But…I don't know Grace…"

Robert turned away from Grace, to look out at the frozen lake as he thought, *is it possible. Will father allow me to see and read the agreement. Why wouldn't he, the agreement involves Grace and me.* With a quick nod, it was decided.

Robert turned back to Grace and said, "I will agree to ask father, but not while you are here. I will wait until you have left and when I find father alone in his study, I will approach him and ask if he will allow me to see, and possibly read the agreement."

Grace was pleased and relieved to hear this, and it gave her hope, hope she didn't have before, and it allowed her to relax and release the tension and uncomfortableness she had felt.

"Thank you, Robert. You have given me…us hope, and I will pray you will find the answers that will free us from what will be an unhappy union."

Robert smiled, "Yes, Grace. Let's hold on to that until we meet again, and hope when we do, I will have good news to relay to you." Robert said as he put his arm out to Grace, "Shall we take a turn in the garden?"

Grace took Robert's arm, no longer feeling squeamish, "Yes, if you make it only one turn, and then we return to the manor where it is warm and cozy," she said, pulling her cloak closer together.

***

Later that evening and before dinner, Robert was sitting on his bed thinking about the past few weeks. He hated his situation, how he had no control over his life and future, and thought, *will it be possible for me to see the agreement? Why would it not be? It is an agreement involving Grace and me. I should…we should have every right to see it. Father though, he may not allow me to read the agreement. I will be so lucky if I'm even allowed to see it.*

Robert felt unsure about his decision to speak to his father. He stood and walked over to his window, then opened the shutters and took a deep breath, taking in the crisp cold night air, then slowly let it out. He looked towards the dark forest and was surprised to see a figure emerging from the forest, and on closer inspection, it was Elizabeth.

Sighing, "I wish I were with you," he whispered. "This has been too hard for me. I wonder if it's been for you. I am sorry Elizabeth. I cannot continue without spending time with you…with speaking to you. Our times together have been the most incredible times of my life, that has filled me with great joy and happiness. There is no question, I must speak with father. I must try, for you and for me."

Robert continued to watch Elizabeth until she was out of sight, then closed the window and went down for dinner.

***

Back at Dunham Massey and in Grace's chambers, Elizabeth and Grace were sitting on the edge of the bed, as they talked about their recent visit at Bramhall Manor and how miserable Elizabeth had been. As they talked, Grace was wondering – hoping Robert would be able to convince his father to let him see the agreement, with the possibility he would find a way to replace her name with Elizabeth's. In doing so, would bring happiness to them all.

My Lord, I pray Robert will be allowed to see and read the agreement, and in doing so, he will find a way for him and Elizabeth to marry. Elizabeth deserves to be with Robert and he with her, with the happiness they have found and deserve to share, Grace thought.

Aloud, Grace said, "Elizabeth, you do not fool me. I know how miserable you have been since you stopped spending time with Robert, and I can confirm, he has been just as miserable."

Elizabeth looked at Grace, she was prepared to deny what she said, but she could not, nor did she want to.

Watching Elizabeth, Grace placed her hand on her leg, "He is miserable too, Elizabeth, he told me so."

Elizabeth was going to object to what Grace said, but Grace stopped her.

"No Elizabeth do not try to deny what I am saying. I know you have feelings for Robert. What does it matter that you do?"

Again, Elizabeth tried to argue, but Grace stopped her by putting her hand over Elizabeth's mouth.

"I know what you are going to say, but you are wrong. I am pleased…happy you and Robert have feelings for each other. It is okay, I what this for you, for you both. Please Elizabeth, do not use me as an excuse. You cannot deny that you are a better choice than I am," Grace said with joy.

Shocked and confused by what her sister said, as Elizabeth tried to deny them, and it irritated her that Grace stopped her each time. Yes, from what she said, it gave her hope, but still, how can Grace be so at ease with their situation.

With anger, "Grace!" Elizabeth yelled. Realizing she was too loud, she lowered her voice, so she would not be heard. "How can you so easily dismiss your situation? You act as if you have a choice when you do not. You and Robert will marry, no matter what my feelings are for him, or his are for me. It is the way things are done," Elizabeth said firmly.

Elizabeth was angry and frustrated, wondering how her sister could be so blind to her situation?

"Neither you nor I can change this, no matter how much we may want to," she said.

Yes, Elizabeth wanted more than anything to return to the way things were, but they could not, and what right did she have to wish it. If Elizabeth continued spending time with Robert, her feelings would only grow for him, so why would she put herself in that position, knowing no matter what she did, she would lose Robert to her sister, and this she could not do.

Seeing how her words caused Elizabeth anguish, Grace tried to ease her, "Elizabeth?" Grace said, placing her hand on Elizabeth's shoulder. "It is true, I care naught for our situation, but Elizabeth, I believe in time, once our families see the feelings you and Robert share, they will allow us to make the change in the agreement, so you and Robert will be allowed to marry.

Robert told me he would talk to his father, to see if he will allow him to see and read the agreement, in hopes he will find a way to change my name to yours."

Elizabeth snapped her head up shocked by what Grace said. She looked at Grace stunned, but at the same time she allowed herself to hope.

Wanting to make sure she heard her sister right, "Grace, what do you mean?" she asked, leaning in, and placing her hand on Grace's arm. "How can what you say be possible?" Then with hope in her voice, "Robert is willing…to talk to his father…to try and change the agreement?" she asked with amazement. "He wants this. He truly wants this." Elizabeth said, but she was afraid to hope.

Grace could not help but smile, "Well, when Robert and I last talked, he was going to wait until after we left Bramhall Manor before he spoke to his father and ask to see the agreement. If he does, he's hoping to find a way to change the agreement that will allow him to marry you." Grace said, placing her hand over Elizabeth's that were resting in her lap. "Elizabeth, he loves you, this I am sure of. He wants to be with you, not me. He is, as I am, wants out of this arrangement. He wants out of our betrothal so he can marry you. Can you not see that?"

"Grace?" Elizabeth started to say, but then looked away, unsure what.

What would she do if it were possible? Does she dare allow herself to hope? With this, she needed to know, and she needed to understand. "What do you mean he is going to speak to his father?"

Grace held back a smile; she knew Elizabeth was trying to understand what she told her.

"It is, as I said. Robert plans to talk to his father about allowing him to see the agreement, so he can find a way to marry you instead of me."

Grace saw Elizabeth's confusion, her fear, and her hope. Leaning in close to Elizabeth's face, as she placed her hand under her chin, forcing her to look at her, "Elizabeth, there is hope for both of us."

I am so afraid. Do I dare hope? Elizabeth thought.

"Grace, I do not know. What if his father refuses, then what?"

"My dear sister, all we can do is hope and pray he will. We will learn if he was successful on our next gathering," Grace said.

Elizabeth nodded in agreement, and then Grace hugged her sister.

***

After the Massey's left Bramhall Manor, Robert without hesitation went directly to see his father before he lost his courage.

Lord Davenport was not an easy man to deal with. He was a hard man, and his word was never challenged. No one argues or questions his father; after all, he is Lord Davenport of Cheshire, the law of the land. If anyone were to go against him, they paid severely, by torture, and would be released to return home if they survived. Other times, they would be tortured, and if they survived, they would be tossed in the dungeon until his father was satisfied. And if their crime were severe, their lives were immediately forfeited.

Robert recalled a specific time; it was one of the days his father insisted he attend court with him, wanting him to watch and learn how he ruled the people of Cheshire.

***

On one occasion, one of his father's tenants, a farmer – Robert could not recall his name, but this farmer had come upon hard times after being ill due to the plague, and was unable to work his land; therefore, he failed to pay his rent. The farmer was desperate, and since he was one of a few farmers to survive, he hoped his father would show mercy, by giving him another season to farm his land, that will allow him to pay his rent.

The problem with this, his father did not show any man or woman mercy, no matter the reason. To his father, the farmer signed an agreement to pay his rent with money or a part of his harvest, and the terms to his agreements were always upheld, with no exception, no matter the reason. The man begged and pleaded with his father to show mercy, if not for himself, then for his family, for his children. Robert recalled the man telling his father he had a pregnant wife and three small children, whom, by God's miracle, survived the plague.

"You knew the consequences of failing to pay your rent. You are aware of the terms of our agreement, are you naught? The one you willingly signed?" asked Lord

Davenport.

"Yes, My Lord, but —"

Lord Davenport cut the man off, "No but!" He roared, standing up to his full six foot four inches, a giant to most people in the land. "You! Dare!" he said through clenched teeth with eyes the look of evil. "Come here to beg me! To plead with me!" he yelled, sitting back down in his throne. "Because you failed to honor your signed agreement!"

The poor man was shaking with fear. Robert looked at his father, wanting him to show the man mercy. But his father gave him a stern look that said, 'I show no one mercy.'

"Yes, My Lord," he said in a shaky voice, filled with fear. "But my wife is with child and our three small children…I was ill…suffering from the plague and was one of the lucky ones to survive. As you are aware, My Lord, with such illness, there was no way I could work my land," said the farmer with pleading in his voice.

The man was trying – fighting to keep his emotions in check, knowing Lord Davenport would see this as weakness, and for a man to show weakness was asking for death.

Robert again turned to look at his father, and as he watched the man, he saw there was no care or feeling for the farmer or the story he told. For Robert, it broke his heart to watch the poor man, and he wanted his father to show mercy to him, knowing he would not.

Many people in Cheshire – in North England lost their lives to the plague. It was by God's good mercy the Davenport's and the Massey's, along with many other noble families were saved from such a disease, but many of the lower families, the unfortunate ones, were not.

"Stop!" Lord Davenport yelled. "If you were unable to work your land, you should have found someone to help you! I was very much aware of the plague! How dare you presume otherwise! If you took better care of yourself, as

my family did, as well as many others, you would not be here right now! Begging for something you know; I will not agree to! You failed to pay your rent; therefore, you forfeit your rights! Per the signed agreement of the land you rented from me, you are in default of your responsibilities! I order you and your family to vacate my land immediately! And, because you decided to come to me and beg me for mercy, I, therefore, sentence you, as the law in the land, to thirty days in the dungeon! Maybe in the future, if there is to be a future for you, you will remember this, and not repeat the error of your ways!"

Lord Davenport so ordered and waved his hand for the guards to take the man away, and without a second thought, he went on to the next order of business.

As Robert watched the proceedings, he could not help but look at the man in need, then to his father, and this was the first time he first felt ashamed of his father. He was shocked that his father was so uncaring to the man's unfortunate circumstances, that Robert, from that day, promised himself and to God —

When I become Lord of Cheshire, I will not govern with such a hard fist. Instead, I will govern with a caring heart, this I promise you, Robert thought.

When the ruling was given, afraid, the farmer panicked, he was desperate for Lord Davenport to see reason, needing him to understand, so he began to plead with Lord Davenport.

"My Lord, please!" The farmer pleaded.

But Lord Davenport ignored the man's pleas and again, with a wave of his hand, he motioned for his guards to take the man away.

"Guards! Take this man and throw him in the dungeon! Get this pitiful sight of a man out of my sight!" he ordered, and the guards carried out his orders, dragging the poor man away.

Lord Davenport called for another guard. "Gather men

and ride out to the farmer's house and throw his family out of their house and off my land!"

And without further thought, his father went on with business.

Robert was shocked, and prayed that God would see this man's family through the hardship he knew was upon them.

After that man, he did not want to see anymore and asked his father if he could leave, but his father refused.

Lord Davenport believed this was part of Robert's learning process in becoming a man, as a man and future lord and law of the land, it was his duty to bear witness to such proceedings.

Robert must learn to rule with an iron fist, Lord Davenport thought.

***

From that day forward, Robert could never forget the look on that man's face, the pain, and his fear. The man was so broken, and Robert hated to see what that poor man was brought down to.

For Robert to remember this, along with the promise he made that day, he decided to reiterate that promise once again. *My father may be a hard man, but I promise you Lord, I will not be,* he thought as he arrived at his father's study and knocked on the door.

"Come," called Lord Davenport.

Robert entered his father's study and said, "Father, may I speak with you about the agreement between you and Baron Massey regarding my marriage to Grace?"

Robert's father eyed him with suspicion, "What agreement do you mean?" he inquired.

Surprised, Robert asked, "You mean there is more than one agreement regarding me marrying Grace?"

"No, of course not. I thought…of course, you do not know yet, as we just completed it. I thought you were referring to the marriage agreement Baron Massey and I completed on this visit, regarding the settlement between you and Grace, before and after you are married. The one you speak of is not for your eyes. It has nothing to do with you. That agreement is between Baron Massey and me."

"Father, how can it not be for my eyes? Is the agreement not about Grace and me?"

"Yes. The agreement was made between the Massey's and the Davenport's. It was not intended for your eyes."

"How can you say that!" Robert yelled. "It has everything to do with Grace and me."

Robert's outburst angered Lord Davenport and he yelled, "Enough Robert!"

"Father!" Robert yelled back. He felt frustrated; he didn't understand how an agreement involving him, would have no right to see it? Robert began to wonder, questioning the contents of the agreement. *How can this be?* he thought.

Lord Davenport was outraged with Robert's persistence and again reiterated in a firmer and harsher tone. "No Robert! Now get out! I have work to do!" Lord Davenport ordered, and when he speaks, you listen.

No one argues with Lord Davenport, not even his family, especially his son. For Lord Davenport, order and obedience were vital, and those who did not adhere to his order paid severely. It did not matter if you were family or not, as his uncle learned years ago, and Robert had the not so pleasure of bearing witness to what happened.

***

Robert's uncle, who was the Earl of Stafford and a solicitor, went against his brother Lord Davenport to defend one of Cheshire's villagers who Lord Davenport called his people.

Roughly ten years ago when Robert was around five years old, and his father believed he could not be too young to learn how to deliver justice.

Earl Stafford agreed to defend a man Lord Davenport

had arrested for failure to pay his rent. The Earl never agreed with Lord Davenport's methods, and the man he arrested was a family member of one of his servants. The accused man's brother went to the Earl to ask for his assistance.

The Earl of Stafford was a good man who treated his servants with respect and was well taken care of, the opposite of Lord Davenport, and something Lord Davenport never could understand.

It was told when a servant was hired by the Earl, and if were ever in need of assistance – help, and the Earl would do what he could to help them without question. The servants were his responsibility, and he trusted them. If a servant came to him for help, he knew it was for a good reason, which bothered Lord Davenport. Lord Davenport believed servants were servants with no rights or privileges, with one titled such as he.

The day of the court proceedings, Lord Davenport had no intension of adhering to the matter as he already passed judgement, but for his people, he felt it was necessary to put on a show, so they would bear witness to his power.

During the hearing when Lord Davenport saw his brother enter the hall where he was conducting court, it surprised him to see his brother, since there was no advance notice of him visiting.

At first, he believed his brother was there as an impromptu visit to surprise him, though at the most inconvenient time, until he recalled his brother was not only an Earl but a solicitor as well.

It must be the reason, why else would he arrive on a day I am to pronounce judgment, he thought. Lord Davenport shook his head, pushing the idea out of his mind. It is a long journey to travel to perform his duty as a solicitor, he further thought.

He knew this was impossible, as Lord Davenport never performed his court on any specific day. He wanted to keep those accused scared, never knowing what or when their fate would be determined.

Lord Davenport looked around to the people he was to pass judgment on but could not see anyone of title that would bring the services of a solicitor, especially one of his brother's stature. At this, Lord Davenport allowed himself to relax.

Lord Davenport made eye contact with his brother and nodded in acknowledgement, but his brother did not return the acknowledgement, nor did he smile. It was all about business for the Earl. He wasn't there as a brother but as a solicitor to support and defend a client.

Once Lord Davenport was done with the current matter, Earl Stafford approached, "My Lord," he said bowing. "I am here to defend this man," pointing at a man standing among the commoners, "Mr. Byron Hutchinson," motioning for the man to come forward.

Mr. Byron Hutchinson was a short man with dark hair. He was a simple farmer, a man of no consequences.

"My Lord, I understand Mr. Hutchinson failed to pay his rent."

When Lord Davenport heard this, he was angry at his brother for taking such liberties.

He took control of his anger and said, "My Lord, I will hear the matter in private."

Lord Davenport turned to the man standing next to him, "Sir Owen, hold any further proceeding until after I speak to my brother. I will return shortly," he said.

Lord Davenport left the throne and took his brother aside, "What do you think you are doing here brother? And how dare you come to my land and into my court to defend a man I have already pronounced judgement on. You make me a fool, for my own brother to defend one of my people," Lord Davenport said firmly, pointing at the man in question.

The Earl looked at his brother with disgust, "It does not

matter what you think. The man has a family member in my service, and you know, if a member in my service comes to me for help, I provide it. This man's…" pointing at the man… "family came to ask for my assistance, and I could not say no. John, I know how you are…you are a ruthless man. For this man to come before you without a good solicitor, he will not survive, because you will condemn him to a sentence, I am sure he does not deserve, and all because he failed to pay his rent.

I am here to ensure this man receives a fair trial. If you agree, here and now, we can come to an agreement. I will pay what the man owes you in back rent, and you will release him and his family into my care. I will take them to Stafford where they will be employed in my service far away from you and this land."

Lord Davenport was outraged that his brother would take such liberties, but what was he to do. His brother was not only a solicitor but an Earl, who clearly outranked him in every way.

"Very well! You have left me with little choice. When court resumes you may make your request, and I will…after a short time, agree to your terms," Lord Davenport said with a crooked smile. "After all, these are my people, and I must maintain authority. Brother, I must warn you, this will be the last time you are to show yourself in my land, and in my court ever again! You choose to go against me, and as so, you are no longer welcome in my land nor my family! I take this action as a complete and utter betrayal!" Lord Davenport said firmly.

Earl Stafford formerly bowed to his brother, but his brother's words did not affect him. He knew his brother and was prepared for the outcome.

Lord Davenport's anger towards his brother never wavered, his brother made him look weak, that his own brother brought down a man of Lord Davenport stature – Lord of Cheshire, and he had to ensure his people understood what seemed like weakness, changed nothing of his authority and control in this land – his land. His people. After all, he was the law of the land, feared by everyone.

After the proceeding was over and the court was dismissed, Lord Davenport called for one of his guards to approach.

With anger between clenched teeth, he said, "I want you to go quickly before my brother takes this man and his family! Destroy everything they own, leaving them with nothing behind! Do Not! No matter what happens, allow my brother to see you! If he does, he will retaliate, and unfortunately, his title and power are greater than mine!

Right now, he is in my land! Go! Do as I command! My dear brother will learn, you do not mess with Lord Davenport! The Lord and Law of Cheshire!" he said, with an evil smile on his face.

Lord Davenport or Robert never knew how well Earl Stafford knew his brother. He prearranged for guards to be situated at the man's house protecting his family and belongings.

Robert was shocked by what his father did, and he knew his father was not a man to be reckoned with, that not even family were safe if they went against him.

***

After Robert left his father's study, he went to the pond furthest away from the manor needing to think about what he was going to do, and how he could possibly get out of this agreement, when he heard his brother Edward approaching.

Edward saw Robert standing by the pond and thought it was an excellent time to practice swordplay. For Robert, he picked the worst possible time.

Robert turned, and when he saw Edward with his sword in his hand, he knew what he was after…*seriously!* Robert thought, shaking his head. *This is not the day, Edward.*

With his sword in hand standing at the ready, "Robert

come on, let us have a go around?" Edward said, twirling his sword in a circular motion.

Rolling his eyes, "Edward, you do not want to fight me right now. I am not in the mood."

Bouncing back and forth, "Oh, come on Robert, you're not a chicken, are you?" he said, going into a fighting stance and firming his position. Edward pointed his sword at Robert as he wiggled it around, "What, are you afraid I will beat you?" he said to taunt him.

"Beat me?" Robert said, raising an eye, as he watched his brother. "You can never beat me Edward, and you know it."

"Well then, why are you still standing there," Edward said, smiling.

Robert let out his breath in frustration but decided – *This may be what I need to release my frustrations. Edward may be the key. He picked the wrong time for this though,* Robert thought as he smiled, with a smile that was filled with sinister and humor. Robert drew his sword and goes into a fighting stance.

Before Robert went into a fighting stance, Edward went at Robert, and swords started clashing. Robert gave as good as he received, even better, but it was clear that Edward had improved from the last time they dueled together.

However, what first started out as playful, had quickly turned to anger, and Robert allowed his anger to get the best of him. His anger and frustration regarding his situation, with the agreement and the conversation he had with his father, caused him to lose all rational understanding.

Something in him took over, something he was unfamiliar with, hatred, anger, such fierce anger. He was no longer play fighting; instead, he'd become a fierce warrior going after an enemy that needed to be destroyed. He no longer saw his brother Edward, but the enemy he sought to destroy. It went from a game to a life and death battle. It wasn't Edward Robert saw but his father, who was the enemy standing between him and what he wanted, which was Elizabeth.

When Edward saw the change in Robert, fear engulfed him. No matter how much he mocked Robert, he knew Robert was a better swordsman. Whatever changed Robert, Edward knew they were no longer play fighting; he was now fighting for his life.

Edward was yelling at Robert, trying to get him to snap out of whatever had taken hold of him. "What…" Edward tried to scream, as swords clashed, while maneuvering around Robert trying his best to avoid his sword. "…are…" he spun around, trying to keep out of Robert's path. "…you…" clash, "doing!" swords clashing, then Robert swung his sword at Edward's head, missing it by mere inches from taking it off. But thanks to Edward's excellent footwork, he managed to avoid the lethal blow.

Now he was screaming, in fear of losing his life, "Robert Stop!" Edward yelled, ducking another almost lethal blow. Realizing Robert wasn't fighting him, but a fictitious enemy, he must try to get Robert to see it's him, his brother, not an enemy he is fighting.

"Who do you think you are fighting!" Edward yelled, barely blocking Robert's next blow, afraid, since he is starting to tire.

Edward was scared, worried he would not get through to Robert, not understanding what was happening, to why he was so aggressive. Who did Robert think he was fighting? To Edwards horror, what he was doing was only increasing Robert's aggression.

Robert was fighting with such fierce as if he were in a battle for his life. Already fearing for his life, Edward started to believe Robert could kill him. So, Edward did everything he could to get Robert to stop. He screamed at the top of his lungs, desperately trying to get him to snap out of whatever had a hold on him.

Robert was blinded by rage; he had Edward pinned down on the ground ready to run him through with his sword, when suddenly he heard Edward yelling, as if it was from a great distance, yelling for him to stop. Robert was not sure what was happening or why, but then, he snapped out of his rage and realized he was not fighting his father but was fighting his father for the feelings he had for Elizabeth – fighting for the need to destroy the agreement and fighting for his freedom. But it wasn't his father; it was his brother he was actually fighting.

Realizing this, he quickly came to a stop and started to panic, afraid of what he almost did. "Edward, oh God Edward, I am so sorry. I do not know what came over me?" Robert said.

Robert could not believe what he was capable of doing, in almost killing his brother. He moved off Edward and turned away, sitting down on the ground with his arms on his knees and his head in his hands. He was frightened of how his anger blinded him, to where it almost killed his brother, his own brother.

"What is wrong with you Robert! You were going to kill me!" Edward yelled, breathlessly. "What is wrong with you! Are you crazy!"

Edward was angry, but more frightened that his brother tried to kill him. When he looked at Robert and saw the fear in his eyes, with the knowledge he almost killed him, Edward reigned in his anger and decided to find out why, to what caused his brother to go crazy.

"Robert, what has you acting so crazy?" he asked with sympathy.

Shaking his head, "I am sorry, Edward. I am so sorry," holding back his emotions. "It's that stupid agreement!" he said with anger. "I went to father and requested to see the agreement, but he refused, and was angry for me asking. When I insisted, telling him I have the right to know since the agreement involves Grace and me. Father said I do not have the right; the agreement is between him and Baron Massey. How do I not have a right to see something that's about Grace and me," he said, shaking his head.

Edward had no understanding, nor did he care that the agreement bothered Robert. He didn't care what was in the agreement and felt it was Robert's duty as the elder son and heir to do what was asked of him.

"I can very well imagine what father did. You were wrong, Robert. You know how father is. There is no arguing with him. What father says is what will be done." Edward sat next to Robert, "It does not matter what the agreement says. Grace is a beautiful girl, and I am sure she will be a beautiful woman, who, I am sure, will be incredible in bed."

Robert turned to look at Edward, and he was shocked by his words. But before he could respond, Edward went on —

"She looks like the type, that with the right man, would be wild in bed," Edward said with a sinister and lustful smile. "You know, you are right, maybe you should look at that agreement and see if brothers will have sharing rights. I would love to play with Grace once you are done with her." Edward said, wanting to rile him up.

Robert swung around to look at Edward, appalled with what he said. "Edward! What is wrong with you! Is bedding women all you think about!"

Laughing, "Well, yes. What else is there? A woman is only good for one thing, to please a man and have babies. What does it matter what the agreement says, so long as she pleases you, and gives you an heir? Marry her Robert and enjoy her."

Robert looked at Edward shaking his head, *and this is my brother. My blood,* he thought. With this, he knew Edward could not be trusted; he was too much like his father.

"Edward, you are wrong in your thinking! You will be

lucky to find a woman who will want you. I am the heir, and as heir, I have the right to know what that agreement says."

"Robert, I do not need luck. I have father, and he will arrange a marriage for me. So, until that day, I plan on having as much fun as I can, maybe even after."

Robert again shook his head; he did not understand Edward's way of thinking and wondered how he could be his brother.

"Something is wrong with you Edward. Maybe mother dropped you on your head when you were a baby."

Edward just stood there smiling at Robert, then returned to the subject of their father. "Robert, you know you cannot force father to do anything he does not want to do."

Robert nodded in agreement. Edward stood up and reached to lend Robert a helping hand, and together they return to the manor. Robert decided Edward was right, and he needed to forget what the agreement said.

***

During the visit at Dunham Massey, and after Robert told Grace about what happened when he asked his father to see the agreement, they both gave up hope of changing the fate that had been tossed upon them and continued the charade.

Once Elizabeth heard the terrible news, she refused to see Robert, feeling it was too much for her to see a man she had no future with.

A month after Robert and Elizabeth agreed to stay away from each other, it was also the time when Robert decided a month was long enough. He needed to see Elizabeth – to talk to her.

The Massey's were due to visit Bramhall Manor, and Robert decided he would give Grace a message to deliver to Elizabeth on the last day of their visit, asking Elizabeth to meet him at their lake.

***

It's their final day at Bramhall Manor, and Robert was with Grace in the small garden next to the manor, to ask her to deliver a message to Elizabeth on his behalf, but found he was nervous.

"Grace, will you do something for me?"

Grace looked at Robert, "Yes, if I am able to."

Relieved, Robert allowed himself to relax a little. "Will you ask Elizabeth to meet me at our special place on the first morning of our arrival at Dunham Massey."

Grace smiled; she was pleased, and more than happy to honor his request and to deliver his message to Elizabeth.

"Robert, of course I will deliver your message," she said with joy. "Robert, may I inquire to what this special place is?"

Robert smiled, but did not answer Grace, instead said, "Thank you, Grace."

Grace was disappointed that Robert did not answer her question and decided not to push. She will deliver Robert's message to Elizabeth once they return to Dunham Massey and are both safely in her chambers.

***

Once the Massey's returned to Dunham Massey, Grace took Elizabeth's hand and guided her to her chambers. Once they were inside, she relayed Robert's message, still wondering what this special place was, and so she asked, "Elizabeth, what is this special place Robert spoke of?"

When Elizabeth received Robert's message, at first, she hesitated, but then after a few moments, she became ecstatic. She missed Robert and could not wait to see him.

When Grace asked about their special place, Elizabeth smiled, she would never reveal her and Robert's special place, but knew she had to tell her sister something.

"Grace, I am sorry, I am unable to tell you. It is a place between Robert and me, and we promised never to share it with anyone, not even you."

Grace was frustrated, and she took a deep breath and

blew it out, knowing she would not learn of their special place and decided to leave it alone.

"Very well, I am going to prepare for bed, and we will talk morrow. Good night sister," she said, giving Elizabeth a kiss on the cheek.

Elizabeth turned to leave, then stopped. She turned back to Grace and said, "Grace, maybe I should not go. If what Robert said about his father, in not allowing him to see the agreement…" shaking her head, "…it may be best I do not go," Elizabeth said as sadness filled her heart.

Elizabeth wanted desperately to go, but the thought of going, knowing they will have to remain apart, would only hurt her more than it already did.

"Elizabeth, you must go. Robert desperately misses you, and you are no better off. If you do not go, you will be miserable, and in turn, you will make me miserable. So please, do us both a favor, and go!" Grace said.

Knowing Grace was right, Elizabeth nodded and left Grace's chambers without further words.

***

Once Elizabeth was alone in her chamber, her thoughts turn to Grace, recalling Robert's message and it made her smile. Grace was right; she missed Robert. This last month has been the hardest days of her life not having her friend, and she desperately wanted him back.

When Elizabeth spent time alone outdoors, it wasn't the same when she was with Robert, and so, it was decided, she would meet Robert at their lake, but it must be after the morning meal. So, Elizabeth prepared a message for Grace to deliver to Robert when the Davenport's arrive at Dunham Massey.

Chapter Nine

Robert was overjoyed to get Elizabeth message agreeing to meet him at their lake. That evening, after retiring for bed, he tossed and turned all night, anxious to see Elizabeth. Once it was close to dawn, he was unable to wait another minute, so Robert decided to rise and dress, then headed for the lake.

While Robert was waiting at the lake, his thoughts returned to the night he arrived at Dunham Massey. Once he settled into his chamber, he walked the halls seeking to find a servant to deliver a message to Grace, and inside that message was a personal message for Elizabeth.

The servant Robert found was one of his father's, who reported directly to him on everything that conspired around his home and family. This was good news for Robert, knowing the servant will inform his father of the message he sent to Grace. This will tell his father their relationship was going well.

And so, the message said —

Elizabeth, I am unable to wait until after morning meal to meet with you, and request you meet me at our lake at first light. I promise to have you back before morning meal. I will wait until the sun is bright in the sky, and if you are unable to come, I will return to the manor and wait until after morning meal as we previously arranged.

*You
r
dearest
friend,
Ro
bert.*

After sending this message, Robert was confident

Elizabeth would meet him at first light.

When Elizabeth received Robert's message, she was thrilled and excited that he wanted to meet her earlier than they had planned, and she too found it difficult to sleep. So as soon as it was close to time, Elizabeth dressed and headed to the lake.

***

When Elizabeth approached the lake, she was surprised and yet pleased to see Robert was already there, standing facing the lake, and it didn't appear he heard her approaching. At seeing him, it caused her heart to race, and she felt nervous and frightened, then she started to wonder if she should go through with meeting him. As she was about to turn and leave, Robert turned and saw her.

Robert was standing facing the lake anxiously waiting for Elizabeth to arrive. When he heard a noise, he turned, and his heart sank at the sight of Elizabeth. Without delay, Robert rushed to her, and before she could make her escape, he took Elizabeth in his arms and swept her off her feet. When he felt her in his arms, it felt as if that part of him that was missing, had now been found – whole once again.

Although Elizabeth thought of leaving, when Robert grabbed her and had her in his arms, she was glad she did not.

For Robert and Elizabeth to see each other after what seemed like years, then a mere month was gratifying. It was Robert who spoke first —

"Oh, Elizabeth, I cannot express enough how much I've missed you. There was not a day that passed that I did not think of you, nor could I get our last time together out of my mind. To see you, and not be able to speak to you…" Robert said, but had to stop. He needed to take a moment to gather his thoughts and ease his heart. He was filled with so many mixed emotions. Then, in a shaky voice, he said, "Those days we were not together, was like a knife in my heart, a heart that ached for you," he said swallowing the lump in his throat.

Robert needed to tell Elizabeth of his feelings for her, and he needed to before he lost his courage. So, he took a deep breath and after he let it out, and before he could change his mind – "There were so many times I wanted to speak to you about what happened between us the last time we were together. Not being able to, was torturous…" Robert looked away for a moment, then he turned back and said, "To part from you again, I don't think I can bear it." Seeing the concern on Elizabeth's face, he quickly went on, "I know the love you feel for your sister is great, and the thought of hurting her is unbearable…but, with the way Grace and I are when we are together…it will never work. Grace and I are too different…she knows we have feelings for each other, I am sure she will give us her blessing."

When Elizabeth saw Robert standing at the lake, her heart stuttered, and then, as she was about to leave, the way Robert rushed to her and took her in his arms, left her weak in her knees, and was grateful she was not standing. The way he held her as if he hadn't seen her in years. And then, when he spoke, to hear his voice caused flutters in her stomach. She loved him. She could not deny it any longer, and she savored every word he said, causing her heart to race, as she enjoyed the feel of Robert's arms around her. She missed him, more than she realized.

Once Robert stopped talking, Elizabeth said, "Robert, I must tell you…" she started to say, but stopped when she felt Robert tense, causing her to hesitate, but her words needed to be said. *He needs to know,* she thought.

"Robert, I spoke with Grace on the day we parted, and I told her what happened between us," she said, needing to look away for a moment. When she turned back, she continued, "I was shocked and surprised by her reaction. She was happy for us. Grace told me, if we have feelings for each other than it should be us to marry, in doing so, will free her.

Grace went to father and asked if it would be possible to change the agreement...” Elizabeth stopped, shaking her head as she said, “The agreement cannot be changed. You and Grace will marry,” Elizabeth said with sadness, as tears stream down her face. *We cannot be together,* she thought, and this thought broke her heart.

At hearing what Elizabeth discovered, Robert's heart sank to the pit of his stomach and wondered, *do I tell her what father said? Does she even know I went to father? Would Grace have told her? Ah, but of course she would have,* he thought with a smile.

But then when Elizabeth told him she had something he needed to know, he was engulfed with fear, concerned it would be bad news, and then when she continued, the only words he heard were 'if we have feelings for each other,' he was elated.

But then, if what she said was true – his happiness turned to sadness, with a realization there was no chance for them. *Why did Grace not tell me this?* he thought. Can Robert live with this knowledge? He didn't know. *There must be a way. I must find a way,* he thought. He was unwilling to give up on them so easily and was determined to find a way for them to be together.

“Elizabeth, are you sure? I went to father and asked if he would allow me to see the agreement…to my disappointment, he refused,” Robert said with sadness.

Elizabeth felt anger, not at Robert, but at their situation and said, “Yes, I am sure!” with a bite in her voice. Her feelings for Robert were tearing her apart. What was she going to do? What were they going to do?

Robert saw Elizabeth pain and sadness, he wanted to slay those responsible, but then, he would have to slay himself.

“Forgive me, Elizabeth? I didn't mean to cause you pain.”

No! Elizabeth thought.

In a panic, she grabbed Robert's arm and quickly said, "No Robert, it…" she attempted to tell him it was not his fault, but Robert cut her off.

Robert hushed Elizabeth by placing his fingers over her mouth. He knew what she was going to say, but he could not allow it. It was not her fault. Robert pulled her into his arms with the need to hold and comfort her, as he remembered how beautiful she looked when he first saw her after she arrived at the lake, how it took his breath away.

At that moment, he could no longer deny his feelings for her. He loved her, and when you love someone, you take on their pain as your own, but in this case, it was their pain.

"If I had not kissed you that day, it would not have come to this. It is I, who has caused you this pain. Will you forgive me? If I controlled my desires, you would not be in tears right now."

Feeling ashamed, Elizabeth said, "No, Robert, it is not your fault. We were both to blame. I wanted you to kiss me, and I was angry at myself for allowing you to. If you want to blame someone, then blame me."

Robert pulled Elizabeth tighter to him, needing to ease her pain, at the same time needing to ease his own pain. "Then let us agree, we are both to blame," Robert said, then for a few moments, they stood in silence enjoying the feel of their bodies against each other.

It was Robert who finally broke the silence. "I am surprised your father said anything about the agreement to Grace, when my father refused to let me see it, and how angry he was for asking."

Elizabeth leaned further into Robert; he felt so good and so right, she loved the feel of his warm body against hers.

"You know how my father adores Grace, and there isn't

anything he would not do for her. She could almost ask him for anything, but this agreement…the power of it…father could not be swayed, not even by Grace. This said more to me than seeing what the agreement says."

Robert refused to accept there was nothing they can do. *There must be a way.* Robert pushed Elizabeth out to arm's length and said, "Elizabeth, I am not willing to give up so easily. There must be a way. I will speak to my father again and insist he show me the agreement. Then I will destroy the agreement by tossing it into the fire if he refuses to change the terms of the agreement, by allowing me the woman of my choosing," he said with a smile.

Without understanding why, Elizabeth was engulfed with fear, as it was beyond her understanding, she knew if Robert did what he said, it would doom them all, so she had to stop him.

With desperation, "Robert no, you cannot. When Grace asked father about changing the agreement, he said it was impossible and not without severe consequences. Don't you see, if you go to your father knowing the man he is, it will be our undoing," she said, grabbing Robert's arms.

Robert was stunned by what Elizabeth said, it felt as if he'd been slapped in the face, and wondered what she meant by 'severe consequences', this, he did not understand. But the fear she displayed in what she said concerned him, and he needed to understand what she meant.

"Elizabeth, what kind of consequences do you speak of?" he asked but did not give Elizabeth time to answer. "If what you say is true, then I must see this agreement, more than I did before."

At this, Robert felt Elizabeth tense in his arms, but refused to relent, and pushed her out to arm's length, keeping hold of her upper arms, "Are you sure Elizabeth? Could Grace have misunderstood what your father said?" he demanded.

Robert's tight hold on Elizabeth's arms was hurting her, "Robert you are hurting me," she said trying to get out of his grip, as his words increased her fears. If he did what he said he would do, it would be a grave mistake.

Not realizing he was hurting Elizabeth, Robert released his hold on her, then started rubbing her arms trying to ease the pain he caused.

"And yes, I am sure!" she said with anger. "When Grace told me, she was distraught; she wants out of this agreement as much as you do…as much as I do," she confessed, filled with sadness, she reverted her eyes to look at the ground.

To hear Elizabeth, he relents, "I am sorry, Elizabeth. If this is the case, then there is nothing to be done," Robert said with disappointment.

When Elizabeth heard his words, it eased her fears a little.

However, for Robert, his thoughts were still – *I must try…I must find a way. There must be something I can do to change our fate.*

For Robert, his thoughts became the better of him, and with anger, he yelled, "So, no matter what feelings I have for you, I will be forced to marry Grace!" He held nothing back, "I do not want Grace! I want you! Do you not understand that!" Robert turned and walked a short distance away from Elizabeth, "Why should we not have a say in what we want!"

Elizabeth flinched at Robert's sudden anger, and yet, at the same time, she understood where his anger was coming from, because she was feeling the same way.

Elizabeth wanted to ease Robert's anger, wanting to take it from him, so in a soft and gentle voice, "Robert, you mean a great deal to me, but you should not be talking about such things," she said, walking over to him and placing her hand on his arm. "Robert, please," pulling on his arm to force him to turn and look at her, but he does not. "There is nothing we can do. You are to marry my sister." Although she said the words to comfort him, instead, it only fueled her own anger. Recognizing this, Elizabeth quickly changed her approach and did something drastic. "I love you, Robert! Nothing can ever change that," then she turned away from him.

Robert turned around when he heard Elizabeth declaration – he was shocked, and yet elated, allowing his anger to dissipate. Robert needed to see her face, to look into her eyes. He touched Elizabeth's arm and turned her to face him, and when he looked into her eyes, he let out his breath – there, he saw an overwhelming amount of love that weakened him. He needed to hear those words again, wanting to be sure he heard what he thought he heard.

Robert took Elizabeth's hands, "Elizabeth, will you please…will you please say those words again?"

Elizabeth smiled; she was more than happy to comply. "I love you, Robert. I love you so very much. You are in my heart, and there you will remain until the day I die."

Robert was overjoyed to hear Elizabeth's declaration and with excitement, "I love you, Elizabeth," he said as his heart screamed with joy. "Oh, Elizabeth, you truly do love me," he said, placing the back of his hand on her cheek giving it a soft caress. "I love you more than I can possibly express. There is nothing I wouldn't do for you, and I want to make you happy in every way." Then he kissed her, throwing all he'd been holding back into his kiss. All the love and passion he felt for Elizabeth.

Elizabeth was overjoyed when Robert kissed her, and she returned his kiss with the same fierce and passion, he was giving her.

When they finally came up for air, Elizabeth said, "As for Grace, she wants me to be happy. You and I know, if it were up to her, she would gladly step aside." Then gently, with her hand resting directly over Robert's heart, "But Robert, she is to marry you, this we both know, and must accept," she said in a softer gentler voice.

Robert looked down at Elizabeth, not wanting to believe what she just said, *how can she*, not after what they just shared.

Elizabeth did not miss this, she clearly saw the concern and the question on Robert's face, she stepped back from their embrace, and with her finger, she poked gently at Robert's chest, "Neither of you have a say. Do you not understand that?" she said firmly.

But then, something happened after she said those words, and there was a pain that pierced the center of her heart, breaking through her calm decorum, allowing her anger to breakthrough.

Robert did not miss the change in Elizabeth, how she went from someone calm to anger. Wanting to help Elizabeth, he quickly took her into his arms, never wanting to let her go, with the need to feel her body against his again. To feel her heart beating in rhythm with his own.

"Elizabeth, I know you are right, but do you honestly believe you can forget and ignore what is happening between us?" he said in a gentle and calm voice, but instead of calming Elizabeth as he intended, it had the opposite effect, his words had only increased her anger.

"No!" she yelled.

The pain Elizabeth was feeling was too much for her to bear. What was happening between them was too much, and she started pounding on Robert's chest. She was hurt and angry, with tears streaming down her face. She wanted Robert with every breath in her, it felt right, but what were they to do? How could they be together?

No, it is impossible, she thought.

To see how angry Elizabeth was, Robert knew there were no words he could say that would help, not this time. Robert did the only thing he could; he pulled Elizabeth to him and held her tight, allowing her the release she desperately needed.

With Elizabeth's head resting on Robert's shoulder, she cried, releasing the pain she was feeling, her anger, and her frustration, not only for herself but for Robert as well.

Robert felt as Elizabeth did, he too wanted to cry, but instead, he allowed Elizabeth to release her pain for the two of them.

When Elizabeth finally gained control of her emotions, she said, "Robert? I am sorry, will you please forgive me?"

Elizabeth sighed, then pulled away from Robert and looked up at his face and into his eyes, as she placed her palm on his cheek, "How can I say this," then looked away for a moment before turning back to him. "I…I want us to be together," she said, looking behind him at nothing in particular. After a few moments, she redirected her focus on Robert. "I want nothing more than to allow these feelings to grow…but…" finding it too difficult to look at him; she averted her eyes from his —

Elizabeth knew she needed to say what was on her mind, and if she was to tell him, she had to face him, he deserved nothing less. So, she looked directly in his eyes and when she did, "How can I? How can we? How can I do this to my sister?" Elizabeth said, feeling so torn – she was confused by her mixed feelings. She wanted Robert, but her sister. She loved her sister, how was she to choose? She could not.

"Robert," she said with a shaky voice, "You know Grace is not only my sister, she is my best friend, and I love her very much. You are her betrothed, bonded by an agreement between your father and mine, and soon you will be married…her husband. We cannot do this, even though I know she wants this for us, but…" no longer able to look at him; she turned away, "It's not right."

Robert's heart broke at hearing Elizabeth and knew where this was going. He disagrees with what she was doing, but what could he do. What can he say? He knew she was right, and so he did the only thing he could do, he placed his hand over Elizabeth's and looked directly in her eyes, wanting her to see what he was feeling.

Elizabeth did not miss anything; instead, she saw what he wanted her to see, and what she saw almost knocked her off her feet. His love for her was deeper than she could imagine. She could see straight into his soul. He loved her as she loved him.

Robert saw her love for him, but what he saw, which was stronger than her love, was her pain, her guilt for what they were doing. She struggled with her feelings, wanting to do what was right by their families, and wanted to do what was right by her heart. How was she to choose? In truth, there was no real choice, and he understood that. It did not have anything to do with Grace, not really, because Grace wants this as much as they do, and Robert does not want Grace.

Elizabeth's guilt was a sign of her good heart and good nature. She always thought of others, never of herself, and showed this on more than one occasion, and Robert recalled a particular event in Chester's village market.

***

After Sunday mass when they were in the village, Elizabeth noticed a group of unfortunate people, men, women, and children – families. At seeing this, it broke her heart, and found she needed to speak with them, to understand why they were in such dire straits.

Elizabeth was shocked and surprised when she learned it was due to Lord Davenport tossing them out of their homes and off their land for failing to pay their rent. Elizabeth had always known Lord Davenport was a hard man, but to do this to his own people, she was appalled to be associated with such a man, but what choice did she have? She had none.

Elizabeth listened intently to these people's tragic stories, then turned to Robert looking for confirmation to what she'd heard, and the look he gave her confirmed their

***

From that day and every Sunday after, Elizabeth would do the same, continuing to this day, helping those in need when they could not help themselves. Robert was so proud to have a person like Elizabeth as a friend, a person with such a large and caring heart.

Robert turned to Elizabeth and said, "Elizabeth, I am sorry, I know this is difficult for you. I know you do not want to do anything to cause conflict between you and Grace, nor do I want to be the cause of such conflict." Robert gently took Elizabeth's hand, "Elizabeth…" he attempted to say, then took her face in his hands and looked directly in her eyes, "Maybe..." again he tried, but found it was too difficult, but knew it must be said. It must be done. "…we should take more time to understand what is happening between us. We must be sure of our feelings for each other."

It hurt him to say this and caused his heart to ache, but for Elizabeth, if it helped to ease her pain, he would do anything for her, even if that meant sacrificing his own pain. His own happiness. It's the last thing he wanted to do, but it was necessary. He could not bear to see Elizabeth so torn between him and her sister. It's what she needed, and at that moment, he knew there was nothing he wouldn't do for Elizabeth. He loved her.

To hear Robert's words, Elizabeth felt ashamed. She knew his decision caused him great pain, and although she wanted to deny it, Robert was right, they both needed more time.

"I am sorry Robert. You are right. We need to be sure. If

it turns out we are unable to ignore what we are feeling for each other, then we will open our hearts to the idea, and then we must find a way to tell our parents."

Robert and Elizabeth were young and new to what was happening between them, confused, not knowing what they were doing. They wanted to be with each other and yet, they could not. They wanted to do what was right, and yet, it proved to be too difficult. If only they had someone they could have talked to, to explain to them, to help them understand what was happening between them, but it was impossible.

If Robert and Elizabeth had someone to confide in, allowing them to reveal their secret to, someone who understood what they were feeling and experiencing. Robert and Elizabeth knew they could not consult with anyone without Grace's consent, and they knew she would not give it.

Neither Robert, Elizabeth, or Grace could deny what would happen if their families were to find out, knowing Baron and Baroness Massey would be angry and disappointed, but Lord Davenport, now that was a different story, he was the most ruthless man in and across the land. There was not one man, nor woman who would question Lord Davenport unless he was the King of course. He was a man not to be reckoned with, which was why the Massey's wanted this merger, to align themselves with a man such as Lord Davenport, who, once Robert and Grace were married, would make Baron Massey as powerful as he.

"Elizabeth, I know what you are thinking, and you are right, we cannot tell our families, no matter how much we desire to. I too, want more than anything to tell our families, in the hope they can help us, but you know as much as I do, we cannot."

Watching Robert, Elizabeth knew he was right, but if there was another way, another person who they could talk to, who could help them understand what was happening, but unfortunately there was none.

"We will agree to remain apart for another thirty days, and if after that time we still have these feelings for each other, nor could we bear to be apart, then we will open our hearts to what is happening and see where it takes us. With this said, I know without a doubt, what I feel for you is real. I love you Elizabeth," Robert said with such emotion, his eyes were filled with love and passion.

Elizabeth gasped as her heart skipped a jump, it was strange for her, it's not like she hadn't already heard his declaration, but the way he said it this time, along with the look in his eyes, it affected her so.

Robert didn't miss anything, "How can I not. You are everything I could wish for in a wife. Elizabeth, you are my perfect match. We are the same, you and I."

Elizabeth was so affected by Robert's words; she was unable to speak, and so she did the only thing she could do, she nodded in agreement. He loved her. Robert truly loved her. At this, it caused Elizabeth to smile. It was all she could do with her emotions so close to the surface.

Robert did not need Elizabeth to speak, as it was clear she loved him, from the look in her eyes, and for Robert, it was enough. So, he pulled her into his arms, and held her tight, not wanting to let her go. He knew this moment with Elizabeth must last him until they meet again, and didn't believe the time apart will help, because what they felt was real, even if Elizabeth doesn't know it yet, and she needed time to see that for herself.

As Robert and Elizabeth were in each other's arms, they could feel their love for each other, with a sensation, a power that flowed from one heart to the other. What it was they didn't know, it just felt right. It felt as if two puzzle pieces that were once separated were found, fitting perfectly together, home once again.

Robert and Elizabeth found it difficult to part; it was harder than before. With resistance, they stepped back from each other as they still held hands, slowly sliding them apart until the tips of their fingers were touching, and they too parted, allowing Elizabeth and Robert to go their separate ways.

Chapter Ten

It's been ten days since Robert and Elizabeth went their separate ways when Robert found himself struggling, hating their decision. Not understanding why, Robert felt Elizabeth was struggling with their decision as well. The one thing he did know, for him, the wait was over. He needed to see Elizabeth and was sure she wanted to see him as well.

During their visit at Dunham Massey, Robert decided once he was alone with Grace, he would ask her to deliver a letter to Elizabeth.

Later that evening, Robert's father presented him with the perfect opportunity, by arranging for Robert and Grace to go horseback riding the following morning.

That evening, since he was unable to sleep, Robert wanted so much to go to Elizabeth, but he knew it was impossible. It wasn't proper. He must wait, but the waiting was killing him. Unable to relax, Robert struggled to sleep, and after a few moments of tossing and turning, he threw off his covers, and for a few moments, he sat at the edge of his bed before finally standing, then he made his way to the window. Once there, he opened the shutters and the window, then stuck his head out to allow the crisp cold air to brush his face as he inhaled.

Robert's window overlooked the forest behind the estate, but he could not see much beyond a few feet without the moon. After a few moments of taking in the fresh air, Robert shut the window and the shutters and returned to his bed. He laid down and closed his eyes as he thought about Elizabeth, and before he knew it, he was sound asleep.

The next morning, Robert was awakened from a deep sleep by his servant, who was there to help him dress for morning meal.

"Giles, what time of day is it?" Robert asked.

Standing at the open wardrobe gathering clothes for Robert to wear, he said, "My Lord, it is mid-morning, and you are late for morning meal."

Robert was surprised since he had such difficulty falling asleep the night before. "Very well," he said, unable to believe how late he had slept. With his servants' help, Robert quickly washed and dressed, then rushed down to join the others.

***

The dining room was an oval table with an extensive buffet, situated at the left side of the room filled with an assortment of pastries, fruits, eggs, bacon, bread, muffins, and croissants. Lord and Lady Booth were at the head of the table with Baron and Baroness Massey and their children at Lord Booth's side, while Lord and Lady Davenport and their children were seated next to Lady Booth. For Robert and Grace, their seats were arranged so they sat across from each other. However, Robert had yet to arrive.

When Robert did arrive, everyone was seated at the table engaged in conversation as they were eating their meal but looked up when he entered the room. For Elizabeth though, she kept her head down, it was apparent she was avoiding him.

Robert sighed; *she is avoiding me,* as he took a few moments to watch her. *She is beautiful.*

"It is nice of you to decide to grace us with your presence?" Lord Davenport said with a burst of slight laughter.

"Good morning, father, mother, Baron and Baroness Massey, Lord and Lady Booth, Grace, John, Rachel, Daniel, and Elizabeth. Please forgive me for being late."

Everyone said, "Good morning," with a snicker from the children.

Robert smiled as he proceeded to fix himself a plate of food, then sat across from Grace.

"I hope you slept well, Grace?" Robert asked.

"Yes, I slept very well, and you?" she asked.

Robert glanced at Elizabeth, then returned his attention to Grace, "At first I was restless, but then I finally fell asleep. I must have been more tired than I realized because I only woke upon my servant entering my chamber. To tell the truth, I was sleeping so soundly he had to rouse me," he said with amusement.

Grace looked at Elizabeth, and she was still eating with her eyes down. *Oh Elizabeth, this is hard for you, I know. My dear sister, I rather it be you than me,* she thought.

Grace knew what Elizabeth was doing; she was avoiding Robert, doing everything she could to keep herself from looking at him.

Grace turned her attention back to Robert, "Yes, I see. We were wondering what happen to you, since you had not arrived for morning meal when you are usually the first one here," she said with a smile.

Robert smiled in return, "Are you ready for our ride this afternoon? I am looking forward to it myself," he said with excitement.

Grace looked at Robert, then at her father, as this was the first she heard of this. Grace turned to her father, who gave her a look that said, 'do not argue.' Grace hated going horseback riding, but she had no choice and must endure it the best she could. She looked at Elizabeth, wishing she could join her, but she knew that was impossible.

"Yes, I look forward to it as well."

Robert knew Grace was putting on a display for their mother and father's benefit when in truth, he knew she hated the idea.

"Good. I am pleased to hear," Robert said, and with that, they finish eating their morning meal.

***

Once Robert and Grace were far enough away from the manor, Robert reigned in his horse and brought it to a stop.

When Grace saw this, she followed suit, "What? What is it? Why are we stopping? We have only travelled a short way," Grace asked with concern.

Robert, anxious to give Grace his letter, could not wait, so he pulled his horse to a stop once they were out of sight of the manor. He knew when he asked Grace his question; she would do anything to help him.

"Grace," he said, pulling the letter from his pocket, "Will you give this letter to Elizabeth for me?" then handed the letter to her.

Relieved to know why Robert stopped, she smiled and happily took the letter from Robert, "But of course I will," she said.

Robert and Grace continued their ride in silence, not knowing what they were going to talk about – Elizabeth? No, that they could not do. Their time together was awkward but necessary, because if they returned too early, it would raise too many questions.

Once Grace and Robert did return, they parted at the stables and went their separate ways. Robert walked towards the forest, and Grace went to find Elizabeth. It didn't take her long, as she found her sitting in her chamber, drawing trees from the view of her window.

"Good day Elizabeth."

"Good day Grace. How was your ride with Robert?" she said with a smile. Elizabeth knew how much Grace hated riding a horse.

Grace growled at Elizabeth and said, "You know how much I hate riding. I cannot believe Lord Davenport was able to talk father into Robert taking me riding, knowing how much I hate it," she said with disgust.

Elizabeth laughed, "Well, there's nothing to be done of it, is there."

Ignoring Elizabeth, Grace proceeded to tell Elizabeth the reason for her visit. "Here," handing Elizabeth the letter from Robert. With a smile, "Robert asked me to deliver this to you," she said with satisfaction.

Elizabeth was surprised but pleased. Instead of snatching the letter from Grace, she carefully took the letter as if it were a delicate rose that would wilt if not appropriately handled. When Elizabeth fully had the letter in her hand, for her, it was as if she was touching Robert's hand. It felt strange since it was only a piece of paper, but for Elizabeth, it was a part of him. What it meant, she did not know, nor did she understand.

After taking the letter, Elizabeth stepped away from Grace and went to stand next to the window. With delicate care, she carefully unwrapped the letter, and it said:

Elizabeth,
I know we agreed to stay apart, but I beg you, meet me at our lake morrow at first light. I shall be waiting for you. Please come.
Yours truly,
Robert

As Elizabeth read Robert's letter, it was almost as if she could hear his voice, and it caused her heart to swell, with fluttering in her stomach. She loved Robert; there was no denying it, not anymore. And there was no doubt he loved her.

The anticipation to see Robert deprived Elizabeth of breath. She needed him. She needed to see him, to touch him, and so her decision was made, she could no longer deny her feelings for Robert, and from his letter, it was apparent he couldn't either.

Grace was watching Elizabeth intently as she read Robert's letter when she noticed a change in her sister. Although she wanted to inquire, but she decided not to, and patiently waited before reminding Elizabeth she was still in the room. When Elizabeth lowered her hand with the letter in it, Grace coughed.

This startled Elizabeth. She had forgotten her sister was still in the room, and when she turned around, she saw Grace smiling. *She knows,* she thought.

"It is alright, Elizabeth. I want this for you. I can see how Robert makes you feel." Then softly and gently, she said, "You love him, don't you?"

Elizabeth quickly goes to her sister and takes her hands, then pulls Grace to the edge of the bed, and sits down. "Yes, Grace, I do. I love him. I never thought this could happen, but it has. I love him so much it hurts."

Grace looked at Elizabeth; she was happy for her sister but found herself, just a little, resenting what Elizabeth found with Robert and hoped one day she too would find love.

"I am happy for you, Elizabeth. I believe when the time is right, we will inform mother and father, who I am sure will accept you and Robert. With their acceptance, father will speak to Lord Davenport, and together they will change the agreement, replacing my name with yours, thus, allowing you and Robert to marry."

Elizabeth grabbed her sister's shoulders and pulled her into an embrace, at hearing the truth in her sister's words. "Thank you, Grace. I love you very much."

"I love you too, Elizabeth," Grace said, returning the hug. She smiled, pleased that her plan worked perfectly.

***

When Elizabeth arrived at the lake, she knew they were going to see where their feelings would take them, and when the time was right, they would find a way to inform their families of what's been happening and pray they will understand. If not at first, within time, they will come to accept her and Robert, and allow them to marry instead of Robert marrying Grace.

As Elizabeth approached the entrance to the lake, her heart started racing with excitement, and when she saw Robert standing facing the lake, she was filled with love and happiness. Robert apparently heard her because as soon as she cleared the trees, he was already rushing towards her, smiling and happy to see her.

When Robert saw Elizabeth, his heart stopped for a moment, and once it restarted, he was unable to stand still while waiting for Elizabeth to approach him. So, without hesitation, he quickly went to meet her, and once he was upon Elizabeth, he took her in his arms and held her tight, never wanting to let her go.

Elizabeth's heart jumped when she saw the love in Robert's eyes right before he took her in his arms, sweeping her off her feet. He held her tight as if he didn't want to let her go, and she fell into him, happy to finally be in his arms and touching him. It felt right, perfect as if they were one.

It seemed a lifetime before Robert and Elizabeth parted, and once they did, Robert took Elizabeth's face in his hands and looked deep into her eyes. *There, there it is*, he thought. He found what he was looking for, the love she felt for him.

Robert stood back as he took in every inch of her as if he saw her for the first time. Her beautiful brown eyes, with those amazingly long lashes, then he moved down to her lips, those full, beautiful heart-shaped and kissable lips.

For a few moments, Robert's eyes were locked on those lips, desperately wanting to kiss them. Never had Robert noticed Elizabeth's beauty more than he did then – how beautiful she truly was. No longer able to wait, he placed his lips to hers and kissed her, long and deep, with all the passion within him, pouring all the love he felt for Elizabeth, and to his wonderful surprise, she returned his kiss with the same desperation and passion, it was explosive, a power fusing them together in a way they could not explain.

When Robert and Elizabeth broke their kiss, he rested his forehead against hers and said, "Elizabeth, I have missed you so much. My heart has ached, as if someone pierced it with a dagger, and when I saw you, it was as if seeing you freed my heart from that piercing pain."

Elizabeth's heart was racing, filled with overwhelming emotions, not wanting to open her eyes, as she wanted to savor the moment.

Robert removed his forehead from Elizabeth's and placed his fingers under her chin, pulling her head up, so their eyes met, but he found her eyes were still closed.

"Elizabeth, my love, will you naught open your eyes for me so that I may gaze into those beautiful eyes of yours."

Elizabeth smiled, then opened her eyes to meet his.

Upon Robert seeing her eyes, it slammed him in the chest, at seeing the pure and utter love she had for him, and it caused his heart to race.

"My god Elizabeth, how did I not see it before…your love for me…you truly are a great beauty."

Robert's words sent shivers through Elizabeth's body, and with the way he touched her with the back of his hand, softly caressing her cheek, as his other hand softly rubbed her arm. When he wrapped his arm around her waist, his touch caused her to blush, along with feeling bashful, shy, even a little embarrassed, but she smiled; she found it funny to hear Robert's words 'a great beauty'.

This wasn't new for Elizabeth, as she heard people say this before, but she never believed it to be true. The way Robert said it though, and the way he looked at her, with so much love and passion, it mattered a great deal.

When Elizabeth finally found her voice, she said, "Robert, I am no great beauty. I am just me. The same girl you once saw as a friend. Are we naught still friends?"

"No, you are not wrong. Does it not feel different between us now, since we've declared our feelings for each other? What I felt when I kissed you, was a feeling like no other, is now embedded deep in my heart. Did you not feel it?" Robert asked as he searched for the answer in her eyes.

He smiled. *It's there.*

What Robert said was true; she felt it too.

Filled with emotions, in a soft voice, "Yes, yes I do," she said with a wide smile.

Robert kissed her again, and when he finally pulled away, all Elizabeth could do was stare up at him feeling stunned.

Robert smiled at her; he loved the effect he had on Elizabeth, as she had on him.

The way Elizabeth felt when Robert kissed her, left her feeling numb and breathless, leaving her feeling exhilarated and happy, so very happy. It left her speechless as well.

It felt as if time stopped for Robert, leaving him with a great deal he wanted to say but found he could not speak the words. So, instead of words, he pulled Elizabeth close to his chest and wrapped his arms around her, desperately needing to hold her, to feel her body against his, wanting their love to flow through them, a mergence of two souls, making them one.

This time it was Elizabeth who spoke first, of words neither of them wanted to hear. "Robert, the sun is rising. We must return to the manor before we are missed."

Robert put his forehead against Elizabeth's. He wasn't ready to leave, not wanting this moment to end, but she was right; they needed to return. Robert stood back and nodded, but neither one of them moved. They just stood there holding each other.

After a few moments, Robert said, "Elizabeth, must we? How can I leave you after this moment we've shared? To be apart from you once again is too much to ask of me."

Unable to let her go, Robert didn't release Elizabeth. He loved the feel of her body against his and wanted to savor every moment of it. He felt if they parted, it would leave him bereaved.

"Robert, look at me?" Elizabeth asked.

Robert pulled away from Elizabeth, just enough to look

down at her, as he was a great deal taller than she was, and at times it amused him. With sadness, Robert looked at Elizabeth as he met his eyes with hers, and the love he saw warmed his heart; knowing it was all for him, it left him breathless.

Elizabeth put her hand on Robert's cheek, and when she did, he felt a surge go through him, sending shivers down his body, but her gentle touch also smooth away his sadness and replaced it with love.

"I feel what you are feeling, and I don't want to leave," squeezing her arms around him, "Nor do I want to leave your arms…to be parted once again, separated until our next meeting, hurts me more than you know. How can I want to be anywhere else but right here in your arms? But my love, we must return, so we are not discovered."

With reluctance, Robert released his hold on Elizabeth, and took her arm and placed it into the crook of his, and together they began their walk back to the manor. Once they reached the outer edge of the manor, that was hidden by the forest trees, Robert turned to Elizabeth and looked directly into her eyes, then he pulled her to him and kissed her, wanting to remind her of what they recently shared.

When Robert finally released Elizabeth, it took them a few moments to bring their emotions under control. Once they were ready, they parted and returned to the manor, with Elizabeth going to her father's cottage and Robert to Dunham Massey Castle.

***

It had been several months since Robert and Elizabeth acknowledged their feelings for each other and agreed to pursue them.

Before the Davenport's returned to Bramhall Manor, Robert and Elizabeth managed to sneak away for a few moments before he returned home.

"Elizabeth, I don't want to go another day without seeing you and ask for your permission…will you allow me to come…to meet with you every day here at our lake." Praying she will say yes, "Will you, will you agree to this?" he asked.

Elizabeth was so happy and excited at the idea, and the thought of being with Robert every day, made her want to fly.

"Robert, yes, of course I will. But will it not be far for you to ride on horseback?"

"Nay, it will not. I am an excellent horseman, and the journey will be nothing to me, especially knowing I will be seeing you. It would hurt me more if I could not. I would risk everything to be with you Elizabeth."

***

And it was done, from that day forth, Robert and Elizabeth met at their lake, allowing their feelings to grow to a powerful love, a bond, a passion, with a closeness they believed no one has ever felt before.

Chapter Eleven

<u>Summer 1533</u>

Not knowing the contents of the agreement, Robert and Elizabeth, no matter how much they wanted to tell their families, knew it was impossible. Their relationship must remain a secret, with hope, that one day, when the time was right, they would be able to reveal their feelings to their family. But will there truly ever be a right time?

After Robert arrived at their lake and saw Elizabeth, he was unable to contain himself. He pulled his horse to a stop, then jumped off and ran to Elizabeth, taking her into his arms, and she leaned into him, closing her eyes as she savored the feel of his touch.

Standing in each other's arms, Robert and Elizabeth could feel the wind blowing in a mild breeze, as it was brushing their bodies in a light embrace. It's as if an unknown force was welcoming them through the feel of their bodies by merging them with a love so powerful; it was beyond time and space.

Their lake was a place they've come to know and accept as their sanctuary. Their safe haven. A place they could be together, allowing them to express their love fully and completely. They allowed their feelings to grow, and it grew into an unexpected, rare, and passionate kind of love, surpassing any, and all love known to man.

Robert kissed Elizabeth, and when he did, there was a spark of emotions he didn't recognize. Was it love, or was it something else? It was both, a bond of two souls connected through the emergence of their bodies, intertwining their love with every aspect of their being, merging their souls, bonding them as one, in a soul-to-soul connection.

Robert pulled her body close as she welcomed his to hers, with the power, passion, and love they felt embracing them, sending a wave of utter lust. Embracing this feeling, Robert touched Elizabeth's face with the back of his hand, softly caressing her beautiful silky skin as he stared at her lips, desperately wanting to kiss those luscious kissable lips. And before he could change his mind, he leaned down, brushing his lips against hers, not once but twice, giving her a chance to pull away, and when she didn't, he used his tongue wanting her to open her mouth for him, and when she did, she tasted sweet as honey.

Elizabeth was surprised by Robert's touch, but once he brushed his lips against hers, a surge went through her, and she welcomed his kiss with a need she didn't understand, with an unknown desire and passion, but it didn't matter, and allowed herself to melt into him.

Robert took his time, relishing in the feel of Elizabeth's lips and the taste of her mouth. With the passion flowing through them, his kiss became demanding, as if he was desperate to be a part of her. The hunger he felt was beyond anything he could imagine.

Once they broke the kiss, Robert said, "Elizabeth, how can I love you this much? Although we see each other every day," stepping back, needing to look at her. "When we are apart," placing his hand over his chest, looking directly into her eyes, "My heart hurts, with a pain so severe, it's as if something is missing. This transpires from the moment I leave you until I am with you again. Here, with you in my arms."

"Robert, my love, how can one person feel so much love for another as I do for you," Elizabeth said, raising her head to look at him. "As you say, my heart feels as yours, incomplete until I am with you again."

Robert met her eyes with his, and they gazed into each other's eyes, seeing deep into their souls, and what they saw was a love so explosive, it frightened them, but it was very much welcomed.

Robert kissed her again, but found he wanted more than her kiss, he needed to merge their bodies, as well as their souls, completing them as one body and soul. To his welcoming surprise, Elizabeth returned his kiss with the same demand and passion, and he felt she wanted it as well.

In the previous months when Robert was with Elizabeth, he was careful to hold back his desire, not wanting it to overtake him, afraid of pushing her to do more than what she was willing to give. But every day he was with her, it became harder and harder. He wanted her with every breath he took. It's only his love and respect for Elizabeth that's kept him from giving in to his desires, not wanting to take what he had no right to take.

Today though, today was the hardest yet. He desired Elizabeth more than he had before and was finding it harder and harder to resist. This time, this time though, he could see she desired him as well. Both their bodies calling and craving each other.

In this, Robert kissed her again, and this time, he took their kiss to the next level and was delighted when she welcomed his kiss as if one needed the other to breathe.

Feeling breathless, Robert stopped before he did something he would regret and stepped back to look at Elizabeth, and what he saw nearly knocked him off his feet. There was a hunger searing through her, and she wanted him as much as he wanted her.

As Elizabeth watched Robert, she smiled; she knew what he wanted, as she saw the pleading in his eyes, hoping she'd say yes and accept him, but afraid she would not. So, without words, she gave him the answer he was looking for, by kissing him, throwing all her love and passion into her kiss.

When Elizabeth looked at him with acceptance in her eyes, he smiled. He did not want to rush her, so he waited, glancing from eye to eye. There was no fear, but he wanted to be sure she was ready, then she kissed him. Showing she was ready.

Robert picked up Elizabeth without removing his eyes from hers. He looked for any hesitation as he carried her to the blanket beneath the tree near the lake. Once he laid her down, he was pleased to see no hesitation. She wanted him as much as he wanted her.

Robert and Elizabeth's unbridled passion pierced deep into their souls. They made love for the first time, a penetrating convergence of two bodies and two souls becoming one, sealing their love for eternity.

Spent from making love, Elizabeth snuggled close to Robert, feeling happier than she believed possible. "Robert, to love you is a gift I never imagined possible. Being able to feel every aspect of you fully and completely, connecting us in a way…" closing her eyes, remembering how she felt when they made love, "Oh Robert, I cannot explain what I am feeling in words. It was magical."

Robert smiled, "Elizabeth, making love has connected us in a way no one can ever destroy. We merged our bodies…" looking away for a moment, not understanding what he wanted to say, only it felt right. "…our passion…god Elizabeth, to feel what I felt when we made love, no other can claim such a powerful feeling…a feeling that…" he let out a laugh, "I do not know what I am saying. Forgive me, Elizabeth…I cannot seem to find the right words."

Touching Robert's face, "Oh, Robert, I say you found the perfect words. Making love to you was…incredible. The way I felt when our bodies merged…sent waves of emotions…love, happiness as if our bodies bonded us…penetrating deep into our…souls."

Robert smiled and pulled Elizabeth closer to him, and they laid in each other's arms basking in the after-effects of making love. After a time, they prepared to leave, and after a long hug and kiss, they left the lake and went their separate ways.

When they parted, it was a struggle, and they were anxious for when they could be together once again.

***

Each time they returned to 'their lake', they allowed the power of the lake to fill them, enforcing and sealing their love and fate for all time.

After arriving home, Elizabeth sat in her chamber, thinking about what happened between her and Robert, and found this was something she couldn't keep to herself. She needed to share their magical moment with her sister.

After taking a few moments to gather her courage, Elizabeth went to see Grace. Once she was at Grace's door, she knocked but did not wait for her to answer. Once she entered her chamber, Elizabeth saw Grace on the bed reading one of her books.

When Elizabeth entered her chamber, Grace put up a finger needing a minute to finish what she was reading. When she finished, she looked up at Elizabeth, "Alright," she said, putting her book down in her lap, "How was your time with Robert?" she asked.

When Elizabeth told Grace about her and Robert's decision to see each other every day, it was the best news she heard or could have hoped for, and she was pleased their time together was going so well.

"Grace, it was amazing. We…" rushing to Grace, sitting on the bed next to her. "Oh, Grace, I cannot contain myself. Robert and I made love. It was the most wonderful and amazing feeling. It was magical."

Grace wanted to be happy for her sister, but she feared Elizabeth made a grave mistake and had to tell her so.

"Elizabeth, I want more than anything to be happy for you, but I cannot. What were you thinking? What will you do if you become with child? Did you not consider that to be a possibility? You became a woman last year, and I know you are aware of what happens once you did, and you have…" Grace stopped, not able to say the words. Instead, she pointed at Elizabeth's private area… "Done that," she said with disgust.

Elizabeth looked at her sister, and she was stunned by her suggestion. A child, it wasn't even on her mind when she made love to Robert. And that therein lies the problem. Yes, it was ignorant and irresponsible – Elizabeth turned away, unable to look at her sister.

"Grace, I did not think…I was only thinking of being with Robert. What am I going to do if making love to Robert…if I become with child…mother and father…"

Elizabeth couldn't bear to think of it; she was engulfed with fear. She leaned forward and grabbed her stomach as she suddenly felt ill. If she were with child, there would be no hiding her situation. Tears started running down her face, and she felt like a fool. What was she going to do?

Grace saw how afraid Elizabeth was and tried to reassure her. "There is only one thing we can do. We pray this one event does not cause the unspeakable to happen. Elizabeth, you must understand, you cannot engage in such behavior again." Seeing Elizabeth's hesitation, Grace reached for her hand and tried to make eye contact with her. "If you become with child, it will destroy us all."

Elizabeth could not speak. The only thing she was able to do was nod in understanding. Elizabeth knew if she and Robert made love again – their behavior could destroy both families.

***

The following morning when Elizabeth met Robert, she wasn't excited as she usually was, instead she was afraid, knowing what she needed to do, she started to shake all over.

Upon seeing Elizabeth, Robert noticed something was wrong, so he immediately took her in his arms, and when he did, he could feel her shaking all over.

Concerned by this, he asked, "Elizabeth, what is

wrong? What has happened?" he asked worried, not understanding what's caused her to be so upset.

Elizabeth tried to be strong but failed as tears streamed down her face, "Robert...Oh Robert," she said, shaking, as her voice cracked. "I am so afraid!"

Robert held her tight against him, not understanding why she was so afraid as he wondered, *what could have happened? Did someone find out?*

Aloud he said with concern in his voice, "Elizabeth, what happened? What has caused you to be upset? What do you fear?" Robert asked. He too began to feel afraid.

Elizabeth does her best to pull herself together and tried to explain. "Robert, what we did...in making love...what if I am..."

How can I tell him? I cannot say the words. I must, I know I must. I am sure he did not consider what could happen either. If he did, he would have told me? she thought.

"...with child?" she finally said, then started sobbing, no longer able to continue.

Grace, he thought.

Robert knew what happened and wasn't surprised; after all, Grace was Elizabeth's sister and her best friend. She was one person she confides in.

Grace must have said something to make Elizabeth feel this way, he thought.

He knew if she did, she did not have ill intent, but something she said affected Elizabeth, causing her to feel afraid.

Robert held Elizabeth tight in his arms, rubbing her back, trying his best to console her, wanting to ease her pain, at the same time, ease his own fears. After a while, Elizabeth's crying started to ease some, and Robert tried to understand what exactly happened.

"Elizabeth, why do you fear being with child?"

"Robert, you cannot be blind to what I say?" she said

with a bite in her voice.

"Well, no, I do understand. Making love can result in a woman having a child, but Elizabeth, I do not believe you will become with child. As there are certain things a man can do to prevent a woman from becoming with child, and…I…"

Robert was having difficulty explaining this to Elizabeth but knew he must.

"…well…I ensured you did not receive that which will cause you to be with child," he finally said with a slight smile.

What? she thought. Elizabeth was confused, she did not understand what he meant. His words though, gave her some relief.

"Robert, I know…I am sure…I am going to feel sorry for asking this question, but…what do you mean by what you say?" Elizabeth asked, moving back so she could look at him.

Robert smiled; how was he going to tell her? To explain to Elizabeth what he meant. Knowing it must be done, he released his breath and attempted to explain.

"Well…Elizabeth, there is something a man does when…well…"

Elizabeth put her hands over her ears, realizing what he was going to say, and didn't want to hear it. Her mother had explained this when she became a woman, the way a man may try to induce her into having sex.

"Stop. I do not wish to know. I get it. I truly do," she said, feeling a bit embarrassed.

All Robert could do was smile at Elizabeth. When he decided to make love to her, he did not consider the consequences in the possibilities of giving her a child, but he ensured he did not leave his seed inside her.

Once Robert attempted to explain and realized she had nothing to worry about, she started to relax, allowing her fears to wash away. Robert and Elizabeth enjoyed their remaining time together, but she could not allow their passion to consume them again.

"Robert, you know I love you and what we did…it was the greatest, beautiful experience in my life, an amazing and magical moment. But Robert, we cannot allow our passion to consume us again, not until we are married."

Robert felt disappointed, he wanted to make love to Elizabeth again and share that magical feeling they had, but she was not wrong in what she said. Her fear was justified, and with that understanding, he reluctantly agreed. For Elizabeth, he would wait until they were married, and he was confident they would marry. After their families see the love they share, how could they deny them.

Robert and Elizabeth believed they'd been blessed with a true miracle, a gift from God, and from that moment, they decided to enjoy their time together by living in the moment, thinking only of themselves.

***

After the times Robert and Elizabeth have shared, on more than one occasion, they've thought about telling their families, and they believed if they knew how much they loved each other, how can they not allow them to marry. This, a constant topic when Grace and Elizabeth met after Robert and Elizabeth's time together.

Grace and Elizabeth were in Elizabeth's chambers, situated on the cottage's northeast side at the end of the hall. It was the safest place that allowed them the best privacy, so they would not be overheard.

"Grace, the times I spent with Robert have been incredible. How can we convince our families to allow Robert and I to marry instead of you and Robert?"

"Elizabeth, I do not know. It may not be possible, after what father said…" shaking her head as she was unsure of the right words, "I do not know Elizabeth. If you choose to tell father, you must pick the right time when he's in a good mood."

"It may be better if you are there with me," Elizabeth said with a smile.

Grace was their father's favorite, and if she could use her sister's relationship with their father to soften him, then she would.

Grace looked at Elizabeth and smiled, "If there is anything I can do to help you and Robert, then I will. As you know, helping you is helping me."

Elizabeth was suddenly worried and scared; if their families discovered what they've been doing could be disastrous. "Grace, how long do you think we can get away with deceiving our families? How long do you think you can go on pretending to spend time with Robert? I worry that one day we will be discovered before we tell them," Elizabeth said, as she began to panic.

Placing her hand on Elizabeth's shoulder, Grace stopped her. "It's impossible for us to be discovered. I assure you. You know the servants. They dare not say a word to father. Also, you know how much they love us. They want to see you and me happy," Grace said with a smile.

For as long as they could recall, the servants have loved and adored Grace and Elizabeth, and with Grace being their father's favorite, they wouldn't do anything to hurt them. Not with something as little as this.

If the servants believed what Grace and Elizabeth were doing would bring them harm, they wouldn't hesitate to tell their father. And for the servants at Bramhall Manor, they were too afraid of Lord Davenport's wrath to say anything, not to mention how much they loved Robert, so much so, they would do anything for him.

"When mother and father inquire how Robert and I are getting along. I simply tell them, yes mother, we are getting along fine. After that, no more is said. To them, what matters is we are getting along. It does not matter if we like each other, let alone fall in love. Love has nothing to do with us getting married, in what's required for us to be husband and wife."

"Grace, what if they start asking more questions? What will you do?"

"It will not happen," Grace said with confidence.

She understands her position. This marriage is an arrangement, how Robert and her felt was of no consequence.

"If they do, I will simply tell them, why does it matter so long as we marry as you wish. That is all they care about, Elizabeth. I want love. I truly do. I knew Robert was not the one when we first met. But, with you and Robert, I saw something between you two, and knew it was you who was to be with him, not me."

"Grace, how could you know that?" Elizabeth said with surprise.

"It was not hard, Elizabeth. It was the way you were with each other," Grace said. "Elizabeth, what about you? What will you do when the time comes?" Grace gently asked.

"The time…" she started to question with confusion. "…oh, you mean when you and Robert are to marry. Oh, Grace, I do not know. I have not thought much of it, but I should have," Elizabeth said, looking down at her hands as they rest in her lap. "I am not ready to think of it yet. I just want Robert and me to enjoy our time together with the time we have left," Elizabeth said.

Then with understanding, she wondered, "How much longer do you think we can continue our deception? We have been avoiding our mother's every time they've asked us to spend time together. I know this is done because you don't want to slip and say the wrong thing," she said, as she placed her hand on Grace's, "As we grow into women, we are required to do what women are expected to do."

"You mean become boring," Grace said with disgust.

Elizabeth laughed, "Yes, Grace, become boring women.

Soon, we will no longer be able to use the excuse; we are only children. We are to be women, and Robert is to be a man."

As far as Elizabeth was concern, Robert was already a man. After all, at thirteen, boys were already considered a man.

"I am sure we will figure something out," Grace said.

However, for Elizabeth, lost in her own thoughts, she did not hear Grace.

Grace saw Elizabeth wasn't listening to her and had to yell, "Elizabeth!" to get her attention.

At hearing Elizabeth yell her name, she quickly snapped out of her thought, "Oh, sorry Grace," she said, returning her focus to her sister. "Yes, I am sure we will."

There was no question, the closer the event became, Elizabeth, Grace, and Robert's arrangement would have to change. In the meantime, Robert and Elizabeth continued with the way things were, basking in every moment, of every day they were together until the day they were forced to stop.

***

For the next couple of years, prior to Robert and Grace turning seventeen, then shortly after, their wedding. Robert and Elizabeth were the happiest they thought possible, living each moment as if it will be their last. Cherishing their time together, knowing any day could be their last. And in this time, their love continued to grow to a love so rare, that for them, it had surpassed all love known.

No one could ever feel the love Robert and Elizabeth had come to know. A love prevailing, that enabled their love to transcend beyond heaven and earth. A love so powerful, it surpasses the fabric of time and space. An eternal love that not even death itself could destroy the love Robert and Elizabeth felt. Their heart and soul connected as one. The times they were not together felt as if their hearts were being ripped from their chest, as if an invisible string was stretched out longing to reunite, connecting them once again.

***

<u>Spring 1535</u>

On one beautiful and unusual bright spring day, while Robert and Elizabeth were at their lake, Robert felt the need to mark their tree, wanting all who were to come after them, hoping they will see this lake as a place of love.

Robert took the knife from his belt and carved his and Elizabeth initials on the side of the tree that was facing the lake. Once he was done, he climbed the tree until he was at the highest he could go, and was unable to go further, at the top of his lungs he yelled, "I love You, Elizabeth Massey, with all my heart and soul!"

Elizabeth watched Robert and thought he was ridiculous to climb the tree, and when he yelled, declaring his love for her, she laughed at his ridiculous and childish behavior, but at the same time, her heart jumped at his declaration. At that moment, she could not have loved him more than she did that day.

When Robert jumped out of the tree, he landed right in front of Elizabeth, then swooped her in his arms. As they stood there gazing at each other, there was an ache in their chest bursting with love.

Suddenly, there was a feeling, as if the heavens opened up, shining its light directly on them, blessing their love. In this, they felt as if no one else existed in the land. That the world was closed off, leaving just the two of them.

***

Soon Robert and Grace would be seventeen, then shortly after, married. One afternoon during the Massey's and Davenport's gathering, while sitting in the great room discussing Robert and Grace's upcoming wedding, Robert and Elizabeth glanced at each other, fear showing clearly in their eyes.

When Robert marries Grace, there was no doubt it

would affect their relationship – it would be non-existent. With their eyes, they asked the question, should they tell their families what was happening between them, of the powerful love they found? And if they did, would their families approve? Or should they continue their relationship in secret, and when the time came for Robert to marry Grace, they would do the right thing by ending their relationship and try to forget each other and their feelings?

With one look and without words, Robert and Elizabeth refused to say anything. They were not ready to forget the love they've come to know. It was too unbearable.

The following afternoon Robert and Elizabeth met at their lake, with the need to discuss what happened the day before. They need to determine if they should inform their families about their relationship and the love they found? They believed if their family saw the love they've come to know, then there would be no question that their families would accept them and allow them to marry.

It was hard for Robert and Elizabeth to understand why they could not be the ones to unite their families by allowing them to marry? The way they saw it, the agreement was for a Massey to marry a Davenport. So, why couldn't Grace's name be changed for Elizabeth's? This, they could not understand.

With this, they wondered if their families would understand the reason Robert and Elizabeth kept their relationship a secret. Maybe it was best they told their families and took the chance and hope it wouldn't be as bad as they thought it would be. After all, Grace had no interest in marrying Robert. An arranged marriage between two families; what does it matter what daughter married Robert? Elizabeth knew they needed to decide if it was time to tell their families, and when they did, pray, they would allow them to marry. To Robert and Elizabeth, the agreement was more of a curse than a merger.

***

Standing at the edge of the lake facing each other, Elizabeth said, "Robert, soon you and Grace will marry. When this happens, I will lose you forever." Then she turned away from Robert to look out at the lake. "How can I live…" she looked down at her hands, twisting the front of her gown. "…The thought of not being with you? To touch you..." Elizabeth turned and looked up at Robert, as she placed her hand on his face with the need to touch him. "To kiss and hold you? To feel your arms around me as you hold me close to your body. My ear to your chest, as I listen to your heart beating faster," she smiled, "Knowing it's beating for me."

Filled with fear, Robert pulled Elizabeth closer to him. He needed to feel her body against his, and was afraid of letting her go, because if he did, he would lose her forever. He smiled; his heart would beat faster when he was close to her. It wasn't only when she was near her, but when he saw her as well. When he thought of her or knowing he was going to see her. And of course, any time she touched him.

Robert understood her fears as they were his own. What would they do if he was forced to marry Grace? Robert heard of those couples who were forced into an arranged marriage, how the man, at times, took a mistress. Robert wondered, should he do that with Elizabeth? Was he capable? Was she capable? If he took Elizabeth as a mistress, it would dishonor her and ruin her forever, preventing her from finding happiness with another because he was selfish. No, he could never do that. Elizabeth was right; it would be over when he married Grace.

Had I not already dishonored her when we made love. He shook his head, *No! I cannot allow this! We must find a way! God, there must be a way!* he thought as he squeezed his arms tighter around Elizabeth.

"Elizabeth, my love…I cannot bear what is to happen? The thought of losing you…No! I will not allow this to happen! I will refuse to marry Grace if it means losing you forever. No, I will not…I cannot do this!" Robert said feeling frustrated.

Robert tightened his hold on Elizabeth, crushing her body against his, as he was filled with fear. He was afraid of letting her go, thus, if he did, he would lose her forever. *No! I cannot! I will not!*

Hearing Robert's words, Elizabeth could feel his fear, and it brought tears trickling down her face. Although Robert was crushing her, she didn't care. She needed him as much as he needed her. She closed her eyes, not wanting to think about the possibilities, as she clung to him for dear life. She too, was afraid of letting him go, thus, losing him forever.

Robert suddenly felt wetness on his shirt and heard sniffling. "Elizabeth, my love," he said, pulling away to look at her, and when he saw her tears, "Do not cry, my love, for I am with you now. If it is Gods will, I will never leave you."

Hearing Robert's words, Elizabeth tightened her hold on him, terrified of letting him go. *What if it is God's will for Robert to marry Grace,* she thought, as she dug her nails in his back, piercing his shirt and breaking his skin.

Robert felt the pain on his back from Elizabeth's nails, but he did not move. Instead, he said, "Elizabeth, my love, I feel your fear, as it is my own. Please know this, I will do all I can to prevent this from happening. What I feel for you…the love I have for you, I will not easily relinquish. So, my love, if you will, please release your nails which are piercing my skin."

Elizabeth was shocked, "I am sorry," she said, quickly releasing her hold, not realizing she was hurting him. "Oh, Robert, I am so sorry. I did not…"

Robert stopped her with a kiss. Once they broke their kiss, Robert held Elizabeth while stroking her beautiful long brown hair, as he stared at the lake, "If our families know of the love we found…we share, they may be willing to listen and allow us to marry instead of forcing me to marry Grace. With Grace having no desire to marry me, even more now knowing how we feel about each other. For our families to force us into an unhappy marriage because of some agreement forged long ago, in doing so, taking away our will and our right to choose who we love and marry."

"Robert, I agree with what you say. I do not understand this as well, but what are we to do? It is done, and what is done cannot be undone. We have no choice," she said, choking on her words as her emotions got the best of her. "And once you are married, I will lose you forever," she said with tears running down her face. She cried so hard; it allowed her to release everything she felt; anger, fear, and sadness, holding nothing back. She cried in Robert's arms as her heart broke, knowing soon she would lose him forever.

There was nothing Robert could do but hold Elizabeth tight, so tight he thought he might break her. He needed the closeness, as she did, with the need to comfort each other.

After some time, Robert said, "Elizabeth, what...now...I am only thinking, but...what if we inform our families of our feelings and the love we share, with the hope they will agree to change or break the agreement, thus, allowing us to marry. Does it matter which sister I marry so long as she…" he pushed Elizabeth away just enough to look at her. "…you are a Massey, are you naught?" he said with a smile.

"Oh, Robert, I want that more than anything…do you think they will agree?" Elizabeth said, giving her a little relief at the idea, and it allowed her to hope.

"I do not know. We can only try and pray they will," Robert said, tightening his hold on Elizabeth. He too, felt relief – hope.

Chapter Twelve

<u>Winter 1535</u>

It's the last month of the year and a month before
Robert and Grace's wedding. The Massey's and
Davenport's decided the best time for the wedding to
take place was in the New Year of 1536. What best time
to start a New Year, then with a wedding. A beginning
of joy and happiness for all involved.

For Robert and Elizabeth, with the wedding closely
approaching, were worried. One day during their time
together at the lake, they discussed Robert's upcoming
wedding. Months ago, they planned on telling their
mother and father about their relationship and the love
they found, but they couldn't find the right time. When
Elizabeth tells her father, it must be when he's in a
good mood and with Grace by her side. For Robert, due
to the man his father was, he would only tell his father
after Elizabeth told hers, in hopes, Baron Massey would
be able to influence his father to their side.

The problem with this decision, was there was too
much happening in the kingdom after King Henry's
decree, declaring his new Church of England to be the
one and only church. Thus, outlawing the Catholic
religion and ordering all Catholic Churches to be
destroyed.

Lord Davenport and Baron Massey being loyal
supporters of King Henry; when they received orders, Lord
Davenport, as the law in the land and with Baron Massey's
assistance, were to enforce the king's decree to the people
of Cheshire and Manchester, demanding they conform to
the new Church of England. If they refused, the people
were to be immediately put to death and forfeit all they

own to King Henry. Baron Massey and Lord Davenport did not believe in the king's new law since they were strong followers of the Catholic faith, but accepted the change because their king declared it.

***

Robert and Elizabeth were sitting under their favorite tree, the one closest to the lake, discussing what they were going to do about Robert and Grace's closely approaching wedding.

"Elizabeth, I do not think I can go through with the wedding. I cannot marry Grace. There must be something we can do to stop this wedding from taking place," Robert said, looking out at the lake.

Elizabeth tensed at the word 'wedding', shaking her head, "Robert, what can we do?" she said with sadness as she twisted the front of her gown. "The wedding is quickly approaching...I don't know how we can prevent it from happening."

Elizabeth wanted this more than anything, but there hasn't been an opportunity to tell their mother and father about their relationship before this wedding was to take place, and they were running out of time. Elizabeth could not help but feel defeated and before the battle has even started.

Robert thought about this a great deal, and with what was happening in the land, he did not believe there was ever going to be the right time, especially with the wedding closely approaching. But he felt he could not, he would not marry Grace, not with the way he felt about Elizabeth. He loves her with all his heart and soul, and the thought of marrying another, her sister, was reprehensible. He has an idea, though; one he's been thinking about a great deal. It's a considerable risk, and one he doesn't think Elizabeth would agree with, but he needed to tell her what he was thinking and see what she had to say about it.

Looking at Elizabeth he said, "I want to talk to you...I

have an idea, but it will mean going against everything we know and believe in."

As he was about to explain himself, he stopped and found himself restless and needed to move away from Elizabeth. He wasn't able to look at her in what he was about to suggest, knowing if she were to agree, it would cause a great scandal.

"Well...Elizabeth," he began to say, then hesitated. He looked over and stared out to the lake before continuing. "What I am thinking…is, well...what if…" Robert lowered his head and took a deep breath, then continued. "We were already married?" There, it was finally said, but he did not give Elizabeth a chance to respond. He quickly continued, "If we marry before I marry Grace, our family will have no choice but to accept us and our relationship."

Robert was still unable to look at Elizabeth and wondered what she must be thinking.

I know she is shocked, but what other options do we have? Do we tell them and hope they will agree? Robert thought, shaking his head, knowing they would not agree.

As Elizabeth watched Robert, she wanted him to look at her, but he did not. After hearing what he suggested, she should have been shocked, but she wasn't. She was more surprised than shocked; she did not expect Robert to want to marry her in secret. If they were to marry in secret, it would undoubtedly cause a scandal that could lead to the ruin of both families.

Elizabeth walked over to Robert, stopping just behind him as she placed her hand on his shoulder, "Robert…please tell me again? I want to make sure I heard you right," she said, pulling on his shoulder, wanting him to look at her, but he doesn't move. So, Elizabeth continued, "You cannot mean what I think you mean?" she said. Then thought, *how can he? The scandal it will cause. Our families will be ruined, and we will be to blame. How can he expect me to live with that?*

Elizabeth wanted to be wrong with what Robert suggested, but she knew he was serious. Then she wondered, *or did I hear what I wanted to hear?* Shaking her head, *no, why would I want to hear such a thing.* She was confused and began doubting herself, but she could not deny what he said; he wanted to marry her without their parents' consent. Elizabeth knew, if they were to marry without their parent's knowledge or permission – it was something she could never consider.

Robert did not turn around. He couldn't. He couldn't bear to look at Elizabeth. To let her see his fear and desperation. He meant what he said, but he was afraid she wouldn't want it. Not realizing he had moved, Robert looked down to find he was standing at the edge of the lake. He kicked at the water, and in the water's reflection, he saw Elizabeth. She was worried. Unable to bear her image, Robert looked up and to the forest on the other side.

Elizabeth tried to will Robert to turn around; she needed to look at him. To look into his eyes and see the truth. "Robert, please look at me?" she finally asked.

Robert still refused to turn around, so Elizabeth tried to move in front of him, but noticed they were too close to the lake's edge to do so. Again, she gently placed her hand on his arm, pulling harder to force him, so he would turn around and face her.

With reluctance, Robert finally caved in and turned his head to look at Elizabeth, though he refused to make eye contact with her.

Upon seeing Robert's face, Elizabeth saw his agony, and his pain was so clear. What he mentioned was not an easy decision for him, and her heart swelled with love for this man standing in front of her. *Her love.* Elizabeth took her hands and gently placed them on his face with a soft caress, willing him to look at her. Instead, he closed his eyes; he did not want her to look to close. Then she said, "Robert, please look at me? Let me see your eyes?"

Although he was hesitant, Robert opened his eyes and looked directly into hers, and what Elizabeth saw broke her heart. She saw his anguish, and she didn't want him to see how his pain affected her. Elizabeth gathered her emotions so she could be strong for him and tried to ease his pain.

"Robert, I can see this was not an easy decision for you. I love you, Robert. I love you so much that my heart aches when I am not with you. I want more than anything to be your wife. But you know we cannot do this." Elizabeth brushed Robert's hair with her fingers. It pained her to say those words to him, but it had to be said.

Robert closed his eyes; it hurt him to hear her words, but she was not wrong, and after hearing her, he wished he could take back what he said. It was done though, and he needed to face it.

It hurt Elizabeth to see how much Robert was struggling, and she didn't try to force him to open his eyes, but she needed to make sure he understood what he said was wrong.

"Our families will never accept a marriage done without their knowledge and consent. You know this to be true. How angry they will be when they learn what we did. To learn of our deception…" Elizabeth stopped, as she was unable to continue.

Robert nodded in acknowledgement.

"…To have their own blood, their own children go against them will dishonor them in a way…shows disrespect. We are to honor and obey our mother and father. How can we," pointing to Robert and herself, "If their son and daughter do this to them?"

Elizabeth's intent to ease and smooth Robert's pain failed. Robert turned away from Elizabeth, unable to look at her. He didn't want her to see his shame. Nor could he deny her words, and he hated to admit she was right, and he could not bear to hear anymore.

In a shaky voice, Robert said, "Please, Elizabeth, say

not another word. I cannot bear to hear any more."

Although it pained Elizabeth to hear this, she had to continue. Her words must be heard. "Robert, please look at me?" she pleaded. Her voice started to crack as her strength was abandoning her.

At hearing her plea, Robert finally turned around to face her.

"What about Grace?" Elizabeth asked. "If we marry in secret, how will this decision affect her? To marry in this way…you know as I do, it will destroy all of us. Robert, I love you, you are my heart and soul, the one my soul is bound to," Elizabeth said, but her own words confused her. This, she did not understand, nor did Robert from his confused look.

"Do not ask me how I know. I just do. It is the same belief…God had brought us together," she said, taking both of his hands in hers. "We must pray God will help us find a way."

Robert knew what Elizabeth said was true. What can he say? There was nothing he could say. Robert was confused by her words, 'the one my soul is bound to.' She was right, God brought them together, and he was the one who could help them find a way to make this happen.

Robert laid his head against Elizabeth's shoulder, not knowing what to do, feeling hurt and defeated. He loved Elizabeth with every breath he took, and the thought of losing her by marrying Grace – to see and speak to her, never again be allowed to touch her, hold her, or kiss her – *nay, this is too much for God to ask me to bear,* Robert thought.

Elizabeth carefully raised Robert's head and wrapped her arms around him, pulling him close to her, with the need to hold and comfort him, at the same time she needed him to hold and comfort her.

Robert lost all his strength and fell into her embrace. In silence, they held each other, and enjoyed the feel of being in each other's arms.

In unison, they said each other's name, then burst out laughing, giving them a moment of relief.

Robert was the first to pull away from their embrace and said, "Elizabeth, I am so sorry. I did not mean to cause you so much pain." He took her face in his hands, "I just love you so much, and the thought of losing you —"

Elizabeth silenced him by saying, "Robert," as she placed her hands on his face, wanting him to look directly into her eyes. "You, my love. You will never lose me. This, I promise."

For unknown reasons, something in Robert snapped with a rage he didn't know was possible. A rage that had been silently building until the right trigger brought it to the surface.

"NO! I may never lose you, but I will never have you!" he yelled. Robert stepped away from Elizabeth and began to pace. "Not the way we are now!"

He was unable to look at her. He did not want Elizabeth to see how angry and frighten he really was. Robert turned his back on Elizabeth; he felt frustrated and pushed his fingers through his hair, trying to get his anger under control. He wasn't angry at Elizabeth. He was angry at their situation, and he needed to make her see —

"It will not be the same! Will you be able to bear seeing me with Grace! She, who is your sister, the one you confide in! Can you two still maintain your friendship knowing she has me in every way you cannot; with her in my bed, not you?"

His words were harsher than he intended, but he had to say them to get a reaction from her because he felt she was being too light about their situation. Was this the right way? No. But he didn't know what else to do.

To see Robert explode in the way he did, shocked Elizabeth. At the same time, she was not surprised. After all, he was only expressing what she herself was feeling.

He is angry, as I am angry. How can I blame him? I cannot, she thought.

Then his words about her sister pierced her heart, ripping it in two. For a long moment, all she could do was stare at him. Then, out of nowhere, everything she was feeling exploded in an anger – a rage she did not know she was capable of, holding nothing back, allowing all she was feeling to rise to the surface.

Did Robert go too far, and will he be happy with the reaction he pushed her to have?

"Robert, how can you say that to me!" Elizabeth yelled, with pain lacing her voice. "You think I want you to marry Grace! To know you will be with her in ways I want you to be with me! Knowing you are sharing her bed and not mine! How do you think…do you think I can live feeling that pain every minute of every day!"

She started crying as she placed her hand over her heart, gripping her gown, wishing she could rip out her heart. She was doing everything she could to keep from falling to the ground.

"My heart hurts so much," pounding at her chest, "At the thought of you with Grace! My sister!" she yelled as she leaned forward. "Who I love with all my heart! How can I bear to know, the two I love most in this world are together! How am I to endure it! God knows how much it kills me to even think of it!" Elizabeth was yelling at the top of her lungs; her throat became sore, making it hard to talk.

Elizabeth's anger was so great she was shaking with furry. This was everything she feared since the day she and Robert allowed their feelings to flourish. She didn't want to cry, but the tears flowed beyond her control. The rawness of her emotions was too overwhelming to hold back. She had always been strong and good at hiding her feelings, but now, she allowed her pain to surface in the way it was – in hearing herself; she had no idea how angry and scared she was until this very moment. Elizabeth could no longer hold back her feelings, and by voicing what she felt, it allowed her to release all the pain she'd been holding back.

Elizabeth was overwhelmed by her emotions. With all her strength gone, she fell to her knees and leaned over with her face in her hands as she wails. She cried for herself. She cried for Robert. She cried for her sister. She cried for her mother and father, and she cried for the situation they've put themselves in.

Robert was horrified and ashamed of what he forced Elizabeth to face. Watching her tore his heart to pieces. To see her in such agony – he had no idea what Elizabeth was enduring. How much she was holding back.

What was I thinking! I did this! I caused her this pain! he thought.

At the sight of Elizabeth falling to her knees, Robert immediately went over and dropped to his knees in front of her. He grabbed Elizabeth by the shoulders and pulled her to him, desperately needing to comfort her. To make right the wrong he did, in pushing her to reveal what she's been feeling. Robert had no idea how much pain Elizabeth was in, and his ignorance allowed this to happen.

Elizabeth pushed Robert away, wanting nothing to do with him at that moment. Robert refused, ignoring her pushing at his chest. She did not want comforting and fought him with all the strength she had. She punched at his chest to get him away from her, but Robert was too strong, and Elizabeth was too weak.

Robert needed to help Elizabeth and find a way to comfort her. He needed to ease her pain. Not only for her but for himself as well, and he refused to let her go. He would endure whatever she threw at him.

Elizabeth fought and fought, but Robert refused to let her go. Only after she exhausted herself did she relent and allowed herself to relax into him.

After a short time in the comfort of Robert's arms,

Elizabeth gathered herself together and pushed herself away from Robert. Still angry, "Move away from me, Robert! I need room to breathe! I am too angry with you right now, and I do not want you near me!"

Reluctantly, Robert released Elizabeth. He was full of sorrow and regret for what he did. Had he known this would be her reaction, he would never have been so presumptuous in pushing Elizabeth to such anger. Yes, he wanted a reaction – *but not like this,* he thought. He loves Elizabeth. How could he make this right?

"Elizabeth, please...I am so sorry. I did not mean —"

Once Elizabeth was calm, she stood. When she was steady on her feet, she put her hand up to stop Robert from saying another word. She needed a moment to regain her composure, so she said, "Please, Robert, I need a moment."

Robert nodded in acknowledgement and allowed Elizabeth the space she needed.

Elizabeth turned away from Robert and began to brush the snow off her gown, giving her time to gather her thoughts. After taking a couple of deep breaths, and after letting them out slowly, and when she was sure her emotions were under control, is when she turned back to Robert.

"No, Robert, I know you did not mean what you said," she said, shaking her head. "But Robert, how could you?" With tears threatening to resurface, she tried her hardest to hold them back but failed, and they began to trickle down her face. She believed her feelings were under control, but it was apparent they were not. It was too much, and her heart was breaking.

I thought I had control of myself. How can I...it hurts too much, she thought.

Robert's heart was hurting from the pain he's caused Elizabeth. He was ashamed for what he did, and it was tearing him apart to see how much pain she was in. How could he make it right? What words could he say that would help?

Way to go, Robert. You wanted a reaction…I hope you are happy with what you received. You received more than you expected, he thought.

Robert tried to talk to Elizabeth again. "Elizabeth, please? I am so sorry," Robert said as he slowly reached for Elizabeth. He wanted desperately to hold her. To comfort her. To make right the wrong he did. Robert needed Elizabeth in his arms, with the need to feel her body against his.

Elizabeth saw Robert reach for her, and this time she allowed him to pull her into his arms. She didn't realize it at first, but she needed him as much as he needed her.

Robert was relieved when Elizabeth allowed him to take her in his arms, and they remained where they were, holding each other, unable to let go, with the need – the feel of each other's touch. There was no question; their fear was great, along with the anguish they both felt. For them to love each other this much, with the thought of never being allowed to be together in this way ever again, was unbearable.

"Elizabeth," Robert whispered in her hair. "We will do nothing now. We will wait and hope that the right time will present itself. We will pray and ask God for his help. There will be a way. I know there will be, and we will not speak of it again. We will find a way to help our families see what we already know. When they do, we will pray they will accept us and allow us to marry."

Elizabeth looked up at Robert and smiled. *God, I love him so much,* she thought. Then she placed her arms around his neck, and on tiptoes, she reached up as he lowered his head until their mouth touched. She put everything she felt for Robert into her kiss with her love and passion, allowing her anger, her fear, and her sorrow to fall away. Elizabeth kissed Robert as if it would be their last, and Robert accepted her kiss and returned it with the same love and passion until they were both out of breath.

After a few moments, Robert took Elizabeth's hand and together, they returned to the manor.

***

The following day, with the clouds in the sky threatening to rain, however, this would not deter Robert and Elizabeth from meeting at their lake as they've agreed to every day. At first, they just sat under the tree staring out at the lake, and for the first time, Robert and Elizabeth felt shy around each other. They did not know what to say or do; with so many feelings running through them, they were unsure what to do or how to express them. They were too afraid to say a word, worried it would cause what happened the other day to happen again. Robert wanted more than anything to take Elizabeth in his arms and kiss her as he held her close to his body, and he never wanted to let her go, but he fought the urge.

Since the first time Robert made love to Elizabeth, it was all he thought about, even after Elizabeth told him they could never make love again, not until after they were married, if they were allowed to marry. Not to mention Elizabeth's fears of becoming with child. After that day, it has taken all his strength to honor her wish, but lately, it was becoming harder and harder each time they were together.

When Robert and Elizabeth merged their bodies through making love, for Robert, it had only solidified his love for her, proving beyond doubt he loved her with all his heart and soul. Robert had to rid himself of his thoughts as they only fueled his desire for Elizabeth. He needed to rid himself of any, and all thoughts of making love to her, and it saddened him to know he could never make love to her again.

Ever since they parted, Elizabeth could not stop thinking about what Robert said. Although they left on good terms, it still affected her more than she was willing to admit. The thought of Robert with her sister still angered her, and she thought, *do I have the right to him? No, of course not. How can I stop loving him? This, I cannot do.*

Elizabeth gave herself a mental shake. She knew they could not be together in any way but friends, but still —

How can I deny what I feel for him? she thought as she looked at Robert from the corner of her eye. *No, I cannot. I should not have to. So, what do I do?* Elizabeth thoughts were tearing her apart, but she knew it was the right thing to do.

Suddenly, it began to rain, then the rain turned into a downpour, pushing all thought from her mind except for the need to find shelter.

With the amount of rain falling, Robert knew he needed to get them out of there and to shelter right away. Robert jumped up and pulled Elizabeth off the blanket, then wrapped it around her to shield her from the rain. It did not help; the rain was coming down too hard, and there was no way to prevent the rain from soaking through their clothes. Robert needed to get them back to the manor – to shelter, but he felt selfish; he didn't want the rain to disrupt their time together.

Robert took Elizabeth's hand and said, "Elizabeth, we must make a run for the manor." Elizabeth nodded, but then he had another idea. Turning to Elizabeth, "Do you trust me?" he asked.

Elizabeth nodded again, believing she knew what he had in mind. She too didn't want their time to end. Yes, she knew the proper thing to do was to return to the manor and walk away from him forever, but she couldn't. She was not ready, not yet.

Elizabeth's gown was soaked and was becoming too heavy for her to continue to run.

Robert saw her struggle and said, "Elizabeth, I know it's difficult, but you must run so we can make it to shelter." But then he saw how difficult it was for her, so he swept her off her feet and carried her the rest of the way. It was difficult with her gown's additional weight from the rain, and the slippery mud made it even more difficult to run.

Elizabeth was grateful to Robert for carrying her the rest of the way and noticed they were not going towards the manor. *If not the manor, then where?* she thought. "Robert, where are we going?" she asked.

There was only one place they could go that would shelter them from the rain, and it was the old woodshed that was a short distance from where they were, which would allow them more time together. Once there, he would build a fire to give them warmth.

After a time, carrying Elizabeth became too difficult for Robert, so he put her down to run the rest of the way on her own, which now, they were only a few feet away from their destination.

As they ran to the shed, Elizabeth lost her shoe and started slipping in the mud as she tripped over branches. Her legs became too heavy, and she began to tire. Robert saw Elizabeth struggling, so he grabbed her around the waist and pulled her close to his side, helping her the rest of the way to the shed.

"Look, Elizabeth," Robert said, pointing to the shed lying directly ahead. "We are close. Can you make it?"

Elizabeth saw the woodshed and willed herself to make it. "Robert, with your help, I will make it," she said, breathing heavily.

In all the years they spent together in the forest, and their time at the lake, never had it rained. Was this their good fortune, or was it more, another power intervening? If so, then why on this day did it rain. Rain that forced them to seek shelter. Was it fate pushing them together, or was it something else? Robert and Elizabeth believed natured wanted them there. Now, with the rain, was nature kicking them out because of their sadness. This, they both wondered.

Robert felt Elizabeth start to shiver, and it worried him. If he didn't get her out of the rain, he was afraid she would become ill. At this, his thoughts ran wild, *what if I lose her because I wanted more time with her? If she dies, it will be on my head. No, I cannot think of such a thing. I will get her to the shed, where I will build a fire, and then help her shed her clothes and mine, and use our bodies to warm each other.*

Robert smiled, "We will make it. Once we are there, I will build a fire to warm us. Elizabeth, we are going to need to shed our clothes. Your clothes are soaked through. If we do not, you will become ill."

Elizabeth didn't speak. The idea of being undressed in front of Robert and he in front of her, the temptation would be too strong. *What am I thinking?* she thought. Then to her shock and surprise, she smirked at the idea of them being undressed together.

By the time they arrived at the woodshed, the rain finally stopped, and Elizabeth was shivering with her teeth chattering. When they entered the woodshed, it was nothing more than a small room – a shack. One side of the shed had a stack of wood with an axe resting on the side, and in the center of the room was a small table with a fire pit, and above the wood stack, at the far corner was a small open window.

Once they were inside, Robert sat Elizabeth near the fire pit on a small stack of wood, then began gathering small pieces of wood and stacked them in the pit. With a couple of strikes to his flint, a fire started. Once the fire was going strong, Robert took the blanket from Elizabeth and laid it on the shed's floor. It may be wet, but it was better than them sitting on the dirt floor.

"Elizabeth, you must remove your gown, leaving only your shift on."

However, if it were up to him, he would have her

remove that as well. Although, if he were to see Elizabeth completely undressed, it would have undone him. The temptation was too strong.

After Elizabeth removed her gown, Robert took it and hung it over a stack of wood, then removed his own clothes, hanging them next to hers, leaving only his stockings on.

Although Robert kept his stockings on, it revealed enough of him to cause Elizabeth to blush. She turned away, trying her best not to look, but found she could not resist.

When Robert was ready, he took Elizabeth, and together they laid on the blanket near the fire and allowed their body heat to warm them. He rubbed Elizabeth's arms, doing his best to warm her, but it made it difficult for Robert to concentrate with their bodies so close together.

"Elizabeth, are you alright? You are still shivering."

"I will be fine. Having you close to me…I am already feeling warmer," Elizabeth said with a shiver.

With Robert and Elizabeth so close together, Robert found it difficult to ignore his sexual desire for her. He desperately wanted to make love to her. The connection he felt was unbelievable. Ever since the first time they made love, Robert's been wanting to re-experience what they felt, wanting to know if it was real.

It was real. How could it not be? he thought.

He struggled, trying everything he could to fight those feelings, and not give in to his desires for Elizabeth by making love to her.

Elizabeth felt something hard against her backside, and she knew what it was; he wanted her as much as she wanted him.

"Robert, I love you," she whispered.

Robert was filled with joy to hear her declaration. "I love you too, Elizabeth, so very much."

With those words, he could no longer resist his need for

her. Unable to restrain himself, he thought, *I will only kiss her, nothing more.* He turned Elizabeth to face him and placed his fingers under her chin, pulling her close until their lips touched, then kissed her, holding nothing back, putting everything he felt into his kiss, with the heat and the passion he felt for her.

When Robert kissed her, Elizabeth stopped shivering as her body warmed to the heat of their passion. With the warmth of their combined bodies, they were blinded by their passion. Elizabeth ached for him. She knew what he was doing and welcomed it. At that moment, they had no care in the world. There was only Robert and Elizabeth in the woodshed, and no one else existed. It was only the two of them.

Robert suddenly panicked. *What am I thinking?* he thought as he pulled away from Elizabeth. I must be sure she wants me as I want her. Robert searched Elizabeth's eyes for him to stop, but instead, what he saw was desire. She wanted him as much as he wanted her. At that moment, there was no more doubt – *she wanted this as much as I do.*

With that thought, he kissed her again, pouring all of him into her and her into him, both giving in to their desires, and they made love. It was as it was the first time – no, it was more powerful than the first time, as their souls intertwined, merging their souls as one.

What Robert and Elizabeth did not know; was each time they made love, their connection – their bond would continue to grow, merging not only their bodies but their minds as well, connecting them spiritually. Their lives would never be the same again, merging their hearts and souls, sealing them for eternity.

***

When Robert left Elizabeth after their time together in the woodshed, and during his ride back to Bramhall Manor, he relived the time he spent making love to her, vowing the next time they made love, it would be in a better place. A comfortable place. Then he thought about their lake and how muddy it would be when they met in the morning.

I will build a bench for Elizabeth. With the rain, the grounds will be too wet and muddy to sit on. With the bench, we will always have a place to sit and won't have to miss a day being together, he thought with a smile.

***

Later that evening at Bramhall Manor, Robert immediately sent for his trusted servant to deliver a message to Elizabeth through Grace. In the message, he asked Elizabeth to meet him at their lake, later that afternoon, outside their regular time.

Robert had a talent he had yet to share with Elizabeth. He was an excellent woodcarver. He was known as one of the best in the land. He could take a piece of wood, small or large and carve it into something extraordinary. He could carve the tiniest bird with exquisite detail, and once for his mother's birthday, he carved a basket with various flowers, similar to the ones in her garden. Robert's talent became known throughout the land, to where his father received requests to commission Robert to carve a small pipe to a large piece of furniture. His father was proud of his talent and had a display of his work in his study. His carvings were magnificent, true pieces of art.

The following morning Robert woke before dawn and rode to Dunham Massey forest, going directly to the woodshed. He chose the woodshed for two reasons; one, it was far away from everyone, so he would not be seen. Two, it was the last place he and Elizabeth spent their time together making love, and he wanted the essence of that love in their bench.

Searching through the wood pieces, Robert found a nice long thick and strong piece, then grabbed the axe and began axing away the bark. Once the bark had been removed, he took out his carving tools and began his tedious work in carving the bench. Once he was finished, the bench would be strong enough to hold two people. The legs of the bench looked like tree branches, as if they were spurting up through the ground. The seat itself was a simple one with branches wrapped around the seats edge as one continuous branch. And there was a saying hidden beneath the seat that said, *our love, our hearts, merged as one, an eternal bond, death itself could never destroy.* A secret Robert would keep to himself for many years until after they were married and had children, and then he would reveal his message to Elizabeth. This, another proof of the love they've shared at their lake.

Robert had the perfect place in mind. It was several feet to the north of the tree, placed at the edge, so it overlooked the lake.

After Robert carved the bench to his liking, he smooth out the rough edges and protected it against the harsh weather by using the oil he made by mixing animal fat and soil. It took Robert most of the morning and a good part of the early afternoon to complete the bench. He didn't even stop to eat. However, he had the kitchen prepare a small picnic with meat, bread, cheese, and wine.

Robert lost track of time while he worked on the bench, and before he knew it, it was time to meet Elizabeth. Robert quickly tied the bench to the back of his horse and rode fast to the lake. He barely made it before Elizabeth arrived and had it in place with him sitting on it before hearing Elizabeth approaching.

When Grace gave Elizabeth the message from Robert, asking her to meet him at the lake in the afternoon, she did not understand why, but when she saw Robert sitting on a bench at the edge of the lake, she thought, *a bench, how wonderful.*

Now standing just behind Robert, she called out, "Robert, my love, what is this I see before me?" she asked but did not give him time to answer. "What a wonderful surprise. How…how did you…when did you have the time to make this?" she said, pointing at the bench admiring the beautiful artwork. "How beautiful?"

Robert smiled when he heard Elizabeth's voice and jumped up, pleased to see her. He reached out his hand to her and thought, *this woman is my gift from God.*

Elizabeth took his hand, and with his other arm, he pulled her into an embrace, and she fell into his arms to the warmth of his body.

"My love, I am so happy to see you," he said with his arms around Elizabeth, turning them towards the bench, "I am pleased you like it. With the heavy rain, I wanted to make sure we have a place to sit without shortening our time together.

Elizabeth let out a giggle as she was filled with joy, "Oh Robert, you are such a wonder to think of me." Turning to the bench, "How thoughtful of you," she said smiling.

Elizabeth was full of joy at Robert's thoughtful gift, and the time it must have taken him to make it. Although he believed she was unaware of his talent, but she knew. How could she naught. Everyone in the land knew of Robert's talent. He was the talk of the villagers near and far.

Robert looked at Elizabeth as she admired his gift and saw the smile on her beautiful face, which had always brought him great joy and warmed his heart. *To have this great beauty before me, and she is all mine,* he thought.

There has never been a day that's gone by where he hasn't felt her love, in the way it flows from her body to his, piercing deep in his heart. His heart was beating so hard as if it would burst from his chest.

Filled with joy, Robert guided Elizabeth to sit on the bench as he sat next to her, then placed his arm around her and pulled her close to his side. With his other hand, he put his fingers under her chin and turned her face towards his, and he kissed her.

For a long time, Robert and Elizabeth sat quietly on the bench, staring out at the lake, taking in the beauty surrounding them. They listen to the sound of the rippling water, along with the wind blowing through the trees with the birds singing. To Robert and Elizabeth, it felt as if the birds were singing directly to them. Their Lake was their sanctuary that surrounded them with a feeling of peace and happiness. They believed this place was given to them by God. A place where everything outside could be forgotten as if nothing else existed but the two of them and their love.

Elizabeth looked up at the trees, and to her shock and surprise, she saw a beautiful pure white dove. "Robert, look," she said, pointing at the dove sitting on the branch in the tree. "It's a blessing. A wonderful gift from God, is it naught?"

Robert looked in the direction she was pointing and smiled, "Yes," he said, then took Elizabeth face in his hands and kissed her long and hard.

Chapter Thirteen

As Lord and Lady Davenport were preparing themselves for bed, Lady Davenport talked with her husband about Robert and Grace's upcoming wedding.

"John, our arrange marriage did not turn out as I wished it to be. We never came to love each other, but instead, we came to an understanding," she said.

Lady Davenport pulled her long dark hair over her shoulder and began braiding it. Usually, this was done by her ladies' maid, but she wanted time alone with her husband.

"I accepted my duties as your wife…as Lady Davenport. For Robert and Grace, I want more for them. I want them to have the love we do not."

Lord Davenport tensed as he rolled his eyes. "Mary, love is not important. Robert must…nay; he will do his duty as my son and heir. If he is lucky to find love with Grace, then I will be happy for him. If he does not, I am sure Grace will honor her duty as the next Lady Davenport as you have, my dear. As the lady of Bramhall Manor, it is your responsibility to ensure Grace adjusts to her role and become a proper Lady Davenport as you did," he said.

Mary finished braiding her hair and was holding the ends as she listened to her husband, then she started to say, "But John —" before John interrupted her.

"There is no but. It will be as I said," he said firmly.

Mary conceded to her husband, knowing there was nothing she could say that would matter.

"Will you talk to Robert and see how he and Grace are faring?"

Growling, *women!* he thought. "Do you not obtain this information from the Baroness? I am sure she is on top of everything. Why do you require me to speak to our son?"

Tying the end of her hair with a ribbon, she said, "Yes,

we talk when we are together. From what Grace tells her, they are getting along well. She does not care for details and feels as you do, as long as they do their duty…is all she cares for."

Mary stood and moved to her side of the bed and crawled in. "I need more, John. I know you are a hard man, but if you never do anything for me again, please consider this?" she asked with pleading in her eyes.

John watched his wife as he thought, *she is a beautiful woman, even after bearing me four children. How can I deny her this?* He watched her walk over and climb into bed.

"That is not the man you married, Mary. I do not speak of such things," he said as he watched his wife straighten her covers over her lap.

There was only one thing on his mind. John grabbed his wife and pulled her on top of him. "I will agree to do this, but only this one time," he said as he kissed her. "I want to ensure this merger will take place. I will take Robert hunting and ask him then," he said, kissing his wife, then he had his way with her.

After their lovemaking, as Lord Davenport was asleep, Lady Davenport laid in bed thinking about her son, how she wanted more for him. She wanted him to have the love she never had.

Lord Davenport pretended to be asleep when he cracked his eyes to look at his wife, and she appeared to be deep in thought. He knew what she was thinking; she wished he'd love her. Although he wanted to, he never came to love his wife. He didn't understand why, after all, she was a beautiful woman and a good wife. A perfect Lady Davenport. He believed it was due to him being a hard man with a hard heart, a heart that would not soften, not even for her.

Times like this, he wanted to love her, and wished he could give her what she's always wanted, his love. For

Lord Davenport, the most important thing was his duty to king and country. Love was inconsequential. A weakness he could not afford.

I am a man of duty…a man of law. My responsibilities have nothing to do with love, nor should it be for Robert. His first duty and responsibility as my heir should always come first, he thought before subsiding to sleep.

***

Robert was with his father hunting pheasant as they were engaged in conversation about his future, his responsibility in becoming a man and later the next lord and magistrate of Cheshire.

After the 'talk' of becoming a 'man and duty' was over, Lord Davenport ask Robert how things were proceeding with Grace.

"Robert, how are you finding Grace? Will she satisfy you?" his father asked.

Robert cringed at his father's question. He knew one day he would be asked this question, but he was not ready to answer. When his father asked, 'will she satisfy you,' this disturbed him.

"Satisfy me, father? What do you mean?" Without giving his father a chance to answer, he went on. "She is a good person. We do not have much in common, but we are resigned to honor our responsibility of your agreement," he said with cynicism, "To you and Baron Massey," he said, as he thought, *that you believe I have no right to see or have any knowledge about, which I do. It is my life, not yours.*

The problem with this, it was not his life; it was his fathers to do with as he chose, until the day his father left this world. This was something Robert could not understand, a young man, oblivious to the ways of the world. Why was that? Did his father not make it clear to him? Of course he did, Lord Davenport had always been very clear, but Robert had a different way of thinking. A man who believed he should choose the woman he wanted, not one forced upon him, regardless of his station in life.

Lord Davenport ignored Robert's question and continued. "Before you marry…" he started to say but felt uncomfortable with this line of questioning, but he had promised his wife. *Why should I care?* he thought. He hated the idea, but he needed to know how things were progressing with Grace.

"Your mother wants you and Grace to have feelings for each other. If not before, then after you are married. She feels as time passes, so will your feelings for each other," Lord Davenport spit out as the words discussed him. Nor did he believe them, as it mattered naught. He must, though; he promised his wife. *Why do I give that woman any leave to have me speak as a woman?* he thought. "Grrr," he growled.

Robert wasn't sure what to say, so he decided to be somewhat honest. *I hate this deception,* he thought.

"I hope we will find love," Robert said, being careful with his words as his thoughts were with Elizabeth.

Irritated, Lord Davenport spit out his next words. "Well, love is not important. I married your mother without love, and it has worked out fine. She understands me. She understands who I am and what's expected of a wife to lord and magistrate of my standing," he said, then under his breath, "She is the perfect wife." These words surprised him, but he shook them off and continued. "You will make me proud by doing your duty in marrying Grace. With your marriage, it will allow our families to merge, creating a great power in the land. In this, we will own this land and its people. To do this will please me greatly," he said.

Lord Davenport was an arrogant and pompous man who strived for power and couldn't get enough. What does that do to a man like him?

Lord Davenport saw a stag crossing their path, and all thoughts and conversation stopped, turning his attention and focus on the stag. He raised his rifle and took aim.

Once he had a good shot, he fired, hitting the stag directly between the eyes, killing it instantly. After the stag fell, he motioned for a servant to attend it before carrying it back to the manor.

Walking side by side with his father, Robert was focused on the ground as he listened to his father, but Robert's thoughts were elsewhere.

Can I do what father expects of me? What would he do if I told him of my feelings for Elizabeth? Would he allow me to choose? I need answers. I must try again, Robert thought.

"Father, can you…" Robert started to ask his father when he realized his father was no longer speaking to him but was in the middle of shooting a stag.

Robert's eyes widen with surprise, "Father, where did that stag come from?"

"I do not know. It was a great surprise though," he said, turning to his son with a broad smile.

The first thought Robert had when he saw his father smiling was to drop his mouth in surprise, never before could he recall a time he saw his father smile. Robert quickly shook off the shock, so his father didn't notice.

"Well, it looks like you hit him right between the eyes."

"Yes, it's turned out to be a great day for hunting after all."

Lord Davenport put the strap of his rifle across his shoulder and swung it to rest on his back. He turned to Robert and asked, "You were saying something?"

Robert hesitated but then cleared his throat and proceeded to ask his father. "Yes, father, I was wondering, will you tell me more about this agreement between you and Baron Massey? Or, if you will allow me, I would like to see it?" he asked.

Robert knew he was treading on dangerous ground, but with the mood his father was in, since it was a rare one, it might possibly be the best time to ask his father.

Lord Davenport's smile disappeared at Robert's request and said, "Robert, why do you ask? I have already told you it is impossible." Sighing, he went on, "When I die, and you take my title and become Lord of Bramhall Manor, only then will you be privy to what the agreement entails. Until that time comes, know, by marrying Grace, you will honor us all."

Robert shrugged his shoulders as if his answer did not matter. As if his response wasn't tearing him up inside, desperately wanting to know what the agreement said.

Robert sighed. *I know this is a risk, but I must try,* he thought and proceeded to ask his father. "Father, I am wondering what will happen if Grace and I refused to marry?"

When Robert saw his father's head jerk and the anger on his face, he wanted to take back his question. However, he was a man now, and he could not allow his father's anger to deter him, so he continued to push.

Swallowing the lump in his throat, he asked, "What if…one of us fall in love with another?"

Okay, now he did it. He could practically see the steam coming from his father's nose.

Lord Davenport looked at Robert as if he just stabbed him in the back, then in a strong and firm voice, "That! Will! Not! Happen. Do you understand me," he said between clinch teeth.

Robert stepped back. The man before him was no longer his father but the one who was magistrate, the man who held all the power in the land.

"Love! What is love! Love is for fools and women! You are not a woman, are you?" Lord Davenport yelled. Robert, unable to speak, shook his head no. "Do not be a fool! Love! If you fall in love with another woman…by all means, do so, if you choose..." he said in a calmer, more sinister voice, "…she can become your mistress."

What? Robert thought, shocked by what his father said.

Then he thought, *does…*unable to fathom it…*does father have many mistresses? Do I want to know?* Robert had to clear these thoughts from his mind; this was something he does not want to know.

"You can have many mistresses if you choose. Mark me, Robert, hear my words carefully. You will do your duty by marrying Grace. There is no negotiation on this." he said in a calm yet firm voice. Lord Davenport turned away from Robert as they began their walk back to the manor. "Now, there will be no more talk of such foolish ideas. Let us see if we can find where those pheasants are hiding. If God," looking up to the sky, "Can be so good to send another stag our way, he will bless us with enough food to get us through the winter."

After his father's reaction, Robert dare not tell his father that he had already fallen in love with another woman – with Elizabeth. And after that day, he knew there would never be a right time to tell his father about him and Elizabeth.

***

The Massey's and Davenport's were throwing a grand party to celebrate Robert and Grace's upcoming wedding, sparing no expense. The Massey's arrived at Bramhall Manor two weeks before they initially planned, so that Baroness Massey could assist Lady Davenport with the preparations.

The great room was beautifully decorated with the finest furnishings, with four pillars that were beautifully wrapped in purple and red flowers intertwine with green dressing. There were gold and silver chairs lined against the walls with seats wrapped in royal blue and dark red strips, along with small two-seat chairs covered with red floral roses, situated between every two chairs stretched around the room. The great room walls were filled with family portraits, beginning with the current Davenports, going as far back as Orme de Davenport.

It was a grand room with seating enough to comfortably fit up to twenty people and even more standing. It was the perfect place for a party. When entering the room, directly ahead was a wall of windows going from ceiling to floor, as if merging the indoors with the outdoors, with seating and storage below. Looking out the windows, you could see green grass as far as the eye could behold, with beautiful green lushes' bushes, and beyond those bushes was a small pond.

When you return to the main room, at the back of the room were French doors beautifully framed with the same marble as the pillars, along with another beautiful view of green grass and a large oval pond with boulders resting on each side.

To the right of the French doors in the corner sat a magnificent piano, accompanied by a tall, beautiful golden harp decorated with golden roses. To the left of the French doors and in the corner sat a large gaming table surrounded by six gold armless chairs with seats covered in solid royal blue. And in the center of the room was an eighty-four by sixty inch richly made French rug edged in royal blue with solid golden lines. And inside those lines were golden leaves intertwined with pink and yellow roses, while the rest of the rug was spattered with blue and white daisies, and right in the center was a large solid gold medallion framed with the same laurel leaves and pink and yellow roses. It was exquisite.

Grace and Robert were dancing – doing and saying everything right to please their families. However, every now and then, Robert would glance at Elizabeth, and when he did, he saw how unhappy she was. It's been hard for them both not being together, as they desperately wanted to be in each other's arms. But no matter how much they want to be together, for tonight, they had to stay away, so their feelings would not be discovered, not before they were ready to tell their parent's.

When the party started to wind down, looking as if it would end soon, Robert went to where Elizabeth had been sitting, which was in a chair closest to the back of the room near the French doors. He smiled, he knew she could not resist looking outdoors, and if she needed to, she could easily sneak out without being noticed, as she did earlier that evening.

Once Robert approached Elizabeth, he placed one arm behind his back and bowed. "My Lady, may I have this dance?"

When Elizabeth saw Robert approaching, she became nervous and yet excited. Elizabeth tilted her head forward and said, "My Lord, I am honored."

Robert put out his hand, and Elizabeth gently placed her hand in his, then he helped her up from her seat, placing her arm in the crook of his, and guided her to the center of the room where they dance a basse with the last few couples.

No one seemed to notice or care they were dancing, as they saw Elizabeth and Robert as

future brother and sister and nothing more.

After a few moments of dancing, Robert whispered, "Elizabeth, I want to be alone with you."

Elizabeth looked around, "Robert, we cannot," as Elizabeth noticed her mother and father were with Lady and Lord Davenport near the ballroom's entry, saying their goodbyes to their guest. "They will see?" she said.

"No, they will not. They are too busy saying goodbye to their guests. We can slowly move our way to the French doors and sneak out."

Elizabeth looked around again and realized he was right. They could make it out the door before they were noticed. "Very well, Robert."

Robert and Elizabeth managed to get out the French doors without anyone noticing, and once they were outside and out of sight, they ran as fast as they could until they were halfway to the lake, where they stopped to catch their breaths.

Elizabeth felt breathless as she said, "Robert, what were you thinking?" she asked in a firm voice before busting out laughing.

Robert looked at Elizabeth, smiling; he was happy to have her to himself and said, "It bothered me to see you sitting by yourself all night looking so unhappy. I decided if we were going to enjoy each other's company, we had to create our own party here at the lake." Robert looked up at the sky. "And look, it's a beautiful clear night with the stars shining bright." He turned back to Elizabeth and reached for her hand. "Come, let us go to the edge of the lake."

Elizabeth smiled as she took Robert's hand. "It is beautiful," then looked at him and said, "Alright."

As Robert and Elizabeth stood near the lake, Robert turned to face her, then bowed at the waist as he asked, "My lady, may I have the honor of this dance?"

Elizabeth smiled with a giggle. She curtsied and said, "But of course, My Lord. I am honored and pleased to accept," as she placed her hand in his.

Standing facing each other, they placed their palms together as they took a step forward and then a step backwards, then connected their arms, turning right, then switched arms turning left, never taking their eyes off each other. Although there was no moon, the stars were shining so bright; it felt as if a light was shining directly on them.

After a few more steps, Robert stopped and pulled Elizabeth into his arms, needing to feel her body against his, changing their dance to a close and intimate basse. Robert and Elizabeth basked in the moment, feeding off each other's energy, igniting their passion that pierced deep in their souls.

Robert abruptly stopped dancing and took Elizabeth's face in his hands, lowering his lips until they were touching, then he kissed her. At first, it started out slowly, before their passion overpowered them, and Robert deepened the kiss, taking Elizabeth's breath away.

That night, their lake became a magical place where Robert and Elizabeth made love, feeding their desires that possessed them, turning that beautiful clear night into a magical night, one they would never forget.

***

Back in the great room where Baron and Baroness Massey, along with Lord and Lady Davenport, were sitting enjoying the peace and quiet after their guest left and their children had retired for the evening. They did not see Robert and Elizabeth, but Grace informed them they had already retired to their chambers.

The Davenport's great room was a wondrous place where one could relax after a long day of family events between wedding preparations and family to-dos.

***

It was two weeks before Christmas, then shortly after, Robert and Grace's wedding. Since Robert and Elizabeth haven't found the right time to tell their parents about their relationship due to the upcoming wedding, they began to worry. And so, it was decided, on the next family gathering, which would include all their relations who's travelled near and far for the wedding, Robert and Elizabeth, knowing there would never be a good time before their wedding took place, prayed their parents would accept and allow them to marry instead of Robert marrying Grace.

The following week at Bramhall Manor, the family finished dinner and were heading into the great room, and Robert was gathering his thoughts on what he was going to say once everyone was settled in their seats. Although it took mere seconds to arrive in the great room, for Robert, it felt like an eternity.

Earlier that morning, Robert, Elizabeth, and Grace decided it would be this night when Robert informed their families of his and Elizabeth's relationship. The plan was:

once everyone was seated in the great room after dinner and everyone were in high spirits with the excitement of the upcoming Christmas celebrations, and thereafter, wedding, Robert would inform them of his and Elizabeth's relationship.

As Robert was waiting, he thought back to the conversation he had with Elizabeth before they headed down for dinner.

***

Robert, Elizabeth, and Grace were in the hall heading to the dining room when Robert leaned in to whisper in Elizabeth's ear, "Elizabeth, once everyone has entered the great room and are seated, I will remain standing to inform them I have an announcement to make." Robert glanced at Grace and saw her beaming with delight in what was going to happen, but then returned his attention back to Elizabeth before he continued, "They will believe my announcement is about Grace and my upcoming wedding," he glanced back at Grace, who was still smiling but was now bouncing on her feet as if she was standing on hot coal. Robert smiled as he turned his attention back to Elizabeth. "Before I continue, I will glance at you to ensure you still want me to go through with the announcement. If you agree, give me a slight nod." Robert turned to Grace and said, "Grace, you will sit next to Elizabeth, so no one will question who I am looking at, and they will believe I am looking at you.

Grace was Jumping up and down like a little girl. "Wonderful idea," she yelped.

"Robert, I am..." Elizabeth attempted to say, but Robert stopped her by putting his finger on her lips and smiled.

"Shh, my love. When I see you nod, I will continue to tell our families we are in love and wish to marry."

Elizabeth didn't attempt to say another word, but instead, she smiled and nodded in agreement. Then Elizabeth reached for Grace's hand, and together they continued to the dining room while Robert waited a few moments before following.

Elizabeth was excited, she was ready for what was to happen, and nothing would change her mind. Grace and Elizabeth looked at each other and smiled, knowing what was to come, and Grace was excited to be released from her betrothal, one she never wanted, and she wanted nothing more than for Robert and Elizabeth to be happy.

Elizabeth squeezed Grace's hand, "I love you, Grace."

Grace squeezed her hand in return, "I love you too, Elizabeth. Tonight, we will both have what we want and the happiness we deserve."

***

After everyone was in the great room and seated, Robert remained standing. He cleared his throat and said, "May I have everyone's attention, please?"

Everyone looked at Robert with interest and excitement.

"As we are gathered this evening," Robert began as he glanced at Elizabeth, looking for reassurance.

Elizabeth smiled and gave him a slight nod for him to continue.

"As we know, Grace," turning to look at Grace, who was smiling, "And my wedding was planned from the moment of our births," shifting his eyes back and forth, making sure to look at everyone before him. "No one could have known or predicted at the time the agreement was forged, what would happen when this day arrived, what it would bring, and where we would be on this day, nor how we would feel. The question on everyone's mind, would Grace and I form an attachment? Will we find love?"

Robert looked at everyone, especially his mother and father along with Baron and Baroness Massey, and saw they were on pins and needles in what they believed he was going to say. When his attention went to his mother, she was smiling.

She thinks I am going to say Grace and I have fallen in

love, he thought. Robert sighed.

Robert glanced back at Elizabeth as he thought, *do I dare say the words, or shall I reach for Elizabeth and run with haste.* But when he saw Elizabeth's beautiful smile as she gave him a slight nod, it gave Robert the strength to continue.

"Well," he started to say but found he could not look directly at them, so he redirected his eyes towards the floor. "I am afraid that's not to be."

There, it was said. Robert stood there, expecting a reaction, any reaction, but was surprised when there was none. When he looked up and saw everyone was watching him with great interest, he thought, *hum.* There didn't seem to be any reaction except for his mother. *Who looks sad,* he thought.

Robert looked at Elizabeth, and she too was watching him, anxiously waiting for him to continue. With her smile and slight nod, he looked at his feet, waiting, expecting them to start moving, ready to take her and run away, but they did not move.

Robert slightly shook his head. *Nay, even if you moved, I would never make it. Father will have me in seconds,* Robert thought.

Sighing, Robert glanced at Elizabeth one more time before he continued, and when he saw her smile, again it gave him the courage to do so.

"I believe, what I am about to say, I speak for Grace as well…" Robert looked at Grace. She was smiling, and she too, was ready for this situation to be over.

Grace nodded in agreement, then said aloud, "Yes, I do."

Grace did this, wanting to ensure everyone knew she was in complete agreement with what Robert was about to say, while sending up a prayer for when he made his announcement it would be in her favor. Yes, this was risky, but one she was willing to chance, willing to do anything to get out of this agreement, preventing her from marrying Robert, a man she did not choose nor wanted.

In the meantime, Robert continued, "Grace and I failed to form an attachment, let alone love, even with the time given to us. Nor do we feel," looking at Grace, "Any additional time together will change this. Now, we know this comes as no surprise…to form an attachment and or even love is welcomed, but not required for us to marry. However," he paused to glance at Elizabeth, and everyone believed he was looking at Grace.

Although he received Elizabeth's approval to continue, he wondered, *are we ready for this now?* Shaking his head slightly, he took a deep breath, and after he released it, he continued. "What has happened," Robert took another deep breath and gathered his strength. He looked and made eye contact with each person in the room, "Is something wonderful, a blessing from God."

At this, everyone looked at each other with confusion but said nothing, waiting for Robert to explain.

"You see...well...Elizabeth and I —"

Immediately everyone turned to Elizabeth, wondering what she had to do with Robert's announcement. Elizabeth's face turned red with embarrassment to have so many eyes on her. With this, fear began coursing through her, as her nerves were getting the best of her, causing her to twist her kerchief.

"I have fallen in love…" Robert started to say before his father interrupted him.

Confused by what Robert said, Lord Davenport asked, "Boy, you just told us you are not in love with Grace. What are you talking about? And what does," glancing, as he pointed at Elizabeth, "She has to do with this?"

Standing straight as he pulled his shoulders back. Robert looked directly at his father and said, "I have fallen in love with Elizabeth." Robert stepped back after seeing his father's anger, he practically had steam coming out of his nose, but Robert continued. "We ask," Robert reached for Elizabeth, and she rushed to be by his side.

Robert pulled her to his side with the need to protect her. "We ask you to allow us to marry instead of me marrying Grace."

Grace immediately jumped up after Robert's announcement to show her support. "I agree!" she yelled. "I have no objection for Robert marrying Elizabeth. To make Robert and I marry will be a great tragedy," she said, putting her bottom lip out in a pout. However, Grace's words were ignored as if she never spoke.

After Robert's announcement, Lord Davenport, along with Baron and Baroness Massey, lashed out at Robert and Elizabeth, and the only one who remained seated and silent was Lady Davenport.

With Elizabeth by his side, Robert could feel her start to shake with fear. So, he tightened his hold on her, trying to ease her fears, knowing his father was not a man to be reckoned with, and he knew he must do everything he could to protect her from the eruption of anger that was taking place.

Lord Davenport was outraged and wasted no time to show his displeasure. Yelling at the top of his lungs, "How dare you! You dare go against me!" Slamming his hand against his chest. "Us," he turned and motioned with his arm to include Baron and Baroness Massey, "This agreement was forged at the time of your births, and it cannot be broken! You will marry Grace! You will end this," pointing at Elizabeth, "So-called relationship at once!"

While Lord Davenport was yelling at Robert, Baroness Massey managed to pull Elizabeth away from him, even with Robert's attempt to stop her, but Lord Davenport took hold of his upper arm and squeezed it hard, forcing Robert to release Elizabeth, then motioned with his head for Baroness Massey to take her away as he thought, *they need to get that girl in check! That harlot seduced my son! She must be dealt with!*

Robert tried to fight his father's hold on him but stopped when he saw his father's anger and immediately relinquished his hold on Elizabeth, as he gave her an apologetic look.

After Baroness Massey pulled Elizabeth away from Robert, she took her away from the others to the back of the room where Baron Massey was waiting. Baroness Massey was the one to do all the talking, as she was the one who wields all the power in the Massey home. Although Baron Massey has a temper, he was gentle as a cat compared to his wife's.

At first, Baroness Massey talked to Elizabeth in a calm voice. For Elizabeth, this concerned her more than if her mother had yelled at her.

"Elizabeth, how could you do this to your sister? To fall in love with Robert, who is your sister's betrothed. Do you have any idea how much you have hurt your sister?"

"Mother, I care naught —" Grace tried to intervene.

Baroness Massey cut her off, "Quite Grace! This has nothing to do with you!" she snapped.

Grace flinched at her mother's harsh words and stared at her as she thought, *how can this not be about me. It has everything to do with me.* Angered by her mother's words, Grace folded her arms and watched the events take place before her.

After Grace's interruption, Baroness Massey went from being calm to being outraged, believing Elizabeth was to blame for Grace's lack of concern for their situation. Baroness Massey thought it was best to protect Grace, then to allow her to do or say something that would anger her even more than she already was. After all, Grace was her father's favorite and could do no wrong.

"How could you fall in love with your sister's future husband! How can you be so selfish!" her mother yelled.

As Elizabeth listened to her mother's words, pain seared through her with a weight on her heart, as if her mother pierced her heart with a dagger. Elizabeth put her hands up, trying to get her mother to stop, wanting her to hear her out, but her mother ignored her attempts, refusing to allow her to say a word.

No matter how hard Robert and Elizabeth tried to get their parents to listen to reason, in wanting them to understand, the love they shared was a love like no other. A blessing from God; thus, there was nothing they could do to stop it.

While Lord Davenport was yelling at Robert, he sought to find Elizabeth, and when he found her, she was being bombarded by her mother and wanted to save her.

Robert decided he's had enough. He took a deep breath, and when he exhaled, at the top of his lungs he yelled, "STOOOOOP IT NOOOWW!"

Everyone was shocked by Robert's outburst, bringing the room to utter silence. Once he had everyone's attention, he took another deep breath, then slowly released it to get himself under control, and once he had his anger under control, he attempted again to explain what happened between him and Elizabeth.

"What happened between Elizabeth and me…it was not planned, nor did we expect such a gift. Elizabeth and I fell in love. This is not an ordinary love, but a love like no other. A love beyond all love. A powerful bond most can only hope or pray for. A blessing bestowed to us by God.

Yes, you planned and wanted Grace and me to marry, and in our marriage, bring the Massey's and Davenport's together, making our families the strongest in the land. Why cannot Elizabeth and I…"

Robert looked at Elizabeth and saw tears streaming down her face. At seeing this, he immediately broke away from his father and went to be by her side. With her hand in his, while looking directly at her, he said, "Our marriage can still unite our families as you wish," turning back to look at his father. "So, what does it matter which sister I marry, so long as I marry a Massey?"

Robert's words meant nothing to Lord Davenport and Baron and Baroness Massey. Their anger clouded any reasonable thought, refusing to hear anything other than their own anger. There was an agreement that was not to be broken, and it does not matter what reason Robert had. All they understood was Elizabeth and Robert's relationship must end, and it must end immediately.

Robert and Elizabeth looked at each other, knowing what was coming next.

Lord Davenport was outraged. "You and Elizabeth, from this day forth, are hereby forbidden to be together! This relationship you speak of is over, here, and now! When our families gather in preparation for your," looking directly at his son, "Wedding to Grace will be the only time you and Elizabeth will be allowed to be in each other's company!

Robert, you will always be at Grace's side! If there is even a look between you and Elizabeth," Lord Davenport looked at Elizabeth, "Elizabeth will be banned from any future attendance! If you are discovered alone, or we learn you have continued this relationship," he said with discuss, "Then," pausing to look at Baron Massey to ensure he had his attention and understood what was coming next. With a nod from Baron Massey, Lord Davenport continued. "I believe I say this with Baron Massey's full understanding and support, if we discover you went against our decision," walking over to where they were standing, "Elizabeth will be shipped off to France, far away from you and temptation! Do I make myself clear!"

Lord Davenport was so outraged, that it took all his strength to keep from beating his son into acceptance. It was only because of his wife's love for their son he held back. *Why do I do what I do for that woman?* he thought, disgusted with himself.

Robert turned and attempted to walk away from his father, but his father grabbed his upper arm and stopped him, forcing Robert to turn around and face him. "Boy, do not be a fool! You will not walk away from me or ignore what I tell you! You will marry Grace as planned! Whatever you and Elizabeth had is over! There is no you and Elizabeth! Do you understand me!" Lord Davenport said between clenched teeth.

Lord Davenport was angry, outraged, but he controlled his temper with all the strength he could muster when he wanted nothing more than to beat sense into his son. However, in this situation, he believed his words were more powerful than his fist. If Robert goes against him by continuing his relationship with Elizabeth, then, and only then, will he take severe action.

Even if that means locking him in the dungeon for a week, no son of mine will disobey me, he thought.

Robert could only stare at his father, knowing there was nothing he could say or do that would matter at this point.

As Elizabeth watched, she was in utter shock and in disbelieve at what happened. What was she going to do? What were they going to do? They have been forbidden to have any further contact with each other. Could she do this? Could he?

Baroness Massey did not like what she saw and took Elizabeth by the arm, pulling her out of the room, to just outside the main entrance where she continued to voice her disappointment to her daughter, how she expected a great deal more from her as the daughter of a Baron and Baroness.

"You have behaved as nothing more than a harlot!" she yelled in a soft yet firm voice.

Elizabeth flinched as if her mother slapped her in the face. She tried pulling away from her mother and found she could not speak with her emotions so raw.

Elizabeth had no delusions of how their parents would react when they told them about her and Robert's relationship – that at first, her mother and father would not be happy, but this, this she did not expect, nor did it make any sense to her. Elizabeth turned to seek her sister's support but found she too, was confused.

Grace was watching the scene before her with complete and utter shock. This was not at all what she expected, and it made her wonder, *what is in this agreement? There is something of great importance for Lord Davenport and mother and father to act in this way,* Grace Thought.

The look Grace gave Elizabeth; words did not need to be said. There was more to this then what they were told.

As Grace continued to watch what was happening, she felt defeated as she thought, *why will they not allow Robert to marry Elizabeth? Allowing them to marry will free me from a life of unhappiness. And to hurt my sister, who I love so much.* Looking at Elizabeth, Grace's heart was breaking. *There must be a way. There must,* she further thought.

With a look between Grace and Elizabeth, then at their mother and father, together they said, "Why can this agreement not be changed?"

The look they both received from Baron and Baroness Massey and Lord Davenport was as if they just committed treason, so they quickly turned away, thinking it was best not to push the question. They were women who had to do what their mother and father told them to do. They had no say.

Lady Davenport was the only one outside the children who remained silent. She disagreed with what was happening. As she watched her son, her heart broke to see the pain in his eyes. She turned to look at her husband – his words were harsh but not altogether unexpected.

God, why can he not, this one time, have a soft heart? she thought.

Even after all these years, Lady Davenport still believed

in love. Although, even after all these years knowing there had been no love between them, some part of her had always hoped that would change. *A girl's silly dream,* she thought.

Could Lady Davenport allow her own son to suffer the same fate? When her marriage was arranged, she was young, never having the chance to experience love before she married Lord Davenport. She had no understanding of what love was or how it felt. She married Lord Davenport to honor her father in hopes in time; they would both grow to love each other. When love never came, she chose to be the best wife she could to a man of title and power such as him. Could she standby and remain silent and allow the suffering she's endured to fall on her son.

Whatever I do, I must do it slowly and quietly. I must choose the right time. But with John, there may never be a right time? I must try. I must do what I can to help my son. It is clear he loves Elizabeth and she him. I must learn more of their feeling for each other before I decide to act, Lady Davenport thought.

Lord Davenport never came to love his wife, but after time she has proven herself to be the proper wife of a man with his status and power. With this, he came to respect his wife, and there were times he wanted to love her, but after a time when love never came, he believed it wasn't to be.

Lord Davenport looked for his wife, wondering where she was with all this happening and found her still sitting where he left her, showing concern but with doubt on her face.

Could Lord Davenport claim to have been faithful to his wife. No, he could not. After all, he was a scoundrel, a man known for his harsh and cruel nature? His wife had turned out to be the right woman for him, never arguing or questioning his authority. What was to be done was done.

For his wife to remain quiet throughout this whole ordeal, he wondered, *could now be the time she chooses to question my decision? If she does, will I listen?* Lord Davenport thought.

For Lord Davenport, this was an extremely hard question. He respected his wife since she's proven to be an intelligent and at times, wise woman.

If she does, I will give her credit and listen before passing judgment, he thought.

Chapter Fourteen

Later that evening, Lord Davenport invited Baron Massey to join him in his study for a drink and to discuss the recent events.

"How did this happen, John?" Lord Davenport asked as he poured him a drink. "Can you naught keep a rein on your daughter?" he said, turning to face Baron Massey as he hands him his drink.

Baron Massey was shocked that he was being blamed for what happened, so he too strikes back. "Me? It's obvious your son seduced my daughter!" Baron Massey fired at Lord Davenport.

"Quiet, both of you!" A voice said from behind Baron Massey.

Baron Massey turned to find his wife standing in the doorway.

Baroness Massey was waiting for her husband to join her in bed, but when he failed to show up, she searched for him and was not surprised to find him in Lord Davenport's study.

When Baroness Massey saw her husband, she had intended to wish him only a good night until she overheard Lord Davenport blame her husband for what happened. This, she could not ignore, nor was she able to hold her tongue.

"Neither of you are to blame. It's Robert and Elizabeth who are to blame, as is," looking at her husband, "Grace. I believe she had a hand in what happened between Robert and Elizabeth. She had no intentions of spending time with Robert, and I am sure she convinced Elizabeth to take her place," said Baroness Massey.

Baron Massey opened his mouth to object, but his wife stopped him.

"Do not try to defend your daughter," eyeing her

husband, "However, we must return to Elizabeth and Robert. Once they knew they were developing feelings for each other, they should have stopped. They both knew better. Instead, they chose to allow their feelings to grow."

Baroness Massey looked at her husband, and he gave her a look of agreement along with a nod.

"What we need to discuss now is how we will handle what happened," said Baroness Massey.

Lord Davenport turned to pour himself another drink while Baroness Massey was talking. When she finally finished, he said, "What is there to discuss? I already passed judgement. Was I not clear?" he asked, turning to look at Baroness Massey, with a look that said, 'do not question me.' "Robert will marry Grace as planned; thus, honoring our agreement."

Baroness Massey rolled her eyes and thought, *pompous man.*

"We may have to disclose the full contents of the agreement. If they understand why it cannot be changed, maybe it will be easier for them," Baroness Massey said.

Lord Davenport gave Baroness Massey the evil eye, causing her to take a step back, as Baron Massey quickly moved to protect his wife, knowing what was coming.

"Woman! Are you mad! There is no need to coddle them! The agreement is not their business!" he yelled, turning to Baron Massey. "John, this is not woman business! Escort your wife to your chambers!" Then he turned his back on them. "We will talk more in the morning. Good evening," he said in a calmer voice.

This was not easy for Baron Massey, for a man with a status below him to speak to him in such a way. But he needed Lord Davenport for his status and power within the land if he was ever to regain Dunham Massey from the Booth's.

As Baron Massey turned with his wife to leave, they saw Lady Davenport standing in the doorway.

"My Lady," Baron and Baroness Massey said as they bowed and curtsied.

"My Lady, we were just heading to our chambers. We bid you good evening," said Baron Massey.

Lady Davenport placed her hand on Baroness Massey's arm, "Will you postpone retiring for the night just now. I wish to address what happened this evening and what I overheard a moment ago."

Baron and Baroness Massey stepped aside as they said in unison, "But of course, My Lady."

Lady Davenport entered the study and moved over to stand next to her husband. "My dear, please apologize to Baroness Massey for your sharp tongue."

Lord Davenport stared at his wife for a moment, astonished that she was so bold to ask him to apologize, but instead of correcting her of this, he decided to let go of his anger and did as his wife requested. "Forgive my sharp tongue Baroness Massey," he spits out. "I am very disturbed after tonight's events."

Baroness Massey smiled, "There is nothing to forgive. We are all upset and angry with what happened this evening."

Lady Davenport knew speaking this way was bold, but it had to be said. "Do you feel we must force Robert to marry Grace?" she asked, then tensed when she saw the look on her husband's face. She knew this was brash, but it had to be said, and she was surprised he didn't try to stop her. So, she continued, "We forged this agreement, why can we not change it to allow Robert to marry Elizabeth? Clearly, he loves her, and she loves him. Why should we force a marriage between two who will be miserable?" she said, looking at her husband with sadness.

Lord Davenport had expected this from his wife, and although it angered him, something else happened, there was a tightness in his chest, a feeling that he was unfamiliar with.

"Mar…" he attempted to say but was interrupted by Baron Massey.

"I was thinking the same," turning to look at Lord Davenport, "Yes, why can we not?" Baron Massey asked.

Baroness Massey was appalled at her husband's suggestion and looked at him and then to Lady Davenport.

"John, Mary, you are foolish in your thinking. Robert must marry Grace. There is no question to that," Baroness Massey said in a calmer yet firm voice. But at mentioning Elizabeth's name, she became angry.

"Elizabeth will leave Robert alone! If this proves to be too difficult for Elizabeth, we will send her to our family in France!" Baroness Massey yelled.

Lord Davenport was appalled by Baroness Massey yelling at his wife, but he couldn't disagree with what she said and was surprisingly pleased to know she agreed with him. When he makes an agreement, it is final, and there was no changing it, regardless of circumstances.

Lord Davenport turned to look at his wife. *What in God's name is happening? How can this woman weaken me so? I must be clear and not allow any woman to influence me,* he thought.

After his moment of weakness, although no one knew, Lord Davenport returned to the hard man he was and said in a firm voice, "No! The agreement will not be changed! Robert will marry Grace, and we will not discuss this any further!

Are we to allow our children to dictate how things are to be? No! I, for one, will not! If we learn it's too difficult for Robert and Elizabeth to stay away from each other, then Baron and Baroness Massey will remove temptation by sending Elizabeth to France."

Baron and Baroness Massey nodded in agreement, except for Lady Davenport.

I need to find time to speak with John once tonight's events have calmed down, Lady Davenport thought.

"We shall take our leave. Good evening," Baron Massey said, putting his arm around his wife, and they left Lord Davenport's study.

***

Later that evening, as Lady Davenport was preparing for bed, her thoughts kept returning to her son. She was unable to forget the pain she saw on his face when his father forbidden him to be with Elizabeth.

What am I to do? I want to help my son. He has clearly found a love…a love I will never know or understand. Why do we have the right to take this away from them. For us to destroy such happiness…is this not wrong? God, help me know what I am to do? I do not want my son to live the life I've been forced to live, never knowing what love is or feels like. I must speak to John and do my best to help him understand that his decision is a grave mistake, Lady Davenport thought.

Later that evening, while Baron Massey was lying in bed after making love to his wife – still smiling, he turned to look at her, who was now sound asleep.

She looks so beautiful, he thought, sighing. *I am a lucky man. God has blessed us both.*

Unable to sleep, Baron Massey quietly and with care left his bed and walked over to the window. He looked up to the night sky, to the moon shining bright, then out to the forest; as he thought about his daughter, and he felt sadness for Grace. He was one of the lucky ones to have found love with the woman he married. He looked back to his wife, and he wanted this for Grace. He hoped that she would find love with Robert once she was married, but when he learned she hadn't spent any time with Robert, it disappointed him.

How can she even know if she could love him or not? If she has not spent any time with him. If she told me how she felt…and what? What would you have done? He thought, arguing with himself. Then his eyebrows raised as realization hit him. *Did she naught come to you and ask you about the agreement?* Feeling like a fool, *she did you fool, and you shoved her away. But what could I have done? The contract is set.*

If Robert and Elizabeth were unable to forget the love they have come to know, then what? Can I force Grace to marry a man who loves her sister? And her sister…my daughter Elizabeth, what were you thinking? he thought, shaking his head.

His wife was right; Grace set Elizabeth up, dooming her marriage before it started. It could never work, not with Grace and Elizabeth being so close. It truly will be a great tragedy, and what was he to do?

Is it possible for the agreement to be changed, as Lady Davenport recommended? She is right, and we are the ones who created it, so why can we not change it? he thought as he continued to argue the situation to himself. *You know why? If you were to change it, it would be yours and your family's death, not to mention you will lose Dunham Massey Castle.*

Can he give up Dunham Massey Castle for his daughter? Baron Massey turned to look at his wife. *No, I cannot. I promised her when we married; I would do what was necessary to regain Dunham Massey Castle, giving her the power she felt she deserved to have.*

Baroness Massey had plans, plans he began to wonder if they were obtainable.

After several minutes, Baron Massey yawned and returned to his bed. Once he crawled under the covers, he scooted close to his wife, then pulled her against his body as he finally allowed sleep to take him.

***

The following morning Lord Davenport summoned Robert to his study before the rest of the manor woke, needing to speak to his son without interruption.

When Robert received the summons from his father the

night before, telling him to meet him in his study before sun break, he was nervous. He feared his father's wrath was so great; he would send him to the dungeon at Chester Castle. Robert loved Elizabeth. How could he let her go? There was nothing he could do at that moment, so he would see his father and face whatever was thrown at him.

Upon arriving at his father's study, Robert noticed the door was ajar, so he walked right in. "Father, you requested to see me?" Okay, maybe it wasn't a request – he was summoned.

He decided to downplay the reason for his father summoning him, feeling it gave him a little control of the situation.

Lord Davenport did not waste any time getting to the point. "Robert, you will marry Grace! There is nothing more to be said about the matter!" Lord Davenport said without looking at his son.

Robert opened his mouth to speak, but his father stopped him.

"Do not even try!" he said as he thought, *if I give him Watch Hill Castle now, this may encourage him…help him to see that marrying Grace is the right thing to do. It will also keep him busy since the castle is in desperate need of repair, which the time he spends repairing the castle will keep his mind off Elizabeth.*

"I was going to do this after you and Grace were married, as it was intended to be a wedding gift, but I believe now is the best time," he said, as he signed the documents that lay in front of him. "I am giving you Watch Hill Castle, and this will be yours and Grace's home once you are married."

Lord Davenport put down the quill, rolled up the document and looked up at Robert as he handed it to him. "Here is the deed giving you ownership of Watch Hill Castle." He also tossed Robert a large pouch of coins, "Here's half of Grace's dowry to hire the men and materials you will need to repair Watch Hill Castle, since it has stood empty for many years and is in desperate need of repair. Do what you need to make it ready."

Robert carefully took the documents and the pouch of coins. "Father, Eliz —" Robert tried to discuss his relationship with Elizabeth, but his father cut him off.

Lord Davenport slammed his fist on his desk. "Stop! You need to forget about Elizabeth! There is nothing you can say or do that will change my mind!" he yelled, looking directly into Robert's eyes. "You are forbidden to have anything to do with Elizabeth! Do you hear me!" Giving Robert a look, that said his word was not to be questioned.

Robert closed his mouth and stared at his father in disbelief, but he knew nothing was to be said or done. Feeling defeated, Robert nodded as he took the deed and pouch of coins, then said, "As you wish, father."

Robert turned with his head hanging low and left his father's study.

As Robert walked out of his father's study, he saw Grace walking down the hall towards the morning room. Robert smiled. *I have no intentions of staying away from my beloved,* he thought.

Robert quickly went to catch Grace before she made it to the morning room. Once he was close enough, he softly called, "Grace?" When she looked at him, he motioned for her to come over.

Grace turned when she heard her name, then smiled when she saw Robert motioning for her.

"Good morrow Robert?" she said, as she curtsied.

Robert bowed, "Good morrow to you, Grace," he said, turning to make sure no one was coming or was able to hear him. "I have a favor to ask of you?" he whispered as he looked over to the window and realized what time it was. "Grace, the sun is not up yet. What are you doing up so early?"

Grace smiled, knowing what he was going to ask her.

So, before he had a chance, she said, "You want me to ask Elizabeth to meet with you?" Giving him a big smile. Grace turned to look out the window and lowered her head, "I could not sleep after what happened last night," she said, then wondered why Robert was up so early. "Why are you up so early? Could you not sleep either?"

"You know me too well," Robert said with a smile. Then with seriousness, "Father requested to see me before anyone else was up. And no, I could not sleep as well."

"Oh." Was all Grace could say, then realizing she had not answered Robert about Elizabeth, she said, "Sorry, Elizabeth asked when I saw you, to ask if you would meet her at your special place." Then she decided to try again, to learn of this special place. "Robert, what is this place? Elizabeth will not tell me, and she tells me everything. Well," looking down at the floor, "At least she use to," she said with a bit of sadness in her voice.

Robert smiled as he thought, *she never told Grace about our special place.*

"I am sorry, Grace, but I cannot tell you. This place is only to be known between Elizabeth and me," he said, touching her arm slightly before pulling it back. "Do not be sad, maybe one day Elizabeth and I will tell you. Please tell Elizabeth I will meet her at our special place when the sun is high in the sky, in seven days hence."

Robert quickly looked around to make sure they were still alone. "But Grace, I will need you to brave the outdoors since you will need to be with Elizabeth. It will be suspicious if she went on her own, and I was nowhere to be found. As you recall, we are always required to be together. If you are seen alone, and Elizabeth and I were nowhere to be found…well, you know what will happen. When you leave, make sure you are seen leaving together, and I will seek permission to ride to the village at the break of dawn, knowing you will be spending the day with your sister. Once I am safe and out of sight, I will cut through the forest and meet Elizabeth at our special place," he said, as he placed his hand on Grace's shoulders in a loving way, in case anyone was to appear.

For Grace, this made her feel uncomfortable, causing her to flinch.

"I am sorry, Grace. I know this is uncomfortable for you, but if anyone were to see us…you understand?" Robert said, giving her an apologetic look, and felt her relax a little. "Grace, you must remain at the place Elizabeth leaves you until she returns. Can you put aside your fears…your discuss for the outdoors. Can you do this for Elizabeth and me?"

Robert's explanation of why he touched her the way he did, made sense, and she forced herself to relax. Grace looked up at Robert as she thought, *can I do this,* twisting her kerchief in her hands. *Oh, Elizabeth, you will owe me greatly for this,* she thought until she realized, *oh no, I owe you, sister. I owe you very much.*

Grace sighed in resignation and nodded in agreement.

After leaving Robert, Grace went directly to see Elizabeth and deliver Robert's message, forgetting where she was initially going.

Once Grace arrived at their shared chamber, she walked in and was surprised to see Elizabeth asleep, as she too struggled to sleep. Grace walked over to Elizabeth's bed, "Elizabeth, wake up," she whispered, shaking Elizabeth's shoulder and was surprised Elizabeth did not immediately wake up. Again, Grace whispered in her ear, "Elizabeth, I have a message from Robert. You must wake." But still, she did not wake up.

Grace rolled her eyes as she thought, *how can she sleep and so soundly.* "Elizabeth," she said louder this time, shaking her more vigorously. Finally, Elizabeth's eyes started to flutter, and Grace thought, *finally.*

Elizabeth heard Grace calling her name, but she didn't want to wake because she was having such a wonderful dream of marrying Robert. Then, when she heard 'Robert has a message for you', she finally tried to open her eyes, but then her dream pulled her back, confused at what she was hearing. To her, Robert was already with her.

He can tell me his message himself, she thought.

Elizabeth was obviously confused between dream and reality. Then, she started to feel as if she was falling out of bed, so she opened her eyes.

"Grace, what is it? I just fell asleep and was having the most beautiful dream," she said, perturbed as she rubbed her eyes.

Grace smiled, "I just spoke with Robert, and he has a message for you."

Elizabeth jerked up, now fully awake, anxious to know what his message was. "What message? Tell me?" she asked, touching Grace's arm. "Well, what are you waiting for. Come on, Grace, tell me."

Grace smiled, watching her sister's sudden burst of excitement, causing her to burst out laughing, but then quickly covered her mouth with her hand.

"I was waiting for you to wake up," she said, rolling her eyes, then sat on the bed next to Elizabeth. "Robert wants you to meet him at your special place, when the sun is high in the sky, in seven days hence."

Elizabeth squeezed Grace's hand, "Really, Grace," she asked with excitement. Then realizing their situation, "How are we going to do this? I didn't consider how difficult this will be now that our parents know about our relationship," she said, feeling worried.

She was now feeling uncomfortable. "You and I are to leave the manor together after Robert leaves for the village at dawn. He will use the excuse, since you and I are spending the day together he will travel into the village. Once he is out of sight and is sure he will not be seen, Robert will cut through the forest and wait for you at your special place. You are to leave me in a place where I will

not be discovered, and there, I will await your return," she
said, looking at Elizabeth with worry. "Elizabeth, I beg of
you, please choose a safe and clean place for me to wait,
and I beg you, do not take long with Robert. Mother and
father will know something is wrong if we are gone too
long."

Elizabeth smiled, "Grace, I know the perfect place. I
will leave you at the pond Robert and I go swimming in."

Grace was shocked, "You go swimming with Robert.
Elizabeth!" she yelled, louder than she intended. Lowering
her voice, she whispered, "Elizabeth, you undressed in
front of Robert?" she asked. Grace was shocked; although
she knew what they have already done, it still was a
surprise.

Elizabeth laughed, "Yes, Grace, I did, but I kept on my
shift. I actually wore two, so when I was wet, he could not
see through, and Robert was very respectable."

"Oh Elizabeth," she said, shaking her head. "I must
leave you now. Get some more sleep, then join me and the
rest of the house downstairs for morning meal. I believe I
will go down to the morning room and read for a while,
while I wait for the rest of the house to rise." Grace bent
down and kissed her sister on the cheek then hugged her.

Elizabeth was ecstatic to receive Robert's message and
found it amusing that he had the same idea she did. She laid
down in her bed and pulled her covers up to her neck as she
thought, *we are the same. For anyone to know us could not
deny what we feel.*

After what happened last night, Elizabeth was desperate
to see and speak to Robert, to know they will meet in seven
days hence – yes, it's going to be difficult to wait so long,
but the thought of being able to see and be alone with him
gave her the strength she needed to endure the separation.
With her excitement, there was also sorrow.

*Will it be the last time we spend together? The last time
I ever feel his touch and his love. There must be away. God*

could not have given us this love, to only have it taken away, Elizabeth thought.

***

Since Robert and Elizabeth spent every day together for the last several months, it was hard for Elizabeth, and her heart hurt from missing him so, and it's only been a day. How was she to endure seven days, let alone the rest of her life? Her heart felt as if it was being ripped from her chest, in a desperate need to find that part which was missing, with the need to make it whole once again, and Elizabeth knew Robert was feeling the same.

For anyone to understand Robert and Elizabeth's pain – try imagining a string tied around your tooth and someone several feet away was pulling and pulling with such ferocity, desperately needing it removed from your mouth. It fights, resisting as if it did not want to be expelled from where it laid, but at the same time, it knew it needed to be free.

This was how Robert and Elizabeth felt as if their hearts were being pulled apart with an invisible string that was tied around their hearts constantly pulling, wanting desperately to be reunited to the one who holds the other end – to be whole once again. When Robert and Elizabeth met every day, it allowed their hearts to reconnect and ease that pain.

***

It's finally the seventh day, and Elizabeth was practically running to the pond as she pulled Grace along behind her.

Grace was irritated with Elizabeth eagerness, so she planted her feet to the ground and yanked on Elizabeth, forcing her to stop.

"Elizabeth, I know you are in a hurry to see Robert, but we must move like ladies going on a casual stroll."

Elizabeth was frustrated, but Grace was right. "You are right Grace, I am sorry. I am just so excited to see Robert after all this time."

Grace rolled her eyes, "Elizabeth, you saw Robert when they arrived last evening."

"Yes, Grace, I know, but I could not touch him or even look at him more than to acknowledge his arrival."

When Grace and Elizabeth finally arrived at the pond, Elizabeth helped Grace by laying down the blanket, along with their small picnic, while taking a little for her and Robert, then she quickly rushed to see Robert.

Grace was not happy being left alone in the outdoors, but she will endure it for her sister and Robert. She will have her lunch, then read her book she brought with her.

***

When Elizabeth finally arrived at the lake, she was surprised that Robert had not arrived yet, so *she stood overlooking the lake waiting for his arrival.*

He must have been delayed. I expected him to be here already. What if he was unable to get away, she thought.

Elizabeth shook her head; she could not think that way. She knew Robert would find a way to meet her. She just had to be patient.

As Elizabeth was staring at the water watching the ripples, she was deep in thought —

I stand here today, facing this lake, as I look out to what is before me, to the beauty of this lake and the trees surrounding it, and the love it yields. The same love Robert and I felt when we first found this place. Nothing has changed. You wrapped us in your love, allowing our love to grow. A love…a wonderous gift, given to us by God. It is a love of the purest kind, so powerful it surpasses any, and all love, and anyone who wishes to destroy our love.

***

Robert was at the stables saddling his horse when he heard footsteps, and when he turned around, he found Edward standing at the entrance watching him. "Edward, what brings you to the stables?"

Edward leaned against the doorway, smiling at Robert, "Well, I heard you are riding into town, and I thought I would join you."

Robert froze. *This cannot be happening. How can I keep Edward from going with me?* he thought.

Robert turned to face Edward, "Yes, I thought I would ride in town to seek men who can help me with the repairs on Watch Hill Castle," he said, smiling.

Since it has nothing to do with women and drinking, Edward will not want to go with me, so I should be safe.

However, that was not on Edwards's mind. His father sent him out here to join Robert to ensure he wasn't sneaking off to see Elizabeth.

Edward watched Robert closely, trying to decide if he wanted to play nursemaid? No, he doesn't, but he must do what his father told him to do.

"Great. I will go with you," Edward said, then went to the stall to ready his horse.

Robert tensed, *seriously,* he thought. This was not good. If Edward went with him, he wouldn't be able to turn off to see Elizabeth. He had to figure a way to get rid of him.

Robert gathered himself together, not wanting to show Edward his disappointment. He turned and said, "Wonderful. Do you have any ideas where to find good men to help me with the repairs?"

Edward rolled his eyes. *Father, you are wasting my time,* he thought. Then, he came up with an idea.

"I do. If you want to find men, then you should go to the tavern."

Robert smiled and thought, *this is perfect.* "Agreed, then our first stop shall be the tavern."

Edward turned to look at Robert. "Our first stop?" he asked with concern. He did not want to spend the whole day with Robert, and he had to find a way to get out of this.

"Yes, then we must go to the carpenter and other places to arrange for supplies to be delivered," Robert said, feeling confident, knowing Edward would not want to leave the tavern.

Once we arrive at the tavern, Edward will not want to leave. He will find a reason to stay behind, Robert thought.

"Very well," Edward said, climbing on his horse. "Let us be on our way. I am eager to get to the village," he said, smiling, as he thought, *I have no intentions on spending the day shopping for supplies.*

Robert climbed on his horse, and the two of them rode to the village.

Once they arrived at the village tavern, and Robert hired a few men, Edward found an excuse to remain. Robert rode away from the tavern, and once he was out of sight, he kicked his horse to a run, racing his way back to the forest and his beloved, and he prays she is still waiting for him.

***

Elizabeth looked up to the sky as she pours out her heart. "I ask you, God, what test do you seek from us to have us go through such pain? How can you bring Robert and me together to only have us torn apart?" Elizabeth shook her head. "I do not understand why this is to be. You brought us together and gave us this amazing, unbelievable love, to what, to only have it ripped from us? How can this be? What are we to do?"

Elizabeth's emotions were overpowering her, bringing her to the verge of tears. "How can we live with this?" she said, then stopped, finding it difficult to express what she was feeling, and began to sob, with tears running down her face, as her heart was breaking.

After a while, Elizabeth took her kerchief and blew her nose, then took a deep breath, letting it out slowly, as she pulled herself together.

"Are we to accept what is to be, by allowing Robert to marry Grace?" Elizabeth shook her head as she rolled her hands into fists. "I am sorry, but I cannot. I cannot bear to see my love, who is my heart and soul, marry my sister," she said, filled with anger, as well as shame.

Elizabeth felt torn up inside, and decided not to hold anything back, and released everything she was holding inside, allowing her anger to explode.

"My sister!" she yelled, then lowered her head as she closed her eyes, then in a whisper, "Why my sister?" she said, shaking her head.

Elizabeth pulled her head up as she raised her voice. "Who has no interest in Robert! Nor does she desire to be with him! Our families are demanding…nay, they are ordering Robert to marry Grace!" she yelled, allowing her anger to engulf her. "For what? For status and power, in hopes one day, my father will reclaim Dunham Massey as his own!" As her tears were streaming down her face, her chest ached, and she was finding it difficult to continue.

After a great deal of time had passed, Elizabeth tried to pull herself together but stuttered as she tried to regain control. Elizabeth took a few deep breaths, and once she released them, she was able to bring her anger under control, and what she was feeling needed to be said. "The thought," her voice cracked, so she closed her eyes and tried again. "Of never being able to touch him. To feel his arms around me," she said in a softer voice.

Elizabeth placed one hand over her heart as she stretched her other arm out, reaching for Robert as if he was standing directly in front of her; she whispers, "To hold him. To love him. How can I let him go?" She's fighting back the tears as her anger once again took over. "I cannot! I just cannot do this!" she yelled.

Elizabeth's emotions were all over the place, up and down, with no control.

Again, she lowered her voice to a whisper, "Please do not make me do this?" she pleaded, as she felt defeated. Elizabeth shook her head, "You ask too much of me. Too much of Robert. If you are asking us to forget the love you blessed us with, to allow this marriage between Robert and Grace to take place…" she lowered her head, wrapping her arms around herself, slightly hunching over. "How can we do this? How can we allow this to happen?" she said, as tears once again flowed down her face.

Elizabeth's mind was racing, desperately trying to understand how this love she found with Robert, a gift given by God, one, she could not believe God would give such a gift, a miracle, to only rip it from them. No, she could not believe this. There must be a way; they only had to find what that was.

What was happening between Robert and Elizabeth was inconceivable, and they did not understand why it had to be this way. Elizabeth felt – no, she believed love this strong, one of the greatest power – God's greatest gift could not have been bestowed to them if it wasn't supposed to be. A love this powerful should dissolve any agreement. But their mother and father were too blinded by their need for power, in what money and land could give them to see that.

Elizabeth suddenly had an idea. *Wait. I will pray and ask God for his help, to help our mother and father see reason. Yes, that is what I must do,* she thought.

With renewed strength, she turned back to the sky, "God, I beseech thee, to help our mother and father. Bring your light to their eyes and hearts. Show them in the way you know, so they too will know this love we feel is a gift from you. Help them see it's right for Robert and me to marry and that our marriage can still merge our families." she pleaded, but felt it was not enough and turned her plea to one of desperation. "God, please help us. Help us to know what to do and how we can make this right? This love you gave us cannot be lost, nor can it be allowed to be taken away. For what? A foolish tradition – power?" Elizabeth emotions again turned to anger. "You saw our families would not listen, nor do they care! Their only concern is to honor this agreement! What agreement can stand before…rule over love! Should love not matter? Should it not be included in this decision! Why should our love not continue to grow! A love that can bring happiness to us all!"

Elizabeth was angry, lost, her heart was breaking, and it was tearing her apart. She urgently needed the other piece of her heart. She needed Robert. *Where is Robert?* she thought, looking around, wondering where he was. When she did not find him, she did not know what to do, what else she could say that would help them, and wondered if she said enough, that she expressed her feelings enough to be heard?

Suddenly, Elizabeth heard a noise, and when she turned around, it was Robert walking towards her. She didn't waste any time - Elizabeth ran and jumped into his open arms, burying her face in his neck.

***

Once Robert reached the tree line, he tied his horse to the tree, and as he was walking to the entrance, he thought about the night he informed his family of his feeling for Elizabeth —

How can I let Elizabeth go? Shaking his head, *I cannot. It's impossible for me to do so. God, tell me what I am to do? How can I make this right?*

In mid-thought, Robert stopped at the entrance to the lake when he heard Elizabeth's voice. She was angry and talking to God. Robert tried to listen to what she was saying, but he could only hear bits and pieces. From the sound of her voice, she was upset and angry at what happened. When Robert heard the pain and desperation in her voice, he picked up his pace and ran, needing to be by her side.

When he approached Elizabeth, she must have heard him, because as soon as he neared her, she ran and jumped into his waiting arms. Robert held her tight, providing her with the comfort she needed.

For what seemed like an eternity, Robert and Elizabeth just stood in the same spot holding each other, not wanting to let go. They feared if they parted, they would lose each other forever, and there was no life without the other.

Robert relaxed his hold on Elizabeth, and with reluctance, he released her. When he saw Elizabeth's face, it was clear she'd been crying, with tears still under her eyes, and it tore at his heart to see her in so much pain. He wanted to comfort her and ease her pain, at the same time ease his own. But he knew there was nothing he can do to ease his heart – their hearts, since they were forbidden to be together.

Suddenly Robert felt a chill as fear started coursing through his body with the uncertainty of their future.

It was Elizabeth who ends their long silence. She looked up at Robert and said, "Robert, I cannot…" but found she could not look at him. Instead, she turned to look at the ground, "I cannot walk away from you, from what we have. It is too much for them to ask this of us. The thought of never being with you. To never feel your arms around me again." Elizabeth gathered her courage and looked up at Robert, with tears in her eyes. Robert pulled her close to him, and wrapped his arms around her.

"To feel your heart against mine," she sniffled. Robert handed her his kerchief, and after Elizabeth wiped her nose, she laid her head against his chest as she placed her hand over his heart. "To never hear this heart beating, knowing it beats for me. I cannot think of this heart beating for anyone else but me." Elizabeth tightened her arms around Robert, "What are we going to do? I do not understand why they will not listen to us. Why will they not allow us to marry? Why are they so determined to keep this agreement as it is? Why are they unable to change it? Why is it so important for them to keep it so, thus, forcing you to marry Grace? Robert, try…help me see and understand…" choking on her words, "Please?" Elizabeth pleaded, desperate for answers.

Robert did not have the answers, and it tore him apart to hear her in so much pain. His pain was great, but his anger was greater. How could he help her when he couldn't help himself? She needed answers, as did he, but he had none to offer her. What was he to say? How could he help her? None of what happened made any sense to him either. He understood how Elizabeth was feeling, so what could he say to her that would help, when he had no answers? He needs to comfort her, to ease her pain.

But how? How can I help her…what can I say that will help her, in turn, help me? he thought.

Robert knew he'd been silent for too long and had to say something. Anything.

"Elizabeth, my love…I…I am not sure what to say," he finally said with honesty. "How can I give you the comfort you seek when I do not understand it myself? How can this agreement be more important to our families than to our own happiness? I am seeking the answers to the same questions…why will they not see? Why will they not allow us the time to show them that instead of Grace, it should be you and I who marry. By marrying you, it can still honor the agreement. Our marriage…" Robert pulled away from Elizabeth to look at her, to see her beautiful brown eyes, her eyes that's always brought a smile to his face. In her eyes, he saw everything: her love for him and the pain of losing him.

Since they've been together, he believed to be the luckiest man in the world to have a woman such as her. To know the love she has for him was the same love he has for her. This, he cannot understand. Robert smiled at Elizabeth as he lightly rubbed her face with the back of his hand, and she leaned into the warmth of his touch.

"…And in doing so, will still merge both our families. I am so ashamed Elizabeth to be connected to such a family."

Elizabeth listened to Robert's heart when he was

talking, and she heard it start to beat faster, so she tightened her hold on him, wanting to show him without words, she understood.

Chapter Fifteen

Then suddenly, she became upset, as Robert's words sunk in. No, she was not upset; she was angry, so very angry, that she pushed at Robert's chest, wanting him to release her, and when he did, she exploded.

"This is not right, Robert!"

Robert was surprised by Elizabeth's sudden outburst, and he tried to pull her back to him, with the need to hold and comfort her, but she refused and stepped out of reach.

Elizabeth looked at Robert, "No! Now is not the time for comfort! This is not fair! The love we share is the strongest and powerful love that anyone would be lucky to have! How can they dismiss it as if it is nothing! Our love is a gift from God!" she said, pacing back and forth, twisting the front of her gown. "Why can they not see that! We both know what we feel is real! God gave us this love! Why do they have the right to take it away! Is it not going against God for them to deny our love by not allowing us to marry?"

It broke Robert's heart to see Elizabeth so upset. He knew he had to do and say something – "Elizabeth, I feel what you are feeling. It is hard to understand. Maybe we are not meant to understand, but to trust God, and trust he will help us. Maybe this is a series of test, to prove our love is strong and real, and our family's reaction was our first test," he said, rubbing his hand over his face. "This is the only way that any of this makes sense." Robert walked over to Elizabeth and placed his hands on her shoulders. "Elizabeth, please, have faith?" he pleaded.

Did Robert believe his own words? There were doubt and uncertainty, but he needed to do something to help Elizabeth. The pain and anger she was feeling was deep, more profound than his own. For Elizabeth, it wasn't just about him; it was about her sister as well. Her pain would be great if he married Grace. To see her sister with the man she loves would destroy her.

Elizabeth was no fool; she pushed Robert away from her and yelled, "Robert! You cannot truly mean that? This is a test of a series of test, truly?" she said, with her hands on her hips.

When Robert saw Elizabeth's hands on her hips with her sassy attitude, he couldn't help but start laughing. He liked this fire in Elizabeth and found at times; he would purposely ignite that spark.

"Robert, you laugh at me! What is it about our situation that makes it so funny?" she asked, with her hands still on her hips, as she tilted her head a little to the side.

Robert dropped his smile, "I am sorry, Elizabeth, but when you stand like that, I cannot help but laugh," he said with a broad smile. Then in a serious tone, he returned to what they were talking about, "I do not know if what I say is true…it's possible, is it naught?"

Robert moved to stand in front of Elizabeth, forcing her to look up at him; as he looked down at her, his eyebrows raised with a smirk.

Elizabeth shook her head, "What I think, Robert Davenport —"

Robert smiled; he loved it when she said his full name, either in anger or in fun. When he heard this, he knew her anger was subsiding,

"— is you are trying to find a reason, any reason! And I know why? she said, softening her voice, "I asked you for an answer, a reason, and being who you are, you were trying to give me one, and I thank you for that." Elizabeth lowered her hands from her hips and reached for Robert's hand.

"I am sorry, Elizabeth," he said, as he thought, *if it makes her feel better to believe what I said to be true, then it shall be.* "You are right. I wanted to ease your pain and anger," looking down at the ground. With his eyes only, he looked at her, "It worked, did it naught?" he said, with a wink and a smirk.

Elizabeth gave Robert a questionable look and said, "Well, I guess it did." Then, Robert and Elizabeth burst out laughing, allowing the tension in their bodies to relax.

"Elizabeth, I am afraid there is more to this agreement then what they have told us. There must be, and I must find a way to discover what it is."

Elizabeth grabbed Robert's arm and squeezed it hard, but not enough to hurt him. "No, Robert! You cannot!" she yelled.

For some reason, an overwhelming amount of fear slammed deep into Elizabeth's stomach. She was afraid if Robert pushed the issue with his father, it would do more harm than good.

If he pushed his father to see the agreement, he would know we are still seeing each other. If that happens, then they will send me away…to France! I cannot allow this to happen, Elizabeth thought.

And with this thought, a flash of memory surfaced, recalling a conversation she overheard between her mother and father after returning to Dunham Massey.

***

Elizabeth was walking by her father's study when she heard him say her name, so she stopped to listen. Her mother and father were talking about her and Robert, and she wanted to know what they were saying, and maybe, they would give her some insight as to why they were so insistent on maintaining this agreement.

"We cannot allow Robert and Elizabeth any levity for them to continue this relationship. What were they thinking?" her mother said, sounding disgusted with the situation.

"My dear, Elizabeth is a smart girl. She loves her sister, and I am sure she will do the right thing. All she needs is time to think on the matter, and when she does, I am sure

she will come to see reason. Elizabeth's loyalty to her family is strong, more so than Grace's."

"My love, you may be right, but mark my word, if I find any sign there is still anything going on between her and Robert, we will have no choice…she will be sent to our family in France, far away from any temptation."

***

Robert noticed Elizabeth's distance stare, and he didn't understand what was happening but feared it was not good, so he tried to get her attention by calling her name over-and-over again, but failed to break whatever spell she was in, but he refused to give up.

When Elizabeth did not respond, he started shaking her, afraid he was going to lose her. Feeling desperate, he grabbed Elizabeth's shoulders and started shaking her harder, as he screamed her name, at the same time praying, *oh God please, do not take her from me. I cannot lose her.*

***

Elizabeth was shocked by what she heard and thought, how can I give him up? But if she didn't, and they were discovered, she would be sent to France, far away from Robert.

Send me to France? No! I cannot allow that to happen! she thought, feeling defeated. What am I to do then?

***

"ELIZABETH!" Robert screamed at the top of his lungs.

While Elizabeth was lost in her memory, recalling the conversation between her mother and father, she barely registered Robert was trying to get her attention. When she heard him screaming her name, she snapped out of her past and returned to the present.

Once she found her voice, she said, "I am sorry, Robert. I was remembering a conversation I overheard between mother and father." Elizabeth looked up at Robert and saw his fear. Then with a sudden feeling of desperation,

"Robert, you cannot say anything to your father!" she said, grabbing his arms. "Robert, the morning after we returned home, I was walking past my father's study when I overheard mother and father talking about us. I stopped and stood outside the door to listen. Robert, if we are discovered, they will send me to France. You cannot say anything to your father! If you do, they will send me to France, and I will never see you again, and I ca…can…not…" Elizabeth stuttered as she tried to keep herself from crying, but her fear was too great as tears started rolling down her face.

Robert wiped her tears, as his heart was breaking to see Elizabeth so upset, so he did what he could, he reached for Elizabeth, and this time she did not pull away from him and allowed Robert to pull her into his arms, and she rested her head against his chest, hoping the beating of his heart – with his love, thus, calming her, at the same time, easing her pain.

As Robert and Elizabeth were standing holding each other, Robert looked out at the lake, the lake he believed was full of love – *this place, which was given to us by God, a place where we found our love and the happiness we share. This place…our place, should not be spoiled by our pain and sorrow, but should always be a place of love and joy,* Robert thought.

Robert pushed Elizabeth away from him, enough so he could take her face in his hands and said, "Elizabeth my love," looking deep in her eyes, "I know your pain, as it is my own. This place," he looked back to the lake, "Was given to us by God, where we discovered our love," he said, turning back to Elizabeth, "And our happiness. This place has given us nothing but joy," turning to look back at the lake and the surrounding area, "We cannot allow our pain and sorrow to taint this place, a place of great beauty that's filled with peace and love."

Robert turned back to Elizabeth and softly rubbed her

face in a gentle caress, "My love, this is our safe-haven, our sanctuary, a place created by God. I believe this place pulled us here and filled us with such happiness; I wanted to tell the world. Do you remember?" he said, not waiting for an answer. He smiled and continued, "It opened our hearts to a love we did not know was possible. So, my love, let us leave our pain and sadness outside of this place, so we do not affect it with our sorrow. This place is our paradise, and when we come here, we will leave all our pain and sadness behind, leaving it as pure as the day we found it. A place that is protected by God shall not be tainted by our pain and sorrow.

"As far as we are aware, there is no one across the land who knows of this place. Our place. Elizabeth, no matter what life we live, we will always remember this place," Robert said, motioning with his arm to indicate the lake and its surroundings. "This lake is our lake," looking directly into her eyes, "Here and now, we will promise each other, no matter what happens, we will always remember this place. How one day, when we are reborn —"

Elizabeth raised her eye in question, not understanding what he was saying.

Robert noticed this, but he did not stop. He found he could not stop. "We will return to this lake in our next life and every life after. We will find each other, Elizabeth, again-and-again. We will promise here and now, on this day, that we will be together for eternity. Elizabeth, I know what our faith says, but I feel…for some reason…" shaking his head.

Robert did not understand what he was saying or why the words needed to be spoken, only that they must; they needed to be said.

"…I know what I say must sound mad, but I cannot explain it…I feel…"

How could Robert possibly explain something he had no understanding of? Something that went against everything they were both taught to believe in, to now try and explain what he's been feeling, something that is unknown to him. He knew it's against what he has always known and believed to be true, but something told him what he was saying was real.

How does one explain something you just feel to be true? he thought.

"How do I explain this in a way that will not sound as if I've lost my head. I feel…we do not just live one life Elizabeth," he said, and saw her confusion. "I know what I say is hard to believe. I too, find it hard to believe, even though I speak the words, but Elizabeth," taking her face in his hands, "I feel it's true. I cannot explain it. It's a feeling I have deep inside." Robert let out his breath, "I am not explaining this well. I sound as if I have lost my head."

Robert turned away from Elizabeth, unable to bear the look of confusion and concern on her face. He rubbed his hands over his face, trying to get control of himself, to figure out the best way to explain what he's feeling to Elizabeth.

How do I make her see? I must though, it's essential, but I do not understand why, only that I must, Robert thought.

Robert turned back to Elizabeth, and took her by the shoulders as he spluttered, and before he lost his nerve.

"Elizabeth, I know we were taught to believe one way, but is it possible, just possible, there is another way? That there is more at work here…between us…there is something in me that is telling me we live many lives. Our soul continues living until God decides otherwise.

Elizabeth, I know…no, I believe we will find each other again. When we leave this life to meet God, we will ask God if he will allow us to remember our love and this place. This place where our love first began and flourished. We will ask him, with the love we have, which is embedded in our souls, for it to be allowed to guide us back here, so we can find each other once again.

Elizabeth, I do not know if you believe what I tell you to be true, but I hope, if not now, then in time you will come to feel as I do. Something is urging me, a feeling deep inside my soul, something I cannot explain. If you were anyone else, I could never say what I am feeling, but with you, you, I can say anything. Please Elizabeth, do not think me mad."

As Elizabeth was listening and watching Robert, she didn't think him mad from his words, but instead, there was something – a feeling behind them. There were passion and certainty in his words. Yes, at first, she was confused and a little concern for Robert, worried he was losing his mind; at the same time, she felt so much love and passion radiating from him, that he trusted her, and was able to tell her his deepest secrets, of his feelings, he'd dare not share with anyone else.

Elizabeth was not sure she could believe what he said but – *can I believe this? Is what he says…can it be true?* she thought.

Elizabeth did not want to interrupt Robert, so she waited patiently for him to finish before she spoke. If what he said was true, she wanted more than anything to believe him, but how could she.

If we leave this life, do we…can we be reborn? Is it possible? Elizabeth thought.

For Elizabeth's whole life, she was taught to believed; when your life has come to an end, you go before God and await his judgement, and once he pronounces judgement, you either go to heaven or to hell, depending on how you lived your life. So, can she believe in what Robert said?

Is he right? Is there more out there? she thought, then there was this feeling in her heart. *I do feel something, but is it what he says? As I listened to his words, I feel…I feel as if someone is screaming at me, telling me to listen, that he speaks the truth. Believe him,* Elizabeth thought.

Elizabeth could not deny there was something to Robert's words – *I need to take the chance. I need to believe.*

After Robert finished, he watched Elizabeth and waited for her reaction, a response, anything.

Elizabeth knew what she was going to say, so, without delay, "Robert, I cannot say I understand everything you said, but something is screaming at me, asking me to believe you." Elizabeth smiled, "So, yes, yes Robert, I believe you. And yes, I promise to remember this place no matter what happens. If God wills it, I will find my way back to this place and to you."

Elizabeth reached up to place her hand on Robert's face, and she felt exhilarated by what she said. It brought her happiness, great and utter happiness.

"We will be together for eternity, Robert," then, rising on her tiptoes, she kissed him.

Robert felt relieved to hear Elizabeth's words. He placed his hands on her hips and lifted her into the air, and swung her around, feeling happier than he had before. How could he believe she'd think him mad?

Once Robert placed Elizabeth on the ground, he pulled her into his arms, into a tight embrace, needing to feel her body against his. There was hope, and in this hope, it gave him a sense of peace in his heart.

Then, a sudden idea hit him. Without a word, Robert released Elizabeth abruptly, it left her unsteady, but she managed to catch her balance, preventing her from falling over.

Robert walked over to the edge of the lake as Elizabeth watched, wondering what he was doing. At the edge of the lake, Robert knelt on the ground, just beneath the tree branch and pulled his dagger from his belt.

What is he doing? she thought as she watched Robert use his dagger to dig a hole in the ground. *Why?* she wondered. Elizabeth decided she could not wait any longer. She needed to know what he was doing.

"My love, what…what are you doing?"

But Robert did not respond to her question. He simply said, "Wait, and you shall see in a moment."

Shrugging her shoulders, Elizabeth stood waiting for Robert to finish as she watched.

After Robert was finished, "Elizabeth, will you remove your bracelet on your wrist?" he asked.

Elizabeth hesitated, as she looked down at her wrist, rubbing her bracelet with her thumb, then she looked back at Robert, twisting her bracelet on her wrist, wondering what he could possibly want with her bracelet.

Elizabeth's bracelet was a gift from her sister. It was an inch thick, made from the strongest metal, with a white stone resting in the center.

Still hesitating, she asked, "Robert, what do you want with my bracelet?" Unable to take her eyes off her bracelet, as she waited for his response, and when he did not answer her, she lifted her head a little to look at him.

After Robert finished digging his hole, he looked at Elizabeth and said, "Please, my love, you will soon see."

Robert felt anxious as he waited for Elizabeth to hand him her bracelet. He knew the bracelet was precious to her since it was a gift from Grace, and she has never parted with it. For Robert, it was the perfect object to bury. To leave a part of her at their lake.

Although she hesitated, Elizabeth trusted Robert, and so, she removed her bracelet and walked over and handed it to him. Robert took it from her and placed it in his kerchief, and then removed the ring he wore on his fourth right finger and placed it in the kerchief with her bracelet.

Robert's ring was a gift from his father, so all who saw it would know he was Lord Davenport's heir. As Robert placed the ring in the ground, he wondered if his father would notice it was missing? Possibly, but at the moment he did not care. What mattered was leaving something of his with Elizabeth's bracelet, and the ring was all he had on him.

Robert's ring was a thick gold band with a large golden square jewel with a splash of orange and red, symbolizing fire – power, particularly Davenport power. On each side of the jewel had the Davenport's coat of arms.

Once both items were in the kerchief, Robert wrapped them up and placed them in the hole, then covered them with the soil, where they will remain buried until the day they return in their next life to reclaim them.

Robert stood, then took Elizabeth's hand. He pulled her close to him, and as they stood directly over the buried ring and bracelet, he looked directly into her eyes.

"My love, when we return to this lake, our lake," Robert motioned with his arm to encompass the lake. "I will ask God if he will allow us to remember this place and these items," pointing to the place directly under their feet, "We buried here today, as proof of our existence and our love. To retain our memory, allowing us to carry it into our next lives and each and every life thereafter, so we will always find each other." Robert used the back of his hand to caress Elizabeth's face softly. "My love, we will carry our love for all eternity."

At hearing Roberts words, Elizabeth was thrilled and felt she was the happiest woman in the land. To have the man she loved to do such a thing truly touched her heart. She was not sure if what he said was possible, but she trusted Robert, and she trusts her heart in how it felt when she was with him.

Elizabeth placed her hand over his heart and kissed the center of his chest – his heart. She was grateful to have a man such as him love her so much that he wanted to be with her in life or in death. This, if so blessed, she would remember for all time.

Then suddenly, "Oh my, Robert, how long have we been here? Grace? I must return to Grace! She must be frantic. I have left her longer than intended," she said in a panic.

Robert took Elizabeth's hand and quickly dashed for his horse.

"Come, my love, up you go," Robert said, helping Elizabeth on his horse, then climbed up behind her. "We will be there in no time, but I must stop just out of sight, so I will not be seen."

Elizabeth nodded in understanding.

When Elizabeth arrived at the pond where she left Grace, she was surprised to see Grace was asleep. Slowly and quietly, she approached, "Grace, I have returned."

Grace woke up and looked at Elizabeth; she was angry. Grace stood and brushed off her gown, then bent down to pick up the blanket and began folding it.

"Do you know how long you left me here? she scolded Elizabeth, "Hours. How could you leave me like that? Mother and father must be wondering what happened to us?"

Elizabeth laughed. She couldn't help it. "Oh, Grace, it could not have been that bad. After all, you were asleep when I arrived. You must have enjoyed it enough to allow yourself to relax and fall asleep."

Grace threw up her head with a "hump," then turned and started for the manor. "Do not expect me to do this again. If you plan on spending time with Robert, you have to do it without me." And with that, they returned to the manor, with no one being the wiser.

***

Since that day, Robert put a great deal of thought in what happened and of their current situation. He had a right, more than a right to know what existed in that agreement. For his father to believe in it so strongly, to force him to give up Elizabeth, the one and only love he would ever have. He had more than a right to know and understand the sacrifice his father was demanding of him. So, it was decided, he would demand answers from his father and insist he be shown the agreement to read it for himself.

Did Elizabeth words concern and worry him? Yes, of course they did. Regardless, it was something he had to do. He believed by reading the agreement, maybe, just maybe, there would be something in the agreement that would save him and Elizabeth from a horrible fate their parents placed upon them.

With determination, Robert went to his father's study to demand to see the agreement.

"Father, I demand to speak with you!" he yelled, not giving his father a chance to respond, nor an opportunity to stop him. "As your eldest son and heir…this agreement involves me, and I demand you tell me…nay, you show me the agreement so I may read it for myself! You have asked me to give up a love…the only love I will ever know, to marry Grace, a woman who cannot stand me, due to this agreement! With this, I have a right to see and read this agreement for myself! To understand why I am being forced to sacrifice my happiness for you…for money! I have a right to know, and so does Grace! If…you expect me to marry Grace, I…we have a right to know!"

Lord Davenport was fuming by Robert's interruption when he barged into his study, making demands he had no right to be making. Lord Davenport, being a powerful man – no one talks to him in a manner as Robert did, even if it was his son.

"If!" he yelled, slamming his fist on his desk as he stood up. "Boy, do you have a death wish!" Lord Davenport was outraged at Roberts fastidious behavior. "Boy, you are walking on dangerous ground with me! There is no 'if', and you will marry Grace!" Slamming his hand down on the top of his desk again. "Son, no one speaks to me as you have done! I am the Lord of this land and your father! To speak to me in the way you have, I should beat you right where you stand! YOU DO NOT

demand anything from me! I am your father, and you will
do as I say! You will honor and obey me by marrying
Grace! There is no question, no 'if', as you put it! This will
happen! As far as the agreement…no, you do not have a
right to see it! The agreement was forged between Baron
Massey and me, and it has nothing to do with you! You do
not get to decide your life. I do!"

Lord Davenport was so outraged; he was shaking with
fury.

Knowing his father was a ruthless man, it still shocked
Robert to hear his father's words. Robert was not afraid of
his father. He knew, as heir, his father dared naught do
anything to harm him, so he pressed on.

"No right! You cannot be serious! I have every right!
This agreement involves me! You father, who decided my
life before I was of age to agree or disagree! What gave you
that right to decide who I marry! It should be my choice!
Grace has no interest nor desires to marry me! She never
once spent time in my company! Instead, she chose solitude
so that she could read her books! You both made this
decision for us, and it turned out to be the wrong one! What
does it matter who I marry! Are Elizabeth and Grace not
from the same house…both a Massey! Tell me father, help
me understand why I am to give up a love given to me by
God!" Robert yelled.

Robert's anger began to recede, to one of sadness and
desperation, and Robert knew this was a grave mistake, to
show such weakness in front of his father, and if it were
anyone besides his son, Lord Davenport would have
forfeited his life.

Lowering his head, "Please, father, help me understand
this? I need to know," he pleaded.

At first, Lord Davenport was outraged by his son's
boldness, but then, he admired him for being so courageous
to come before him – showing no fear.

He will make a great lord, he thought. But then, when

Robert showed his weakness, it again stirred up his anger, and he was quick to jump on it.

"You lower yourself to plead with me! Are you naught my son! My son has a backbone! He does not show weakness, such as this!" he yelled as he pointed at his son in disgust. "This woman, Elizabeth Massey, has found a way to bewitch you!" he bellowed.

This refueled Roberts anger, "Bewitched! You are a man of power, who's never known love, nor can you understand what real love is! So yes, to you, I appear to be desperate. If my pleading to allow Elizabeth and me to marry is a sign of weakness, then so be it! But father, know this, this weakness you call it, is a sign of one's heart, being greater than one's strength in appearance! I show great strength, from the power of my heart, in my willingness to lower myself, even to a man such as you! A pure and powerful love that was given to me by God! This father, not even you can rebuke!"

Robert was angry and desperate, and he needed to know and understand why his father would force him to give up such love and happiness. He knew speaking so would risk his father's wrath, but it had to be done. He needed answers and answers, that only his father could provide.

Lord Davenport was angry for his son to take such liberties, but, at the same time, it showed backbone. "You are a young and foolish boy! Get out and speak no more of this to me again! Or…I will demand Baron Massey ship Elizabeth to France, and you will never see her again! Now get out!" Lord Davenport hollered.

Robert knew his father's threat was no idle one, and it should not be taken lightly, so he felt defeated. In this, Robert left his father's study without the answers he sought but refused to give up. He was determined to get the answers he needed, even if that meant going behind his father's back. Robert was sure he knew where his father kept his agreements, and the next time his father was away from home, he would search his father's study and find the agreement, then finally he will know the truth.

***

Shortly after Robert left Lord Davenport's study, a rider arrived with an urgent message from King Henry the Eighth, ordering Lord Davenport to London immediately and without delay. When Robert heard this, it was the answer he was looking for. Once his father left, he would return and search his study for the agreement.

After the express rider delivered King Henry's message to Lord Davenport, ordering him to London, he called for the housemaid and began yelling out orders.

"Have Lady Davenport brought to my study at once! After, instruct my manservant to ready my trunks! I ride to London as soon as they are ready!"

The housemaid rushed out of Lord Davenport's study and quickly went looking for Lady Davenport. Once Lady Davenport was informed, she ran to find her husband's manservant.

When Lady Davenport entered her husband's study, he wasted no time informing her of the urgent message he received from King Henry.

"My dear, I must go to London at once, by order of the king, on urgent business that requires my attendance, with no time to delay. I am not pleased to leave after recent events, but it cannot be helped. How can I be sure there will be no issues while I am gone? Before the message arrived, Robert came to me, asking questions about the agreement, and I am afraid he is not finished. Robert is determined to find a way out of marrying Grace. Mary," he said, raising his head to look at his wife, giving her a fierce and firm look, which would send most men and women shrieking to the ground, but for Lady Davenport, his wife was no shrinking violet. She had not once shown him weakness in the face of danger or an emergency.

Thus, is why I admire this woman. She is a strong and

fierce woman in her own right, he thought as he laughed silently.

There was no doubt that Lady Davenport proved to be the right woman for a man such as Lord Davenport. She was used to her husband's fierce looks and anger; therefore, they did not affect her, but it told her he was very serious, that if his orders were not obeyed, there would be repercussions. Lady Davenport never grew to love this fierce man but came to respect him.

"Mary, this cannot happen. I am counting on you to ensure there is no contact between Robert and Elizabeth."

"My husband, do not worry, all will be well. Robert is your son, and he won't do anything that would gain your disapproval. He knows his place as the elder son and heir."

"My dear, I hope you are right. What about the wedding…I will not be back in time?"

"Husband, you must be here for the wedding. It would not be the same without you," she said, then pondered an idea – *if it can be postponed, then it will give me time to understand more of what Robert feels for Elizabeth. Yes, this is a good plan,* she thought.

"My husband, why do we not postpone the wedding until you return. We can plan for the wedding for two months after the new year?"

Lord Davenport looked at his wife, and there was something in her voice, something suspicious. "My dear, what are you planning?"

Lady Davenport only smiled at her husband, then said, "My dear, I have no plans. I only wish to have time to speak to Robert. If anything, to help him see and understand his place, in a manner…from one not so fierce," she said, with a slight smile, as she eyed her husband.

Lord Davenport watched his wife – a chuckle raised inside of him. *Yes, she has no fear of me. Ah, what a powerful woman. I shall give her this,* he thought.

With a slight smile, he said, "Yes, very well. You are

right. It will be best since I do not know how long I will be gone, nor do I know of the urgent business the king has called me for. I shall return as soon as possible. Do what you can with our son Mary, but mark me, that boy will marry Grace," he said in a firm, yet softer voice.

Lady Davenport only smiled as she turned to leave her husband's study. Then in realization, she turned back to her husband, "John, shall I inform Baron and Baroness Massey that the wedding has been postponed?"

"Yes, that is wise. Now, I believe I have everything. The servants should have my trunk packed and tied to a horse. I must go now. It will take me several days to reach London," he said.

Lady Davenport curtsied and left her husband's study. She was pleased the wedding had been postponed and believed the delay would prove to be the correct decision, as she thought it was too soon for Robert and Grace to marry.

Since Robert announced his feeling for Elizabeth, she hoped for more time to understand what happened between her son and Elizabeth. *Maybe with more time, it will help John see reason as well,* she thought. Lady Davenport wants her son to have the love he found, something she never had. *I will pray that God will help me find a way to make this work for everyone's concern,* she thought.

Chapter Sixteen

<u>**Christmas 1535**</u>

It was two weeks before Christmas, then after Robert and Grace's wedding, and they were relieved to learn it's been postponed.

When Robert's mother told him the wedding was postponed, he saw it as a sign, a chance to find out the truth. His mother did not miss the relief and excitement on his face, and he knew his mother noticed, and he was grateful she said nothing of it. Instead, she requested to speak with him.

They went into the parlor, the room his mother enjoyed sitting in during the day. There, she inquired about his feelings for Elizabeth, and Robert held nothing back. To his relief, his mother agreed to help him, but she would give him no guarantees. For if she failed, he had to prepare himself to marry Grace after the new year.

Robert used this opportunity to ask his mother about the agreement and requested permission to see it. He wanted to understand why it was so important for him to marry Grace. At first, his mother hesitated, but after a few moments in considering his request, she agreed to show Robert the agreement.

Lady Davenport's reasons weren't to scare Robert but to show him the seriousness of the agreement. She knew if her husband found out, it would be his wrath, and she would deal with it, but she did not fear it. *I wonder why that is?* she thought. Whatever her feelings are of the matter, it was important that Robert understood the severity of the agreement. Unless his father and Baron Massey agreed to change it – *no, it is unbreakable and unchangeable. He must see and understand that,* she thought.

Lady Davenport took Robert to his father's study and

showed him the bookshelf behind his desk. On the third
shelf from the top, and behind a couple of books was a
small panel, and inside that panel was the agreement. Lady
Davenport took the agreement and handed it to her son.

Robert didn't know what to expect when he took the
agreement. At first, he hesitated. *Do I need to know what
this says?* he thought. No matter if he wanted to or not, he
needed to know what it said, and so, he read the agreement.
What he read sent chills through his body, and it scared
him.

What Robert read was: is that Grace and he were
married after their births by a priest. Although not legal, it
was a powerful binding. He also read that if he didn't marry
Grace, and it was determined to be the Davenport's fault,
then his family would lose everything they knew, title, land,
and power. If it was found that the Massey's were at fault,
it was the same, but more severe. His father agreed, if
Robert and Grace married, thus, merging both families, for
his father would increase his power within the land. For
Baron Massey, he would gain his father's help in regaining
Dunham Massey Castle from the Booth's.

*Baron Massey has a great deal to lose if he was
determined to be at fault,* Robert thought.

After the Massey's reclaimed Dunham Massey Castle
as their own, they've agreed with a future descendant, and
through marriage, a Davenport would be given Dunham
Massey Castle.

*Ah, now I see. It was not enough father already owned
most of the land...he also wanted Dunham Massey Castle,*
he thought.

After reading this, Robert knew, unless his father and
Baron Massey came to a mutual arrangement to change the
agreement, one or the other would be destroyed.

Lord, what am I to do? he thought, but then, *what if the
blame falls on both of us? There would be no winner or
loser. Could this be what I need?* Robert thought.

Robert asked his mother, "Mother, what if both the Massey's and the Davenport's were at fault, of equal blame? Would it void the agreement?"

Lady Davenport stared at her son, stunned by his question. What was she to say? *Could it be possible?* she thought, but she didn't know. But then, *no!* she thought.

"Robert, I do not think there is anything that can be done," she said, but then she wondered what he was thinking. "How would it be for both Baron Massey and your father to be at fault? I do not see how that is possible. In declaring your love for Elizabeth, and Grace confessing her disinterest in marrying you, it had no bearing. So, explain, what are you referring to?"

Robert put his finger to his chin as he thought, *marriage! If Elizabeth and I were already married before Grace and I were to marry, they would have to change the agreement, or it may nullify it altogether.* At this thought, Robert smiled.

Lady Davenport saw Robert in deep thought, but when she saw him smile, fear consumed her. "Robert, what are you thinking?" she asked with concern.

"Mother, I think I have a plan, but I dare not tell you. It is best you know nothing of this," Robert said.

Robert could see his mother was concerned, so he placed his hand over hers, which were folded in her lap. "Do not worry, mother. If my plan goes well, we shall all benefit. I must go." Robert rose and kissed his mother on the cheek, then left her, leaving her with many questions.

With concern and worry, *what have I done,* she thought?

The love Robert and Elizabeth found was rare, and he was unwilling to let it go, not a love as powerful as theirs. They believed it was a gift from God, and for their family to push it aside as if it were nothing – forbidden to be together, was traumatic. Robert could not turn his back on Elizabeth, nor the love they found. He was not going to lose her, and after reading the agreement, he knew exactly what he had to do.

There is only one way I can keep Elizabeth and stay in good standing with my family. I know in doing this, they will have no choice but to accept us, Robert thought.

Although his plan was risky, he believed it would force their hand to accept his and Elizabeth's relationship.

***

During Robert and Elizabeth's relationship, Robert proved to be a true romantic and poet. His poems were original, created just for her. Times when she couldn't be with him, she would pull one from memory, in doing so, it made her feel close to him.

For Robert and Elizabeth, it was difficult for them not to see each other every day as they had been doing before their families learned of their relationship. They had to be extra careful when they arranged to see each other during their family's gatherings. It was risky, but they managed to pull it off.

One day while lying on her bed thinking of Robert, with her need to be close to him, Elizabeth pulled up a couple of Robert's poems from memory.

Elizabeth, my fair, fair lady, where art thou. Oh, here thy are, in front of my eyes. What beauty I see, and all thine beauty is mine. God giveth me such pure beauty, a love, no man has known. My fair, fair lady, my heart thee own.

Elizabeth smiled. Yes, it was silly, but it was all hers – a gift from her beloved.

And this one reminded her of their promise.

My heart is yours for all eternity. Death cannot taketh away, thy love I feel for thee. Elizabeth, Elizabeth, who art thou, but my heart and soul. My heart swells every time I think of thee. I ache, until thy day, I have thee in my arms. Elizabeth, my sweet, sweet Elizabeth, my heart thou own.

"Oh Robert, my heart aches for you now," Elizabeth whispered as she shivered at the memory. *Sighing, how can*

I not love him, she thought.

On the seventh day, when the sun was high in the sky, and once church services had concluded, Robert needed to pull Grace aside to give her a note to deliver to Elizabeth. Robert took Grace's elbow and escorted her away from the others, one to make a show of them being together, and two, he needed her alone and out of earshot.

"Grace, will you give this note to Elizabeth for me please?" Robert asked, slipping Grace the note, which she took and slipped in her sleeve until she could put it in her chatelaine.

Grace looked at Robert and smiled, "Yes, of course I will," she said, touching Robert's upper arm lightly. "Robert, I am sorry for what happened. As you know, I want more than anything for you and Elizabeth to be together. It should be Elizabeth you are marrying, not me. I wish there were a way to change what's happened."

Their situation saddened Grace, but there was nothing to be done. She was doomed to marry Robert, and at the same time, destroy her beloved sister's heart.

God, I wish there were something I could do, she thought.

"Yes, Grace, I know, and thank you. Your support during this time means a great deal to Elizabeth and me. I am sorry for everything. To be forced —"

"Stop, Robert! There is no need to explain."

"Thank you, Grace."

Robert and Grace looked away, not wanting to think about what was to come – their wedding.

***

After returning home from church, Grace grabbed Elizabeth's hand and rushed her through the manor, heading directly to her bedchamber. After Grace closed the door, she handed Elizabeth Robert's note. With excitement, Elizabeth snatched the note from Grace's hand.

With the note in her hand, Elizabeth walked over to the

window, and before she opened it, she took a moment to absorb the feel of the note, knowing, only a short time ago, Robert's hands were where her hands are, and before that, concealed in his tunic close to his heart. Finally, when Elizabeth opened his note, it read:

My love,
I ask you to meet me when the moon is high and join me on a magical sleigh ride around our lake this evening.

Your beloved,
Robert

Elizabeth, in a rush, turned to Grace. "Grace, Robert wants to see me tonight!"

"Elizabeth, what about mother and father, not to mention Lord and Lady Davenport?"

"It is of no matter. We are to meet after everyone's to bed."

"Very well."

Without hesitation, Elizabeth left Grace's chambers to her own. After Elizabeth entered her chamber, she tossed Robert's note on her bed, as she was filled with excitement in what was to come.

Wow, a magical sleigh ride. Robert thinks of the most romantic things, she thought, while wondering how he was going to make it possible.

Elizabeth laid on her bed thinking of what was to come, and due to the lateness of the day, she fell fast asleep without realizing it. She only woke at her sister calling her name. "Elizabeth! Get up! It's a few hours before dinner! You must dress and quick! I will call for your maid!" Grace yelled.

Elizabeth sat up quickly, "Grace, stop! I will dress myself if you will help me?" Elizabeth said with a smile.

Grace nodded and helped Elizabeth dress, then per her request, Grace left her chamber, giving Elizabeth a few moments alone.

As Elizabeth rushed downstairs for dinner, she ran into her mother and father at the bottom of the stairs.

"Elizabeth, why are you rushing? You need to behave like a lady, not a wild child!" her mother scolded. "Ladies, do not rush down the stairs. They glide gracefully," her mother said, in a firm, almost heartless voice.

Elizabeth rolled her eyes, "Mother, father, I am sorry. I did not want to be late for dinner. I know how you feel about being on time," she said, walking next to her mother and father to the dining room.

In a firm voice, "Very well. It is time you start to act like a lady, Elizabeth. You are too old for this wild behavior."

Again, Elizabeth rolled her eyes. She nodded as she said, "Yes, mother."

At the tone of her mother's voice, Elizabeth wondered, *will they ever stop hating me?* Then she sighed, *do not think of them and how they feel. Think of tonight and the magical sleigh ride you will have with Robert,* she thought.

Elizabeth smiled and forgot about the way her mother talked to her and proceeded to have a nice dinner with her family and the Davenports.

When Robert saw Elizabeth enter the dining room with Baron and Baroness Massey, it took all his power to keep from looking at her, except the brief moment when she entered the room, he noticed how beautiful and radiant she looked.

Their time with their family in the same room was the hardest time for Robert and Elizabeth. They knew if they were caught looking at each other, Elizabeth would be shipped off to France. Therefore, they used all their power and strength to maintain control, knowing they were closely watched, not only by their families but by the servants who were ordered to do so. Robert and Elizabeth were reduced to using the corner of their eyes, or when they roamed around looking at the others during conversation, would they glance at each other.

Later that evening, when everyone was in bed, Elizabeth went to her wardrobe, knowing the exact gown she was going to wear. She pulled out her gown and tossed it on her bed. Normally, she would call for her maid to assist her, but she couldn't take the chance – too many questions would arise – *and she might tell father,* she thought.

Elizabeth sat at her dressing table fixing her hair the way Robert liked it, and after a quick wash, she began the tedious effort of putting on her gown, *only the best will do for a magical sleigh ride,* she thought.

Her gown was made of red and gold french silk. The front of her gown had gold with red cross-stitching throughout, along with red strips on each side, and the back of her gown was solid gold. It was the perfect gown for the Holiday season and a magical sleigh ride.

After dawning her gown, Elizabeth grabbed her white fur cloak and gloves, and before walking out of her chamber, she stopped in front of the mirror to admire herself, to make sure she looked perfect.

"Perfect, now I am ready to see my beloved," she said to her reflection.

Before Elizabeth left her chamber, she quickly looked around, and this was when she noticed Robert's note sitting on her bed. She snatched it up as she thought, *oh God, I left this when I went down for dinner, and if any of the servants saw this* – she shook her head and pushed that thought out of her mind, then proceeded to fold Robert's note back up and carefully placed it inside the bottom of her chest.

***

While Robert was at the lake waiting for Elizabeth, knowing winter was her favorite time of the year, and how she loved the coldness of the snow. Robert shook his head; he always thought she was mad in the way she loved the cold so much.

With the fresh snow, after a recent snowfall, Robert thought, *this is perfect. Elizabeth is going to love the fresh snow, as she would say, 'it's the best time, nothing nor anyone has spoiled it. To be the first one to touch or play in the snow is glorious.'*

The freshly fallen snow made this night even more magical, with what he had planned, more so than he first hoped. *Our lake will truly be a romantic and magical of all nights, he thought.*

When Elizabeth arrived at the lake – just the sight of her left Robert breathless, as his heart seemed to stop beating.

God in heaven, how beautiful she is, the way she is standing there in her white fur cloak, and her dark hair peeking through her hood, falling over her shoulders, Robert thought.

When Elizabeth saw Robert, she was beaming with excitement, her happiness radiating through her eyes. Even though Elizabeth was standing right in front of Robert, he found he could not move. He just stood there staring at her.

Elizabeth smiled; she loved the way he looked at her and decided not to speak. Instead, she waited patiently for Robert to say something. *He likes it,* she thought.

When Robert finally broke his hypnotic stare, he took Elizabeth's hand in his, and when he did, he got a glimpse of her gown, but a glimpse was not enough, he had to see all of it. So, he slowly and carefully pulled open her cloak, revealing her beautiful gown.

"Oh, Elizabeth, how beautiful you are. You are truly breathtaking. Will you remove your cloak, so I may see the fullness of your gown?" he asked.

Elizabeth smiled. She was pleased with Robert's reaction and did as he asked. It didn't matter that it was freezing; she felt nothing except Robert's love.

"Oh, Elizabeth, it is exquisite. Beautiful."

Robert loved her gown; she was the most beautiful sight he has ever beheld, and he took a step back to admire her better.

"Your gown radiates with your golden skin and brown hair…beautiful," he said, as he thought, *God, thank you for this beauty, of this woman standing before me.* Then realizing the cold, "You must be cold, how foolish of me. Here," he wrapped her cloak around her, then took her hand to help her into the sleigh as he slid in next to her. Unable to wait any longer, Robert gathered Elizabeth into his arms and kissed her. It seemed as if time stopped, with fluttering in their stomachs. The beating of Elizabeth's heart escalated as she felt the softness of his mouth against hers.

Their kissing ignited their building passion, and Robert knew he had to pull away, but found it was too difficult to tear himself away from her, but he must. So reluctantly, he forced himself to release Elizabeth, then hit the reins for the horses to start moving, thus, beginning their magical sleigh ride around their lake.

Elizabeth was left breathless after Robert's passionate kiss, but once she gathered herself, she looked around and was amazed by the beauty of their lake. Then a question came to her, "Robert, how did you get a horse and sleigh through the trees?"

Robert smiled, "It was with great difficulty. I had to move the tree branches, with having to cut some away, but not enough to reveal our secret place, as I am sure you noticed when you arrived."

Elizabeth shook her head no; she could not tell anything had been disturbed.

As they continued their sleigh ride, it was a beautiful night, with the stars and moon shining bright. Elizabeth looked around and noticed how peaceful and beautiful their lake was, more so than any other night.

"Robert, this is a wonderful surprise. It is so beautiful this evening, more so than any other night. Would you not agree?" Elizabeth said, looking around in awe.

At first, Robert could only smile, but then he said, "Yes, Elizabeth, it is. It's as beautiful as you are."

Elizabeth turned to look at Robert, "Robert," she said in a small whisper, as she turned to look at the lake and its surroundings, "Thank you, Robert, this is a beautiful and wonderful gift."

Robert was filled with pure and utter joy as he watched Elizabeth admiring the lake.

"Robert," she said, turning to look directly in his eyes.

He saw there was something important she wanted to say, so he pulled on the reins and brought the horse to a complete stop.

"Robert," she said again, placing her hand on his, "I love you so much. My heart hurts from the love I feel for you."

Without taking his eyes from Elizabeth, he said, "Elizabeth, I love you more than life itself. There is nothing I wouldn't do for you. And yes, I have never seen our lake look more beautiful than it does right now. Though, I believe it is due to your beauty."

Elizabeth smiled. She was amazed that she could feel so happy after what happened, but she was, she was so very happy and very much in love with Robert Davenport.

After a moment, she returned her attention to the scene around them, then pointed to the trees, "Robert, look at how the icicles are hanging from the trees. See how the light from the moon and stars are piercing through, shimmering off the icicles to the water below, glistening off the icy lake. With the beautiful fresh snow…ah…it is…breathtaking. Robert, our lake has transformed into a beautiful and magical place.

Robert marveled at the sight of Elizabeth, the way she found pleasure in the littlest things. He couldn't help basking in her beauty. How her beauty intermingles with the beauty of this magical night. To see the look of pure joy and excitement shining in her eyes, and after recent events, made his heart swell, sending tingles through his body.

"My love…to know…to feel…to know I can bring you such joy and pleasure, warms my heart. The look in your eyes makes my heart burst with the love I feel for you," Robert said, placing a hand over his heart as he caresses her face.

As Robert resumed their ride around the lake, with the moon and stars glistening off the icicles to the water and snow below, Robert and Elizabeth felt as if heaven itself was shining down on them, blessing them and their love. A love that started as friendship, then grew into the most powerful, amazing, and unbelievable love, that anyone could ever imagine. To have such a love, given to them by God, truly was one of the greatest gifts anyone could ever have bestowed to them.

After Robert and Elizabeth marveled at the beauty of their night together, Robert again brought the horse to a halt. It was time to reveal his reasons for asking her to meet him. Once the horse was at ease, Robert turned and took Elizabeth's face in his hands.

Looking directly in her eyes, "Elizabeth, my love, you are the love of my life, my heart and soul. There are no words enough to express the love I feel for you or how much you mean to me. You are my reason for being. Our hearts are connected, in a way, for when we are apart, it feels as if my heart is being ripped from my chest, trying to find its way back to you."

Elizabeth felt his love and knew exactly what he was saying, as she felt it too. Her heart ached until they were together again. Filled with emotion, Elizabeth was unable to speak; instead, she nodded in understanding.

"What I am about to do will be going against our families," Robert said, staring into her eyes, caressing her face while softly rubbing her hands. "For us to deny what we feel, in the love we found, this gift is given to us by God…how can we forget and walk away from this love?" shaking his head, "We cannot. We should not. Not after God has given us this love," he said, as he thought, *beautiful, and she is all mine, and soon to be my wife.*

Robert was mesmerized by Elizabeth's beauty and her smile. He didn't need her words; he could see how she felt for him, and he could see her love for him in her eyes.

"God Elizabeth, I love you so much," he said, placing his hands on both sides of her face.

Elizabeth, suddenly feeling bashful, closed her eyes as she slightly lowered her head, unable to look at him. She needed a moment to absorb his words, his feelings for her, combined with her feelings for him. Then, she slowly placed her hand over his, giving it a soft caress.

Robert lifted her chin to face him, and when Elizabeth opened her eyes to meet his, and their eyes connected, a feeling unknown struck them with a sharp pain that penetrated the center of their hearts, deeper, as if it pierced their souls – a remembrance of two souls, bonded for eternity.

"There is not a day when we part…when I count the days when we are together again. To touch you, to have your arms around me…" he had to stop. His love for this woman was overwhelming him – taking his breath away. Once he gathered his emotions, he continued?

"…the thought…" his voice cracked, "…of life without you. Not being able to hold you. To kiss these beautiful lips," he rubs his thumb across her lips, causing Elizabeth to smile.

For Elizabeth to see Robert become so emotional, it filled her with joy, as well as pain.

To never again touch or feel him. To never again know of his kiss, nor have his arms around me, she thought. This broke her heart as she was engulfed with fear.

"…To never be able to make love to you again. The three times we made love…" seeing her fear, "…do not fear my love, our love and passion connected us in a way no marriage could. Our love and passion are of the highest level…" they were no longer one single soul, but two souls intertwined as one. "…there is no Robert without Elizabeth." Picking up Elizabeth's hands, "…Elizabeth, will you…with all my heart," placing his hand over his heart, "Will you honor me, by excepting to live your life with me, in becoming my wife?"

Elizabeth gasped as her eyes widened. She was shocked, stunned at hearing his words. She could not believe it, and it left her breathless. She had prepared herself for a life without Robert, then to hear him ask her to be his wife, she did not know what to say, all she could do was stare at him, as she looked deep into his eyes, wondering if he was serious and if she heard him correctly.

Yes, I did. He means what he says, she thought.

Robert was right; there was no Robert without Elizabeth. What he was asking of her, she knew was wrong, but at the same time, she could not resist.

Robert watched Elizabeth intently. It was clear he shocked her. It wasn't what she expected, and this pleased him, but he also saw her struggling to give him an answer. It didn't matter, as he knew what her answer would be.

She will say yes, he thought.

As Elizabeth watched Robert, she saw the assurance and the confidence on his face. He knew what her answer would be, and he was right. There was no Elizabeth without Robert. Their love was original, unique. There were no words to express how they felt, for the love they felt for each other had no words. When this day came, Elizabeth always knew what her answer would be if Robert asked her to marry him and at that moment, right or wrong, it didn't matter. Only their love did.

With tears in her eyes, Elizabeth jumped into Robert's

arms and said, "Yes-yes, oh God, yes, with all my heart, I will marry you!"

Robert laughed as he thought, *well, it appears she is over her shock.*

Elizabeth clings to Robert, wanting to be a part of him, body and soul as she thought, *to be with Robert for the rest of my life…to marry him, it will be perfect. There could be no question if we married on the holiest day in the land, Christmas Day.*

Elizabeth released her embrace from Robert and looked directly into his eyes. "I will only marry you…if you promise to marry me on Christmas Day. To marry on the holiest day in the land and in a church, a house of God, no one will dare question us. It will be a blessed union," Elizabeth said, filled with excitement.

Robert burst with joy at Elizabeth answer as he thought, *yes, she is right. We will marry on the holiest day in the land.*

Robert took her in his arms and held her tight against his chest. "Elizabeth, you have made me the happiest man in the land. Yes, you are right. We will marry on the holiest day in the land. You could not have picked a better day."

***

After returning home from her magical night with Robert, Elizabeth couldn't wait to tell her sister and share her happy news. Once she reached Grace's chambers, she didn't waste her time in knocking and opened the door. Once she was inside and closed the door behind her, she blurted out, "Grace, I have great news!" she said with excitement.

Grace was unable to sleep, so when Elizabeth barged into her chamber, she was seated on her bed reading her book. Although she was irritated by her sister's disturbance, she quickly put aside her irritation and book after seeing Elizabeth's joy and excitement.

Elizabeth rushed to her sister and sat on her bed, pulling

her into a tight embrace. It was so tight; Grace felt as if she couldn't breathe.

"Elizabeth, what is it? What happened?" Grace asked.

Elizabeth released her sister and sat back on her heels, "Oh Grace," she said, looking away, recalling every detail of what happened. "Grace, it was the most beautiful night I have ever experienced," she said, moving away from Grace's bed, going over to the window, to stare out into the night as she recalled what happened. "Grace, Robert took me on a magical sleigh ride," turning back to look at her sister, "It was as if God opened the heavens and shined down it's light, wrapping Robert and me in his love, giving us his blessing."

Grace moved off her bed and went directly to her sister and took Elizabeth's hands in hers, then pulled her to the edge of the bed and sat down. "Tell me, sister? Tell me what happened?"

After sitting for a few moments, but feeling too excited to sit, Elizabeth jumped off the bed and started pacing.

Do I tell her? What would she think? Would she think I was mad? No, of course not. She loves me and will support me, she thought.

Elizabeth calmed herself, then returned to the bed and sat down. She put her hands over Grace's, which were resting in her lap. "Grace, Robert asked me to marry him," Elizabeth said. Without waiting for a response, "Can you believe it? I am to be his wife. Oh, Grace, this is what I have dreamed of."

Elizabeth leapt off the bed and pulled her sister with her, then spun them in a circle until Grace became too dizzy to stand anymore.

Grace pulled away from Elizabeth, then carefully walked to the edge of her bed and sat down. After Grace gave herself a few moments for the dizziness to subside, is when it hit her, she could not believe what she just heard. *This is mad. What was she thinking?* she thought.

Grace was flabbergasted by Elizabeth's news. Unable to speak, she just sat there watching her sister, seeing how happy she was. *How can she be so foolish?* she thought.

Grace sighed, knowing what she had to do. "Elizabeth, what you told me cannot be true. You cannot marry Robert. If mother and father discover —"

Elizabeth rushed to Grace and stopped her. "Grace, do not worry. It is as I said. It will be all right, you will see. We will be careful. Once we are married, mother and father, along with Lord and Lady Davenport, will have to accept us. And you, my dear sister, will be free," she said, but still saw the worry on Grace's face, "Grace, we will marry on the holiest day in the land, and in Gods house, by a priest. A marriage done so cannot be broken, nor could it be denied."

"Elizabeth, I —" Grace attempted to say before Elizabeth stopped her.

"Grace," she took her hands and placed them over her heart, "Do you feel my heart beating?" Grace nodded. "This heart, in my chest, beats for Robert. When we are not together, it feels lost, broken, as if a part of it has been torn from my chest. Right now, it beats with joy. It knows once we are married, nothing can tear us apart again."

Grace watched and listened to her sister, and her words affected her. Elizabeth and Robert have genuinely found a powerful love. One, no one should be allowed to deny. But she couldn't help but think of the ramifications if they were to marry.

Elizabeth still saw the worry and fear on her sister's face, so she continued, "Grace, do you believe Robert and I should be together?" she asked, looking at her sister with so much love in her eyes.

"You know I do," Grace said, not being able to look at Elizabeth.

"Then you must be happy for me, sister. I will have my love and happiness, and you will have your freedom."

Grace could not deny what Elizabeth said. She wants her freedom more than anything. She doesn't want to marry Robert, the one her sister loves so much.

If only I could be so lucky to find the love Elizabeth found with Robert, she thought and felt a little jealous at Elizabeth's good fortune.

Elizabeth was still watching Grace; then, she began to worry as she was engulfed with fear. If her sister isn't with her, she doesn't know how this will work. "Do you want to marry Robert, knowing how he feels about me and me about him?"

Grace shook her head. No, she didn't and reflected on what Elizabeth said. No, she could not deny what she said. Grace wants this for her sister and herself, but to go against her mother and father, not to mention Lord and Lady Davenport, was wrong.

Oh, now you feel it is wrong. Not before all this happened. It is all your fault, so you should support your sister and Robert's decision, she thought. But the thought of what could happen when they are discovered, *she knows I do not want to be married to Robert. A man who clearly loves my sister. But for what they are thinking of doing is wrong, but how can I deny them.* Shaking her head, *I cannot.*

Elizabeth understood her sister's fears; it's what she feared as well. But after tonight, it felt right. Elizabeth tried to reassure her sister, "Grace, Robert is the eldest son and heir. There is nothing his family can do to him. There is a chance for mother and father to disown me, and if they do, I will still have Robert and you. Grace, I am safe. We will be alright."

Grace could not look at Elizabeth as she thought, *what am I to say to that?*

Elizabeth patiently waited; at the same time, she was on edge about what her sister will say. She wanted Grace to look at her and see the joy and happiness in marrying

Robert would bring her. She needed to try again to convince her sister.

"Grace, have faith in God and us. God brought Robert and me together, he gave us this great love, and once we are married, we will be bonded as man and wife."

Grace finally looked at her sister. She wants this for Elizabeth, *and I want it for myself,* she thought with sadness. Seeing the joy on Elizabeth's face when she first told her they were to be married – it was decided that she will stand by Elizabeth for the love of her sister, no matter what happens.

"Alright, Elizabeth," was all Grace said? But it was all Elizabeth needed.

Chapter Seventeen

Soon, the Massey's will travel to Bramhall Manor to celebrate Christmas, and then in spring, the upcoming wedding of Robert and Grace. For Robert and Elizabeth to marry, they had to find a way, an excuse to keep them from attending the Christmas celebrations. The only reason they could think of was their raw feelings for one another. This excuse was ideal for Elizabeth, but for Robert, it may prove to be fruitless. However, it was imperative they did not attend such a happy celebration.

Since Lord Davenport was in London, the only person Robert could speak to was his mother. Although Elizabeth's mother and father were cordial to her, it was clear they were still angry, so Elizabeth would need to elicit her sister's help before approaching her father since Grace was his favorite.

Before Robert went to his mother, he went to his special place in the woods. He needed to think, to figure out what he was going to say. How he was going to make this happen. He needed to be able to sneak away from Bramhall Manor without being seen by anyone in the household or in the stables, but then, how would they explain his horse being missing. Would they even question it? Possibly. However, they might think his horse was stolen and alert his mother, which he could not allow to happen.

I could pretend to go for a ride, with the need to clear my head. Or, I need to get away, unable to bear...seeing the joy from everyone, when I'm in so much pain, and to see Elizabeth...wait... shaking his head, no, that will not do. Elizabeth will not be here. They will know this once the Massey's arrive.

Robert had to think; he needed another idea, but what?

Well then, I will use the excuse, with the pain I feel in my heart, I am broken from the loss of Elizabeth, I could not bear to be around so many happy people. If only for a short time, I need to stay away from the festivities.

And so, it was decided, by the time his absence was noticed, he would be far away from the land.

The next obstacle was to decide how to get to Elizabeth and then the church.

A church, where am I going to find a church that will marry us, and without the churches consent, or with the need to travel to Scotland. Go to Scotland! Shaking his head, *it would take too long, and we would surely be discovered since father would send his best men after us, but father is in London, and by the time he learns we are missing, it would take him several days to arrive, let alone find us in Scotland before we are married.* Robert shook his head. *No, it is still too far to travel.*

Robert continued to pace in a circle as he pondered where he could find a church. There have been many places he's travelled in his young life, so there must be a place. He just has to recall one from memory.

The church must be a reasonable distance away from Cheshire and Manchester and would not notify our families before marrying us.

After walking several rounds, it suddenly hit him —

Robert snapped his fingers – *I have it. The Tavern. I heard of a church near Yorkshire the last time I was there with father and Edward. It will be a long and hard ride…* he stopped in mid-thought – *for this, it might prove too difficult for Elizabeth.* Robert smiled, *no, not for my Elizabeth. She is strong and determined and would endure whatever pain if it means we'll be together. From what I heard, the distance and seclusion of the church would be perfect. From what the man said in the Tavern, it was a church that stood…that survived after the great battle during War of the Roses. I must learn more information, but how, and without stirring up questions. Maybe I can return to the Tavern and find the man who mentioned the church.*

If they were to go to this church, Robert knew it would take more time than they had. After further consideration, Robert decided he would inquire about hiring a driver and carriage in a village outside of Cheshire and Manchester. Hopefully, it will be one on the route they would be travelling. There was much Robert had to do. For the moment, he needed to gather his courage to speak to his mother.

***

Back at Bramhall Manor, Robert approached his mother in her parlor.

"Mother, may I speak with you?" he asked.

Lady Davenport was sitting in the chair next to the window in her parlor, that gave her the light she needed to do her needlework. When she heard Robert enter, she immediately put down her needlework, to give Robert her full attention.

"Yes, Robert, how may I help you?"

"Mother, I am sorry, but I cannot attend the Christmas celebration. It is too much to ask of me," he said, lowering his head. He felt sorrow and shame in lying to his mother, but he had no choice. "I am sorry, but to ask me to do so…to force me to pretend that Grace and I are this happy couple…to do so with Elizabeth…no," shaking his head. "It is too much to ask of me and too cruel. I am a strong man, but only for so long. Please, mother, do not ask this of me? I cannot do so. To do so would cause me great pain, not to mention Elizabeth's pain. This, I could not bear," he said, unable to look at his mother.

Lady Davenport watched her son as he made his request, and it broke her heart to see how much pain he was in. What should she do? Does she give in, or does she force him to attend the party and bear the pain she knows he would suffer?

No! I cannot do this. Before I decide, I must know more, she thought.

"My son, before I decide," Lady Davenport stood and took her son's hand, then led him to the two-seated chair, "Sit with me and tell me more about your feelings for Elizabeth? I know we have talked of this after your father left, but…help me see…to understand…tell me more?"

Robert sat next to his mother, debating how much he should tell her. Yes, he told her much after his father left, but was it enough?

"What I feel for Elizabeth…how can I put this in words, to where you will understand," Robert said, taking a moment to gather his thoughts on the best way to tell his mother of the love he found with Elizabeth.

"Our love is wordless. It's a feeling deep in our heart and souls. Never did I believe I could find love, let alone the deep and utter love I feel for Elizabeth."

Lady Davenport watched her son intently, watching his expression, the look in his eyes, to see if the feelings he claims is true.

"Mother, the love Elizabeth and I share," Robert said, deciding to hold nothing back, wanting his mother to see his feelings for Elizabeth is real. "It is a gift from God. When we are together, my heart swells when I am near her," he said with excitement. "And when we are apart, it feels as if my heart is being ripped from my chest," as pain laced his voice, "Wanting desperately to reunite with hers. It's as if an unknown thread was pulling at my heart, a need to re-join with hers, and in doing so, connecting our hearts, making them whole once again."

When Lady Davenport heard this, her heart ached to feel what her son felt and thought, *to be able to feel such a love.*

"How can Elizabeth and I be asked to endure such pain. To do so would be as if you are asking me to thrust a dagger in my chest, piercing my heart."

Robert's anger began to swell, along with his pain. He sighed, letting go of his anger, then turned away, unable to look at his mother. His feelings – the emotional loss he was feeling; he could not bear for his mother to see.

When Lady Davenport heard her son's words and saw the love and pain in his eyes, her heart ached for her son. She wanted to help him – *but how?* she thought.

"Robert, I want to help you, but my hands are tied. There's nothing I wouldn't do for you," she said.

What could I do for him? Yes, I can speak to John, but will he listen to me? This, I know naught, she thought.

Resigned, Lady Davenport was willing to try. "When your father returns from London, I will speak to him. I do not believe it will do any good, but I am willing to try. For now, I grant you leave, but only this one time." Touching her son's arm, "But Robert, once you and Grace are married, you will not be able to avoid Elizabeth. You need to be prepared for this," she said in a soft and gentle voice.

No, I will not, because Elizabeth and I will already be married, Robert thought.

"If my conversation with your father proves no good, as I believe it will, you must find a way to let go of your feelings for Elizabeth."

Lady Davenport reached for her son, placing her hand on his face, looking at him with so much love and sorrow, then she embraced her son.

"Oh, mother," falling into his mother's embrace. "I will pray father will listen to you and accept Elizabeth as the one I should marry."

If mother is on my side, once we are married, father will eventually accept us, if not at first, then in time, he thought.

***

Each day as Robert and Elizabeth's elopement – their wedding day grew closer, Elizabeth struggled to keep hold of her excitement. She knew if her mother and father discovered their plans to marry in secret, she would be shipped off to France, losing Robert forever. Understanding the seriousness of their secrecy, she took hold of herself, reigning in her excitement, and decided to seek her sister's help to bring her emotions under control.

Once at Grace's door, Elizabeth walked in without knocking.

"Grace, I have need of your help?"

"Elizabeth, what is it?" Grace said, sounding irritated.

Elizabeth hesitated for a moment, but she knew that her sister would help her no matter what.

"Grace, I am so excited to marry Robert that I am afraid mother and father will discover the truth. Have you heard or noticed anything of my behavior that would have given me away?"

"Elizabeth, if you are determined to marry Robert, then you must be careful. To be careless now, you risk being shipped off to France. No, I have not noticed anything for you to be concerned about, and I do not believe mother and father suspect anything."

"I know. I know. Oh, good. There is something else I need to ask you."

Grace looked at Elizabeth with a questionable eye, but she nodded for her to continue.

"I need your help…I need an excuse that will keep me from going to Bramhall Manor for Christmas celebration. I think…well, if I ask father if he will let me stay home so I will not be a distraction to Robert…this will allow everyone to relax so they could enjoy the Christmas festivities. What do you think?"

"Elizabeth —" Grace attempted to say, but Elizabeth interrupted her.

"Grace," stopping her sister from speaking, "Do you really think they will mind? I believe they would be grateful for me to stay behind. Grace, I know this is a great deal to ask of you, but I must stay here. Robert and I are going to meet at our special place before we leave to marry. It will be easier for Robert to travel on horseback alone from Bramhall Manor than the two of us…it will be less chance of us being seen on the road."

Elizabeth hesitated on what she needed to ask her sister next. "Grace…well, I also need you…well," Elizabeth looked down at her hands, twisting the front of her gown, "I need you to be the one to tell father."

This is mad. I cannot believe I am helping them, Grace thought, then she heard a voice in her mind, *if you had not forced them together, this would never have happened.*

Grace rolled her eyes, but she could not deny the truth. Shaking her head, then turned to face Elizabeth, "What…no Elizabeth! That is too much to ask of me," Grace said, but the little voice in her head said, *it was you who forced this to happen.* Grace knew when she was defeated, "What am I to say?" she asked.

Elizabeth flinched by her sister's outburst, then was surprised and pleased she was willing to assist her.

"Grace, father adores you. For him to hear it from you…well, he would be more amenable, when…if it were me, he would yell at me. Please, Grace, you must do this for me?" Elizabeth pleaded.

Grace was looking at her sister with utter disbelieve, but Elizabeth was not wrong to fear their father, after all, their mother and father were still very angry with her, but Grace could not be the one who talks to their father; it must be Elizabeth.

She let out her breath, "Elizabeth, I don't agree that what you are doing is right, but I will speak to father," she said, taking Elizabeth's hand. "Elizabeth, I am afraid for you," looking directly into her eyes, "There are times when mother and father, not knowing I am near, speak of this agreement, that if they allowed you to marry Robert, it would destroy everything they worked so hard for."

When Elizabeth heard this, she looked away from Grace, unable to bear to see the fear and anguish on her sister's face.

Grace pulled on Elizabeth's hand and upper arm to force Elizabeth to face her. "Elizabeth, I am afraid, and I fear when they find out you married in secret, they will be furious. I cannot bear to think about what they will do, but you are right, they will disown you, and when that happens, I will lose my sister, and I am not sure —"

"Grace, stop. You will not lose me," she said, placing her hand over Grace's, "If mother and father disown me, which I am sure they will…Grace, you are your own person. You will visit me. This I am sure of," she said with a smile. "Have faith sister, God will see us through this, this I am sure of. Please trust me and believe in God."

Although doubtful, Grace agreed to help Elizabeth but was afraid that Elizabeth doesn't understand the seriousness and the ramifications of what they were going to do. What else can she do? She loves her sister and doesn't want to marry Robert. This will save her and bring Elizabeth the happiness she deserves. Grace would do whatever was necessary to make that happen.

***

The following day, When Elizabeth arrived at their lake, she saw Robert waiting for her.

Robert turned when he heard footsteps and was pleased to see Elizabeth. "Elizabeth!" he shouted, rushing to her as he took her in his arms, "You look beautiful as always."

Elizabeth beamed at the sight of Robert, and when he took her in his arms, she melted into his embrace. "Oh, Robert, I love you so much. I have missed you terribly."

Robert and Elizabeth remained in each other's arms for a few moments before Robert released her and guided her to the bench.

"Elizabeth, I discreetly made inquiries, and in those inquiries, I found a church with a priest who is willing to marry us without question. Alas, it is a good distance away, and it will take us half the day, if not the full day to reach our destination. If we leave by horse and ride to the village outside of Cheshire, I can arrange for a carriage to take us the rest of the way. We will need to move at high speed for us to make it on time."

As Elizabeth listened to Robert, all she could do was smile, and she was willing to suffer whatever discomfort was needed to be with Robert – to marry him.

"Once we are married, I want to stop at an Inn on our way back," Robert said with a smile, "So we can spend our first night as husband and wife before we face our families."

Elizabeth looked at Robert and blushed at the thought. She wanted the same thing. "I will do whatever is required, so long as we are together…married."

***

After Elizabeth returned home, she went directly to speak to Grace. It was time to speak to their father, but they had yet to form a plan.

"Grace, how can we convince father to allow me to remain behind from attending the Christmas celebrations."

"Elizabeth, it's simple enough. We simply tell father it would be best to keep you and Robert away from each other, not wanting to cause any uneasiness."

Grace's reasoning for this was: to have Elizabeth presence around Robert would be a distraction, a painful reminder they could not be together. A holy day as Christmas should be surrounded by the merriment of people. It was not right, nor fair, to force Elizabeth and Robert to endure such a joyous occasion when they would be miserable – too painful.

Elizabeth couldn't believe it could be so simple and had to ask, "Grace, do you believe it's that's simple?"

"Yes. Mother and father would do anything to prevent further conflicts by having you and Robert in the same room. This, I am sure of."

"Do you believe I am the one to speak to father…alone?" Elizabeth hesitantly asked.

"Yes, I do. Since I already agreed, I will accompany you."

Elizabeth let out a sigh of relief, "Oh Grace, thank you."

That evening after dinner, when their father was in his study, Grace believed it was the best time to speak to their father. With Elizabeth by her side, Grace knocked on their father's study door.

Baron Massey was busy at his desk, dealing with the day's matters, when he heard a knock on his door. Usually, when his doors closed, it was a sign he was not to be disturbed. But he recognized the soft knock to be his daughter Grace. If she came to see him during the evening, it was important, and he could not deny her.

"Come," he called.

Grace entered her father's study with Elizabeth following behind, "Good evening, father. I am sorry to disturb you this evening, but I have Elizabeth with me," Elizabeth stepped from behind Grace to stand by her side. Her father gave her a questionable eye, but this did not deter Grace, "We wish to speak with you about Elizabeth going to Bramhall Manor for Christmas."

Baron Massey was not surprised by this request, nor that Elizabeth elicited Grace's help, knowing Grace was his favorite. He always had a soft heart for Grace since the day she was born. He wanted to show the same favoritism to Elizabeth and his son, but it never happened, and he never understood why.

"Very well," Baron Massey said.

Grace and Elizabeth looked at each other, confirming they were really going to do this. Without hesitation, Grace turned to her father and began explaining their reason for disturbing him.

"Father, with what happened between Robert and Elizabeth," looking at Elizabeth, "Elizabeth and I, well…we were talking and…well, we feel…" Grace glanced at Elizabeth, "For everyone's best interest, Elizabeth should not accompany us to Bramhall Manor. Instead, she should remain here."

Baron Massey raised his eye in question as he asked, "What brought this on?" turning to look at Elizabeth. "Elizabeth, you cannot continue hiding from Robert. Once your sister and Robert are married, hiding out in your woods or in your chambers will not do," Baron Massey said, seeing the surprise look on Elizabeth's face. He smiled, "You think I did not know you go to those woods every day. I know your every move around this manor and land. There is nothing you can hide from me," he said.

Elizabeth looked at Grace as she thought, *does he know?* Grace did not have the answers, so they did their best to remain unaffected by their father's words.

Elizabeth turned to her father and said, "I am sorry, father."

"You cannot go the rest of your life, by avoiding your sister and Robert being together. If you feel it's too difficult, then we will send you to —"

"No!" Elizabeth interrupted her father. Then knowing she had to be careful, she regained control of her feelings. "Father, please," she pleaded, trying not to panic. "I know I must deal with them, but sending me away will not help. I promise father, I will come to terms with what is to happen. With Christmas being a time of joy and happiness, to be forced to watch Robert with Grace will be too difficult. I do not want anything to happen that would ruin the festivities. It is best for everyone I do not attend," she said.

Baron Massey watched his daughter intently, looking for something, anything that would give him a reason to be concerned, but saw nothing. He only saw a scared child who made a grave mistake. He didn't hate Elizabeth; he loved her. Yes, it's true he didn't treat her the same as he treated Grace, but he came to admire her. She was a strong girl who did not need to be coddled.

Maybe, that was my mistake. Maybe, I should have paid more attention to Elizabeth. But in this matter, I need to be firm. To show weakness would be a grave mistake, he thought.

"Elizabeth, if that is how you feel, it will be best to send you to France before Grace and Robert are married. The distance might do you both good," Baron Massey said.

Elizabeth panicked – Grace and Elizabeth looked at each other, and Grace saw Elizabeth's fear, and they had to find a way to change their father's mind.

"Father, please do not. I promise, before Grace marries Robert, I will be fine. Right now, it is still too painful. I only ask, you allow me this time, and I promise to do better," Elizabeth pleaded.

Grace added, "Father, it was my mistake in what happened between Robert and Elizabeth," Grace said, placing her arm around Elizabeth's waist. "Father, you are aware it was not their fault alone. If I had not insisted Elizabeth help me avoid spending time with Robert, this would never have happened. So, I ask you, for me, will you please, this once, as Christmas is a special time, not force Elizabeth and Robert to endure seeing each other. To do so would be a grave mistake and too cruel. I ask you, father, as a favor to me, please allow Elizabeth to remain behind?"

Baron Massey watched his daughters intently, and he too believed it was best Robert and Elizabeth do not see each other.

The temptation would be too much, he thought.

"Very well," turning his attention to Elizabeth, "This will be my only concession in this matter. You either endure it, or you will be sent to France. Is this understood?"

Elizabeth couldn't look at her father, so, looking down at her feet, she said, "Yes, father. Thank you, father." Grace and Elizabeth curtsied, then left their father's study and returned to Grace's chamber.

Once they were in Grace's chamber, she wasted no time

voicing her concerns.

"Elizabeth, be careful, if mother and father find out…oh Elizabeth, I could not bear to think what they might do when they discover your plan, they will send you away, and I could not bear to not have my sister by my side."

"Grace," taking her sister's hands, "Do not worry. Once Robert and I are married…yes, they will be angry, but in time, I am sure they will come to accept us. Once we are married, there will be nothing they can do to us."

"I am sure you are right, Elizabeth, but…I do not know, I have a bad feeling about this. Please, Elizabeth, you must be careful."

Grace did not know what to say or do, only what Elizabeth and Robert were doing was wrong, and it terrified her of what their actions might cause. She cannot explain it; it was a feeling that something terrible was going to happen, in what they were about to do.

However, it didn't matter, and she already committed to helping Robert and Elizabeth. She wanted more than anything for them to be happy, in turn, make herself happy.

But is this the right way to go about it? Is it possible; what I am feeling is nothing, just me worrying too much? Yes, that must be it. Everything will be well, I am sure of it, she thought, but was she really.

Elizabeth hugged Grace and kissed her on the cheek, then to relieve Grace of her worry, she said, "Grace, you will see, everything will be well. Ease yourself sister, do not worry, it will be well." Elizabeth again kissed her sister on the cheek, then turned and left her chamber.

***

Once Elizabeth was in her chamber and lying on the bed, she thought about everything that happened. Was what she and Robert were about to do, was it right? Will this cause more harm than good? These were questions she could not answer. In a way, she knew what she was about to do was wrong, but she didn't care. The only thing that mattered at that moment was her love for Robert and his for her. Their love was rare and should not be denied for any reason.

I love him more than life itself. I could not endure a life without Robert. I could not live without him, Elizabeth thought.

Whatever she was thinking did not matter. She would marry Robert, risking their family's wrath.

Once Elizabeth fell asleep, she dreamed about her future with Robert.

Robert and Elizabeth were married and happy with her sister by her side. What she didn't see was her mother and father, nor the Davenport's. Everyone seemed well, with no unknown disaster, and she was pregnant with their first child. But there was no joy, only sorrow, and she wondered, how can this be? she thought. The dream continued – there was sorrow, pain, but through it all was the love she felt for Robert and the love he felt for her. Their love never wavered; it only grew stronger.

Elizabeth woke up. "What does this mean? Is it a forewarn prediction or my own fears?"

It was decided it was her own fears, so she brushed the dream aside and went back to sleep. The problem with this, her dream was more than just her fears, but a prediction. One that would go awry.

The night before the Massey's were to travel to Bramhall Manor, Elizabeth went to see Grace. She needed her help once again. Her father requested to see her before they left for Bramhall Manor, and she was afraid to face him alone. Since her mother and father found out about her and Robert, her mother was still very angry with her. There wasn't a day that went by; her mother did not show disappointment in Elizabeth. Her mother was adamant the agreement be honored, for if not, it would be of great peril.

For Elizabeth, this made no sense, nor did Grace

understand it as well. *What could be in the agreement to cause such a reaction?* Elizabeth thought. Her mother said it was crucial the agreement be honored. *Why?* she wondered.

Although her father had no harsh words to Elizabeth, it was worse. He ignored her. He refused to look at her and avoided her at all cost. Only when it was necessary, did her father talk to Elizabeth – acknowledge her? Which was why Elizabeth needed Grace's support. Grace, whom her father adores and loves more than her. Yes, it was hard. Even though her father loved Grace more, Elizabeth always knew that in his own way, her father loved her as well. There was never any cause for doubt or question until now.

Why does he behave as if I am the enemy, a stranger he wishes he did not know, Elizabeth thought?

Elizabeth's father's reaction hurt her. She wanted more than anything to speak to him, to find a way to make right the wrong she's done – *but to convince him I no longer want, nor love Robert, this, I cannot do,* she thought.

Elizabeth sighed as she knocked on Grace's chamber door.

"Come," Grace said.

Elizabeth opened the door and walked in. "Grace…I need your help. Father wants to see me, but I am…I am afraid to go alone. Will you accompany me?"

"Elizabeth, there is no need to fear father. He is angry, yes, but you are his daughter, and he loves you very much."

"I know he does, but he is still so angry with me, and he still refuses to acknowledge me when I am in his presence. Do you know how much that hurts? At least mother acknowledges me, even if it is to berate me," Elizabeth said, with sorrow in her voice.

Grace saw Elizabeth's pain and immediately went to her sister's side, with the need to comfort her. Grace wrapped her arms around Elizabeth and pulled her into a tight embrace.

"Elizabeth, I am sure in time it will get better. But…with what you are about to do, you understand, it will only make it worse, before it is better. In time, I am sure they will grow to accept you and Robert and find a way to honor the agreement with you as Robert's wife. I am sure it can be done. They are too stubborn to see it now."

"Maybe you are right. Will you go with me, though?"

"Yes, of course, I will. Now?"

"Yes. Father requested my presence only moments before I came to you."

"Then, we best hurry. You know how father hates to be kept waiting."

Elizabeth nodded, as Grace grabbed her hand and pulled her out the door, going directly to their father's study.

When Grace and Elizabeth arrived at their father's study, they found the door was open. Standing side by side they approached the entry, and Grace cleared her throat to get her father's attention. When Baron Massey raised his head, he smiled when he saw Grace, but when he saw Elizabeth, his smile disappeared. Elizabeth saw this, and it hurt her very much.

"Father, you wished to speak to me?" Elizabeth said in a shaky voice.

"Yes," then looked at Grace. "Grace, what are you doing here? I did not call for your presence."

"No, father. Elizabeth asked if I would accompany her to see you." Before her father could say another word, Grace quickly continued, "Now father, you cannot blame her for not wanting to come alone. You have been angry with her, and as her sister, she requested my support. So please, allow me to be her support. You may be angry with Elizabeth, but you should also be angry with me. If it were not for me insisting Elizabeth spend time with Robert, this would never have happened. She did this because she loves me."

Baron Massey, although he was not pleased, he could not deny what Grace said. He smiled, then motioned for them both to enter and close the door.

"Elizabeth, you requested to remain behind while the rest of us attend the Christmas celebrations at Bramhall Manor. Although I agreed to this, you will remain in residence. If you wish to go on your walks, it must be within sight of the other servants. I have instructed the servants to keep a close eye on you. They will go wherever you go."

It stunned Elizabeth to hear this, but she was also not surprised, knowing he was having her watched. But this, this would make it more difficult for her to meet Robert if the servants were to go wherever she goes. What was she to do? She'll have to figure out something.

Her father continued, "Your sister will marry Robert, and I strongly insist you take this time alone to rid yourself of these feelings you have for Robert and accept what is to come. Once we return, there will be no further excuses. You will be a part of this family and a part of the preparations for your sister's upcoming wedding. Do you understand me?"

Elizabeth stared at her father for a long moment, and when she went to open her mouth, she closed it. What was she going to say? Her father was firm in his words, words that were not to be questioned.

I must bide my time for now. Once Robert and I are married, there will be nothing father could do, as I will no longer be under his care, but the care of my husband —

"Elizabeth!" Baron Massey shouted, breaking her thoughts.

Because Elizabeth was lost in her thoughts, she didn't hear her father was calling her, and thought, *this is terrible. This is really terrible.*

"Yes, father, forgive me…I understand." She said, looking down at her feet while twisting the front of her gown.

"Elizabeth. Look at me and answer me again. I want to make sure you are clear on what I said."

Oh God, he is making me look at him. What if I cannot hide my feelings on my face. I must, Elizabeth thought.

Elizabeth gathered herself before she looked up to face her father. "Father, I understand, and I will do as you ask."

Her father watched her for a few more moments, and during this time, Elizabeth's stomach was twisting inside, fearing her father would see right through her. When her father nodded in satisfaction, Elizabeth was relieved.

Baron Massey turned his attention to Grace. "Grace," he said in a softer voice.

While her father was speaking to Elizabeth, Grace was staring at the floor, lost in her own thoughts. She feared she would be forced to marry Robert, *then what? If I married Robert, the man my sister loves…it is my fault we are in this situation. I do not want Robert. I want Elizabeth to have him. What will I do if Robert and Elizabeth are unable to elope? I will be forced to marry Robert, in turn, hurt my sister. This is all my fault.*

"Grace!" Baron Massey shouted.

Startled at hearing her father calling her name, Grace pulled herself out of her thoughts and looked up at her father, "I am sorry, father. My mind was wandering."

"What is wrong with you both. You both seem to be off in your own little world. Grace, you may not be happy about marrying Robert, but this was arranged at the time of your birth. An agreement sealed in front of God. No matter how you feel, you will marry Robert as planned. I suggest you find a way to accept this before you are married, and you need to start getting to know your soon to be husband. There will be no more avoiding it or using your sister to do so." In a firmer voice, he said, "Is that clear, Grace!"

"Y…yes father," Grace said, lowering her eyes to avoid his. "Father, may I say something regarding Elizabeth?"

Her father raised his eyebrows but waved his hand for her to continue. "Father, I know you and mother are not happy with Elizabeth…I am asking…please do not be angry with her. This is…was my fault. I forced her to spend time with Robert. Because of me, you and mother are angry with her when you should be angry with me." Her father tried to speak, but she prevented him from doing so by quickly going on. "No, father, please let me finish. Elizabeth is my sister. She only did what I asked her to do. I wanted nothing to do with Robert, and I saw how much in common they had. So, I pushed for them to spend time together, thinking…hoping they would fall in love, believing if there were another in the same family, then you and Lord Davenport would see Robert and Elizabeth to be a better match then I was. Father, it hurts Elizabeth," Grace looked at Elizabeth then back to her father, "Much to know her mother and father hate her…are angry with her about what happened between her and Robert."

Baron Massey watched his daughter Grace as she spoke. At first, he was furious, but before he spoke, he took a couple of deep breaths. Once releasing, he glanced at Elizabeth before turning his attention to Grace.

"Grace, you were wrong in what you did. Know this," looking back at Elizabeth, he said, "I do not hate your sister. Elizabeth, know your mother and I both love you very much. It angered us in what you did, but we love you still the same. You are our daughter, blood of our blood," turning his attention back to Grace. "Grace, if you felt this way after meeting Robert, why did you not come to me before invoking this scheme of yours? Your sister was a fool to allow this to happen. You know you can talk to me about anything. We could have worked something out. Your encouragement for your sister to spend time with Robert was a bad choice on your part. But your sister knew Robert was your betrothed. Knowing this, she took it upon herself to allow feelings to form…by falling in love with him." He looked back at Elizabeth, and in a firmer, harsher voice, "She was selfish in allowing herself to have more feelings than those of a soon to be brother should have." Turning back to Grace, "Did she think of you or her family when she did this? No!"

As her father was going on, Elizabeth stood frozen as her thoughts ran away with her. *It was my fault. He is right. I allowed Grace to talk me into this. Why?* Sighing, *because you are a fool, and the idea of sharing your love of the outdoors with another was too much to turn away from, thus, why you agreed. But I did not plan to fall in love with him. It just happened.* Then a voice in her head said, *'it was to be. You were meant to be together. Your souls are connected, a love pure and true. A gift from God.'* This was true, she agreed. *If this is true, and it is meant to be, then what shall I do?* she asked the voice. And the voice in her head spoke again, *place your faith in God, and he will see you through this.*

"But father —" Grace tried to speak but was interrupted by her father.

"No, Grace! Do not try to defend your sister. There will be no more excuses for Elizabeth. She has a mind of her own, and she failed to use it wisely. I suggest you both deal with what is to come. Because Grace, there will be a wedding. You will marry Robert whether you like it or not. Is that understood?"

Grace, staring at her father, swallowed the bile rising in her throat and said, "Y…yes father," then looked at Elizabeth, "We will work it out. This, I am sure," she said, turning back to her father.

Baron Massey waved her off, "Now both of you go. I have work to do."

After Grace and Elizabeth left his study, Baron Massey watched the door close, and then with a sigh, his thoughts turn to Elizabeth. *What am I going to do about that girl? Grace put her sister in a bad position. I know how close they are. Elizabeth would do anything to make Grace happy, as would Grace for Elizabeth. Are we wrong to make Grace marry Robert?*

Baron Massey went to his bookshelf, to a hidden panel, and inside that panel was a small compartment, and inside that compartment was the agreement made between Lord Davenport and himself. He looked it over; then, after he finished, he shook his head. *There is no getting around this. We agreed, no changes could be made. Otherwise, we would lose everything,* he thought.

Baron Massey placed the agreement back in the hidden compartment. He let out his breath, then returned to his desk, forgetting about the idea of the agreement being changed.

As Grace and Elizabeth were walking down the hall to Grace's chamber, Grace turned to her sister, "Elizabeth, I am sorry. I wish there was something I could do to help. Father is determined this wedding will take place. Knowing you are being watched, what will —" Grace stopped when Elizabeth placed her hand on her arm as she put her finger to her lips to hush her.

Once they reached Grace's chamber, Elizabeth spoke. "I know, Grace. I must figure out a way to meet Robert. You must help me. There must be a way."

Shocked, Grace stared at her sister in disbelieve that she still wanted to go through with eloping. Then again – letting out her breath, *I cannot really be surprised. Elizabeth loves Robert. She will do whatever it takes to be with him. I cannot blame her, and I must help her since it was my doing. She is only in this position because of me. Because I pushed her to spend time with Robert. God, please, help Robert and Elizabeth. Help them find a way to be together. Help our families see what Robert and Elizabeth have is right and before it's too late. Before I end up married to him. This will be best for everyone involved,* she thought.

Grace nodded and said aloud, "I will help you, Elizabeth. I think it will be wise to leave after everyone is abed. With them thinking you are asleep, they will not be watching you. I will let Robert know when we are alone and explain what happened, that he must meet you after everyone's abed."

"Oh, Grace, that is a wonderful idea. Yes, it will be perfect. We are to leave the day before Christmas. He must find a way to leave early that morning before everyone wakes. Tell him – I will be waiting for him at our special place."

"Elizabeth, what will you do? It's winter. The snow…it will be too cold to be out there waiting."

"Do not worry, Grace. I have a plan."

Grace nodded in agreement, trusting her sister. "Elizabeth, please be careful. I feel…this…what you are about to do will not go well with father, nor Lord Davenport. I am…I am afraid it will be worse than we both believe."

"Grace, you worry too much. Everything will be well. Yes, mother and father, as well as Lord Davenport, will be angry at first. But…I am sure in time all will be well. You shall see."

Grace only nodded at Elizabeth but couldn't help feeling this would go very wrong, worse than she believed when she first planned for Robert and Elizabeth to fall in love. *And if it does, it will be all my fault. I will be the only one to blame,* she thought.

Chapter Eighteen

When Robert arrived with his grey chestnut horse and saw Elizabeth's chocolate Arabian horse, he knew she had arrived a great deal earlier than he expected, considering how early he left Bramhall Manor. When Robert passed through the trees to the lake, he saw Elizabeth sitting on the bench he made as he thought, *she must be freezing.*

Robert walked the remaining distance between him and Elizabeth, and once he approached her, he said, "Elizabeth, how long have you been waiting for me? You must be freezing. Come, let me warm you."

Elizabeth stood when she heard Robert approach and went directly into his open arms. "I waited until I knew all the servants were abed and asleep before I left. I have not been here for long. I went to the woodshed first since the moon was high in the sky, where I lit a fire and waited until I believed it was the right time to leave. I am cold, but not freezing. I have my cloak, it is enough, and you know how much I love the cold," she said with a smile.

Robert held Elizabeth close, warming her with his body and snickered at her ridiculous love for the outdoors.

After a time, he pushed Elizabeth away from him, "Now, let me look at you," he said, and the sight of her took his breath away, as it always had.

When Robert saw beneath her cloak, he was pleased she wore the same gown she wore the night he asked her to marry him.

"You wore my favorite gown, I see," he said, raising her arms out to get a better look at her, then removed her hood and pulled her beautiful brown hair over her shoulders. "God Elizabeth, you are the most beautiful woman I have ever beheld. This gown…it is…magnificent. Thank you for wearing it."

Elizabeth felt her cheeks heat up at Robert's praise, and

in all their times together, there were only a few times Robert made her blush, and she couldn't believe after all this time, it was still possible.

So, I will be married to this man, she thought, sending shivers through her body.

When Robert felt Elizabeth shiver, he believed it was due to the cold, and pulled her back into his arms to warm her, then being unable to resist; he kissed her.

After their kiss, Robert guided Elizabeth to where their horses were gazing, then helped Elizabeth mount her horse, then he mounted his, and they began their journey to the small church just on the outskirts of Yorkshire.

First, they would stop at a small village outside of Cheshire to board their horses and hire a man and carriage to take them the rest of the way, with as little stops as possible. If all worked out, they would reach the church by nightfall.

***

By the time Robert and Elizabeth arrived at the church, the sun was beginning to rise on the following morning, arriving later than he originally planned. The reason why they were late, it turned out there was no direct road that leads to the church, so the driver took them as close to the church as possible, which was near a small river that stood between them and the church.

After helping Elizabeth out of the carriage, they approached the edge of the river, "Look, just beyond those trees, on the other side is the church," Robert said, pointing in the direction of the church.

Elizabeth looked in the direction Robert was pointing but could hardly see the church, and what she did see, was indeed a tiny church.

"It looks tiny, but it is perfect," she said with excitement. "How did you find this place?"

At first, all Robert could do was smile, but then he leaned down and whispered in her ear, "I have my ways."

"Robert, how are we going to get across the river?" Elizabeth said, looking around, "I do not see a place to cross, nor a place we can go around the river."

"No, we will have to cross," Robert said, pointing down at the river, "Here."

Elizabeth looked up at Robert with fear in her eyes at the thought of crossing a rapidly moving river in her gown.

"Robert, you cannot expect me to cross this river; I will surely fall in."

Robert laughed, "Do not worry, I will help you across. Look there," pointing down to the river, "See the large rocks sticking out. They appear to be close enough to use, allowing us to cross to the other side," Robert said, but this did not reassure Elizabeth. "My love, trust me, we will not fall in."

Elizabeth stared at Robert as if he was mad, but without another word, Robert took her hand and guided her across the river until they were safely on the other side. Once on the other side, there was a better view of the church, and it was indeed a tiny church.

As they approached the church, they could see it was made of different shaped stones, with one door from what they could see, nor did there appear to be any windows.

Robert opened the door, and it creaked as if it hadn't been used for many years. Upon entering the church, it was a single room, and at the far end of the church was a large window with a red painted cross in the center that gave enough light to light up the room.

Though the church was small and looked old and worn – *centuries-old,* Elizabeth thought. Still, Elizabeth couldn't help but admire the beauty of the little church.

"Oh Robert, it is beautiful? A small but adorable little church."

Inside, sitting on each side of the church, were small worn benches with a stone path down the center, that lead to the altar. Once Elizabeth looked up from admiring the path, she noticed the priest standing at the front of the altar smiling, holding an open bible in his hands, as he waited for them to approach.

"Robert, the priest, he looks as if…he is waiting for us. How can this be?" Elizabeth asked with surprise, unable to take her eyes off the priest.

Robert smiled as he watched Elizabeth, then he leaned down, "Yes, my love. He has been expecting us," he whispered in her ear.

Elizabeth looked at Robert and saw the smile on his face, not having any idea to the extent he went through to make this wedding happen, and she admired his efforts and expense it must have cost him.

Robert continued to explain, "When I learned of this church, I sent word ahead, asking the priest if he would agree to marry us on Christmas Day. I gave him a brief description of our circumstances, and when I received his reply agreeing to marry us, you could imagine my relief. To find a church and a priest who was willing to marry us without our family's consent," Robert said with a broad grin.

"What a wonderful surprise," Elizabeth said, looking at Robert with amazement. "Thank you. I love you so much, Robert. God is shining down on us on this day."

With Elizabeth's arm tucked into the crook of Robert's, he guided her down the narrow stone path until they were standing directly in front of the priest.

Elizabeth watched the priest as they walked towards him, and she noticed on the small stone altar behind him was a thick gold cross seated in the center, which appeared to be the only thing of riches in this old rough little church.

How interesting. To see such treasure in such a place, I wonder where it came from? Elizabeth thought.

To each side of the cross stood silver candle holders with a white candlestick, and next to them were two silver goblets. Everything was perfectly set in preparation for their wedding. Elizabeth was amazed at how perfect everything was.

Once they approached the priest, Elizabeth, for the first time, noticed the man himself. He wasn't a very tall man, shorter than Robert at least and definitely taller than her. The priest had straight brown hair that rested just above his shoulders. He had light facial hair as if he hadn't shaved in a couple of days. Elizabeth couldn't help but notice the priests best feature was his crystal blue eyes. He wore a simple long white robe with a red holy cross in the center.

"Well, I am glad you made it. Shall we begin?" said the priest.

Robert nodded as he said, "Forgive me, father, it took longer than we expected."

The priest motioned for them to take another step forward, placing them directly in front of him. "Let us bow our heads and pray to our all mighty lord that he shall come and bless this union on this Holy day."

Robert and Elizabeth bowed their heads, and the priest began, "Our Father, who art in heaven, blessed be on this Holy day, thy birthday. We bring to you, this day, in your house of worship, neigh, tis naught grand, nor richly made, but a house full of thy love. I bring these two young people to you, asking for your blessing to their union today, bonding them in marriage. Bless them with your strength, your love, along with your guidance."

The priest gave Robert and Elizabeth the sacrament and blessed them by making a cross before Robert and Elizabeth. Both Robert and Elizabeth made the cross, then all said, "Amen."

Standing face to face, Robert took Elizabeth's hands in his; as the priest spoke, Robert and Elizabeth gazed into each other's eyes, feeling the love of this day engulf them. It felt as if there was something – a strange sensation circling them – surrounding them from all directions. For Robert, it felt similar to the stories he heard – what a man felt when standing too close when the ground was struck by lightning. It is a power blessing them in a loving embrace, connecting their hearts and souls, bonding them, making them one, and completing the merger of two hearts and souls.

The ceremony wasn't a customary Catholic ceremony but a shortened version due to the time allowed. Once the priest completed the traditional vows, Robert, also in his letter, informed the priest he wanted to add his own words of love and declaration to Elizabeth. When Robert looked at the priest, the priest nodded for him to begin.

Robert turned to Elizabeth and gazed into her eyes. "Elizabeth my love," he began rubbing the top of her hands with his thumbs. "Never in my dreams did I imagine I would find love as powerful as ours. You are my heart and soul, and now we are to be bonded for eternity. In God's house, I stand here today," looking around the church, "In front of this priest," turning his attention to the priest then back to Elizabeth. "I give you my heart and my soul to take into you, to intertwine with yours. If the day comes when we are to part from this world, our souls will find each other again in death. I ask thy God in heaven to seal this union with our commitment to each other for eternity."

Elizabeth was breathless with Robert's declaration, leaving her speechless. With her emotions so high, it took her a few moments before she could speak.

"Robert…that…that was so beautiful. Yes, with all my heart and soul, I offer to you and accept yours in return. Bonded for eternity."

Robert took Elizabeth into his arms and held her tight, and just when he was about to kiss her, the priest cleared his throat, "You may kiss your bride," he said, with a smile, "But my son, you are a little premature, since you have not exchanged bands yet."

Robert and Elizabeth let out a small laugh before exchanging bands. Robert motioned for Elizabeth to go first, and she gave him a small golden band. Although it wasn't the custom to provide the groom with a band, after discussing it, both felt this day was special, not for one, for the two of them, and together would show their fidelity and commitment.

When it was Robert's turn to give Elizabeth a ring, it wasn't a ring he had, but something he felt was more special than a ring.

"I am sorry, my love, but I do not have a ring for you."

Elizabeth looked at Robert with shock and disappointment, but seeing his love for her, she decided it wasn't important. Being his wife was the only thing that mattered.

Robert saw the disappointment on Elizabeth's face and laughed silently, then with a smile, he reached into his pocket and pulled out a necklace. "I am sorry, my love, but will this do?" he said as he raised his hand, dropping the necklace to hang in front of Elizabeth.

Elizabeth gasped with surprise. It was exquisite. It was a gold necklace with circles connecting tiny mini pearls and teardrop rubies. "Robert, it is beautiful and better than any ring. I shall wear it always."

"I am glad you like it. When I found this necklace, it seemed perfect to seal our love with."

With Elizabeth's emotions – her feelings were tremendous. She loved Robert so much, and there were no words enough for her to express her love for him.

With tears in her eyes, she said, "You were right, it's perfect. Thank you. I love you so much."

Elizabeth reached up and put her arms around Robert's neck, then pulled him down and kissed him. Robert wrapped his arms around Elizabeth's waist as he pulled her even closer, as he deepened the kiss, pouring all the love he felt for her that words could never express.

The priest cleared his throat again, and Robert realized where they were, and he quickly broke their kiss. He looked down at Elizabeth and placed his forehead against hers for a few moments before turning to the priest.

"Forgive me, father. I lost myself to where I was."

The priest shook his head but laughed. He understood what it was to be a man and a young one at that. The priest reached for the goblets and handed one to Robert and the other to Elizabeth.

"Now, we shall drink to your union. You are now man and wife, Lord and Lady Davenport of…oh, My Lord, where shall I say you bid from?"

"Oh." Robert hadn't thought of that. His father did give him Watch Hill Castle, so he shall be known as Lord Robert Davenport of Watch Hill Castle, Cheshire. "I am Lord Robert Davenport of Watch Hill Castle, Cheshire."

Elizabeth looked at Robert in awe; she felt so proud of him.

"It is my pleasure to pronounce you man and wife, Lord and Lady Davenport of Watch Hill Castle, Cheshire."

Robert and Elizabeth drank from their goblets, and once they were done, the priest handed them the bible to sign their names and date of marriage in.

Before leaving the church with his wife – Elizabeth, Robert smiled, thanked the priest and handed him a bag of coins. After leaving the church, Robert and Elizabeth took a deep breath of the crisp cool and refreshing air, then he turned and pulled Elizabeth into his arms and kissed her again before they returned to the carriage.

When they reached the carriage, Robert turned to Elizabeth, they were both filled with joy and happiness after their union, having pledged their love before God, were now connected, bonded for eternity, where no man could tear them apart.

With Robert's overwhelming joy, he grabbed Elizabeth, and picked her up at the waist, then spun her around. After putting her down, he pulled her into his arms, "Wife. Kiss me." And she did, with all the love and passion she felt for him.

Elizabeth's joy was overwhelming as she thought, *how can one feel so much for another as I do for this man standing before me? Thank you, God.* Suddenly, her joy dissipated when she thought of them returning home to inform their families. She was instantly engulfed with fear. It crept into Elizabeth like an unexpected villain as Robert was helping her into the carriage.

She stopped and turned to face him, "Robert, I love you, but…I am suddenly feeling afraid…in telling our families we are married. What if…oh, I am so afraid it will not go well. What do you think they will do when we tell them?"

Robert pulled Elizabeth into his arms to ease her fears. "Elizabeth, we both know they will be outraged. I am sure my father will be difficult; this I have no doubt. But I am also sure, in time, they will come to accept us as husband and wife. This, I am certain of."

"Robert, I am so afraid of what they will do when we tell them we are married. This agreement…they said it could not be broken or changed. What if —" Robert stopped her in mid-sentence.

"Elizabeth, we are married. This will force them to reconsider changing the agreement. You are a Massey, as I am a Davenport. A Massey wed a Davenport, thus, sealing the agreement. It does not matter whose name is on it, yours, or Grace's. It makes no difference. Thus, our marriage will merge our families as they wanted, making us the most powerful families in the land. We will make them see that," Robert said with satisfaction.

Should I tell Elizabeth what I've learned after reading the agreement? After a moment of considering this, *yes, she has a right to know, and knowing this, could ease a great deal of her fears,* he thought.

"Elizabeth, there is something else I have not told you." Elizabeth looked at Robert with a questionable eye, but

Robert ignored her and continued. "After father left for London, I talked to mother, and she allowed me to read the agreement." Elizabeth gasped, but Robert ignored her. "My decision for us to marry was from what I discovered in the agreement. You see, it said if either the Davenport's or the Massey's were found at fault, the one at fault would forfeit all they own and must leave the land. If refused, they will be immediately put to death." This caused Elizabeth's fears to only increase, but again Robert ignored her and continued. "You see, if both Davenport's and Massey's are at fault, they would have to void the agreement. Don't you see Elizabeth, you and I together, decided to marry. Neither one nor the other can be held at fault, but both. Therefore, voiding the agreement. It will force their hands," Robert said.

Elizabeth wanted to believe him, but there was something she hadn't felt before creep inside of her, and it refused to leave. An unknown fear that made her wonder, *did we make a grave mistake? God, I pray we did not.* But as quickly as the fear engulfed her, it dissipated.

Robert watched Elizabeth closely, waiting for her to weigh his words and wondered what her thoughts would be. First, her fear increased, and without hesitation, he drew her into his arms to allow his strength and love to reassure her, with a need to bring her comfort, if only a little. When he decided to marry Elizabeth in secret, he knew it would be difficult at first, but in time, all would be well. He hoped his words, the confidence in them, would help Elizabeth. So, he decided to try again to reassure her.

"Elizabeth, my love, please do not fear. You will see, all will be well." Elizabeth only smiled, deciding not to say anything to allow Robert to finish. "Yes, at first it will be difficult, our families will not be happy, this, I am sure. I am sure there will be a great deal of yelling and screaming, but in time they will come to accept us." Robert pulled back and lifted Elizabeth's chin to look at him, "You will see, my love, they will accept us and realize we made the right choice. Once they see the love we have for each other, this love we feel was a gift from God. In time they'll come to accept us. How could they not once they see how strong and powerful our love is for one another. To see us, no one could deny our love, and we must trust our love will endure anything. It will see us through these tough times, I am sure are to come."

Elizabeth sighed, feeling relief in her heart, she nodded in understanding. Robert moved his hand to the nape of her neck, pulling her close until their lips touched. He kissed her, pouring all his love and passion he felt for Elizabeth, wanting to show how the power of their love could put aside any doubts and fears she had. Elizabeth relaxed into his kiss and allowed her fears to completely melt away, turning it into pure passion.

Robert and Elizabeth rode in the carriage in complete silence, enjoying the feel of being in each other's arms. They were married and were together for eternity. Nothing – no man could keep them away from each other.

After what seemed hours, it was Elizabeth who broke the silence. "Robert, earlier you mentioned a conversation you had with your mother when you asked to be excused from attending the Christmas celebrations. You said there was hope…that she might be able to help us?"

"I did, Elizabeth. Mother seemed to understand the love we found. I feel, if she is able to convince father, then your mother and father will accept us as well."

"Oh, Robert, if this is possible, our prayers would be answered."

"Yes, Elizabeth, it's possible," Robert said, smiling, and it filled his heart with joy to see the hope in his beloved's eyes.

***

It was near nightfall when they finally arrived at the small Village Inn that Robert planned to stay for their wedding night. He wanted their first night as man and wife to be filled with love and happiness before having to face their families and what they knew was to come.

The village wasn't much to see, as it had a cobbler stand, stables, a small shop, and the small, yet quaint Inn. Although the Inn wasn't much to look at, it was the best he could find on the road.

Once the carriage came to a stop in front of the Inn, Robert stepped out of the carriage, then helped Elizabeth. After a small word with the driver, Robert escorted Elizabeth into the Inn.

"Elizabeth, we will spend our wedding night here before continuing home. I know it is not much —"

Elizabeth put her hand over Robert's lips to quite him, "No, it is not, but it will do. To have this night with you is all that matters," Elizabeth said.

Robert smiled and kissed the back of her hand, "I will get you settled in our room, to allow you time to freshen up before dinner. I am going to send a message to Grace, letting her know when she can expect us. We should be at Bramhall Manor by nightfall on the morrow. Your family will still be at Bramhall Manor, which will allow us to inform everyone at the same time of our good news – we are married."

"Yes, all right, Robert. I am exhausted from our long journey. To be able to clean up would be wonderful. After, I may lie down for a bit until you return for me."

Robert went to the desk clerk and asked for their best room, informing the clerk they were just married. The Inn keeper's wife, standing next to the clerk, who wasn't just a clerk but her husband and owner of the Inn. She was thrilled to have newlyweds staying at their quaint little Inn. It's been a while since they had newlyweds and the Innkeepers wife wanted to make Robert and Elizabeth's first night together memorable.

"Oh, My Lord, how wonderful. I am Mary and,"

turning to the man next to her, "This is my husband and owner Al. Now, you just wait here a few moments while I go up and make the room perfect for your first night as husband and wife," said Mary.

Elizabeth smiled, "Thank you, that would be wonderful."

While Robert and Elizabeth waited for Mary to return, he instructed the driver to follow her with their baggage.

Mary gave them the top room on the Inn's north side that overlooked the open valley. Once the room was ready, she returned to show Elizabeth to their room.

"Now, My Lady, allow me to show you to your room."

"Robert, are you coming," Elizabeth asked, forgetting Robert was to remain behind to send a message to Grace.

Robert only smiled, "No, my love, I need to send a message to Grace first. Go and settle in and rest a bit. Once I am done, I will return to escort you to dinner," Robert said, kissing her on the forehead before she ascended the stairs.

"Alright, lying down sounds good."

"My Lady, please follow me," Mary said.

Once Elizabeth was out of sight, Robert turned to the Innkeeper, "Kind sir, where can I find a man who can send an express message?"

"My Lord, if you go to the stables, there is a boy who will be willing to take your message for the right amount of coin," Al said with a wink.

"Thank you, good sir, I shall go directly."

***

When Elizabeth walked into the room, she was surprised at how spacious it was. It had a large four-poster bed, with white lace bedding and curtains, and it appeared Mary sprinkled the bed with red roses. *Where did she find roses in the winter?* Elizabeth wondered.

Although Elizabeth was exhausted from their long journey, she found she was too excited to lie down on the bed, plus she wanted Robert to see what Mary had done. Elizabeth noticed a small two-seat chair with comfortable pillows in the corner of the room. She would use this seat to rest until Robert arrived to take her to dinner. Across from the bed was a basin and pitcher sitting on top of a small table next to the room's only window. There were a couple of chairs, and the room was very well cleaned.

"Mary, how did you find roses this time of the year?" Elizabeth asked.

"Oh, My Lady," she said with a chuckle, "It's because we have a place in the back that is closed in, allowing us to grow flowers along with other plants and herbs. It was my husband's idea. He learned it on his travels when he was a soldier with the king's army. I believe it was China, where he learned it," Mary said, chuckling again.

"Amazing. What a wonderful idea. To have roses in the winter. Thank you, Mary."

"Oh, tis nothing, My Lady. I shall leave you now to freshen up," Mary said, curtsying to Elizabeth, then she turned and left the room.

Elizabeth removed her cloak, went to the water pitcher, poured water into the bowl, and then began to wash.

***

After Robert sent the message to Grace, he wanted to give Elizabeth more time to rest, so he decided to check on the carriage and horses, ensuring they were secure. Then to the driver, making sure he was fed and was settled in for the night. After he finished, an hour had passed before he returned to Elizabeth.

When Robert walked into their room, he was amazed at the length the Inn keeper's wife had gone through to make their wedding night special.

Elizabeth heard Robert open the door, and when she saw him, she went directly into his waiting arms, and he kissed her, then after, he released Elizabeth to admire the room.

"Robert, did Mary not do a beautiful job?"

"Yes, Elizabeth, she did a beautiful job. Where did she find roses in winter?" Robert asked, amazed at the number of rose petals spread across the bed, as well as the small places around the room."

"Elizabeth smiled, "I was also amazed, and I asked Mary how it was possible to have roses during winter. She said her husband learned how to grow flowers, plants, and herbs in a building, which was where these roses came from," Elizabeth said, motioning her arm to encompass the room.

"Amazing," Robert said with awe. "I shall thank Mary when we go down for dinner. Are you ready?" Robert asked, then put out his hand, "Shall we go?"

Elizabeth took Robert's hand and placed her arm in the crook of his, then together went down to the dining room.

After Robert escorted Elizabeth to the dining room, he left a few moments wanting to find Mary, to thank her for making their wedding night feel so special and to make an additional request. He wanted to elicit her help, a surprise for Elizabeth.

Robert found Mary at the front desk, "Mary?"

"Yes, My Lord."

"I have a request to ask of you?"

"Yes, My Lord, how may I be of assistance?"

"Thank you, Mary. If you could please place a bottle of wine and glasses and…" Robert stopped to look around, then softly, to not be overheard, "Along with as many candles you can manage, and place them in our room before we finish dinner? Robert asked, then dropped a generous number of coins in Mary's hand.

"Oh, My Lord," eyeing the number of coins in her hand, "I shall be happy to," Mary said, smiling broadly. "My Lord, I shall keep watch, and when I see you and your wife are at the end of your meal, I shall go up directly to light the candles and I will revive the fire in the hearth as well," Mary said, with delight.

"Thank you, Mary, that would be perfect. I want this night," turning back to where he left Elizabeth, "To be extra special for my wife."

Mary smiled as she curtsied, then left to do as Robert requested.

After Robert and Elizabeth were done with their meal, Robert led Elizabeth back to their room. When he opened the door and motioned for Elizabeth to enter before him, Elizabeth gasped at the sight of candles in the room, while Robert stood behind her smiling.

"Robert," Elizabeth said, amazed with the number of candles in their room. "But, when we left for dinner, there were not all these candles…wine," Elizabeth said with excitement.

Elizabeth was astonished by the effort Robert went through to turn their room into a romantic setting. She walked around the room, taking in everything she saw, and it appeared Mary had added more roses as well.

"Robert, how…Mary…" Elizabeth was lost for words.

Robert nodded with a wide smile; he was amazed at what Mary had done to their room. The room was filled with roses and lit candles, with the blazing fire engulfing the room, creating a beautiful and romantic sanctuary. It was breathtaking. It was perfect.

"You like it?" Robert asked.

Elizabeth turned to Robert, "Like it. I love it," she said, then threw her arms around him, and he enfolded her in his arms, then kissed her.

Robert broke the kiss, then took Elizabeth's hand in his and guided her to the bed, then they stood facing each other for a few moments before he took her face in his hands, then brushed her hair off her shoulder. All he could do was stare at her, wanting to take in every inch of her beauty, and the look of love in her eyes. *For me,* he thought. He softly caressed her cheek with the back of his hand, and then with his other hand, he softly rubbed the bottom of her lip with his thumb.

Elizabeth stood with her eyes closed, taking in the feel of Robert's touch as it sent small tingling through her body, awakening her most intimate areas.

Robert watched Elizabeth intently to her reaction to his touch, and saw how much she wanted him, just as much as he wanted her. At seeing this, he slowly lowered his head until his lips were barely touching hers, and Elizabeth tensed with anticipation. At first, he gave her a small and light kiss, then, unable to hold back, he took her in his arms and deepened the kiss, pouring more love and passion then he's ever expressed before, and felt her return with the same passion, causing their combined passion to explode.

When Robert pulled back, ending their kiss, it left Elizabeth bereaved, wanting, nay, needing more. Robert only smiled, then walked over to the small table where the bottle of wine and glasses were, then poured them both a glass, and handed one to Elizabeth.

Raising his glass, "Elizabeth, my love, you are the greatest gift God has ever given me. To have you here as my wife…ah Elizabeth…God knows…I love you so much. I will cherish you for all the days to come. I feel our love will only grow with every minute, of every hour, of every day we are together," raising his glass in the air, as did Elizabeth, "To our future as husband and wife. You are my heart, Elizabeth."

Elizabeth could not stop smiling since she entered their room. She was enamored with Robert, and his words sent shivers down her body. She loved him with all the breath in her; he was her heart and soul.

Robert and Elizabeth clinked their glasses, then took a sip of their wine, but Robert, unable to wait, took Elizabeth's glass from her, then sat their glasses on the table. At that moment, Elizabeth suddenly felt nervous - shy. She wanted to make love to Robert, as much as he wanted to make love to her, and she wondered, *why?* Then she knew why; it wasn't just going to be a few stolen moments, but a whole night together in the same bed with the man she loved more than life itself. Robert was her heart and soul, and without him, she would cease to exist.

***

After Robert and Elizabeth made love, Robert put his arm around Elizabeth and pulled her against his body and held her tight, enjoying the warmth and the feel of their bodies meshed together.

"Robert, no words could ever express how much I love you. It is only in our lovemaking when I can fully express how I feel. My body craves yours as I know yours craves mine," she said, grinning from the memory of making love. "I have longed for this day, the day we made love as husband and wife. To feel your touch, and in your touch, your love. The passion we feel, when —"

Robert stopped Elizabeth, he couldn't wait any longer, he needed to kiss her, and kiss her he did, with a deep and fierce kiss that sent fire through their bodies, reigniting their passion, and they made love again, and many times after, with neither of them ever being sated.

Robert soared with pleasure, and once Elizabeth was asleep, he thought back to the first day he saw her, what they felt – that sting when they first touched. When he took Elizabeth's hand to help her down on the blanket – that instant sting made him wonder, *was that a sign we were destined to be together? Was it a knowing that she was mine?* he thought. He was grateful for Grace in insisting Elizabeth join them on their picnic that day. Never did he believe he would be married to this woman lying next to him.

Robert remembered when they first made love, and again in the shed, then that night after the party underneath the moon and stars. "Ah, love, there will not be a day, nor a moment, I will not want to make love to you," he whispered, then he too succumbed to sleep.

Chapter Nineteen

After Robert returned the carriage and retrieved their horses, together Robert and Elizabeth rode to Bramhall Manor ready to face their families.

Robert turned to Elizabeth and asked, "Are you ready for this, my love? It will not be easy, but I will be by your side. You will always have me. I love you."

"Robert, I am so afraid…but yes, yes I am ready…ready to spend my life with you, no matter what happens, as long as you are always by my side. I love you, Robert. You are my heart, and there is no me without you."

Robert smiled as he reached and squeezed Elizabeth's hand, wanting to give her reassurance.

***

Once Robert and Elizabeth arrived at Bramhall Manor, they noticed the strange looks they received from the servants. However, one look from Robert reminded the servants of their place. Regardless of what they knew, he was still lord and heir.

After they dropped their horses at the stables, arm and arm, Robert and Elizabeth entered the manor, and as they reached the great room, they heard everyone having a merry time. Robert and Elizabeth took a deep breath, and when they reached the doorway, Robert cleared his throat. When everyone looked up, they didn't seem surprised to see them together.

Did they find out? Robert thought.

What Elizabeth failed to realize, was once the sun rose on the following morning, and the servants weren't able to find her, they became worried. It was only after nightfall when worry turned to alarm after she hadn't returned.

After discussing the situation, it was decided that the older man servant would ride to Bramhall Manor and inform Baron Massey that Elizabeth was missing.

***

It took the servant most of the day before he finally arrived at Bramhall Manor. Once Baron Massey was informed that Elizabeth was missing since the morning before, Baron Massey enlisted the help of Lord Davenport, who had returned in time for Christmas, ordered the guards and the servants to search for Robert.

When it was discovered that Robert's horse was missing, and from what they learned from the stable hand, it appeared that Robert took his horse and rode out when the moon was high in the sky the previous night.

Lord Davenport was outraged. It wasn't hard to put together what happened – Robert and Elizabeth were together. Where they were, they didn't know, but Lord Davenport wasted no time and ordered his best men to search the countryside, and once Robert and Elizabeth were found, they were to bring them back no matter what resistance they received. He also sent a couple of men to Scotland in case they went there to get married.

Although everyone was relieved to see Robert and Elizabeth, they were also concerned to see them with their arms locked together. Robert was surprised to see his father, as he was not expected to return until after Christmas or the New Year.

This is not going to go well, Robert thought.

Robert knew he had to say something before anyone had a chance to inquire as to why they were together, so he blurted out, "Elizabeth and I are married."

Was it smart or wise to announce such news as he did? Probably not.

Robert turned to look at Baron Massey, wanting him to know Elizabeth was no longer under his care nor his responsibility.

Robert's announcement sent an uproar through the room. Although Baron Massey and Lord Davenport suspected this was why Robert and Elizabeth were absent, to have it confirmed only infuriated them.

Lord Davenport jumped up and rushed towards Robert and Elizabeth, and Robert put his hand up in an attempt to stop his father but failed, since Lord Davenport charged at him like a man gone mad.

Seeing the look on his father's face, Robert knew he had no choice, so before his father could reach him, he quickly pulled out his sword and pointed it at his father, stopping his father mere feet from where he was standing. Even Lord Davenport knew how much of an accomplished swordsman Robert was.

In the beginning, when they dueled, they were on equal footing, but in recent years Robert proved to be a better swordsman than his father. Robert would do whatever it took to protect Elizabeth, even if that meant facing his father with his sword.

"Hold! Do not come any further!" Robert yelled.

As Lord Davenport rushed towards Robert, he was yelling, along with Baron and Baroness Massey, demanding answers. However, for Lady Davenport, she remained calm as she followed her husband and was surprised when Robert raised his sword at his father.

Lady Davenport tried to calm her husband by placing a hand on his arm, "Wait, let us hear what he has to say."

Lord Davenport usually wouldn't pay heed to his wife, but for some reason, on this occasion, he felt now was the time, and nodded in agreement, ceasing his attack on Robert. He motioned with a wave of his hand for everyone to quiet, giving Robert leave to have his say.

Robert felt Elizabeth shaking and moved her behind him to better protect her from his father, knowing their family's outburst frightened her, although it was not so unexpected.

"You will listen to what I have to say!" Robert yelled.

He noticed his mother place her hand on his father's arm and was surprised that her action stopped his father.

With Lady Davenport by his side, he reluctantly agreed to allow Robert his say.

"Fine! I will give you leave this once! Go on, tell us why you two were together when it was forbidden!" Lord Davenport shouted.

Lord Davenport had the look of a man ready to pounce on them both if he was given the chance, then motioned with his arms for everyone to step back, giving Robert the space he needed to have his say.

"On Christmas Day, Elizabeth and I were married in a church by a priest – in the eyes of God," Robert said.

When Lord Davenport heard this, he wanted to lunge at Robert, but instead, he stood his ground.

Robert didn't miss this action and was amazed at the power his mother had over his father, but Robert ignored this and continued. "We understand this comes as a shock, but you left us no choice. You were willing to force Grace and me to marry when my heart belongs to Elizabeth. There would have been no good in me marrying Grace. Elizabeth and I," Robert pulled Elizabeth to his side, "Hope you will come to see how right it was for us to marry. Elizabeth is a Massey, thus, she can still merge our families as you wanted. What does it matter whose name is on the agreement, so long she is a Massey?" Robert said, turning to look at Elizabeth as she looked at him.

Lord Davenport, along with Baron and Baroness Massey was horrified. Angry. So incredibly angry. However, when Lord Davenport looked at his wife, it seemed she wasn't so surprised. *She must have suspected. What does she know that I do not? I will speak to her about this later*, Lord Davenport thought.

Robert wasn't surprised that his words did not have the effect he had hoped. Instead, his words were ignored and his father along with Baron and Baroness Massey lashed out at them.

They yelled and screamed about how they went against

their orders by continuing their relationship in secret, going against everything they worked so hard for, by marrying in secret. In doing so, he broke an agreement forged at the time of his and Grace's birth. An agreement that was unbreakable and unchangeable.

Robert's father was furious – a rage of a man ready to kill. He felt betrayed, and by his own son, blood of his blood.

"How dare you! You were forbidden to see Elizabeth! For you and Elizabeth to continue seeing each other in secrecy! Not only that, but you also went and married without our blessing or permission!" Lord Davenport could not control his temper, and he lashed out at Robert through clenched teeth, "How! Dare! You! You disrespect me! You disrespect your mother! You disrespect Baron and Baroness Massey, by marrying without our consent…in secrecy!"

Lord Davenport was screaming at the top of his lungs, to the point that the level of his voice – everyone in the land could hear him.

Robert was looking down to avoid making eye contact with his father. He knew their actions were wrong, but Robert felt he had no other choice, though his father's words cut through him like a knife.

"You were intended to marry Grace Massey, not Elizabeth Massey! Boy, do you not know the difference! Your marriage was placed in motion at the time of your birth! An agreement made between Baron Massey and me! Doing so would have merged both our families, making us the most powerful families in the lands!" Lord Davenport yelled, then turned his attention to Elizabeth. He looked at her with death in his eyes. Elizabeth saw this and moved slightly behind Robert. In a menacing frightening voice, "Elizabeth was not part of this agreement! She is of no consequence to any of our plans!"

At Lord Davenport's last words, Robert looked at his father, shocked and angered by his father's words.

How dare he! Robert thought. Knowing how his father's words affected him, he glanced at Elizabeth and saw how his father's words struck her as if he struck her with a blade.

To see this, Robert exploded. No one, not even his father was allowed to speak to Elizabeth, his wife, in such a manner. Robert showed a temper not seen by anyone, including himself. Robert was always a kind boy and man, never harsh to anyone, until now.

"HOW DARE YOU FATHER! You have no right to talk about my wife in such a way! You have no understanding, nor did you care when I tried to tell you how we felt about each other! You would not listen, nor would you give any consideration to allow Elizabeth and me to marry! We sought your approval! You refused! I am disgusted with you, my father! You who only cares about what he wants! What he can get from a marriage between Grace and me! Not once did you, nor would you consider my feelings, my wants, and my desires! I LOVE ELIZABETH! I do not and could never love Grace! I chose love and happiness over honor and respect! You use tradition to arrange my marriage to Grace! But…my dear father, I feel there is more to this agreement, which you and Baron Massey has refused to tell us!"

In what Robert said, there seemed to be an indication – *has Robert read the agreement,* Lord Davenport thought as he looked at his wife, but she refused to make eye contact with him. *Something else I will have to discuss with my lovely wife,* he thought.

"I have tried to get you to tell me, to help me understand the importance of marrying Grace, but you refused! So now, my dear father, you shall face the consequences of such secrecy…in your denial of the truth! I chose not to live my life unhappy, by not being allowed to be with the woman I love, whom, I gave my whole heart and soul to," Robert said this last in a softer, calmer voice.

"You have no right to tell me who I can or cannot love nor marry." Robert looked directly into his father's eyes and in a firm voice, "You, my dear father…you disgust me." Robert was furious. Although he tried to control his temper, it was impossible. "You, who…who would not…could not allow himself to see how much in love Elizabeth and I are! You are a hard man, this I know! Nor did you allow yourself to love! Are you not a man!"

At this, Robert's father eyed him, giving him a warning; he needed to watch his words. Lord Davenport was going to voice this, but Robert stopped him.

"Nay, I am not finished! You will listen to what I have to say!"

Lord Davenport was about to attack his son until his wife touched his arm again, reminding him of his promise to hear his son out. He did not understand why he was allowing his wife to control his actions.

Robert did not miss this action and thought, *is it possible mother means more to father than we knew. At that, more than she even knew.*

Never before has Robert seen such an effect his mother had over his father. Usually, his father would ignore his mother, giving her no heed. Now – this was something for Robert to consider later.

Robert continued. "Father, you may have no heart, but…" shaking his head. Robert took a step back, not wanting his anger to overtake him. He took a few deep breaths to bring his anger under control. "Is it right to believe your own children should suffer the same fate? Father, you say you believe in God, and so our love was given to us by God. You, who preach of God. Who speaks of honoring God…well, my dear father, this is what God chose for us. Now, because it was not as you planned, but God's plan. A God, who brought Elizabeth and me together. Our love has joined us as one, for eternity. There is nothing you can do now. It is God, who had a say, and it is God who has any further say. Right now, I am ashamed to call you father. If I married Grace, thus, would truly have been a sin. A disrespectful arrangement. If I married Grace…" shaking his head, "Nay, there would be no honor to her or to me. Grace knows my heart will always belong to Elizabeth. It would not be right to ask her to take a man who could never give her his heart, nor ever claim her heart. Grace would not want a man as so. A man who will never love her," shaking his head, "Nay, thus not right, for her to marry a man who will always love and desire her sister. Would this be fair to anyone connected to this marriage? No. It would not."

Although Robert's father listened to what he had to say, it made no difference. His words had only allowed his anger to fester and grow. Lord Davenport was infuriated. He looked at Robert as if he wanted him dead.

Death itself would have been better than the betrayal of my son, in this fashion. My first son and heir, he thought.

Robert saw the look on his father's face and took a step back, going into a fighting stance in case his father decided to attack him. He went to move Elizabeth behind him so he could better protect her, but instead, he noticed her mother was behind Elizabeth trying to pull her away. When Robert went to prevent Baroness Massey from taking Elizabeth, his father stopped him.

"Let her go! Her family has a right to speak to her!" Robert reluctantly let Elizabeth go, but he would immediately rush to her if he saw she was in trouble. When he turned back to his father, his father had turned his back on him.

Lord Davenport decided he wanted nothing further to do with his son. To Lord Davenport's surprise, he turned to his wife for support. Lady Davenport was taken back by this jester and took it as a good sign. She rested her hand on his chest hoping it would help calm him.

Robert again saw this action and wondered, *is it*

However, at that moment, Robert could not think of such a thing, as his focus needed to be with Elizabeth, but found he could not move, as he was mesmerized by his mother and father's interaction with each other as he wondered what his father was going to do.

Lord Davenport was struggling with what happened – trying to get control of his anger, at the same time, contemplating on what he should do. No matter how hard he tried, there was no getting around his anger. Regardless of family, Lord Davenport shall never be disobeyed, nor dishonored by his son. At that, he turned back to his son and threatened to disown him. But Robert knew this was a false threat. As elder son and heir, Lord Davenport could not disown him. So, Lord Davenport did the only thing he could do – he turned around and said through clenched teeth, "Get! Out! Take your wife and leave now! And never return, not so long as I breathe!" he yelled, then again turned his back on Robert.

Lady Davenport put her hand on her husband's arm, and to her surprise, he put his hand over hers.

This was unlike him. What has happened to him, she thought?

Lady Davenport looked at Robert and gave him a slight nod to let it go, along with a small smile, letting Robert know this was a good sign. At least she hoped it was. To see her husband show any type of feelings – emotions gave her hope.

Robert looked at his father with hurt in his eyes. This was not what he expected. Anger, yes, but this, no. Robert turned from his father and went to seek Elizabeth, it was time to take their leave. They will go to Watch Hill Castle, their new home.

His father gave Robert Watch Hill Castle believing it would be a home for him and Grace, but instead, Robert turned it into a home for him and Elizabeth. After his father gave him Watch Hill Castle, he discussed it with Grace and they both agreed it would be for him and Elizabeth once they were married.

While Robert was arguing with his father, Elizabeth's mother and father pulled her aside, and were no better than Lord Davenport – they were worse.

Baron and Baroness Massey were angry and disgusted by Elizabeth's behavior. Knowing Elizabeth secretly continued her relationship with Robert, then ran off and married in secrecy – her sister's betrothed was unforgivable.

No matter how hard Elizabeth tried to get her mother and father to see and understand – her words went unheard, but she refused to give up.

"Mother and father, please hear me! Our love is a gift from God!"

"A gift from God! Thus, no gift! You have sinned! You are ruined! And you ruined your family with your disgrace!" Baroness Massey yelled.

Elizabeth was devastated and heartbroken by her mother and father's reaction. They were too angry to hear anything she had to say, but she had to keep trying.

"Mother, please!" Elizabeth pleaded.

Grace watched in horror of the events taking place. She wanted to help her sister, but with the anger between Lord Davenport and her mother and father, she dared not interfere. But when she saw how hurt and scared Elizabeth was, she tried to get Elizabeth to look at her, but with her mother and father practically on top of her, Elizabeth was staring at the floor and not once looked up, and in her direction.

This is not right. I did not want Robert. I did not want this. What have I done? In our deception…was it wrong? As soon as I can, I must go to Elizabeth and do what I can to be there for her, Grace thought.

"How could you Elizabeth! How could you do this to

us! To your sister! From this day forth, you are no longer our daughter! We will have nothing further to do with you or Robert!" Lady Davenport hollered.

Elizabeth looked at her mother, although she was shocked, her mother's anger and behavior were expected, as well as being disowned, but deep down, she'd hope they wouldn't, and it broke her heart.

Baroness Massey was so distraught by her daughter's actions that her emotions threaten to break through to the surface, and she had to fight to regain her composure. Once she had her feelings under control, she yelled, "Get out! Get out of our sight now!"

Baron and Baroness Massey were turning their backs on their daughter just as Robert was approaching.

When Robert saw and heard what Baron and Baroness Massey were saying to Elizabeth, he quickened his pace to get to her side, seeing the horror and pain on her face. Once Robert was by her side, he took her in his arms and held her close to his chest. Elizabeth felt numb and shock from what happened, but once she was in Robert's arms, she allowed her tears to fall.

Robert walked Elizabeth out of the great room, then turned to her, and with his thumb, he wiped away her tears, then took her face in his hands. "Elizabeth, we have each other. I love you. We will get through this," he said, then kissed her lightly. With Elizabeth close to his side, they left Bramhall Manor.

Robert took Elizabeth to their new home at Watch Hill Castle where he planned to spend the rest of his life making her happy. He knew it would be painful, but he would be there every step of the way to help her get through this, starting this evening when he shows her their new home, and the surprise he had in store for her. It will still hurt, but in time, it will hurt less in losing her family.

Our family, he thought.

***

Robert was excited to show Elizabeth Watch Hill Castle after he took great care, in the time he spent preparing the castle to make it their home once they were married.

When Robert and Elizabeth arrived at Watch Hill Castle, to Elizabeth's surprise, lights were glowing in the windows.

"Robert, who is here?" Elizabeth asked.

Robert smiled, "Well, what I didn't tell you when I sent the message to Grace, was I asked Grace to speak to the caretaker and the servants I employed, to prepare the castle for our arrival. So, you see my love, we will have everything we need to begin our life together as husband and wife."

"Robert, how?" Looking at the castle, "Oh, this is so wonderful. I was afraid we were going to walk into a cold and dark castle. What a wonderful surprise."

"Well, prior to the wedding being postponed, which I took as a sign from God, and before we revealed our relationship to our families, father gave me a large sum of money as part of the agreement, part of the dowry for marrying Grace to begin our life as husband and wife. You see my love, we will live comfortably," he said, smiling down at Elizabeth.

"But, what of Grace? As the money was intended for both of you."

Robert, still smiling said, "Well my love, I did talk to Grace about this, and she felt as I did, once our family saw we were…are a better match, then Grace and I would have been…this money would still be for us when they changed Grace's name to yours."

Elizabeth was relieved to hear this, and embraced Robert, as she felt a bit of joy and happiness after the night's events. But then, "Robert," she said grabbing his arm, "After tonight, how can you be sure they will?"

Turning to face Elizabeth, "My love, I know tonight was difficult. Your mother and father caused you great pain.

I am sure after they take the time to consider our situation, they will reconsider. Now my love, shall we enter our new home?" Robert said, motioning his hand towards the door.

"Yes, oh yes, very much," she said with excitement, as she took Robert's arm.

Robert knocked on the door using the beautiful door knocker he carved to resemble their tree, the one he carved their initials in.

"Elizabeth, does this look familiar?" Robert said, pointing at the door knocker.

At first, Elizabeth didn't notice, but after Robert pointed it out, "Oh Robert, how wonderful, it is beautiful. I love it. Thank you," she said, admiring the door knocker, she reached up and gave it a soft caress.

When the door opened, there stood a middle-aged, short-statured woman, who had streaks of grey hair, throughout, what once was black hair.

She greeted Robert with a curtsey and said, "My Lord."

"Good evening Mary, allow me to introduce you to my wife, Lady Davenport," he said with pride.

Mary curtsied to Elizabeth, "How lovely you are My Lady. Please come inside," Mary said, turning to Robert. "Everything is ready just as you requested My Lord. I even had the cook prepare a warm meal just in case you were hungry after your long journey."

"Very good Mary, thank you. Indeed, we are famished. Allow us time to clean up, and we will be down shortly."

"Yes, My Lord," Mary said, as she curtsied to Lord and Lady Davenport, then showed them to their chamber.

Robert took a great deal of care and effort when designing their bedchamber, wanting it to be their own private sanctuary.

After Robert and Elizabeth entered their chamber, Elizabeth paid no mind to the room. Although she had a moment of happiness, she still felt a bit numb after the night's events. She held herself together until Mary left their chamber and closed the door. At this, Elizabeth released the pain and sorrow she'd been holding back and broke down and cried. Robert pulled her into his arms, and for a brief time, he just held her, allowing her the release she so desperately needed.

When he felt it was time, he guided Elizabeth to the side of their bed and sat down. The bed was beautifully made; a four-poster canopy bed was constructed and carved by Robert from solid oak wood. The pillars were made to look like the shape of a tree, with sprouting branches creating the canopy's top. The headboard, which took a great deal of time, was as detailed as Robert could get – he slowly and carefully carved an exact image of their lake. He wanted to bring their lake into their home, to have the place where they found their love, so it would always be a part of them. A reminder that their lake was a gift from God. A place known only to them, they would hold deep in their hearts and souls.

While sitting on the bed, Robert held Elizabeth in his arms as she continued to cry. After a time, Elizabeth finally pulled herself together and said, "I am sorry, Robert. This was supposed to be a wonderful and happy time. A celebration of our union."

"Elizabeth, you have no reason to be sorry. You have every right to express your pain with the loss of your family, just as I do." Robert placed his fingers under Elizabeth's chin and pulled her head up, so she was looking directly at him. "My love, know this, you will never lose me. I will always be here for you. Our hearts and souls are one, bonded for eternity."

Elizabeth laid her head against Robert's chest, needing to feel and hear his heartbeat. "Oh Robert, I could never survive this without you. How can it be wrong to love you the way I do? To love you so, can only be explained as the purest and powerful love, one could feel for another. Oh Robert, why is it so hard for me to express in words the love I feel for you? I love you with every breath I take. With every heartbeat I make. I could not wake up every day if I lost you. I would not want to live without you."

Robert put his arms around Elizabeth and pulled her closer to his body. He needed to feel her body against his and her heart beating to the rhythm with his own.

"Elizabeth, you need naught to use words to express your love for me, but you have expressed yourself beautifully. I know how you feel. I feel it each time I touch you. When I touch your face," Robert gently glided his thumb against her cheek, "When I hold you in my arms and feel you shiver from my touch, and when I kiss you," he leaned down and lightly kissed her lips, "And most of all, when we make love. What we feel then, there are no words, only passion. So, know my love, words do not need to be spoken to know how much you love me. Now come, let us clean up and go down for dinner."

Robert moved off the bed with Elizabeth's hand in his, and pulled her up when he rose. He used his thumbs to wipe away her tears before pulling her in an embrace. Robert gently kissed her on the forehead, then guided her to the pitcher and basin sitting on the table near the door, so they could clean up for dinner. Robert motioned for Elizabeth to go before him, but she was still shaky from her emotional breakdown and waved for him to go first, giving her more time to compose herself.

While Elizabeth was waiting for Robert to finish, she looked around their chamber for the first time and noticed how it was beautifully decorated along with the exquisitely carved bed.

She gasped, *how did I not see this when I entered the room*, she thought, then answered her own question, *because you were so grief-stricken, that is why*.

"Oh, Robert, can you forgive me for not noticing this beautiful room. It's breathtaking."

Robert was pleased that Elizabeth noticed the room. He

took a great deal of time and effort, pouring the love he had for her in the creation of this room – their haven, and smiled at seeing her sudden joy.

"This bed…Robert…how did you ever do such a thing? It's beautiful," Elizabeth said, walking over to the bed where she placed her hand on one of the pillars, wanting to feel the work Robert put into it, along with his love. With tears in her eyes, "Oh Robert, what a wonderful gift. Thank you. This must have taken you a great deal of time to create – a permanent mark of our lake where we first discovered our love. The colors…the blue and white draperies, along with the bed coverings are perfect. When I lie here with you, it will feel as if we are lying at our lake. What detail…oh Robert, a beautiful reminder of our lake. Robert, you have clearly outdone yourself. An excellent replica of our tree and lake, our sanctuary right here in our chamber."

With Elizabeth filled with such mixed emotions, she turned and reached for Robert, throwing her arms around his neck, and she pulled her head down until her lips touched his – she kissed him, wanting to show Robert how she felt about his gift without words, as words would never be enough. She wanted him to feel her joy and love.

Although that night started out painful, it ended with Robert and Elizabeth filled with joy and love for each other, feeling as they did at their lake. Their bedchamber became their sanctuary when they were not at their lake. A place as their lake, should not be tainted by their pain and sorrow, but instead, it should be filled with their love and happiness.

"Thank you-thank-you-thank you, Robert. I love-love-love it. Thank you for my gift, and thank you for making me your wife. I cannot be happier than I am right now."

Robert could not help but laugh at Elizabeth's reaction to their chamber. After Elizabeth took another good look around, taking in the beauty of their bedchamber, she quickly washed, then with her arm in Robert's, they left their chambers and descended the stairs to dinner.

***

After that night, Robert and Elizabeth chose to seclude themselves at Watch Hill Castle. They learned on their first outing in the village that the word of their elopement had spread across the land, into the villages surrounding Cheshire and Manchester. The people snickered, frowned, and looked down at the disgraced couple. However, with Robert by her side, they dared not say a word. Although the people were not pleased with them, for Robert being the heir to the Davenport title, land, and power, the people dare not treat him nor Elizabeth as his wife, when she was in his presence with disrespect. They already felt the wrath of his father, Lord Davenport, and wondered if his son would be as his father was? The people hoped not, but dare not take the chance and risk Lord Davenport's retaliation.

During their seclusion of Watch Hill Castle and the surrounding area, although, they could not visit it daily, due to the distance, Robert and Elizabeth never forgot their lake. When they needed to feel and take in the magic and power of the lake, they would return to feel the love that flowed within and around it, allowing it to pour into them, in a comforting embrace.

On entering the clearing and as they neared the lake, it immediately brought them peace. A feeling of comfort and love, piercing their skin, as it touched their hearts and settled deep into their souls.

This was their sanctuary, their safe-haven, a place that washed away their burdens, allowing them to fully and completely embrace their love, so they could feel free and safe. Free of all anger and pain.

Robert and Elizabeth had promised never to bring their problems to this lake, and in doing so, they allowed it to be filled with the power of their love, and not once did they break that promise.

Their lake was a gift from God, and they feared that

their lake's power would be lost, forgotten from the world once they left this world, and they couldn't allow that to happen. So, together, Robert and Elizabeth asked God to protect their lake. To allow it to survive through time – centuries. For God to allow those who will come after them, be allowed to remember their love, in feeling the power of the love they found at the lake, wanting others to be blessed as they were. For those who find this place will find the same love that Robert and Elizabeth found, along with those who are seeking love, and those who are looking to solidify their love, will be allowed to feel and take in the power of this place, this lake. And for those who already found love, and were struggling with their love, would increase and strengthen their love, bonding them together stronger than before. This, after visiting their lake.

Robert and Elizabeth wanted this to be a gift to the world for others to have a chance at sharing the love they found and were able to share. For those who find their lake would experience the greatest of magic in this powerful place. A place to be known as, "The Power of Love".

Another reason they wanted this power of their love to remain, was also for when they left this world as Robert and Elizabeth, and returned in their next life, praying that the pull of their love will return them to this lake – to their lake, allowing them to take in the power of their love, to remember, and to be found once again.

Chapter Twenty

<u>**Spring 1536**</u>

One early evening as Robert and Elizabeth were exploring their new surroundings, they came across a beautiful open area, that was just off the path of the river that ran near Watch Hill Castle. When they entered, they noticed it was enclosed by large lushes' trees, with a sloping hill to the right – it was beautiful.

As Robert and Elizabeth were standing face-to-face, in a soft voice, "Elizabeth, my love, how are you feeling today?" Robert asked, as he caresses Elizabeth's face.

Looking down at the grass, Elizabeth leaned into Robert's touch. "Robert, my heart hurts so much from the loss of my family. I had always believed I would be able to share this happiness with them," she said looking up at Robert. "Robert, I am surprised to say…I feel very happy. I never thought I could be so happy after what happened with our family."

For a moment Robert could only stare at Elizabeth before pulling her into his arms. In their short time as a married couple, it has allowed their connection and their love to grow. The small touches they gave each other would cause their bodies to tingle – shiver as if they were hit with a cold breeze.

"Robert, did you think when we found our love, it would grow as strong as it has? Every moment of every day we are together, my love only grows for you. Our love," shaking her head in disbelieve, "Even still, is the greatest power bestowed to us. I never thought it could grow as it has. Standing here before you…my love for you is endless. How can this be? If, what I feel for you now is this strong, where will it be years from now?" She turned to face the river, "I still find it hard to express the words I feel for you, there is never enough. The best to express my love is to show you." Elizabeth turned back to Robert and placed her hand on the side of his face, "Through my touch, my kiss, and most of all when I make love to you," she said.

Elizabeth looked directly into Robert's eyes, wanting to see into his soul, then placed her hand on his chest to feel his heart. In his eyes, she saw love, pure and utter love, as well as passion. She felt the pounding of his heart against his chest, and it was clear he wanted nothing more than to make love to her, right then and there, where they stood.

Robert didn't hide what he felt for Elizabeth; there was no need, as she felt as he did. She wanted him as much as he wanted her. Robert smiled, not hiding what he wanted to do, which was to pull her down on the ground and make passionate love to her? But he couldn't, he wouldn't, not there.

Elizabeth remembered how Robert made love to her that morning; the memory sending shivers through her body. "Making love to you is the best way for me to express my love for you. My love," touching the side of his face, "Nothing can ever tell me different. Our love is of the greatest and the purest power given to us by God. God has blessed us by giving us this love, with a power that fills our hearts, allowing it to grow, pouring over us, solidifying the connection in the emergence of our hearts and souls, which created this one love, a bond which can never be broken. The power of this love will flow deep in our souls for eternity."

Robert watched and listened to Elizabeth as he thought, *how can she say there are no words to express her love. On the contrary, I would say she expressed herself perfectly.*

"Elizabeth, your words are perfect. You have expressed how you feel…it is the same as I feel…my love, we are one, for eternity. I understand there are times when you want words to express how you feel, but they are not forthcoming. There will never be enough words to express how we feel for each other. It is not the words that are important, but in our touch…when I touch you, kiss you, and yes, most of all, when we…I make love to you, thus, the best way for me to express the love I feel for you, with the emergence of our bodies…joining us as one body, one heart, one soul, allows us to intensify our love, bringing it to the highest level, a feeling, a passion…I no naught the words. When I try to express the love I feel for you," shaking his head, "Even then, it is not enough. For what I feel for you has no words," Robert said.

Robert softly rubbed the back of his hand against Elizabeth's cheek. He loved touching her, and it was never enough. In their touch, he felt the love flow from him to her, feeling as if his soul wanted to rise, to fly with the happiness he was feeling.

Everyone should have a chance to feel what I…we feel, Robert thought.

Robert and Elizabeth were filled with passion; their love was more than they ever thought possible. This new place was not their lake, but it was a wonderful and beautiful place. A place they could be together and a part of nature.

Although Robert and Elizabeth felt the loss of their families daily, it never interfered with their happiness. They never believed there was anything that could destroy the joy and happiness they felt. They believed, so long as they had each other, they could survive anything.

***

Since Robert and Elizabeth were married, the only person brave enough to visit – well, old enough to visit was Elizabeth's sister Grace. She kept her promise to Elizabeth to visit her, but she had to be careful. Grace managed to sneak away from their cottage at her first opportunity and went to see her sister, with the need to know she was doing well.

There was a knock on the door, and Elizabeth knew who it was, since she received word from Grace that she was coming to visit her. Elizabeth didn't wait for the servants to open the door; instead, she opened the door herself and with excitement, she threw her arms around Grace.

"Grace! I am so happy to see you!"

When Grace saw Elizabeth, she expected her to be an emotional mess, but instead, and to her relief and surprise, Elizabeth was happy. Incredibly happy. Yes, she was hurt and saddened at the loss of her mother and father, but she didn't allow it to get in the way of her happiness.

Once Elizabeth released Grace, Elizabeth took Grace's hand and pulled her into the castle, spitting out questions, wanting to know how the family was. Although Elizabeth did not have her mother and father in her life, she kept up with how they were doing through Grace.

"How is mother and father and little John?" Elizabeth asked as she guided Grace to her favorite room – the sitting room.

Grace and Elizabeth sat on a high back bench that was covered with a forest scene tapestry situated near the window overlooking the beautiful garden Elizabeth created, although it's nothing close to the one Lady Davenport made at Bramhall Manor, it was hers.

When Grace was finally able to speak – peering out the window, she said, "Oh Elizabeth, what a beautiful garden."

"Yes-yes," not caring what Grace thought of her garden. "Now tell me how everyone fairs?" Elizabeth demanded.

Grace rolled her eyes, "Well, I will, if you allow me to speak long enough," Grace said, eyeing her sister.

Elizabeth laughed, "I am sorry, Grace. I am so excited to see you and I have missed you so much," she said, with excitement. Then in a softer voice, "Is mother and father…are they still very angry with me?"

"I am sorry, Elizabeth, they are. I have never seen father in such a state. I am so very worried…Elizabeth…I fear there is more to this agreement, of these consequences that father talks about. I tried to listen when mother and father are talking when they don't know I am near, to try and learn what is in this agreement, but as soon as mother and father see me or hear someone is near, they stop talking and pretend there is nothing wrong, but I know there is."

"Oh Grace, I am so sorry you have to endure this. Robert did read the agreement, and from what he read, Robert believes with us marrying it should void the agreement. It said, if one or the other were at fault, the one at fault would forfeit all they own and be forced to leave the land or face death," Elizabeth said, seeing the fear cross Grace's face, so she quickly continued, understanding her fear, as she felt the same way when Robert first told her.

"Wait, do you not see Grace? We are both at fault. Therefore, the Massey's and Davenport's…not one can be blamed, but both. In this, they will be forced to void the agreement and…or make the change to replace your name with mine," she said with satisfaction.

"Elizabeth, are you sure of what you say? To hear father speak of such a thing, if caused me to think…fear of what I did, of what you did, will do something to harm father," Grace said, but Elizabeth stopped her before she could continue, wanting to ease her fears.

"Grace, I am sure," placing her hands over the top of Grace's hands that were twisting the front of her skirt. "Grace, did you not hear me? I said there is nothing they can do to the other, as it was not just my decision, but Robert's as well, thus, placing both sides at fault. One cannot condemn the other without condemning themselves. So, you see, there is nothing to fear. You shall see, all will be well."

"Elizabeth, what if Robert was wrong in what he believes? To hear mother and father talking…the fear in their voices…Lord Davenport is a powerful man. If he turned on mother and father, he could destroy us all," Grace said when the realization hit her, "Wait, now that I think of it, I did hear father say the only reason nothing's happened, as there was no clear answer to whose fault it is," Grace said with a sigh of relief.

"Grace, do you believe if you married Robert, it would have helped any of us?"

"No Elizabeth, of course not. You know I do not. But if…what we did —"

Elizabeth cut Grace off before she finished. "Grace, stop. In time you will see. All will be well. Have faith that God has a purpose, and in time it will be revealed. It will be well. I promise sister," Elizabeth said, then hugged her.

No more was discussed of the matter, and the rest of their visit was filled with happiness and contentment.

***

One beautiful spring afternoon, while Robert and Elizabeth were at Chester's Village market, Francis first, The King of France, and John Bonnet, a former Catholic Clergyman, were riding through the village at the head of a large party as they made their way to Chester Castle, that will be one of many stops as he makes his way to London to King Henry the Eighth.

King Francis and John Bonnet were engaged in a conversation, when King Francis turned to look at John, he spotted Elizabeth standing next to a stand in the market browsing items for a lady, and he was immediately captivated by her beauty – this woman of great beauty took his breath away, and he knew he had to have her.

John was still speaking to King Francis when he noticed the king's attention was no longer on their conversation, but instead on something he saw at the village market. John looked in the direction he was looking, wanting to know what captured King Francis's attention, and when he saw what it was, he wasn't surprised to find it was a woman.

John laughed; it never failed, wherever they went, King Francis would find a woman who captured his attention.

John looked to make out the woman King Francis was looking at, and when he could make out her features, there was something different about her; she was a rare breed. She had a unique beauty, of one he hasn't seen before. A beauty that could capture a man, any man, even a man such as he, a man of the cloth, he too could not ignore.

John needed to regain King Francis's attention, so he motioned with his hand and pointed at Chester Castle that was directly ahead. At this, King Francis returned his attention to John and their destination, Chester Castle, that will end their long journey.

***

As Robert was making his way back to Elizabeth from the blacksmiths, he noticed the large party parading through the village. From the flags they carried, it appeared to be someone of French royalty.

The king perhaps, Robert thought.

Having no care of the parade, Robert returned his attention to Elizabeth, *my wife*. Saying the words always made him smile.

Elizabeth was standing near a stand browsing those items made for a lady – items for her hair.

Oh, no she does not, he thought as he snuck up behind Elizabeth and grabbed her around the waist, pulling her against him.

"Robert, what are you doing? We are in public. What will people think?" Elizabeth said, smiling.

Elizabeth loved how affectionate Robert was, even the ones he displayed in public. Although improper, she loved them still the same.

Robert laughed as he pulled Elizabeth closer to him, then kissed her on the back of her neck. He whispered in her ear, "My love, what are you doing? Why are you looking at things to put your hair up? You know how much I love your hair down, long and beautiful. It's too beautiful to hide by putting it up."

"Robert, I am a married woman now. It is imperative as a married woman to wear my hair up."

"Well, you are my wife, and I like it the way you have it now. So, you will not put it up. I forbid it," Robert said, as he tried to keep a straight face, but failed and burst out laughing.

"Robert, stop it," Elizabeth said, but she too couldn't help but laugh.

Robert turned Elizabeth to face him, as he pulled her into his arms, then he kissed her again, right there in the market where everyone could see, having no care in the world to what people might think.

Elizabeth pulled away, then looked around and saw people staring with shock on their faces in their display of affection.

"Robert, we should not be doing this. People will talk."

"So, let them talk. You are my wife, and if I want the world to know how much I love you," Robert said louder than he should, wanting everyone to hear, "Then, so be it."

Elizabeth could not help but smile. She loved how Robert was never afraid to show his feelings, in the love he felt for her, regardless of where they were.

***

Upon King Francis and John Bonnet's arrival at the gates to Chester Castle, the gates were opened to allow them entry once they were announced. Once they were inside the gate, a guard directed them to the castle's main entrance, where King Francis and John Bonnet, along with two of the royal guards dismounted, while the remaining party was directed to the castle's side entrance.

King Francis's mind was racing with thoughts of the woman he saw in the market and found he couldn't relax. He needed to know who she was, and so it was decided. He called for one of his guards, then ordered the guard to learn who the beautiful woman in the market village was. At the same time, King Francis's thoughts ran away with him, taking him back to the woman that captivated him in the village.

God, what beauty to behold, and so young and pure, he smiled. *With her beautiful long dark wavy hair, God in heaven, what a beauty. She truly is a blessing from God. Those eyes of hers, brown, I believe, large and sleek like a cat*, he thought, with his excellent eyesight, there wasn't anything he missed.

"Go! Go now! Seek her out! Find out who she is and who her family connections are! Do not return until you discover who that beauty is," King Francis Yelled.

The guard did not have to ask who the 'woman' the king was referring to. It was their duty always to know what the king needed.

"Wait!" John called to the guard.

The guard stopped and looked at King Francis. John didn't miss this, and before King Francis waved for the guard to continue, John quickly went on.

"Your Majesty, allow me to go and seek out this woman? As a Catholic Clergyman, the people here will easily confine in a man of the cloth than one of your royal guards."

King Francis eyed John, he questioned his words, but then, he couldn't deny the truth in what he said.

"Yes, you are right. But John, you are no longer a Catholic Clergyman," King Francis said.

John smiled. "Yes, your majesty, but those of this land are unaware of this truth," John said with a sinister smile.

King Francis laughed, "Go then, bring back the information I seek, and you will be handsomely rewarded."

John bowed to King Francis and with the guard by his side, left the king's chambers in seek of the woman from the market. To John, any woman who could captivate his king was revolting, but this one, this one was different.

It didn't take him long to discover who the woman from the market was, and to John's pleasant surprise, she turned out to belong to one of the two most powerful families in the land. However, there was a slight problem – she was recently married, and a scandalous one at that.

The woman's name was Elizabeth Massey, the second daughter born to Baron and Baroness Massey. Baron Massey was a descendant of the famous Hamon de Massey, a man, and Lord, who once held great power and owned most of the land in Cheshire.

He knew the information would please his king immensely, but to learn Elizabeth was married, would not. John had to think, does he tell King Francis she was recently married, but one of scandal? Or does he inform King Francis all he learned, holding back the fact that she was married, to allow him time to investigate the situation further? If he could discover the wedding was not legitimate, King Francis could still have the woman he desired.

As if being married mattered to King Francis, John thought. *So, do I tell him she is married, or do I keep that from him until I can prove she is or she is not married?*

So, it was decided, for the moment, he would not inform King Francis of what he learned. After all, he could find no one who witnessed the wedding.

It may only be rumors, he thought. At this, it solidified his decision; he would not inform King Francis, at least not yet.

As John was returning to Chester Castle, his thoughts ran away with him – *how glorious! King Francis will be pleased to learn the woman who captivated him is one of French noble blood and a descendant of one of England's greatest and powerful men*. John smiled. He was pleased with himself and his discovery.

Once John returned to Chester Castle, he went directly to see King Francis in his chambers.

John knocked, and when he heard King Francis say 'enter,' he walked in and bowed. Unfortunately, King

Francis had his back turned as he was busy looking at documents.

"Your Majesty, I bring you great news about the woman from the village market."

When he heard this, King Francis turned around and gave John his full attention.

"Well, go on then, tell me what news you have of my beauty," he asked, beaming with excitement.

For John to see King Francis's excitement, it brought a smile to his face, so he informed King Francis of what he learned.

"Your Majesty, she is of French noble blood, and her name is Elizabeth Massey. She is the second daughter of Baron Massey and Sire, Baron Massey is a descendant of the famous Hamon de Massey. Hamon de Massey, who once had great power and owned this great land of Cheshire. There was a time," he turned and looked around as he put his arms up, "He used to own Chester Castle," John said with a smile.

He felt very pleased with his discovery, knowing it would please his king, which would surely bring him great fortune.

"Excellent work John. Call for my horse. I will go at once to speak with Baron Massey regarding his daughter."

John hesitated for a moment and thought, *do I tell him what I learned? That she may be already married?* John shrugged his shoulders and decided not to. *If he discovers she is married, I can claim I was unaware.* At this thought, he agreed not to say a word and pray what he heard in the village was nothing more but idle gossip.

John turned and called for a guard standing outside the king's chamber door.

After the guard entered the king's chamber, he ordered the guard to have one of the stable boys prepare King Francis's horse.

"Be quick! The king rides out on urgent business!"

***

It was an hour when King Francis arrived at the cottage behind Dunham Massey Castle. He learned this after stopping at Dunham Castle first – to himself, he laughed at the reaction of the shocked look Lord Booth gave him when he found the King of France standing in his foyer. But then, Lord Booth was a bit disappointed when he learned he was seeking to speak with Baron Massey.

King Francis thought it was unusual for a descendant of the great man Hamon de Massey to be living in a cottage behind the famous Dunham Massey Castle.

He laughed again, aloud this time —

His guards turned and looked at each other, knowing this laugh meant the king's thoughts were of no good.

This will be too easy. I am sure the man will want to live in the main castle, not a cottage behind it. At this thought, King Francis laughed aloud again.

After King Francis arrived at Baron Massey's cottage, his guard knocked on the door and was greeted by an older woman.

In a commanding voice, "I am Francis the first, King of France. I wish to speak to your master, Baron Massey."

The servant was shocked to see the King of France standing at the door, and after a moment, and once the shock wore off, without further to do, she curtsied and escorted King Francis to Baron Massey's study.

Baron Massey was in his study with the door closed when he heard a knock on the door. This interruption irritated him. Everyone knew when the door was closed, he was not to be disturbed, but before he could say a word, the door opened, and in walked King Francis. Baron Massey was shocked and speechless when he saw the King of France standing in the doorway, not understanding what brought the King of France to his home.

When King Francis saw Baron Massey with his mouth open as he slowly stood, he seemed as if he was going to speak but said nothing, causing King Francis to laugh.

"Close your mouth man, before the flies crawl in."

Embarrassed, Baron Massey immediately closed his mouth, then took a moment to gather his wits before he tried to speak again.

"Your Majesty," he finally said as he walked out from behind his desk to stand in front of King Francis and bowed. "What do I owe the honor of such a visit?" Baron Massey asked, remaining bowed, not rising until King Francis gave him leave to do so.

King Francis smiled, "You may rise Baron Massey. I have come to you on urgent business."

Baron Massey rose with the look of surprise, wondering what urgent business could bring a king such as he to his home.

"Your Majesty, I am honored by your visit, will you please sit?" King Francis waved off the jester. "What urgent business could bring you to my home, Your Majesty?"

King Francis looked around at Baron Massey's study to how small it was. Then, without looking at Baron Massey, he said, "Baron Massey, I come to you about your daughter Elizabeth Massey."

Baron Massey's eyes widened when he heard his daughter's name.

"Upon my arrival in Cheshire, as my party was riding through the village in Chester, I noticed your daughter. Her beauty captivated me, and I wasted no time in seeking her out and learning who this extraordinary beauty was. It was to my tremendous delight when I learned it was the daughter of noble blood, to no other than Baron Massey, a descendant of a well-known and honored man of Hamon de Massey.

I have come with an offer for your daughter. I wish to bring her to France and give her a place at my court for as long she wishes to remain. Is your daughter at home? I want to speak with her directly?"

Ah, to get an up-close look at that beauty I beheld in the village. I am sure her beauty will be nothing to what I saw in the distance, King Francis thought.

Baron Massey was stunned. What was he to say or do? Elizabeth may be his daughter, but she was no longer his responsibility since she married Robert. Baron Massey needed to tell King Francis, *but how*? Whatever he said, he had to tread very carefully.

***

Baroness Massey was sitting in her parlor knitting, when a servant entered the room to inform her that the King of France was with Baron Massey in his study. Baroness Massey's eyes widened at hearing this news, and she immediately put her knitting down and went to her husband's study. She needed to know why the King of France would honor them with such a visit.

As Baroness Massey approached her husband's study, she could hear the conversation between her husband and King Francis, and without waiting, Baroness Massey entered the study.

"Your Majesty," Baroness Massey said as she curtsied to King Francis.

King Francis turned at Baroness Massey's interruption, annoyed that she dared to enter the room and speak without permission.

"Baron Massey, who is this woman who dares address me without permission?" King Francis asked perturbed.

Baron Massey looked at his wife, knowing she made a grave mistake, he immediately rushed to her side. "Your Majesty, I apologize. This is my wife, Baroness Massey." Baroness did not move, and remained in a low curtsy with her head down. "She must have heard us talking as she was entering my study to see me. She spoke only out of respect."

King Francis looked at Baroness Massey then said, "Is

this so, Baroness?"

Baroness Massey realizing her mistake was afraid, but she knew she had to answer with care. "Yes, Your Majesty. Please forgive me for addressing you so."

King Francis looked at her for a long moment, then said, "Very well. I shall forgive you just this once for your impetuous behavior. You may rise Baroness Massey."

Baroness Massey flinched at King Francis's words and knew if this were France, King Francis could have had her head for such behavior.

"Thank you, Your Majesty," Baroness Massey said, as she rose, but stayed by her husband's side.

"Now, Baron Massey, shall we continue the matter regarding your daughter, Elizabeth," King Francis said.

Baron Massey looked at his wife, then to King Francis, and said, "Yes, Your Majesty, as I was about to say before my wife interrupted us. My daughter Elizabeth…I am sorry to say, my daughter Elizabeth was recently married to Lord John Davenport of Bramhall Manor's son and heir, Robert Davenport."

King Francis was very disturbed to hear this news, which Baron Massey did not miss, and quickly attempted to offer King Francis another solution.

Perhaps he will take Grace in replace of Elizabeth, he thought.

"Your Majesty, perhaps your visit will not be in vain."

King Francis raised his eye in question.

"I have another daughter, my firstborn; perhaps you will consider her as a replacement?"

King Francis hesitated, then took a moment to consider this option. *If Elizabeth is beautiful, perhaps this other daughter will be as well*, he thought and decided he would see the girl.

"I will see her. Go now and bring her to me. I will look and speak with her, and if she pleases me, I will accept your offer of replacement."

Baron Massey looked at his wife, "Go my love. Have our daughter ready, then quickly bring her to meet his Majesty, the King of France."

Baroness Massey curtsied to King Francis, then turned and left.

After leaving her husband's study, she quickly called for Grace's maid, then rushed to her daughter's chambers. Once Grace was adequately prepared, they returned to Baron Massey and King Francis. This time Baroness Massey had the servant announce their arrival before entering.

"My Lord, Your Majesty. Baroness Massey and her daughter, Lady Grace Massey," The servant said as she curtsied.

Once Baroness Massey and Grace entered the room, they curtsied to King Francis, and after King Francis permitted them to rise, Baroness introduced their daughter.

"Your Majesty, allow me to introduce you to my daughter Grace."

King Francis looked Grace over as a man does when looking to buy a horse, looking at her from head to toe and back again. Although she was beautiful, she did not compare to her sister Elizabeth.

How can sisters be so different in beauty? Yes, Grace is beautiful, but not enough to tempt me, King Francis thought.

King Francis was disappointed that Grace did nothing to excite him as Elizabeth did. Yes, she would due, but he had no desire to have her, knowing he would grow bored with her too quickly.

"No, she will not due. I will not be extending my offer to your daughter Grace. I bid you good day."

Without another word, King Francis left Baron Massey and returned to Chester Castle, outraged at what he learned, and the ride to Chester Castle did little to ease his anger.

When King Francis returned to Chester Castle, he was

fueled with anger. *How could John be so impetuous? How could he not have learned Elizabeth Massey was married when he made his inquiries. Well, I shall find out, and he had better have an excellent reason for not knowing this vital information,* King Francis thought.

***

John Bonnet was not always the man he was then – he was born in Noyon, France where his father was the financial advisor to the royal family. John was raised with the hopes he would study the law one day, but once John was at university, instead of law, he chose to study religion, which led him to join the priesthood at the Roman Catholic Church, where he thrived and succeeded in his role for many years until he found interest in the Lutheran religion. Once this happened, he wanted out of the Catholic Church's control and to be no longer required to answer to the Pope.

To be a pastor with the Lutheran church, you controlled what you did in how you preached without obtaining anyone's approval. There was no pope to answer to, and this pleased John a great deal. As a Catholic Clergyman, he was forced into celibacy, and John never liked that rule. As a Lutheran preacher, he could have women whenever he wanted and could choose to marry if he so desired, but he never did. This defiantness intrepid John, and he left the Catholic Church to become a vowed Lutheran.

John's life took him to many places allowing him to learn a great deal that gave him tremendous knowledge that earned him respect with the Lutherans across the lands. It also allowed him to serve some of the royalty within and out of France. Which in time he gained King Francis favor and earned him a place at the royal court as one of the king's advisor. He was willing to do whatever was needed to become and remain as one of King Francis's top and trusted advisors.

John wanted to build trust with King Francis, so he

would one day welcome him into his confidence and allow John to be his direct council. When that day came, John was ecstatic; he was finally in a place to put his plan in motion.

King Francis informed John he was contemplating converting himself and his people to Lutheran and needed John's assistance to help him and his people understand the Lutheran religion. If he converted, his people would follow.

John was pleased when this came about, and planned to show the king the benefits of becoming Lutheran, hoping that once the king was satisfied, he would rise in the court and be allowed access to great riches and power.

As John began to rise in status and after gaining the taste of power, it fed on him like a plague, turning John from a man seeking and giving God's wisdom, to a man seeking – desperate to have more wealth and power by finding ways to manipulate King Francis to do his will. In doing so, King Francis continued to feed John's hunger for power.

***

"John, you fool! You failed me! Elizabeth Massey is married to Robert Davenport, the son and heir to Lord John Davenport of Bramhall Manor, who holds all the power within Cheshire and Manchester! This man is not to be reckoned with! He is of high standing with the English king! You made me, the King of France look like a fool! How could you have not known this! I should have you beheaded for your insolence! Leave my sight! Do not call upon me unless I call upon you!"

Although King Francis was initially going to allow John to explain himself, since his anger festered on his way back to Chester Castle, he was too furious to care.

John was furious to be insulted by King Francis and to not be given a chance to defend himself. With the lengths he went through to become the king's direct confidant, it could now be in jeopardy.

Why? Because of this girl! I must find a way to make it right. But how? I shall make King Francis see he was not wrong in bringing me into his confidence! I shall, or there is no God! What am I saying? I am God, John thought. Feeling confident in this thought, he left to find a way to make it right, by finding the truth.

John was an arrogant man, and once he had his first taste of power, he couldn't let it go. It only made him crave more. Although he was the one in error, he quickly convinced himself it was Elizabeth who was at fault.

***

The following morning, at sunrise, John set out to search for information that would regain King Francis's trust in him. John began at the first church he saw, looking to verify a wedding took place between Elizabeth Massey and Robert Davenport. After finding nothing at the first church, he was given directions to the other churches within the surrounding area. To his happy surprise, he found no evidence or proof that a wedding ever took place between Elizabeth Massey and Robert Davenport. What he did learn, was Robert Davenport was supposed to marry Grace Massey, and when he ended up married to her sister, Elizabeth Massey, it came as a shock to everyone around.

Since John Bonnet found no evidence that a wedding took place between Robert Davenport and Elizabeth Massey, John concluded their marriage was a ruse and believed Baron Massey concocted this story to deceive King Francis. John felt this was done because Baron Massey was aware of how King Francis treated the ladies of his court, and therefore, Baron Massey sought to protect his daughter from King Francis.

At this, John smiled. *This is it! This is my way back into King Francis's good graces. To learn this information, I will be handsomely rewarded. Oh, how I shall be his savior. It will restore his belief in me. For me to give him the woman he wants, Elizabeth Massey,* John thought, marveling at his success in discovering Baron Massey's plan. Without haste, he rode back to Chester Castle in leisure, savoring each moment before informing King Francis of his great news.

***

Upon arriving at King Francis's chamber, he ordered the guard that was standing at the door, "You there, inform King Francis I need to speak with him on urgent business. Tell him I have news to contradict the information regarding Elizabeth Massey, to what Baron Massey told him."

After a knock on the door, the guards nodded, and one entered the chambers to speak to King Francis on John's behalf.

When the guard returned, he informed John of King Francis's answer. "Sire, King Francis is busy, and cannot be bothered with other fables you have for him. If it is as urgent as you say, you are welcome to wait outside his chambers until he is free to see you."

This angered John. He stared at the guard for a few moments knowing King Francis was doing this on purpose to punish him by making him wait. However, John reveled in his discovery and knew once King Francis heard his news, he would be back in the king's good gracious. So, he sat in the chair outside of King Francis chambers and waited with a smile on his face.

It was the end of the day, with the sun low in the sky, when John heard the king call for his guard. When the guard entered the king chambers, King Francis asked, "Is that buffoon still out there waiting?"

"Yes, Your Majesty."

"Very well. Tell John I will see him. But, if he is wasting my time, I will have his head on a silver platter." The guard bowed and left his chambers.

"King Francis will see you now. But he says, if you are wasting his time, he will have you beheaded."

For a moment, John stared at the guard, and he knew the guard wasn't joking. John swallowed hard, then put his hand to his neck and smiled. He knew with the information he carried – *I will not be losing my head today*, John thought, then walked into King Francis's chambers.

John bowed and said, "Your Majesty, I bring great news regarding Elizabeth Massey."

King Francis had no care to hear John's babble. He only allowed him in as he was in great need of amusement. Then, with his back turned away from John, he waved his hand for him to continue as he said, "Yes-yes. Be quick, tell me your news so I can have you beheaded for your insolence and for my amusement in your disregard for my orders."

This statement did not disturb John, since what he had to say would change everything. "Your Majesty, I know I did you wrong, and I apologize. I am sure the news I have will redeem me."

John waited a few moments to see if King Francis would respond, then continued when he was met with silence.

"Your Majesty, Elizabeth Massey is not married. I checked all the churches within and outside of Cheshire. Not one had a record that a marriage took place between Robert Davenport and Elizabeth Massey. Therefore, your Majesty, it seems Baron Massey has deceived you."

At hearing this, King Francis turned to face John.

When John saw this, he knew he had King Francis's full attention. He smiled, as he savored the moment before he continued. "You see Your Majesty, when I inquired about Elizabeth Massey, I realized no one mentioned their recent marriage —"

Well, that is not entirely true. What he does not know will not hurt him. John smiled within. *Nor will it hurt me,* he thought.

"Since the Massey's and Davenport's are well known in

the land due to their wealth and status, surely all in the land would have known and been proud to speak of such a supreme union. At this, I thought if indeed they were married, it would have been recorded with the church they married in. So, I made inquiries with all the churches in the land, and in doing so, I could not find one church with a record of marrying Robert Davenport and Elizabeth Massey. What I did learn, a wedding was planned between the eldest daughter Grace Massey and the eldest son Robert Davenport. This made sense, as per custom, the eldest son married the eldest daughter. So, it made no sense for the eldest son to marry the second daughter.

When the people of Cheshire heard Robert married the second daughter, Elizabeth Massey, it was a great shock and apparently, it was one of scandal. So many rumors are spreading across the land as to the reason they married. Were they having an affair, causing Elizabeth to be with child, or was there more to this scandal? There are many questions with no answers."

The whole time John was telling King Francis the news, he noticed the change in King Francis – he was pleased with this news and himself.

I am back in his good gracious, John thought.

"Your Majesty, it seems Baron Massey has deceived you and is keeping you from what you desire, his daughter Elizabeth Massey. You know what this means, Your Majesty?"

In hearing this news, King Francis was pleased, very pleased indeed. *Then he thought, Baron Massey deceived me. You do not deceive the King of France. He will not get away with this deception,* King Francis thought.

"Yes-yes, I know what this means," King Francis said, with lust in his eyes and a sinister smile. *She is mine,* he thought. "With Baron Massey's deceit, he will have no choice but to agree to my terms, and he will want me to take Elizabeth off his hands since she will be considered spoiled goods, and he would want nothing more than to be rid of her, not wanting to ruin his good name and status. I will make him an offer he cannot refuse." King Francis said, with a broad smile.

"Excellent job John! You've done well and will be richly rewarded," Francis said, patting John's shoulder congratulating him on a job well done.

"Now, we must work out the details on this agreement and have it presented to Baron Massey at once. This agreement will force Baron Massey to turn his daughter over, placing her into my care. But, first, you must make further inquiries on the nature of their deception. In doing so, it will seal their fate. There cannot be any questions of deceit." John nodded in agreement. "Good man. Good man. You will set out first thing in the morning and speak to all those who know the Massey's and Davenport's well."

John left King Francis chambers, feeling incredibly pleased with himself. It was as he believed, he regained King Francis good gracious and once again was in his trusted confidant. But, this time, no matter what, he needed to stay there if his plan were to succeed.

***

At first light, John searched for those who were close to both families and did whatever it took to gain the information he needed. In doing so, he made promises on King Francis's behalf even though he had no authority to do so. This did not matter, for even if he had, King Francis would never have honored it.

Those who talked only knew of the upcoming wedding between Robert Davenport and the eldest daughter Grace Massey. No one knew about a wedding between Robert Davenport and the second daughter Elizabeth Massey. What he did learn, although rumors – *Rumors always have some semblance of truth,* John thought.

What the rumor was: Grace Massey had no desire to marry Robert Davenport and convinced her sister to spend time with him, hoping they would form a bond, even love. Thus, they would be allowed to marry, freeing her from an unwanted marriage. However, he heard when Baron Massey and Lord Davenport learned of Robert and Elizabeth's relationship, they were forbidden to continue, but instead of stopping their relationship, they instead married in secret.

Since John could not find any record that a marriage ever took place, he concluded that Robert and Elizabeth deceived their families and were living in sin as an unmarried couple. This information was exactly what John needed to redeem himself with King Francis further, so he wasted no time and quickly returned to Chester Castle to inform King Francis of his glorious news.

Chapter Twenty-One

"Your Majesty, I have great news," John said with glee, bowing to King Francis.

"Well, now is not the time to hold your tongue man! Speak! Be out with it!" King Francis said with utter excitement.

The whole time John was out looking for proof, King Francis was filled with lust, thinking of ways to please Elizabeth and how she would please him.

John smiled, taking in the moment of victory before he informed King Francis of what he learned. Then, he reported to King Francis everything he heard, and once done, he ordered for his legal counsel to be brought to his chambers at once.

When his legal counsel arrived, Francis instructed him to prepare an agreement between him and Baron Massey, which said:

A formal agreement between Francis the First, King of France, and Baron John Hamon Massey the Second of Dunham Massey, that so states:

I, Francis the First, the King of France, do hereby declare one, Elizabeth Massey, will become a part of my French royal court as a lady in waiting. Elizabeth Massey will accompany me to France, where she will be given title and be known as Lady Elizabeth Massey. Lady Elizabeth Massey will remain in my court until I find I no longer have need of her services. Baron John Hamon Massey the Second will release his daughter Elizabeth Massey to my care within a fourth night upon signing this agreement. Baron John Hamon Massey the Second will not dispute this agreement, as Baron John Hamon Massey the Second has lied and deceived Francis the First, the King of France.

Although Baron John Hamon Massey the Second, lied and deceived Francis the First, the King of France, King

Francis will not leave Baron John Hamon Massey the Second with anything for his daughter Elizabeth Massey. If Elizabeth Massey, as Lady Elizabeth Massey satisfies Francis the First, the King of France, in her duties to him, Francis the First, the King of France will aid Baron John Hamon Massey the Second, in his quest to reclaim Dunham Massey Castle, their ancestry home. If Lady Elizabeth Massey does not please King Francis the First, the King of France, she will be returned to her family Baron and Baroness Massey. At such time, Baron John Hamon Massey the Second will receive no further assistance from Francis the First, the King of France, to reclaim Dunham Massey Castle if it has not already been returned to him.

After King Francis completed the agreement, he signed and sealed it with the royal seal.

"Now John, I want you to deliver this agreement to Baron Massey personally. You will take my legal counsel to give witness to Baron Massey signing this agreement. You are to deliver it directly to Baron Massey himself, and you will not return without the signed agreement, is this clear, John?"

"Yes, Your Majesty."

"Give Baron Massey until the second nightfall to sign the agreement," he ordered.

John bowed then left King Francis chambers with the king's legal counsel bound for Dunham Massey.

***

After John arrived at Baron Massey's cottage, he saw a servant walking and called out, "You girl, go inform Baron Massey that John Bonnet's here on behalf of Francis the First, the King of France."

The maid wasted no time and went directly to inform Baron Massey.

When Baron Massey heard this news, he was surprised to receive such a visit and didn't understand why. He believed, once King Francis left disappointed after learning

Elizabeth was married, he wouldn't hear anything further from the king. To suddenly have another visit from a messenger sent by King Francis, baffled him.

What could he want now, he thought?

"Direct John Bonnet to my study at once," he said to the servant.

When John entered Baron Massey's study, he bowed in respect to a man of his title and noble status.

"Sir, I am honored, and you are most welcomed. What business from King Francis do you bring me?" Baron Massey asked.

John wasted no time, "My Lord, I am here to present an agreement to you from Francis the First, the King of France. First, allow me to introduce you to King Francis's legal counsel, Lord Moreau," John said, and Lord Moreau bowed to Baron Massey.

"Will you and Lord Moreau have a seat? Would you care for a glass of wine?"

John waved off the seat but agreed to a glass of wine, as did Lord Moreau. "Thank you, My Lord, but we will stand as this will not take long. My Lord, I come here with Lord Moreau, who is here to give witness to the signing of," John pointed to Lord Moreau, who presented a rolled-up parchment to Baron Massey, "This agreement. Lord Moreau, please hand Baron Massey, King Francis's agreement."

In receiving King Francis's agreement, Baron Massey wondered, *could this mean King Francis reconsidered taking Grace in replace of Elizabeth?* This thought bothered him; at the same time, he felt a sense of relief. Grace was his eldest daughter and his favorite, and to part with her would be difficult, but for her to have such status with the King of France could bring her a great marriage.

John Bonnet and Lord Moreau waited quietly while Baron Massey read the agreement, and as he was reading, they saw the anger form on Baron Massey's face, which pleased him immensely.

"As you can see My Lord, King Francis will not take no for an answer —"

John slammed his hand down on his desk. "This is not true! So, you are trying to tell me…nay, King Francis is accusing me of lying and deceiving him regarding the marriage between my daughter Elizabeth and Robert Davenport? He believes their wedding did not take place. Well, I tell you sir, if this is true, then I have also been deceived…lied to by my own daughter!"

Baron Massey was outraged by King Francis's accusation and demanded to know how King Francis came to know this information, and that his daughter was not married to Robert Davenport.

John related the information he learned regarding the marriage between Elizabeth Massey and Robert Davenport, and how he was unable to find proof they were ever married. Baron Massey was shocked and outraged to hear such news. It left him feeling like a fool, for him to be betrayed, and by his own daughter. For Elizabeth to go to such length, in pretending to be married, only to prevent Robert from marrying her sister Grace, this did not make any sense to him.

Although Baron Massey's anger was great, a thought popped into his head – *she did not do such a thing. She would not go to such length to live in sin as man and wife when they are not married.* Then he thought, *but how can I deny it.* He looked at John, *in what this man of God said.* In this, he believed what John said to be true. He believed that no man of God could create such a lie. *How could she betray us in such a way! God no! It must be true, and Elizabeth has ruined us all! God forgive them and me for what I am about to do.*

Baron Massey loved his daughter more than Elizabeth ever knew, and it broke his heart to hear what he believed she had done. With this decision, his heart that once was filled with love for her was replaced with hate. Hate for his own daughter. A daughter to him no longer.

"I will sign this agreement only if I can make one change? Well, two," Baron Massey said.

John looked at Lord Moreau, "Before we agree, what is the change you are proposing?" John asked.

"If, or when King Francis no longer finds Elizabeth satisfactory in her duties to him, he does not need to return her home. King Francis may do whatever he deems fit with Elizabeth Marie Massey. Please make these changes, including her full name?" Baron Massey said.

He was outraged and embarrassed in what he learned. *I have been made to look like a fool,* he thought. He felt betrayed, and by his own blood – his daughter.

Was it true? No, of course not. But at the time he believed it was. When a man of cloth spoke, it was the truth. It was unthinkable that a man of the cloth would willingly deceive and lie to a man of nobility. *Why, for what purposed did he have to do so?* However, the man Baron Massey believed to be a man of God, was no longer a man of the Catholic faith, but a man seeking his own wealth and power at any means possible.

After John consulted Lord Moreau, they agreed to the changes proposed by Baron Massey, as they were minor changes, and there was no need to obtain King Francis's approval. Therefore, the agreement was signed.

Once the agreement was signed, John informed Baron Massey of what he needed to do next.

"Baron Massey, please have Elizabeth delivered to King Francis at Chester Castle in the fourth night."

Baron Massey was unable to speak as he was fueled with anger, so he nodded instead.

John Bonnet and Lord Moreau bowed to Baron Massey then took their leave with John feeling incredibly pleased with himself by getting Baron Massey to sign the agreement. In doing so, it would redeem him with the king.

As John and Lord Moreau rode away from Dunham Massey, John couldn't help but laugh aloud. Lord Moreau jerked his head at John's sudden outburst of laughter but said nothing.

John and Lord Moreau rode back to Chester Castle in silence, as John was lost in his own thoughts. *I know I will succeed in becoming King Francis's greatest and only confidant. And in doing so, he will allow me access to all he knows. He will listen and trust my counsel, which will put me in a position of great power.*

In this, John was very pleased with himself and the future he saw with King Francis and his beloved country.

When John arrived at Chester Castle, he walked in with leisure with his head held high, knowing he succeeded in getting King Francis what he desired, Elizabeth Massey. John had a broad smile as he approached King Francis's chambers.

After John was granted entry, he presented King Francis with the signed agreement, and as John expected, King Francis was delighted with the success of their visit with Baron Massey. However, King Francis did not expect the agreement to be signed so quickly. Instead, he expected Baron Massey to hold out until the last hour and wondered how John managed to get him to sign the agreement so quickly.

"John, you have done me well. If you continue pleasing me in this way, you will go far in my court, which will bring you great riches and power. But fail me, and I will banish you from France, never to return."

While John was away, King Francis thought long and hard on what he would do to ensure John's continued loyalty. But then it hit him. It was his love for France, his country; he loved more than anything. If he were to have him beheaded, it would cease John's torturous pain, but to banish him from the country he loved most would be a continuous torture until the day he died.

Seeing the look on John's face, *ah, yes, this was the right decision,* King Francis thought.

John nodded in understanding.

"Now John, tell me how you managed to get Baron Massey to sign this," waving the agreement in the air, "So quickly. I believed since this had to do with his daughter, he would have taken the full two days before reconciling with his situation and signing the agreement," King Francis said, with his arm on John's shoulder guiding him to sit at the table in his chamber.

With King Francis's words, John reveled, and at the same time, they caused him great concern. For if he failed again, in a way King Francis deemed unforgivable, he would be banished from his beloved country and lose all hope in what he wanted to achieve.

It's better than being beheaded, he thought. Then he let his thoughts run away with him. *Elizabeth Massey will belong to King Francis, and I will make sure of that.* Then, with a sinister smile, *when the king is through with her, she will be mine.*

John felt pleased with himself and was ready for his next step; to journey to Watch Hill Castle to personally inform Elizabeth Massey she would be accompanying King Francis to France, and become part of his court, a lady in waiting. He also wanted to throw Elizabeth's sin in her face. Therefore, he will go to her as a clergyman, which she will trust and welcome him without further thought.

If this fails, a more forceful action may be required, John thought.

* * *

After John and Lord Moreau's visit, Baron Massey sat at his desk fueled with anger. First, he received an unannounced and surprising visit by King Francis, wanting his daughter Elizabeth. When King Francis learned of her marriage to Robert, he believed it was the end of it, especially when he refused to take Grace in her place, which relieved Baron Massey immensely. He did not want his daughter Grace to become part of King Francis's court, knowing how King Francis was with the ladies of his court, and he did not want that for his Grace. But, if the king wanted her, there was nothing he could have done but allow his daughter to go. No, he didn't have authority but knew King Francis and King Henry's association was a sketching one, and he didn't want to do anything to cause further conflict. But, what was he to do, he was miles from London and King Henry's forces.

With his recent visit from John Bonnet, a Catholic Clergyman, as a representative of King Francis and King Francis legal counsel Lord Moreau, he was forced to sign an agreement giving King Francis Elizabeth. Did it bother him? Did he feel? At that moment, no. He was too angry to see through John Bonnet's lies.

As John was sitting at his desk going over the recent events, his wife entered his study.

"John, I just heard. What happened? Why were the king's clergyman and legal counsel here?"

For a few moments, John just sat there staring at his wife. Does he tell her, or does he not? He shook his head, and he knew it was unavoidable; she had to know what happened.

"My dear, I have grievous news," he said.

Baroness Massey put her hand over her mouth when she saw the look of distress on her husband's face, and it sent fear coursing through her body. *What could it be?* she thought.

Did she want to hear what her husband had to say? No, but she must. She was a Baroness, and as such, she had to endure whatever her husband was to tell her.

Baroness Massey straightened her posture and put her shoulders back. She was prepared to hear whatever her husband had to say. "Tell me. What is it, John? What has happened?"

Baron Massey looked at his wife and saw the fear in her eyes, but he also saw her strength. John related the details in full to the reason for John Bonnet and Lord Moreau's visit. After Baroness Massey heard the awful news of what her husband learned about Elizabeth, it fueled her already existing anger.

First, Elizabeth destroyed their chance to merge their family with Lord Davenport's, and now, now – no, this was too ridiculous to believe. If Baron Massey and Lord Davenport saw through their anger, they could have seen it their marriage was still a perfect merger. It did not matter what daughter married Robert. All that mattered was a Massey married a Davenport, therefore, they were still able to merge both families.

To have King Francis take an interest in Elizabeth, a king, Baroness could not help but think of the possibilities of what they would have received with such an alliance. If they allied with the King of France, would they have still needed Lord Davenport? Probably not, but to have both alliances would have made them unstoppable. It would have placed them far above everyone within and outside the land.

Baron Massey wanted wealth and power, not to mention the return of Dunham Massey Castle. To find a woman to love and who would love him in return was a blessing, along with the children she gave him. He felt content. Yes, Elizabeth did wrong, but in time he knew he could have forgiven her. It was his wife he feared would not.

Baroness Massey was the one who was power-hungry, thus, married a man who had title and power, although he was not as powerful as Lord Davenport. When they allied themselves with Lord Davenport, the power between them both would have been unstoppable.

Baroness Massey had always seen herself married to a man of great power and wealth. No, Baron Massey wasn't all she hoped, but an alliance with a Massey put her in high status, and the merger with Lord Davenport would have put her above all the women in her acquaintance. Although she never believed she would have love or happiness, to have the title and power of being Baroness would have been enough.

She never imagined she would find love with her husband, and to have love, made her situation all too perfect. Their love was powerful, and she loved him with all her heart, and she knew he loved her in the same way. She felt her life was perfect until her daughter destroyed it. Then, a part of Baroness emerged that no one, not even her husband knew she was capable of.

Baroness Massey could not help but think if Grace married Robert Davenport and King Francis took Elizabeth to become part of his court – the power and wealth that would have come from this would have been great indeed. They did not just lose one powerful opportunity, but two. Baroness Massey was fueled with anger and allowed it to explode as it filled her heart with hatred for a daughter she once loved. It disgusted her to think of Elizabeth as her daughter anymore.

A daughter who should have been loved and accepted by her mother and father, no matter the circumstances. Baron and Baroness Massey were too blinded and filled with anger at the loss of the power and status they could have had, but Baroness Massey felt it more acutely than her husband.

Baroness Massey wasted no time, she ignored her husband, who was trying to get her attention, but her anger was too great to listen to anything her husband was trying to say. Without further words, she immediately set off to see her daughter Elizabeth and inform her of the recent events, and how she had destroyed all their hopes of their family being placed above all families, including the Davenport's within the lands.

***

When Baroness Massey arrived at Watch Hill Castle, she wasted no time in lashing out at Elizabeth once she opened the door.

"Do you know what you did! Again, you have ruined us! What do you have to say for yourself! You selfish girl, how can I ever call you daughter!

We recently received a visit from…do you want to know who! Well, I will tell you! The King of France! After seeing you at the village in Chester, he came to see your father with the intent of making you part of his French royal court! In doing so, he would have helped us regain Dunham Massey Castle from the Booths! Along with titles and wealth! This would have increased our status and power within the land!"

Lady Davenport was outraged, and she was pointing her finger at her daughter, not giving her a chance to say a word.

"How can I believe, twice in such a short time, you have managed to ruin us! This, because you choose to deceive us by marrying Robert, who was intended for your sister! You, ungrateful child! You did not just deceive us in your relationship with Robert but this so-called marriage as well! Just so you know my daughter," Baroness Massey said with disgust, "We have learned the truth about your marriage after we received a visit from John Bonnet, a French Catholic Clergyman, who informed us you are not married! He could not find any record nor a witness that a wedding ever took place! We should have known it was a lie! Now everyone will know! You have shamed us! Ruined us! You, sinful child! You and Robert are living in sin!" she screamed.

Before Baroness Massey could say another word, Elizabeth yelled, "STOP IT! Just stop it! You have no right!"

It hurt Elizabeth to hear her mother's words; they

pierced her heart like a dagger, filling it with great pain. Elizabeth loved her mother and father so much, she never wanted to hurt them in such a way. To hear her mother speak to her in such a way, with such hatred in her voice, as if she was a stranger who betrayed them, not someone who was her daughter – this crushed Elizabeth, and she was unable to believe what her mother had said.

When Baroness Massey arrived, Elizabeth was in Robert's study when she saw her mother walking up from the road. It surprised her, and yet she was pleased to see her mother finally come to visit. It gave her hope that her mother wanted to see her home, and she saw this as a sign her mother and father had come to accept her marriage to Robert. It was time to forgive, but when she heard her mother's cruel words, it was too much and too painful for Elizabeth to bear.

Elizabeth was determined not to let her mother see how much she hurt her. She held back her tears and screamed at her mother. "GET OUT! GET OUT NOW! Leave my sight and never return! If you and father cannot accept our marriage, and yes, we are married! Not that you deserve an explanation, but we were married in a small church outside of Yorkshire by a priest! And yes mother, it was in the eyes of God! We are married! If you cannot accept this, then leave and never return!" Elizabeth yelled, then slammed the door in her mother's face.

After Elizabeth bolted the door, she dropped to her knees and put her face in her hands, then allowed herself to release the pain she'd been holding back – she cried, she could not understand her mother's hatred – her mother, the blood of her blood. She needed Robert. She needed him desperately, but he was not at home. She was alone with her pain and grief.

The whole household heard what Baroness Massey said to Elizabeth, and it hurt and angered the servants. Once Elizabeth closed the door, they rushed to her side to help her even though it was not their place, but they couldn't leave Elizabeth sitting on the floor crying.

"My Lady!" Yelled Mary, putting her arms around Elizabeth.

After a few moments, Elizabeth gathered herself and said, "It is okay, Mary. Give me a moment, and I will be fine," Elizabeth said.

After getting herself together and with Mary's help, Elizabeth went to her bedchamber and collapsed on her bed and cried all over again, and she cried herself to sleep.

***

When Robert returned to Watch Hill Castle, he noticed Elizabeth was nowhere to be found, when she usually greeted him at the door with a hug and a kiss, which was something he'd come to look forward to when he arrived home. Feeling concerned, Robert called for a servant, "Hello there!"

A maid answered, "Yes, My Lord," she said with a curtsey.

"Mary, where is Lady Davenport?"

Mary hesitated, but she knew he must be told. "I am sorry, My Lord, but Lady Davenport has been in her chambers all day."

Raising an eye, "All day? Is she unwell?" he asked with concern, but didn't wait for an answer and started to rush up the stairs when Mary called out.

"Nay, My Lord. She's upset after receiving a visit from her mother. After her mother left, I helped her to your bedchamber where she's remained all day."

Robert stopped halfway up the stairs. "Her mother, when did this happen, Mary?"

"Oh, My Lord, I do not know. I think late morning or early afternoon."

"Good God, what happened!" Robert asked, but he didn't wait for a reply and went directly to see Elizabeth.

Once he was standing outside the door, he took a

moment to gather his emotions, then went into the room. He needed to know Elizabeth was alright, and he needed to know what happened during her mother's visit.

What could her mother have said to upset Elizabeth that she did not leave our chamber all day? Robert wondered.

Robert quietly entered their chamber, and once he was inside, he saw Elizabeth lying on the bed sleeping, so he quietly shut the door, not wanting to disturb her, then he gently eased himself on the bed, and as soon as he put his arms around Elizabeth, she woke up.

Elizabeth was startled when she felt someone touch her, and when she opened her eyes, she was grateful to see it was Robert, so she quickly turned around and wrapped her arms around him, burying her face in his chest.

"Robert, oh Robert," then she burst out crying.

Robert just held her until she stopped crying and was ready to tell him what happened. When she quieted, he asked, "Elizabeth, Mary told me your mother paid you a visit. What happened to cause you to be so upset."

After pulling herself together, Elizabeth recounted what happened with her mother, and the harsh and cruel words she said to her.

When Robert heard what happened, it outraged him, and he wanted to go directly to Dunham Massey and give Baroness Massey a piece of his mind. *How could she…her own mother hurt Elizabeth like this. To be so cruel. Elizabeth is her daughter, not some stranger,* Robert thought.

"My love, I am sorry for what happened. I wish I were here…I could have protected you from your mother, from the pain she caused you. I do not understand how an agreement could cause such hatred in someone. To place an agreement above a loved and beloved daughter makes no sense. To me, from what you say, it sounds as if your mother finds power more important than her own blood. I do not understand this," shaking his head, "I hope we would be more open and understanding when we have our children. To never turn against them, as our own has done to us."

Robert knew there were no words he could say that would comfort Elizabeth. They would have each other no matter what happened between their families.

Elizabeth looked up at Robert, and she knew with Robert by her side, she could endure anything.

After a while, and after Elizabeth fell asleep again, Robert went directly to speak to Mary. He needed answers to understand exactly what happened between Elizabeth and her mother.

Robert found Mary in the kitchen helping the cook prepare dinner. "Mary, tell me what happened when Baroness Massey came to visit."

"Oh, My Lord, it was awful. Baroness was very cruel and harsh to My Lady. It broke my heart to hear such horrible words. Baroness Massey spoke with such hatred; in a way, no mother should ever speak or feel for a child."

"Mary, if you would in the future…if anything or anyone upsets my wife I want to be notified at once. If I am not at home, send for me directly. Is that clear?"

"Yes, My Lord."

"I will be sure to let you know where I will be so you will know where to find me if her mother shows up again. I do not want my wife upset as she was today. Do you understand Mary?" he said harsher than he intended.

"Yes, of course, My Lord."

"I am sorry, Mary. I do not mean to sound so harsh. It upsets me that my wife had to endure such pain."

"No, My Lord. I understand. What Baroness said hurt her very much, and it broke my heart to see her in such pain."

"Thank you, Mary. I am depending on you and the rest of the staff to keep an eye on Lady Davenport while I am away from home."

"Yes, My Lord, but of course, My Lord." Mary said, then curtsied before returning to her duties.

"Mary, for this evening, Lady Davenport and I will have our supper in our chambers."

"Yes, of course, My Lord."

Robert left the kitchen and returned to his chambers. He wanted to be there before Elizabeth woke up. After what happened with her mother, he was sure she had not eaten all day, and when she woke, she would surely be hungry.

When Robert returned to their chamber, Elizabeth was still asleep. Not wanting to wake her again, he placed a chair near the door and waited for the tray of food to arrive, and when Mary finally arrived with the tray, Robert thanked Mary and carried the tray into the chambers, then placed it on the table next to the bed. Once Mary left, Robert slowly and carefully eased himself in bed with Elizabeth, and this time when he put his arms around her, she did not wake.

When Elizabeth finally woke up, it was dark outside, and she found Robert with his arms around her, as he was watching her intently, so she turned to face him and saw the unconditional love he had for her in his eyes.

"Robert, what time is it? It looks to be full dark."

Robert smiled, then moved a piece of hair out of her face, "Yes, my love, it is very late. Are you hungry?"

Elizabeth smiled. She had not realized how hungry she was until that moment. "Oh, yes, I am famished. I am sorry I missed dinner."

Robert smiled, "No worries, my love. I had Mary prepare a tray of food for when you woke. There is meat, cheese, and fruit. Shall I make you a plate?"

Elizabeth returned the smile and said, "Oh yes, please. Thank you, Robert. You are so good to me."

Robert just smiled, as he left their bed and prepared a plate for his beloved.

After Elizabeth and Robert had their fill, Robert readied himself for bed, and they fell asleep right before the sun rose with Elizabeth in his arms.

Chapter Twenty-Two

It had been only a couple of days since Elizabeth received a visit from her mother, when she received a visit from John Bonnet.

When Elizabeth heard the knock at the door, she was coming out of Robert's study and waved off the maid who was about to open it, instead she opened the door herself. On the other side was a tall man she did not recognize.

"Lady Davenport, I presume?" John asked, bowing to Elizabeth, and she curtsied to him.

"Yes, Sir, I am Lady Davenport. To whom am I speaking?"

"My Lady, I am a Catholic Clergyman, John Bonnet from the French royal court of his Majesty King Francis the First."

Elizabeth was surprised to receive a visit from a Catholic Clergyman who was in service to the King of France. She recognized the name though and tried to recall where she heard it. *Where did I hear that name before?* She thought about this as Elizabeth made niceties with John Bonnet.

"Sir, what do I owe the honor to receive such a visit?"

"My Lady, I come on behalf of Francis the First, the King of France. Will you honor me on a walk down by the river nearby?"

Elizabeth hesitated; after all, she was a married woman and wondered, *would it be proper to go alone with this man? But, how could I fear him? He is a man of God.*

"Sir, I am afraid you find me home alone, I do not —"

John stopped her, knowing what she was going to say. "You need naught fear me, My Lady, as you can see," turning and pointed to the two French royal guards that accompanied him. "I come with two of King Francis royal guards. As a Catholic Clergyman, My Lady, surely you know you will be safe with me," he said, smiling to himself with the deception of the role he was playing.

He is right. There is no reason to fear a man of God, she thought.

Elizabeth agreed and reached for her cloak, but before she left, she turned and called for Mary.

"Mary?"

"Yes, My Lady?" Mary said as she rushed to her mistress's side and curtsied.

"Mary, if Robert should return home early, please let him know I went on a walk with," she said pointing behind her, "John Bonnet. He is a French Catholic Clergyman. We are going for a walk down by the river north of Dunham Massey Castle," Elizabeth explained, and saw the concern on Mary's face and reached for her hand, "Do not worry, Mary. He is a man of God. If we cannot trust a man of God, then who can we trust." Mary nodded in agreement, and Elizabeth walked out the door with John Bonnet and his two royal guards.

John listened intently to Elizabeth as she gave instructions to her maid, and what he heard, he could not help but smile. 'He is a man of God. If we cannot trust a man of God, then who can we trust.' He repeated her words, as he thought, *indeed, who can you trust, my dear.*

"My Lady, why did you tell your maid we will be walking near the river north of Dunham Massey Castle? Is there not a river right down the way here," pointing towards the river Elizabeth and Robert take their daily walks by?

"Sire, forgive me. Yes, there is, but that is a private river for my husband and myself. You do not mind, do you?"

"No, My Lady, not at all." *The farther away from others, the better,* he thought. "If this is the case, we will take my carriage to the river," John said, then informed the driver of the change in plans. "We will take the carriage to the river north of Dunham Massey Castle," John ordered the driver.

Once they arrived at the river, John assisted Elizabeth out of the carriage and then began their walk. As they walked, John explained the events between King Francis and Baron Massey after they arrived in Chester but purposely left out certain truths.

At this, Elizabeth realized why his name sounded familiar. *This is why his name was so familiar. So, this is the man mother mentioned,* Elizabeth thought.

When John learned how Robert and Elizabeth married, or did not marry, and Baron and Baroness Massey disowned their daughter, it made what he was about to do even better.

"You see, My Lady, King Francis took an interest in you. Your beauty, as rare as it is, captivated him. So, he took the liberty to go himself, to speak with your father. When Baron Massey learned the truth of your deception, he and King Francis came to an agreement." John Bonnet came to a stop and turned to Elizabeth, "My Lady, in a fourth night you will accompany King Francis when he returns to France, then shortly after, become his bride," he said, as he bowed. "You shall become the next queen of France, a great honor to be bestowed to one as you," he said, bowing again.

Elizabeth was shocked; she needed to rectify the misunderstanding and quickly. "Sir, surely, my mother and father informed King Francis of my recent marriage to Robert Davenport, son of Lord Davenport, of Bramhall Manor."

"Yes, My Lady, they did indeed. Of course, King Francis was very much disappointed at first, but when King Francis informed me of your recent marriage, I believed it to be untrue."

Elizabeth looked at John, unable to believe what she heard, and before she could say a word, he continued.

"You see, My Lady; I heard the rumors in the village on how your marriage took place, so I took the liberty to make inquiries with all the churches in and outside of Cheshire. And to my wonderful surprise, I found there was no record of a wedding taking place between Elizabeth Massey and Robert Davenport." Seeing the shock look on her face, he emphasized, "My dear, I assure you; I visited them all," John said, smiling as he eyed Elizabeth, relishing the confusion he saw on her face. "My lady, it is a great honor to have a king such as King Francis's quality to consider you as the next Queen of France. To refuse him is a slap in King Francis's face, not to mention the possibility of war against France and your people."

To hear this, Elizabeth flinched, and John saw her fear and reveled in it.

"My dear, you captivated King Francis when he saw you in the village. You should be honored to have a king as great as he pursues you in such a fashion. For a king, one of King Francis status, to personally go to your father to make his wishes known…which is unknown to be done by any king, especially one of his status."

Elizabeth looked at John with utter shock at what he said. At first, she had no words in response, and for a long moment, she could only stare at John in bewilderment. What was she to say? How was she to prove to this man of God and King Francis she was married.

How can I explain to this man of God that I am a married woman and cannot marry King Francis without insulting him or the king? To tell him his inquiries were wrong, she thought.

Elizabeth took a deep breath and then released it slowly; she needed to help this man of God see the truth. "Sir, I am indeed honored. How could any lady not be sought out by such a glorious and noble king as King Francis. His interest in me is greatly appreciated, and for one to not accept such an extensive offer of marriage to a king as great as he would be inconceivable. But Sir, as I already told you, I am married to Robert Davenport. I am grateful for the compliments and for this glorious king, King Francis, who wants to honor me by making me Queen of France…Sir, it is impossible to accept such an offer of marriage. Again, Sir, I am married. Robert and I were married in a church in the eyes of God. It was not a church within or outside of Cheshire, but a church near Yorkshire, which is a day's ride away, which is why Sir you could not find any proof a wedding took place. Sir, I promise you, here and now, as God is my witness, Robert and I are indeed married. Please thank King Francis for his wonderful compliments and his generous offer, but I must respectfully decline."

To hear this insolent girl refuse King Francis's offer – of course, there was no offer of marriage, but still to refuse was a grave mistake.

Outraged by Elizabeth's response, "I do not believe you!" he said, in a harsher voice than he intended, causing Elizabeth to flinch. He took a moment to reign in his anger and tried again. "My lady, I do not believe you are being truthful with me. You may have fooled your mother and father, but my dear, you do not fool me," John said, as his voice went from soft to firm, giving her a sinister smile.

Elizabeth flinched at John's erupt anger and saw a man with evil intent, not a man of God. Although his anger was short-lived, it sent shivers of fear coursing through her body, and just in that brief moment, Elizabeth realized she had made a grave mistake in accompanying this man who claimed to be a man of God on a walk alone.

John watched Elizabeth intently as he continued; he did not miss how that small amount of anger he displayed had a severe effect on her. In this, he decided there was no need to constrain his true self.

"You are breaking one of God's greatest sins, pretending to be married when you are not!" he said with a growl. "You are living in sin as husband and wife! Your deceit dishonors King Francis, and this, my dear, I cannot allow!"

This sent shivers through Elizabeth as her fear increased; everything in her was telling her to run, to get away from this man now. How could she? What would he do if she tried? This man of God no longer. His demeanor changed to one of evil.

Oh, God, help me! I am afraid to be here with this man any longer! Help me find a way out! she thought.

John smiled at his success in causing fear in Elizabeth, and he could see she wanted to escape. "My dear, you might want to reconsider your decision. You are insulting King Francis…dishonoring him with your refusal and lies! If you do not accept King Francis's proposal, your insolence will result in a war between France and your countrymen!" John hollered, then lowered his voice to one of malice, "You do not want that, now do you, my dear?"

Elizabeth stared at John, horrified by his threat, and she could not understand, *how can my refusing to marry King Francis erupt in a war?* This didn't make any sense to Elizabeth.

Elizabeth felt lost and confused, and she was unsure how to react? What was she to say? Never in her life has anyone accused her of such dishonor and disrespect. Let alone one that could result in a war, in her refusing to marry King Francis.

"Not only will this war destroy your countrymen, it will destroy your families as well! Do you want that on your head?" John said, relishing in threatening Elizabeth. But, to his surprise, he felt a strong and deep sexual desire for her. He knew his threats were unfounded, but Elizabeth – he looked at her – she was so young and so easy to manipulate.

Elizabeth looked at John, baffled and torn by what was happening.

What am I to do? How do I convince such a man? A man who will not listen, nor believe I am married. How can I make this man see and understand I am a married woman? Married in a house of God? I am not free to marry King Francis, she thought, frantic to make him understand.

She couldn't believe this was happening, but she could not give up. She had to keep trying to convince this man of God, to make him see reason.

Elizabeth took a deep breath and began again. "Sir, I know naught why it's essential that I marry King Francis. Again, I am truly honored by King Francis's interest in me, in one of my standing, how could I not be. A king, as great as he, wishing to honor me by making me his wife and queen. But Sir, I employ you to see, it's impossible. I am already married. As I told you, there is no record to be found in the churches within or directly outside of Cheshire. Robert and I married in a church, a house of God, only a day's ride from Cheshire, in Yorkshire.

Being a man of God, how can you dispute what I say? As you know Sir, being married in a church, in the eyes of God, what is done cannot be undone. If I were to agree to marry King Francis, I would be committing a great sin, and you, a man of God, should surely see that?" Elizabeth said, but this was a grave mistake in choosing her last words.

This was a big mistake for John to hear, 'A man of God should surely see that,' unsettled John, it angered him beyond control. A man who saw himself as God, would not contrive to have a woman speak to him in such a way.

"HOW DARE YOU!" Elizabeth flinched and wanted to run at John's abrupt anger. "This is the King of France, you fool! You dishonor him with your lies, and you dishonor me! I, a Catholic Clergyman…you dare continue with these lies! You are beneath King Francis, and you are beneath me! King Francis desires you, and you will not refuse him! You will accept King Francis's offer of marriage or bring war on top of you and your countryman, destroying all you hold and love dear!"

Elizabeth was terrified; she could not believe what was happening to her. She looked around, afraid she could not escape this man who changed before her eyes, from a kind and good man of God to a man of great evil, who possibly worships the devil instead of a good and holy God.

Oh, God, what is happening? How can this man who claims to be a man of God change in this way? God, I am in trouble, and I know naught how to escape, Elizabeth thought, again she looked around, needing to find a way to escape, but there was nowhere she could run where he couldn't catch her. It wasn't only John Elizabeth had to worry about, but the two guards with him as well. She could never outrun them all.

Elizabeth did the only thing she could do; she yelled at the top of her lungs. "I WILL NOT! I cannot marry King Francis! He is not my king, nor does he have a right or the authority to demand…nay, order me to marry him! How dare you, a man of God, to treat me in such a way!"

There was nothing John Bonnet could say or do that would induce Elizabeth to change her mind. Although she feared this man, she could not allow him to continue with his insistence on her marrying King Francis. Elizabeth tried to walk away, with her need to return to the safety of Watch Hill Castle, when John grabbed her upper arm and pulled her back to him.

John clenched his teeth, and in her right ear he said, "You! Foolish! Girl!" he snarled, then he started shaking Elizabeth by her shoulders. "You will accept the king, or —"

John stopped abruptly as he suddenly looked at Elizabeth with such evil – lust in his eyes. He was no man of God, but a truly evil man.

"Ah, I see why King Francis favors you," he said, sliding his hand down her cheek. Elizabeth jerked away, but John held her firm in his grasp. "Yes, you are a true beauty." He grabbed Elizabeth's hair and rubbed it between his fingers, then pulled it to his nose and inhaled deeply; taking in the sweet scent, then he rubbed the softness of her hair against his face. "You will indeed make a great wife. Why should King Francis have all the beautiful women? Why should I not…what he does not know…I think…I shall try you out for myself to ensure you will be good enough to please my king."

Elizabeth panicked, knowing what John wanted to do, and she desperately tried to pull away, but John only pulled her closer, so their bodies touched in a way no Catholic Clergyman should touch a woman. John ran his fingers through Elizabeth's hair, "Ah, my dear, I shall have the first taste. Yes, indeed, I shall." John took his thumb and gently glided it across Elizabeth's lower lip while looking at her with a strong and lustful desire.

Elizabeth jerked away, trying to fight – doing all she could to pull away from John, but he was too strong.

"What are you doing! Stop that!" Elizabeth yelled. "Get your hands off me!"

Elizabeth tried with all her power to get out of John's grip – screaming, kicking, and scratching, trying with all her power to force him to release her, hoping once he did, it would give her a chance to escape and run back to the safety of Watch Hill Castle.

"My dear, you cannot possibly be ignorant of my intentions?" John said as he worked his way down her body with his hands, grabbing and touching everything, and when he reached and lifted the bottom of her gown, he placed his hand where no man, especially a man of God, should place his hand, unless he was her husband.

As Elizabeth was struggling, trying everything in her power to break free from John – her struggles only angered him, causing him to grab her harder – *she wants it rough, well I shall give her rough,* John thought.

John held Elizabeth's upper arms in a firm grip, shaking

her again. "Stop resisting! You know you want this!"

But Elizabeth refused to give in. She would fight with all she had, even if that meant her death, but all her resistance only fueled his anger and his deployable desires. John shook Elizabeth again to stop her struggling but felt more drastic steps were needed, so he threatened her.

"If you do not stop resisting, I will take a knife and cut your throat! Is that what you want?"

Elizabeth froze. *Will he do as he says? Oh God, what am I to do? This cannot be happening, no, no-no-no. This is not happening,* she thought.

"STOP!" Elizabeth screamed at the top of her lungs, causing her voice to echo across the land. Unfortunately, they were too far for anyone to hear her screams. Elizabeth did what she hoped would work, she began to beg for John to stop, but he does not. John continued touching and feeling Elizabeth's body, wanting to touch every inch of her. Placing his hands —

"No-o-o-o! Stop! Do not…No!" Elizabeth looked over to the royal guards, seeking their help, but they only looked away, pretending as if nothing was happening.

At this, John threw Elizabeth to the ground as he fell on top of her, then reached beneath her gown as he slowly slides his hand up her leg, at the same time pushing her gown out of the way. Once her gown was above her waist, he placed himself between her legs as he used his other hand to lower his stockings to prepare himself for his invasion.

The noises Elizabeth was making, John took them as pleasure. For Elizabeth, it was pain and torture.

God, please help me, do not let this man do what he is about to do, Elizabeth pleaded. Elizabeth fought to keep her legs closed, but John was too strong, and he forced her legs open, then roughly placed his hand on her —

"Don't…Stop! Please stop!" Elizabeth was crying as she reached down with one hand to stop John. Then without realizing it, an automatic defense, she used her other hand to scratch Johns' face, still pleading for God's help. *Oh, God, please stop him! Help him see what he is doing is wrong! He, a man of God, should not be doing what he is doing!* But no matter her efforts, John did not stop.

When Elizabeth scratched John, it set him into a rage, and he crawled up Elizabeth and grabbed and squished her face, "Stop! Or I will have those," turning Elizabeth's face to force her to look at the guards, "Guards come here and hold you down! Then after I am done, I will let them have you as well! Is that what you want?" Elizabeth shook her head no. With that, John proceeded to do what he wanted with her. Elizabeth could not bear it; she closed her eyes in an attempt to escape from what was happening to her.

John pulled at the top of Elizabeth's gown, ripping it down the middle, revealing her large lushes' breast – he smiled, then took them in his hands, squeezing them, enjoying the feel and softness of them, but he was not gentle. John puts one in his mouth, biting her nipple; at this, Elizabeth struck him on the head with her fist. She did not intend to; it was another reflex reaction that again angered him. He grabbed her arms to prevent her from hitting him again. He looked over to the guards, and Elizabeth saw this and started shaking her head no, but John ignored her and called the guards over to them.

When Elizabeth finally found her voice, she screamed, afraid of what he was going to do with the other men. "No-o-o-o-o, please no-o-o-o-o-o, don't...I won't do it again!" Her words were not heard, and it did not matter at this point.

When the guards reached them, John ordered, "Take her hands and hold her down!" Elizabeth tried to fight but failed. Once the guards held her arms on each side, John proceeded to rape her. He raped her with all his aggression, his anger, hard and very painful. He held back nothing.

Elizabeth felt as if John was tearing her apart from the inside out. When John was done, he looked up at Elizabeth and smiled with that evil smile, then tossed her aside as if she was no more than trash.

Elizabeth was crying and hurting. At first, she felt a great deal of pain; then, it seemed as if her body went numb from shock. During her rape, it was as if she left her body, turning herself off from what was happening. When it was over, and she returned to her body, she felt lost, not understanding what happened and what she was to do next.

God, what just happened? At this question, it hit her, *no, no-no-no, God, tell me this did not happen? It could not have happened. John Bonnet is a man of God, how could he?* she thought, then closed her eyes and rolled to her side into a fetal position with her hands placed between her legs, not wanting to deal with the agony and the pain of what happened.

Oh God, he did, didn't he? It did happen. At this thought, Elizabeth opened her eyes and turned to look at John. He was basking in triumph at what he did to her. *How could he? Why did he do this? It did happen; there is no denying it.*

After Elizabeth finally gathered the strength to get up, and once she was standing, she looked down at herself and saw her dress was ripped down the front and the rest of it was disheveled. Elizabeth tried to gather the top of her gown, trying to pull it together the best she could, with her emotions in chaos. But tried the best way she could to pull herself together, without saying a word or making a sound. Even if she could, she did not know what to say or do.

Where do I go? Who do I tell? Who can I talk to that could help me understand what happened? How can I live with this? Who can I trust? she thought.

There were so many questions and so many concerns – she was scared. Worried.

Elizabeth was lost, afraid, and so alone.

Maybe…maybe I can go talk to Grace? she thought, then immediately dismissed this thought. *No, no, I cannot! She will want me to tell mother and father, and this I cannot do, not ever! Especially after what happened!* Then suddenly, her thoughts turned to Robert. *Oh God, Robert? What am I going to do with Robert? I cannot tell him. I could never tell him.* Elizabeth's heart sank at the realization there was no one she could go to – to talk to. And if there was, who would believe her? *Robert?*

Yes, he would believe her, but what would he do? He would do what any man would do to a man who hurt his wife. He would try to kill John Bonnet, and Elizabeth could not allow that. She could never tell Robert. This left her heartbroken and feeling defeated.

Oh God, there is no one I can tell. No one I can go to. If I went to anyone other than Grace or Robert…who would believe me, that a man of God did what he did to me.

Elizabeth was shaking, reeled with shock. With her fears, Elizabeth could no longer control her emotions, and finally released what she was holding back and broke down crying, but quickly placed her hands over her mouth to muffle her cry, as she quickly turned to hide the pain and her fear. At that moment, she felt lost and alone, more alone than she ever felt before. To be a woman, Elizabeth knew that no one would believe a woman over a man, especially if that said man was a man of God. There was no man or woman who would believe a man of God was capable of doing such a thing, in what she would accuse John Bonnet of doing.

***

Even though Lord Davenport ordered Robert to stay away, Robert felt he had a right to know and understand why this agreement between Baron Massey and his father could not be changed.

As Robert approached the front entrance to Bramhall Manor, he ran into his brother Edward. Edward agreed with their father, and he too was angry at Robert for what he did, and Edward wasted no time in voicing his disgust with his brother, even if he had to, he would fight his brother to force him to leave. "How dare you come here and show your face after what you did to our family! Get out of here now, Robert!"

"Edward, I understand you are angry, but I love Elizabeth —"

"You love Elizabeth! Well, Elizabeth was not the one you were supposed to marry! Now get out of here, Robert! Or, as God is my witness, I will run you through!" Edward pulled out his sword to show Robert he was serious.

Robert sighed; he didn't want to fight his brother, but if Edward forced him, being a better swordsman, then Edward would lose.

"Edward, get out of my way! You know I am a better swordsman than you!" Robert said, shaking his head. "I do not wish to fight you. I need to speak to father about this agreement! Now move and let me pass!"

Edward refused to back down. "Oh, you mean the agreement you failed to honor! Now you want to discuss this agreement after you already married another and sealing our fate."

"Edward, what do you know of this agreement?"

Shrugging his shoulders, "I know nothing! Only what I overheard father talking to mother about!" Edward said as he thought, *maybe I should let father deal with Robert.* "Fine, you want to talk to father, it is your head! Father is still furious with you! I would not be surprised if he ran you through upon seeing you! And he is a better swordsman than you are!" Edward said, then bowed and jester with his arm for Robert to continue. "Please, proceed," he said, being condescending.

"What a cocky bastard," Robert said under his breath as he moved passed Edward to the manor's main entrance. *And father knows, he is not a better swordsman than me,* he thought.

Robert, with caution, continued through the manor to his father's study. He was not going to be deterred from speaking to his father. When he entered his father's study, he cleared his throat to get his father's attention.

When his father looked up and saw Robert standing in the doorway, he was outraged. *He dares come here after I told him to stay away,* he thought, but then, *however, I must give it to the boy, he has a backbone,* he silently snickered.

There was no doubt Lord Davenport was a hard man, but he admired strength and courage, and Robert had always displayed both. In Lord Davenport's eyes, he believed Robert was the right one to proceed him, although he would never tell him so.

"Boy, do you have a death wish!"

"Father please, I must know and understand why this agreement is so important. I feel that you and Baron Massey have not told us everything about this agreement. I demand to know why it is so important…why Grace's name cannot be changed to Elizabeth's? I should be allowed to see it for myself."

Outraged, Lord Davenport rushed towards Robert as if he were going to attack him, but before he could reach him, Robert pulled out his sword and pointed it at his father.

"Father, I do not think you want to do that," Robert said, staring down his father.

"You have no business knowing the contents of the agreement! However, I understand with your mother's help, you have already read the agreement! Now, get out before I do something I will regret, that your mother could never forgive."

Robert stared at his father for a long moment as he thought, *so, mother told father.*

"Yes, I did. The agreement was about Grace and me; therefore, I had every right to read it. You had no right to keep it from me, and from what I read, I see no reason why the agreement cannot be changed or be considered null and void. I chose not to honor your ridiculous agreement, as I felt love was more important than honor. Tell me, father, why did you believe I had no right to know? How can this agreement be more important to you than your own son? Your own blood. Was I so easy to be disposed of? And father, this concern of yours on how mother would feel, is this not contradictory to the famous Lord Davenport? You have never shown any care or love for mother. How about this, why do you not just kill me. Is that what the famous and great Lord Davenport, magistrate, controller of law would do, and to his own blood, his son and heir?" Robert mocked his father.

Robert did not understand his father nor his ways. He understood as Lord of the land that there was a certain need for control and law, but to the extent his father took it to, this, he did not understand, nor did he approve.

Although his father was a hard and cruel man, Robert knew his father could never hurt him, his own son and heir. If he did, it would make Edward heir —

Humph, Edward heir. Hum, I guess it would be a better choice since Edward is more like father, Robert thought.

To kill his own son, no, he would not do that. Regardless of Lord Davenport's power, he still needed the respect of the people, and to kill his own son, a mob of angry villagers could rise against him, no matter of his title and position. If enough of the people revolted against Lord Davenport, it would be his undoing. No, he would not kill his son.

"Boy, are you mad! You are wasting my time! Now, get out! There is nothing further we have to discuss!" Lord Davenport yelled, then turned his back on Robert.

Just then, Edward walked in with his sword drawn, snickering, "Do as father says Robert, I do not wish to hurt you, but I will if I must."

Lord Davenport turned back when he heard Edward's

voice. "Let him be Edward!" Lord Davenport said, then turned his back on Robert again. "Go Robert, and never return, so long as I still have breath in my lungs!"

Feeling defeated, Robert left his father's study, and as he was walking down the hall, he saw his mother, which caused him to stop abruptly.

"Mother?" Robert said, with sadness in his voice, then he saw the concern on his mother's face. "Worry naught, mother; I am leaving. I will be fine," Robert said as he touched his mother's arm on his way out.

Lady Davenport could not let her son leave. It was the first time she had seen Robert since he left the night he announced he was married to Elizabeth. She had to stop him.

"My son, please stop." Robert turned at his mother's plea. "Robert, I am sorry for what happened, but you have no idea what you did. Your actions have ruined us all."

Robert does not understand this. From what he read in the agreement, to him, in what he did, it should nullify the agreement.

"Mother, when you showed me the agreement… do you not see? In what I did, if everyone would stop and see, they would see what I did can nullify the agreement." Robert saw the baffled look on his mother's face and tried to explain. "Mother?" he said, taking her hand, "Do you not see? The agreement said if the one who wronged, would be the one at fault. It was not one, but both of us. In this, both sides are at fault; therefore, one cannot punish the other without punishing themselves. For me to marry Elizabeth was the perfect solution."

Lady Davenport stared at her son, she could not believe what he said, but what he said made sense. *How could we not have thought of this? Is he right?* she thought.

"Robert, this is what you were talking about when you read the agreement, when you said there was a way out, knowing that marrying Elizabeth would anger your father?"

"Yes, mother, it was. I chose love over honor, as we all should, no matter the circumstances or consequences."

Lady Davenport stared at her son with a feeling of pride. *He will make a great Lord one day. A better man than his father,* she thought.

"I understand why you chose love over honor when you married Elizabeth," his mother said, then turned her eyes away from Robert to look at the floor. "If I could have chosen love over honor…tradition, I would have," she said, twisting the kerchief in her hands. "I do not fault you in choosing love. On the contrary, I admire you for it," she said, then looked up at him with a pleasing smile.

When Robert saw the acceptance in his mother's face, his barriers cracked a little, and he confessed the difficulties it's been for him – his suffering.

"Mother, it is so hard for me…I am sorry mother, I love you very much," Robert said, reaching for his mother's hands and pulled her in for a hug.

"And I love you, Robert," she said, looking up at him with loving acceptance in her eyes. "But now, you must go. Just know, I love you no matter what." Lady Davenport pulled her son in for another hug and kissed him on the cheek before letting him go.

Robert turned and left, and once his back was towards her, she released the tears she'd been holding back. Then, to Lady Davenport's surprise, she felt strong arms wrap around her waist. When she turned, she expected to see Edward, but to her surprise, it was her husband, and she leaned into him and allowed him to comfort her.

***

When Elizabeth returned to Watch Hill Castle, she was afraid to be seen by the servants in the state she was in, so she took a few moments to make herself presentable by pulling up the hood of her cloak, then tightened it around her body in order to conceal her ripped gown.

Elizabeth quietly walked through the front door, and

once she was inside, to her relief, Robert was not at home. She didn't have to see Robert to know this – she felt it in her heart.

Thinking she was safe, Elizabeth started to ascend the stairs hoping to make it to her chambers before she was seen, when she heard Mary call out to her.

"My Lady, did you have a good walk? Is there anything I can get for you?" Mary asked, curtsying to Elizabeth.

Elizabeth took a moment to get her emotions in check, she didn't want Mary to know anything was wrong. She knew Robert asked Mary to send for him if anything was the matter, and Elizabeth could not allow that. She needed time to get her bearings, so she could figure out what she was going to do and say to Robert.

Since they married, there wasn't a night Robert did not make love to her, except for those times when her monthly came, and she knew that excuse would not work this time since she already had her monthly.

Suddenly, she felt fear coursing through her, how was she going to keep Robert from wanting to make love to her.

"It was a lovely walk, Mary, thank you. No, I do not need anything right now. I am tired and will lie down for a while."

Mary curtsied and said, "Yes, My Lady." Then she turned and resumed her duties.

Elizabeth managed to get to her chambers without running into any more servants. After entering her room, she frantically ripped off her gown and shift and tossed them into the burning fire. She went to the table with the pitcher and basin, filled the basin with water, then dipped the cloth until it was soaked, rubbing it with soap. Elizabeth began scrubbing every inch of her body, until she was raw. She wanted to remove all trace of 'his' filth and touch. With each scrub, tears fell until she was crying uncontrollably and had to muffle the sound so she would not be overheard.

Once she believed her body was clean enough, she used

the pitcher to pour water over her head and began the tedious job of scrubbing her hair, trying to get out the filth of his touch. Once she was done, she pulled on her dressing gown and crawled into bed, pulling her legs to her chest in a fetal position, and silently cried until she fell asleep.

***

When Robert returned home, Mary informed him of the visitor Elizabeth received.

"My Lord, he is a French Clergyman named John Bonnet. He —

Before Mary could say another word, Robert stopped her.

"What! What did you say?" Robert asked.

Mary could see Robert was upset at hearing John Bonnet's name. "Forgive me, My Lord, John Bonnet invited Elizabeth on a walk, and when she returned, she was tired and went directly to her chambers, where she's been asleep ever since.

At hearing this, Robert went directly to their chambers, and when he entered, he saw Elizabeth asleep on the bed. Robert quietly and carefully crawled in bed next to her, and when he put his arms around Elizabeth and started to pull her close to him, she woke in a panic and started attacking him.

Startled, Robert gently grabbed Elizabeth's hands and said, "My love, it is I your husband. It is alright. You are safe. Did you have a bad dream?"

Elizabeth was sleeping soundly until she woke up with arms wrapped tightly around her. This caused her to panic, thinking John Bonnet still had her until she heard Robert's voice.

"Robert, I am so sorry. Yes, forgive me; I was having a horrible dream."

"My love, there is nothing to forgive," Robert said as he gathered Elizabeth in his arms.

Elizabeth tensed; she was so afraid, if she flinched,

Robert would know something was wrong, and this she could not allow. But she could not prevent herself from tensing in his arms, and Robert did not miss that.

"My love, is something the matter? Are you unwell? Mary said you have been in bed all day since you returned from your walk with John Bonnet."

At hearing John Bonnet, Elizabeth flinched again, but to her relief, Robert did not notice. "I am sorry, Robert. When I returned, I was not feeling well and thought I would lay down for a short time. I did not expect to be in bed all day."

This is perfect. I can claim to be ill, thus, keeping Robert from making love to me. But how long can I claim to be ill…not long, Elizabeth thought as she sighed, *I must get myself together. I cannot allow Robert to think anything is wrong.*

"I may have caught something on my walk. I do not want you to get sick as well, so, you best not kiss me."

Robert smiled, "My love, I do not care if you are ill. It does not matter. I shall kiss you anyways."

Elizabeth panicked. She did not think she could kiss Robert or be intimate with him, not after what happened. She was hurting and was sore everywhere. If she allowed him to make love to her, he would know what happened. She had to keep him away, just long enough for her to heal, so there would be no evidence of what happened. What was she going to do? How was she going to convince him?

"Robert, stop it. If I am ill, I do not wish you to become ill too. You will not be kissing me until I am sure you will not get what I have," Elizabeth said with confidence, as she thought, *yes, that is it. This will buy me a little time.* She sighed, *but not much.*

Robert laughed but agreed. He would not kiss Elizabeth, nor would he be intimate with her until she told him she was well. *I am sure she is fine. It will not be long before I can kiss those beautiful lips again,* he thought.

"Then, my love, I shall not kiss or make love to you until you give me leave to do so."

At this, Elizabeth smiled, feeling relieved.

"Are you hungry? Shall we go down for dinner, or shall I have Mary bring our supper here?" Robert asked.

"Oh no, Robert, I think I can manage to go down to the dining room with you. I have been in bed all day and would like to get out a bit."

Robert helped Elizabeth out of bed, and after she freshened up and dressed, they headed down for dinner.

Although dinner went well, Elizabeth tried hard to appear as normal as possible. However, she noticed Robert watching her intently and felt he suspected more was going on than what she claimed.

Robert was indeed watching Elizabeth, and he couldn't help but feel there was more going on with Elizabeth than she claimed. Unable to ignore these feelings, he walked over and sat in the chair next to her, but she refused to make eye contact with him, so he reached for her hand, and with his other hand, he placed two fingers under her chin to force her to look at him.

"Elizabeth, what is wrong? I know there is more going on with you than not feeling well. Tell me what it is, love? You know you can tell me anything?"

Anything? No, not this time, she thought.

Elizabeth knew she could not tell Robert she was raped by a man who claimed to be a man of God. A Catholic Clergyman. Elizabeth was terrified Robert would see right through her. But she knew she had to say something to reassure him that everything was well.

I cannot tell him the truth. Not ever, Elizabeth thought, then she sighed in resignation. Unfortunately, there was no choice; she must lie to Robert.

She put a smile on her face and hope it was convincing enough. "Nothing, my love, all is well," she said, praying this would satisfy him. But, from the look on his face, she could see it did not.

Robert didn't by what she said. He knew there was more going on with her than what she was claiming, because she refused to look at him, or make eye contact with him, which told him what he needed to know – *she is definitely hiding something,* he thought.

Although Robert tried to force Elizabeth to look at him, it would only last a moment before she averted her eyes to stare at their connected hands. Elizabeth knew if she made eye contact with Robert, he would see right through her lie and anguish.

Robert again placed his fingers under her chin to force her to look at him. "My love, I know you are not well, but I feel there is more happening with you than only being unwell. So, tell me, love, what has you so upset?"

It broke Elizabeth's heart to see the worry on Robert's face. How could she not tell him? At this, she could no longer hold back her tears and closed her eyes to allow them to fall as she thought, *God, what do I tell him? How can I tell him? How can I lie to him? I cannot...no, but I must. He is my love, my husband. I love this man with all my heart and soul. He has always been there for me, but if he knew the truth, he would go and try to kill John Bonnet, and if he fails...God no, I cannot lose him, not ever.*

Robert could see Elizabeth struggling. It was clear she wanted to answer him, but she was unsure how.

What could it be that she struggles to tell me? She knows she can tell me anything. So, what is it she fears? If she cannot tell me, I will not push...no, I cannot let this go. I must know, he thought.

"Elizabeth, please tell me what is wrong? There is nothing you cannot tell me. I am your husband, your friend. We have been together for a long time. There is nothing you cannot tell me. Love," looking deep in her eyes, "You know you can trust me. Please, my love, tell me what has you upset?" he asked, in a soft low voice. He then took

Elizabeth's hand and kissed it with his eyes locked with hers.

"Oh, Robert, forgive me. I know I can tell you anything. It is only, I…I am only upset…I miss my family." Elizabeth finally said, but she had to turn her face away from Robert, unable to look at him with the shame she felt with her lie.

Robert waited patiently for her to elaborate, and he noticed she could not look at him, but he decided not to push, which relieved Elizabeth immensely.

After a few moments, she continued. "While you were away, I went on a walk with John Bonnet, and he told me what happened when King Francis visited my father and the way my father reacted. Well…it hurt," Elizabeth said as tears continued to fall. Robert pulled her into his arms and allowed her to release the pain – cry that she desperately needed. When Elizabeth finished, she pulled away from Robert and continued. "I…miss them so much. I…cannot believe…they think…they think…oh Robert," she said, falling back into his arms as she rested her head on his chest, with the need to hear his heart beating, thus calming her. "They think we lied, and believe we are living in sin." Elizabeth managed to say before she completely lost it.

Robert held Elizabeth tight in his arms, allowing her to release her pain. He understood how hard it was for her to know her family to believe such lies, and it breaks his heart to see her in so much pain.

"Elizabeth. Elizabeth, it will be all right," he said, rubbing her back, "One day they will learn the truth, and when they do, all will be well."

It took a while before Elizabeth could speak again. Finally, she rose her head to look at him, "I am sorry, Robert. Please forgive me."

"My love, there is nothing to forgive. You are in pain, and you have every right to express that pain."

"I just miss them so much. You are wonderful, and you

are the greatest thing I have in my life. If all I have is you, I do not require anything else, but…" Elizabeth hesitated, lowering her head to avoid looking at him again.

"But what, my love?" Robert asked, lifting her chin to look at him.

"Sometimes, like today, for some reason…although I have you, I still feel so alone. For mother and father not to want anything to do with me…oh Robert, it's just…so hard. I started thinking about how I will never see my mother and father or John ever again. I know they hate me, but I still love them all so very much. It breaks my heart to know they will never want anything to do with me ever again…their own daughter. When we have children, they will never know them. The one thing I am happy about is that Grace has not abandoned me. She is all the family I have right now besides you. But, I can only see her when she visits me, which is not often enough. It is not as if I can call on her whenever I feel the need to see and speak with her…oh Robert, I am so sorry. Please do not think I regret what we did because I do not. If I had to choose again, I would still choose you. You are my heart, and I could never live without you ." Elizabeth clings to Robert, needing to feel his heart beating, knowing it beats for her.

Robert held Elizabeth tight against his body, trying to give her the comfort she needed. He knew there was nothing he could do to replace her pain, but he was determined to do what he could to ease her pain every day until finally, it was barely there.

"My love, it is difficult not to have your family around you, as it is for me. I believe in time; they will come to accept us."

"Do you, Robert? Do you really believe that…that they will accept us?"

Robert pulled Elizabeth closer to him and said, "Yes, Elizabeth, I do. We will continue to pray for God to help them see how wrong they are. In time, they will come to accept our marriage, and when they do, we will be back in their lives."

Elizabeth held on to Robert as tight as she could as she cried in his arms.

God? I prayed to God. I begged, pleaded for him to help me. Why didn't he? she thought.

With these thoughts, although she wanted so much to believe Robert, but it was difficult after her rape.

What Elizabeth didn't understand; God did help her that day. No, he did not save her by stopping the rape; instead, he separated her soul from her body to protect her from being there – being a part of John raping her, which was why when it was over, she was confused and lost, not knowing or understanding what happened. This is what some call shock or trauma. When in actuality, in some cases, was a spiritual intervention. It was a way to protect Elizabeth from permanent damage.

No matter how much Elizabeth wanted to tell Robert the truth, she could not. How could she? When she knew Robert would stop at nothing to seek revenge, to restore her honor. For that reason, she had to remain silent. She was not going to risk losing Robert too, it would be unthinkable.

Chapter Twenty-Three

It's been weeks since Elizabeth's rape, and she's done everything she could to forget about those hours of horror. Yes, there was a gap in what she remembered, although she didn't understand why, she was grateful not to have the full memory of that day.

Elizabeth found solitude during her walks around Watch Hill Castle, especially near the river she and Robert called their own. Finally, after a few days after the rape, Elizabeth was able to make love to Robert. Her love for Robert and his for her, allowed Elizabeth to embrace their love, for when she made love to him, it wiped away any, and all pain, along with the fear she felt that day. Making love to Robert was a renewal of their love, for that which was tainted was now cleansed – purified by the love their hearts and souls shared.

When Elizabeth was with Robert, it was always the two of them; everything else was forgotten, leaving them with a calming and peaceful feeling of that place that belongs only to them. For whatever reason, however it worked, it allowed Elizabeth to forget the event itself, keeping only the love she felt for Robert when they made love.

During Elizabeth's walks, it allowed her time to think about what transpired that day, in her need to understand what happened, when it seemed as if she was removed from the actual 'act' – rape itself.

Elizabeth wondered, *I asked for God's help that day, but I believed he failed me. Now, as I think back to what happened, is it possible he did help me? Is it the reason I could not recall the actual event? It could only be he who could do such a thing. Isn't it?*

Since this time, Elizabeth found peace with God, knowing he could not prevent John Bonnet from raping her, but instead, he somehow gave her the ability to escape from

that moment she was being raped, and that gave her a sense
of peace.

***

One early afternoon as Elizabeth was returning to
Watch Hill Castle after her walk by the river, she heard
horse hooves that seemed like several horses approaching
and wondered who they could be.

Robert was away, so the men approaching could not be
for him. However, when Elizabeth reached the outer walls
of Watch Hill Castle and saw the men approaching, to her
horror, John Bonnet was at the head of several French royal
guards.

Elizabeth froze and was unable to move. What was she
going to do? How was she going to avoid them? But she
knew there was no avoiding John Bonnet and the soldiers,
and as soon as she walked towards the castle, John would
see her. Elizabeth refused to allow fear to rule her, so she
took a deep breath, and once she found her inner strength,
she continued towards the castle.

When Elizabeth was in earshot, she shouted, "What
business do you have here?"

Yes, she was scared, but she focused on Robert's love,
refusing to allow her fears to own her, and his love gave her
the strength she needed to confront John Bonnet.

John looked down at Elizabeth and snickered, "Lady
Elizabeth, you cannot be ignorant to my arrival? I am here
to ensure you will be ready for your journey to France in
seven days hence."

Once Elizabeth was face-to-face with John, for a few
moments, she could only stare at him in utter shock, that he
would dare presume she would go with him to France.

***

When Robert arrived home early, he learned Elizabeth
was on her daily walk. So, while he waited for her to
return, he decided to do some work in his study that had a
large window that allowed a good view of the road, which

would enable him to see Elizabeth when she returned to the castle.

After sitting down in his chair, Robert heard several horses approaching. When he turned to see who it was, he saw Elizabeth walking up to the men on horseback. Robert then turned his attention to the men approaching and saw King Francis's royal flags. Without delay, Robert rushed out to be by Elizabeth's side and to learn why King Francis's men were on his land.

Could it be what Elizabeth told me? King Francis is determined to have her. Are these men here to force her to France to marry the king? If this is so, they will have to go through me first, Robert thought.

Robert grabbed his sword on his way out the door, so he would be ready to fight if it was called for, *royalty or not. They are on English soil and had no true order over King Henry's people,* he thought.

As Robert was walking to Elizabeth, for some reason, he was overwhelmed with a great deal of fear, fear that Elizabeth was in danger. In this, he quickened his pace to get to Elizabeth's side. As Robert approached Elizabeth, he heard John telling her she needed to make herself ready for their journey to France.

What is happening? he thought.

When he reached Elizabeth, he said, "Good day, Sir, what brings you to our land?"

Elizabeth was startled when she heard Robert's voice behind her. *Oh, God, he's home. What am I going to do?* she thought, but she couldn't think of that now. She needed to deal with John Bonnet and not allow herself to be disturbed by Robert being there.

John ignored Robert as he kept his focus on Elizabeth. It didn't matter he was there, and John saw Robert's confusion and he knew Elizabeth hadn't told him what happened, because if he did, his sword would have been drawn, and he would have been forced to kill Robert.

Well, maybe it's time the boy learns the truth, John thought. If he had, John would have been forced to kill Robert. *Which is fine with me; I would have one obstacle out of the way,* he thought as he smiled.

Robert looked at Elizabeth and wondered, *what is going on here?* He was determined to get answers from Elizabeth.

Elizabeth felt Robert directly behind her and was sure he was confused to what was happening, but she couldn't allow his presence to affect her, then she heard him ask —

"Elizabeth what is going on —"

She ignored him and cut him off. "What makes you think or believe I will go with you to France! I told you on your last visit I am married to Robert!"

John was furious. He jumped off his horse and stood directly in front of Elizabeth in an attempt to intimidate her. Robert tried to get between them, but the royal guards, who already jumped off their horses, stepped in his way.

"You will go to France and marry King Francis!" John said in a firm and demanding voice.

At this demand, Elizabeth allowed the anger she'd been holding back to surface. But not only surface, it exploded, showing a side of Elizabeth that she herself didn't know she was capable of, and by the shocked look on Robert's face, neither did he.

"NO I WILL NOT!" she screamed. "I will never marry King Francis! Nothing you can say or do will force me to go against God and my vows to my husband! My heart and soul belongs to Robert! There is nothing you can say or do that will induce me to go with you to France and marry King Francis!"

Robert watched Elizabeth; he was stunned, shocked at what he was hearing. He had never seen Elizabeth behave in such a way before in expressing such anger. He was utterly lost and confused and didn't understand what was happening. Clearly, there was something going on that he knew nothing about, and he was determined to find out what that was, after John left.

Robert, unable to hear anymore, decided to confront John Bonnet directly. He pushed through the guards by stating he was Lord Robert Davenport, the son of Lord John Davenport, magistrate of these lands, and they were on English soil, ruled by King Henry the Eighth. The guards looked at each other, then stepped aside to let Robert pass, and he stood between Elizabeth and John.

"I demand you tell me what is going on here? My wife will not be going anywhere with you or King Francis!" Robert yelled.

John took his eyes from Elizabeth to look at Robert, then gave him a sinister smile. "My dear boy, you are such a blind fool! You and this harlot," turning his attention back to Elizabeth, then eyed her from head to toe, before returning his attention to Robert. "Are living in sin, as you are not married! To be living as man and wife when you are not is a great sin in Gods' eyes! Your wife is nothing but a harlot," turning back to Elizabeth with lust and filthy desire in his eyes, "But a lovely one at that."

Robert noticed the look John Bonnet was giving Elizabeth was not one a man of God should be looking at a woman.

John reached for Elizabeth's face. Robert saw this and grabbed John's arm to stop him as he thought, *what is going on here* – Robert was about to say so, but Elizabeth cut him off before he had a chance.

"Get out of here now!" Elizabeth Demanded.

This infuriated John to have this woman speak to him in such a way. "You are a liar, my dear!" he said with malevolent mockery, "There was no marriage between you and," he glanced at Robert with disgust, "Robert! You are both living in sin! I found no evidence of a marriage you claimed ever took place! As I see it, since you were not married in front of me, you were not married, nor were you married in the eyes of God, since I am God!" John said.

John was blinded by his belief, along with the power King Francis had bestowed upon him, which allowed him to believe himself to be God.

"You are a foolish girl! Your beauty captivated my king, and what my king wants my king gets!"

Robert was stunned by what he heard, and to see his wife in such a furious state – he's known Elizabeth since she was a child, and never before has she shown such fury. Not even after their family forbade them from being together and when they disowned her. It was evident there was a great deal more going on than Robert was aware of.

Elizabeth refused to stand there listening to anything further John had to say.

God, no! I cannot allow Robert to find out what happened! Not this way! Please help me be rid of John and allow me to be the one to tell him! she thought.

"I am married! I will not marry King Francis!" Elizabeth yelled at John. She was outraged and desperate – *I need to calm myself down. I know what I must do to make this man leave,* she thought.

Elizabeth closed her eyes and took a deep breath, and once she released it, she spoke in a calmer voice. "Sir, if my beauty is what your king wants, then I shall rectify that immediately. I will make sure he will never desire me again." Elizabeth grabbed a dagger from Robert's belt and placed it to her face. "Your king is captivated by my beauty, is he? Well then, I shall correct that, then your king will no longer desire me and finally leave us in peace."

Elizabeth placed the dagger to her face, and just as she was about to cut, Robert reached out to stop her, but John got there first and grabbed the knife from Elizabeth's hand.

"You fool! Do you believe that cutting your face will prevent King Francis from desiring you! Foolish girl!" Shaking his head. "Well, my dear, let me tell you, it will not!" John said with a sinister smile.

John threw the knife to the ground at Elizabeth's feet,

then turned and climbed back on his horse. As he turned to leave, he looked back at Elizabeth, "You, my dear, you best be ready to leave for France when I return in seven days hence or —"

John cut himself off, saying nothing further. He wanted to leave Elizabeth with 'or,' wanting her to think what 'or' might be. John turned back to the royal guards and ordered them to depart, leaving Watch Hill Castle in their dust.

After John and King Francis's royal guards left Watch Hill Castle, Robert turned to Elizabeth and demanded to know what happened, and what was really going on. It was clear there were things he did not know about, and he was not going to leave until he received the answers.

"Elizabeth, why was John Bonnet here insisting you be ready to travel with King Francis?"

Elizabeth hesitated; she never wanted Robert to know what happened between them on his visit. But now, after what happened, she knew there was no choice; she had to tell Robert the truth.

Elizabeth was silent for a long moment, unable to look at Robert, keeping her head down as she stared at the ground. Then after she took a deep breath and released it, unable to make eye contact, she began to tell Robert what happened that day John Bonnet paid her a visit.

"Robert, I do not know the right words to tell you…that would not hurt you."

Robert was watching Elizabeth intently, trying to read her face. He was afraid of what she might say. *Elizabeth. What could she possibly tell me that will hurt me? Elizabeth…no, she would never do anything to hurt me. Calm yourself. Just listen to what she has to say,* he thought.

Robert took a deep breath and braced himself.

"I never intended for you to know —"

For me to know. What has she been hiding from me? God give me strength, Robert thought.

"— as I was afraid of what you would do. You see…I…oh God, how can I tell you." Elizabeth broke down crying and Robert took her in his arms as he thought, *God, what is it.*

For the first time, Robert truly felt fear in seeing Elizabeth so distraught, it worried him. Fear was coursing through his body as he thought, *what happened to this beautiful woman? This woman, who is my wife, my heart and soul.*

After a moment, Elizabeth pushed at Robert's chest, wanting him to move away from her. This surprised him, but he did as she requested, and Elizabeth told Robert the horrible details of what happened the day John Bonnet paid her a visit. That John raped her.

After Robert heard Elizabeth's confession, his heart sank into his gut. It was cutting his insides like a knife. He was hurt, furious, and he drew his sword – he was prepared to go after John Bonnet, not caring that the French royal guards were with him. What he did to Elizabeth was a crime, and he intended to enforce the law under his father's rule, as magistrate of Cheshire. John Bonnet may be connected to King Francis, but they were on English soil, govern by King Henry.

Desperate, Elizabeth grabbed Robert's arm, "Robert, please do not do this! If anything happens to you, I will be lost! I only have you now! If anything happened to you, I could not bear it! I could not go on! I would die if I lost you! There is no Elizabeth without Robert! Where one goes, the other shall follow! Please do not do this, Robert! If your love for me is as strong as mine is for you, you will stay with me!"

Robert looked at Elizabeth, shocked; her words cut him like a knife. If anything happened to him, he didn't want her to follow him by taking her own life. In doing so, it would be a great sin. An unforgivable sin that would prevent them from being together in their next life.

Yes, he was angry, hurt, and shocked about what he learned and wanted to do what Elizabeth asked, but his instincts were telling him to go after John Bonnet and kill him for dishonoring his wife. But as he watched Elizabeth, the pain and fear in her eyes were too much for him to bear. Was it possible he would lose against John? Yes, but there was a strong possibility he would win.

Robert was a great swordsman, one of the best in the land, outside his father. Still, if he were to lose, he would leave Elizabeth on her own, with no family to turn to, and Robert pondered this for a long moment.

What would Elizabeth do? Would she take her own life if anything were to happen to me? He hoped not, *but if I were to die, where would she go? Who would accept her?* Robert thought as he watched Elizabeth, then shook his head. No, there was no doubt, Elizabeth would take her own life and follow him to the other side.

Robert sighed, then relaxed his arm as he sheathed his sword, letting go of his anger, then took Elizabeth in his arms. "Elizabeth, my love, I will not go. I will stay here with you."

Elizabeth relaxed, relieved that Robert wasn't going after John to seek revenge in his need to defend her honor.

"Oh Robert, thank you," she said, holding him tight. "I could not live if anything happened to you. You are my heart and soul. You are my life, my only reason for living. I would die if I lost you."

Elizabeth tightened her arms around Robert and held on to him for dear life, never wanting to let him go. With him in her arms, she knew he was safe.

Robert's heart sank at the thought of Elizabeth taking her own life. If anything were to happen to him –

"Elizabeth, look at me?" he asked.

Elizabeth stepped back but refused to release her hold on Robert, so she looked up to meet his eyes.

"Promise me, no matter what might happen to me; you

will not take your own life?" he said, but Robert saw the doubt in her eyes.

Pulling her away from him and holding her shoulders tight, "No! Promise me Elizabeth! You will not take your own life! To take your own life is a great sin, and if we are to find each other again when the time comes…oh God Elizabeth —"

Robert was so scared at the thought, he pulled Elizabeth back into his arms, and held her so tight as if he were to let her go, he would lose her forever.

"If you were to do so, we will not be allowed to be together. Elizabeth, you must promise me, here and now, you will not for any reason take your own life? Please, Elizabeth, promise me?"

As Robert was holding Elizabeth, she could feel him shaking with fear at the thought of her taking her life. Elizabeth pulled back to look at him, and what she saw she did not like, the look of fear and panic in his eyes, and she couldn't bear this.

"Robert, I promise. I will not take my life and jeopardize us from finding each other in our next lives."

Feeling relieved, Robert allowed himself to relax, and pulled Elizabeth back into his arms, needing the closeness of their bodies.

"Elizabeth, know this, no matter what happens, I will always love you. Do you hear me? What John Bonnet did was not your fault. So please, never fear losing me. I promise that will never happen."

Elizabeth relaxed into Robert as relief swept over her, and for a long moment, they stood together in each other's arms, holding on with all their strength, allowing themselves to feel the love and joy of being together.

When they finally parted, Robert took Elizabeth inside to Watch Hill Castle's safety, where Robert made love to her, wiping away everything that happened.

***

Robert and Elizabeth were lying in bed, with recent events put aside, talking about their lives, their future, and life once they left this one.

"My love, I want you to know that no matter what our future holds, I will always love you," Robert said, holding Elizabeth close in his arms, with her head resting on his chest, as he was smoothing her hair. "Even if you become fat and ugly," Robert said with a chuckle.

Elizabeth smacked Robert in the chest, which only made him laugh harder. "That is not nice, Robert," turning her head away, sticking her nose in the air, then said, "I will not get fat," she said defiantly.

"How do you know? Only know I will love you then, as much as I love you now," he said, but then suddenly all banter disappeared, turning to one with a more serious tone. He rose and took Elizabeth's arms and turned her to face him, "Elizabeth, my love for you is beyond our physical form. What you were about to do out there…when you placed that knife to your face…if you had cut your face, it would have hurt me, but it would never have changed how I feel for you. The love I feel for you is deeper than physical appearance.

My love for you comes from deep in my heart and my soul. I know," taking Elizabeth's face in his hands, "When we are born in our next life, no matter how you look, whether you were fat and ugly," he said with a slight smile, "I will love you." Robert placed his hand on Elizabeth's chest, directly over her heart, "Here, is where I will feel it, where I will know it to be true. No matter our physical appearance, this here will tell me what I need to know. Our love is stronger and deeper than our physical bodies." Robert looked deep into Elizabeth's eyes, "Do you not feel it, my love? Do you not believe what I say to be true?" Robert asked, then waited for her answer.

As Robert looked deep into Elizabeth's eyes, he wondered why it was so important he told her this. With the need to be clear and sure, their love being on a higher level than where they were. Why did he believe in something so unfamiliar to him and her? This, he did not know. It was a feeling deep in his soul.

With tears in her eyes, Elizabeth said, "Robert, what do I say, I have no words for, but what I feel, in hearing your words, is yes, I do believe you. Why, thus, I do not know, but I do believe with all my heart and soul."

Robert pulled Elizabeth into his arms and held her tight to his chest, feeling her with his love as he took hers in him.

***

It was a week since John's unexpected visit to Watch Hill Castle. Robert and Elizabeth were walking along the river towards the open clearing, talking about what they were going to do when John Bonnet showed up to take Elizabeth to France.

"Elizabeth, I do not understand this man who claims to be a man of God? This John Bonnet…is no Catholic Clergyman I have ever known. And why would the King of France go through so much trouble for you? Yes, you are from a good and noble family, but you are an English woman on English land govern by King Henry. John Bonnet nor King Francis has any authority to enforce such demands. For this, John Bonnet, to go through such length to force you to marry King Francis when you are already married makes no sense. To why he went through such efforts to search in and out of Cheshire to prove we are not married? None of this makes any sense to me. What kind of man is John Bonnet to claim to be God, in saying, 'You did not marry in front of me; therefore, you are not married, since I am God.' How can a man of God speak of such a thing? This John Bonnet cannot be a man of God, especially after what he did to you, my dearest Elizabeth," Robert said, stopping for a moment along their walk to place his hand on Elizabeth's face in a soft caress.

The entire time Robert was talking, Elizabeth's eyes were pinned to the ground until she heard John Bonnet's name, which caused her to flinch. Robert saw this and took Elizabeth in his arms and held her tight against him.

"Elizabeth, I am so sorry, I was not thinking. I didn't mean to cause you any pain by causing you to remember what that man did to you. Forgive me, my love?"

Elizabeth's love for Robert was so strong and powerful that his love for her could overpower any feelings of fear she might have felt from John Bonnet.

"My love, do not worry; I am well. Yes, when I heard John's name, it startled me, but your love for me will always overpower any discomfort or fear I may have for what John did to me. For when you are with me, I know I am safe, and I can get through anything."

When Robert and Elizabeth finally reached the clear open circle that was surrounded by tall lushes' trees, they stood near the edge of the tree line in a loving embrace.

"For any man to claim to be God is no true man of God, but his own man to do whatever he wants."

"Robert, I do not understand it myself. Why would John, this man who claims to be a man of God, believe I could ever leave you and go with him to France and marry King Francis. Robert," unable to look at him, she turned away to stare out to the river and after a few moments, "I am so afraid," she finally said, "What if…he tries to force me to go with him to France and I am forced to marry King Francis?"

Elizabeth turned back to look at Robert then placed her hand on his face with her eyes pinned on his lips. Then, after a moment, she looked up into his eyes, "I do not know what I would do if I were taken from you…forced to France to marry King Francis," Elizabeth said as she stared into Robert's eyes, seeing the love he has for her, "Oh Robert, what are we going to do if that happens?"

As Robert and Elizabeth discussed what they would do

if John tried to force Elizabeth to France – *was it possible? Could he enforce his power on English soil?* Robert thought.

Robert feared he could, and he thought about discussing what happened with his father, and to induce his help. But then he remembered what happened the last time he went to see his father, and he quickly tossed that idea aside.

Robert feared they were truly on their own. Without his father's help, it was impossible to prevent John Bonnet and King Francis from taking Elizabeth by force, and Robert was sure John Bonnet was aware of this, and feared he would use force to take Elizabeth to France, and the thought of Robert losing Elizabeth was unbearable.

"Elizabeth, if John Bonnet and King Francis try to take you from me, I will do everything in my power to prevent…stop them." Then, after a moment, Robert had a thought, a risky one, but nonetheless a possible solution. "Maybe we should consider leaving England and go to a place far, far away from where no one will ever find us."

To hear this, Elizabeth wanted nothing more than anything to leave with Robert and put everything that happened behind them, and maybe then it would allow her to forget.

No, she thought, shaking her head, knowing it was impossible.

Robert and Elizabeth were walking around the clearing holding hands, and Robert watched Elizabeth intently, looking for a reaction to what he said. He could see she was weighing the idea and saw the worry on her face to what would happen if they were to leave.

As they stood there facing each other, without words, it was clear what her answer would be.

Robert was looking down at Elizabeth, who was staring at the ground. She did this when she wanted to avoid giving him an answer he did not want to hear. With the back of his hand, he gently and softly caressed her face wanting to soothe away her fears and replace it with his love.

At Robert's touch, Elizabeth felt his love flow through her, so she closed her eyes, and turned into his touch, accepting what he offered, his love, in the warmth and sensation of his touch. Elizabeth placed her hand on top of his, then pulled his hand to her lips, lightly kissing the inside of his palm, thanking him for his love and support.

With Elizabeth's kiss, Robert could fill her fear falling away. "Have faith, my love. God will see us through. A God who gave us this love will not allow it to be taken away from us so easily. But, no matter what happens, I promise you I will do everything in my power to keep us together. I will not lose you. I will fight to do what needs to be done to protect you from John Bonnet. I will never let you go. Do you hear me? Never."

Elizabeth put her arms around Robert's waist, and he pulled her closer, so her body was against his, and held her as if at any moment he was going to lose her.

"Robert, I know you will. I love you so very much, and it hurts to think of not being with you. Just the thought makes me feel as if a part of me is being ripped in two."

Robert tightened his hold on Elizabeth – they both felt the fear of the other at the thought of John Bonnet and King Francis being able to take Elizabeth away, and this he could not allow to happen, not after what they went through to be together.

"Elizabeth, my love, we will put our trust in God. He will see us through whatever may happen. But, Elizabeth, you must promise me no matter what happens," Robert pleaded.

Before Elizabeth could answer, there was a sudden noise out in the distance beyond the small ridge of the open clearing they were standing in. Robert and Elizabeth looked to where the noise came from and saw a large group of French soldiers rushing down towards them. Before they could react, two of the soldiers ripped Elizabeth right out of

Robert's arms.

Robert tried everything – using all his strength to hold on to Elizabeth to prevent the soldiers from taking her from him. *No-no, this cannot be happening! Not now!* Robert thought.

He didn't want to let Elizabeth go. He held on, gripping Elizabeth in a death grip as if death itself was coming, but two of the soldiers grabbed Robert's arms from behind, and forced him to release his hold on her, then pulled him away from Elizabeth, while the other two soldiers were pulling Elizabeth out of his grip and removed her from his hold.

When Robert looked at Elizabeth as the soldiers were carrying her away, he saw the fear in her eyes. Robert tried to fight. He used all his strength to try and fight the soldiers off him, but he failed. He had no sword or any weapons on him, and it allowed the soldiers to overpower him easily. Thus, taking Elizabeth away from him and all he could do was watch as they carried her away, kicking and screaming with her arms reached out to him, begging him to save her. His heart sank. He was powerless to help her, and after he promised he would. He felt shame for being less than a man at the time she needed him the most.

As Elizabeth was being carried away, she reached for Robert to help her, but she knew there was nothing he could do since the soldiers were holding him back. While she was kicking and screaming at the soldiers to release her, she yelled to Robert, "I Love You! I Love You! I Love You!" she said over and over again.

Feeling powerless, all Robert could do was watch, helpless, as he was unable to help Elizabeth. He began berating himself – *how could I have not been prepared! It's my fault! My ignorance that allowed this to happen,* he thought. But he refused to give up, and he fought with all his might.

Robert yelled to Elizabeth, "Elizabeth! I will do whatever I must to find you! I will bring you home! Do not give up! Have faith in me and our love! God will see us through this! I love you with all my heart!"

When the soldiers finally released Robert, he took off running after Elizabeth, but it was too late; she was gone.

Elizabeth was hitting the soldiers with her fists as she was kicking and screaming, demanding they release her. She tried so hard, but without success. The soldiers were too strong. They carried Elizabeth up the small hill to the ridge and to a nearby carriage. She could hear Robert yelling at her not to give up.

I will not give up, Robert, I promise, she thought.

The soldiers tossed Elizabeth in the carriage, and when she righted herself on the seat, to her horror, sitting directly across from her, was John Bonnet, the man she feared. The man who raped her.

Elizabeth pulled her shoulders back, refusing to become a scared caged little mouse. "Release me at once!" she demanded.

John watched Elizabeth with a look of such malice, "No!" John said in a firm and powerful voice. His demeanor was cold, as was his soul. "You will sit down and shut up! If not, you will endure my wrath!"

Elizabeth was stunned and could only sit there, staring at the man.

"You will go to France and marry King Francis! You will do everything you are told!" John said, seeing the defiance in Elizabeth. "If you do not…if you want your beloved," John said with a smirk, "Robert and your families to live!"

Elizabeth froze. She looked at John. She was horrified and filled with fear. She was stunned beyond disbelief that this was happening to her. After sitting there staring at him for a few moments, she finally turned away and looked out the window as the carriage began to move away from the clearing and her beloved Robert.

As she stared out the window, she saw Robert standing

there in shock and disbelief, but also saw his anger, sorrow, and the pain in failing to help her. Elizabeth closed her eyes, and she turned her thoughts to the last words Robert said to her, 'Elizabeth, I will do whatever I can to find you and bring you home! Don't give up! Have faith in me and our love! God will see us through this! I love you with all my heart!' Elizabeth opened her eyes, and before she was out of sight of Robert, she lipped, "I love you too," then he was gone. Elizabeth sank in her seat, putting her face in her hands, shaking her head in disbelief to what happened.

He is gone. Robert is gone.

Chapter Twenty-Four

After John Bonnet kidnapped Elizabeth, Robert was lost. He felt as if his heart was ripped from his chest. When the soldiers left with Elizabeth, Robert, without haste, returned to Watch Hill Castle and ordered his horse to be brought to him immediately.

Once he mounted his horse, Robert rode as fast as he could to Bramhall Manor to seek his father's help. Although his father wanted nothing to do with Robert after marrying Elizabeth, he had no choice. Robert needed help, and with his father's power and influence in the land, Lord Davenport was his best and only option he had.

Robert needed to hold on to, that no matter how angry his father was with him, blood was blood, and blood was stronger than anything else, and he was sure once his father hears what happened, he would help him. *He must. He must help me,* Robert thought.

Even if Robert had to beg his father for his help, he would do it. Now was not the time to be proud. All that matter was saving Elizabeth. So, if he had to lower himself to his father, for Elizabeth, he would. There was nothing he wouldn't do for her.

With no time to waste, Robert rode hard and with haste towards Bramhall Manor to see his father.

As Robert rode, he replayed the events that took place when John Bonnet arrived at Watch Hill Castle.

"She needs to be ready to sail to France in seven days hence."

John Bonnet's forcefulness in demanding Elizabeth be ready, with the confidence he displayed, was as if nothing they said would deter him.

Damn, I should have seen it then, Robert thought. Robert realized that the signs were there, as clear as they could be. *If so, I would have been more prepared.*

If he'd realized this before, he would have been more prepared – armed to protect Elizabeth better, than when the soldiers arrived, he would have been able to prevent them from taking her, or at least, given them a good fight, even though he knew he was outnumbered. It didn't matter, and it would have given him a chance to fight until his last breath was drawn if it came to that. There was no doubt John Bonnet was not a clergyman in Robert's mind. He was no honorable man of God.

***

Once Robert arrived at Bramhall Manor, he wasted no time, ignoring everyone around him and he burst through the front door and into his father's study.

When Lord Davenport saw Robert, he was outraged, "What are you doing here! Again, you go against my orders! How dare you show yourself here! Do you have a death wish boy!"

Robert ignored his father's objection – "Father, you must hear me out! I beg you, please! I need your help!"

Lord Davenport refused to listen to anything Robert had to say, as he has been unable to forgive him for marrying Elizabeth.

"How dare you barge into my home! You have no business here or with me! Your betrayal has not been forgotten! Now, get out!"

Robert still ignored his father and began pleading, begging for his father to hear him out. "Father! Please! I come to you on a matter of great urgency!"

"There is nothing you could conceivably say or do that will induce me to help you in any way! Now, get out!" Lord Davenport shouted as he pointed at the door. "And Robert, never return until I AM DEAD! Is that clear!" Lord Davenport hollered, slamming his hand against his chest.

No! I will not allow him to push me out! Elizabeth is in danger! If I must fight him to force his help, then I will! There is nothing he can say or do that will force me to leave! Robert thought.

Robert was so distraught and desperate and scared. He

needed his father's help, and he wasn't going to allow his father to bully him. *I will…I must convince father to help me!* he thought.

Robert braced himself and yelled, "FATHER STOP!" and continued without stopping, not wanting to give his father a chance to interrupt him. "I know you are unhappy with Elizabeth and me for going against your orders, but you are my father! We are of the same blood! You have to listen to what I have to say! Father please?" his plea was filled with anguish as he fought back the tears that were threatening to surface, then Robert blurted out, "John Bonnet kidnapped Elizabeth! And right now, they are on their way to Liverpool to board a ship bound to France!

Once Elizabeth arrives in France, she will be forced to marry King Francis!" Robert yelled as his voice cracked. He looked directly into his father's eyes, "Father Please! I know you do not understand what Elizabeth and I have, but father…please…I love her with all my heart! I would die for her! If I must, I will go after her and die trying to save her! But father, if you could help me by lending me the men I need, it will strengthen my success in bringing Elizabeth home!"

When Lord Davenport heard John Bonnet's name, it captured his attention, and he decided to listen to what Robert had to say.

Even though Lord Davenport portrayed himself as a hard and heartless man, he did have a heart and loved his son more than life itself. What Robert did, affected Lord Davenport's pride, but hearing the desperation in his son's voice and the emotions his son was trying to control, and at hearing John Bonnet, he couldn't maintain his control any longer. At that moment, Lord Davenport let down his guard and decided to listen to what Robert had to say.

"What! How can this be? What you say makes no sense!" Lord Davenport said as he brought his voice to a reasonable volume. "All right, you have my attention. But

Robert, make it quick and tell me what happened?"

Robert sighed with relief; he was thankful his father was willing to hear him out. Robert took a deep breath and let it out slowly, then began telling his father what happened.

"Thank you, father. Earlier today, when Elizabeth and I were standing near the river by Watch Hill Castle, we heard a noise. When we looked to see what it was, we saw King Francis's soldiers rushing down the hill towards us and they snatched Elizabeth from my arms. Right now, they are traveling to board a ship bound for France. I must try to stop them before they leave English shores," Robert said, feeling frantic. He was afraid he would not make it in time due to the time he was spending explaining what happened to his father.

Robert was ashamed of his lack of knowledge and ability to sense danger. Although he was an excellent swordsman, this was one ability he hadn't yet mastered. There was still much he had to learn. Did he want to admit this weakness to his father? No, but what other choice did he have.

"I am ashamed that I could do nothing to help Elizabeth. Two of King Francis's soldiers held me back while two others carried Elizabeth kicking and screaming away. And I, her husband, being unable to help her, was forced to watch instead. To watch in horror as they forced her into a carriage that was waiting at the top of the hill, and for a moment, through the carriage window, I was sure I saw John Bonnet lean over to Elizabeth before the carriage drove away and was out of sight. But then, I saw Elizabeth look out the window…father, she looked so frightened, and I, her husband…" Robert's voice cracked, and he had to look away for a moment. He needed to regather his composer before he continued.

Lord Davenport saw this and did not push for Robert to continue, allowing him the time he needed to gain control of the emotions he was fighting back.

Robert turned back to his father and continued, "Because I was prevented from helping Elizabeth…not being able to intervene…I could not save her! It is my fault! If only I foresaw this, I could have been prepared…to prevent it!" Robert yelled, shaking his head, "But I did not! I failed as her husband to protect her!" Robert looked away from his father again, unable to bear the shame he felt in admitting his failure.

Lord Davenport watched his son intently, and when he heard Robert's admission, he wanted to agree but elected to hold back his tongue. So instead, he tried to understand the events that happened.

"Robert, what you say makes no sense. To my understanding, in what happened between King Francis and Baron Massey…yes, King Francis took an interest in Elizabeth when he saw her in Chester. However, upon King Francis learning she was already married and to you…from what Baron Massey told me, the matter was closed.

Then, a few days later, it appeared John Bonnet took matters into his own hands by making inquiries. He wanted to prove you and Elizabeth were not married, and when he learned there was no record nor a witness of a wedding took place, it convinced John there was no wedding. Then, when he informed King Francis of what he learned, it convinced King Francis, along with Baron Massey, you both lied about being married.

When Baron Massey learned this, it angered him, and without thinking, he was forced to sign an agreement giving Elizabeth to King Francis, making her a part of his royal court —"

Before Lord Davenport could go further, Robert burst out, "He has no authority to do so! Elizabeth is my responsibility, not his, since I became her husband! Therefore, the agreement is invalid!"

Lord Davenport put his hand up to stop Robert. "Allow

me to finish." Robert nodded. "It is impossible for King Francis to marry Elizabeth as he is already married. So whatever John Bonnet convinced you and Elizabeth of it is false. Elizabeth will become a part of King Francis's Royal Court, which means she will become one of his many mistresses until the day comes when King Francis becomes bored with her."

Robert's mouth dropped open when he heard this. He could not believe what his father was telling him, leaving him feeling nauseous, and he felt as if he was going to collapse. So, before he did, he sat in a chair in front of his father's desk and placed his face in his hands as he thought, *such deceit from this man, who claimed to be a man of God.*

After a few moments of silence, Robert finally asked his father, "Father, who is this man John Bonnet who claims to be a Catholic Clergyman, but his behavior shows me he is the opposite. Father, he raped Elizabeth when she refused to marry King Francis."

Lord Davenport was shocked and outraged when he learned John Bonnet raped Elizabeth. Yes, he was angry with his son for what he did, but now, he felt sympathy for his son. So, Lord Davenport did something he knew Robert would not have expected him to do. He went to his son and placed a hand on his shoulder, "Robert, I am deeply sorry for what happened to Elizabeth," he said, squeezing his son's shoulder. "I am afraid John Bonnet is no man of God. It is true that he was a Catholic Clergyman, but he turned away from the Catholic Church to become a Lutheran. You know how those people are…they cannot be trusted. Although King Henry married one and forced this change on his people…this man John Bonnet, for him to rape Elizabeth, deserves nothing less than to be hung. To die, a slow and painful death."

Robert listened to his father and was shocked and horrified to hear the truth about John Bonnet. His heart sank, "Father…Elizabeth, she cannot defend herself against a man such as John Bonnet. Five days passed, John Bonnet paid Elizabeth a visit at Watch Hill Castle and threatened to harm her if she did not go to France and marry King Francis. John Bonnet told us he found no proof Elizabeth and I were married. Although no matter how hard we tried to make him understand we are married, and that we were married in a church, in the eyes of God, he refused to listen. He told Elizabeth since we did not marry in front of him, we were not married, as he is God. This man, who believes himself to be God…" shaking his head, "To claim to be God, is this not a great sin? No true man of God would claim to be God. He would only claim to be God's servant."

"Robert, when I learned of the accusation John Bonnet made about your marriage from Baron Massey. I told Baron Massey I did not believe you would go through such lengths of deception in pretending to be married when you were not. If so, you would have made that clear. No. I believe this, out of all you have done. I told Baron Massey he made a grave mistake. In my saying this, he informed me he would go to King Francis and tell him he did not have the right to give his daughter Elizabeth to him since she was no longer his to give. I cannot say what happened, but I am afraid Baron Massey did not speak to King Francis but instead spoke with John Bonnet, as a representative of King Francis. And that John Bonnet never informed King Francis of the truth, wanting to hide his deceit, therefore, took action to rebuke Baron Massey."

"Father, what am I to do? How can I fight such a man? I need your help, father. With your power and influence, I am sure I can retrieve Elizabeth from King Francis and John Bonnet."

For Lord Davenport to see his son so distressed, he reluctantly agreed to provide his son with a little help, but not to the extent Robert had hoped for.

"Robert, I will help you," Lord Davenport said, putting his hand up when he saw Robert's excitement. "Wait. But not with what I am sure you expect. I can only do so much since I am a part of King Henry's court. I may not be in London, but I must remain outside of what King Henry would want me to do. I cannot be seen, nor can it be known I am assisting you in rescuing Elizabeth from King Francis. For years, King Henry and King Francis have been at odds with each other. First, they are in an alliance, and then they are not. More so now that King Henry has rejected the Catholic Roman Church. If it were discovered I have assisted you, it would surely bring war, and in this, the king will have my head. What I am prepared to do…I will give you five of my best men, along with a ship and crew to have at your disposal. But it will be up to you to rescue Elizabeth, making sure there is no connection to England and King Henry, nor myself.

You will have the use of our family chateau in France. Once you are there, do what you must, but remember, I, as well as England, should remain disconnected. If King Henry were to find out…I will be forced to inform him that you acted without my knowledge or permission.

Heed this my son, if this were to happen, King Henry will indeed have you beheaded or allow King Francis to do what he will with you. If you are to do this, do so quickly and quietly. Be careful," Lord Davenport said, as he watched his son, the anger he felt lessened a great deal, for him to give Robert a small boon. "Go my son and bring Elizabeth home. Once you have succeeded, we will sit down and discuss your marriage and the agreement between Baron Massey and myself."

Robert watched his father, astonished at what he just heard. *God, could it be? Is this a chance to finally regain both our families?* he thought, with hope in his heart.

Robert was grateful for whatever help his father could provide, along with the possibility of making right his marriage to Elizabeth.

***

Lord Davenport took Robert to where his most trusted men were, and to Robert's surprise, they were not men of his guards or soldiers but men he used for unique and secret missions. One's he knew would not be tied to him. After the introductions, the men were instructed to ready themselves for a long and hard ride before nightfall. They needed to make it to Liverpool as soon as possible. Then, if they missed finding John Bonnet on the road, they would immediately set sail for France.

Lord Davenport gave Robert a letter with his seal to present to the captain of his ship. The letter gave Robert full control and authority of his ship and crew as Lord Davenport's son and heir. But first, Robert needed to speak to Baron Massey to learn what happened when, or if he spoke with King Francis about Elizabeth.

***

When Robert arrived at Baron Massey's cottage, he was not welcomed. At first, he was denied entry, but he refused to give up and yelled into the household, "It's urgent! Your daughter is in grave danger!" Then, to Robert's incredible relief, Grace approached the door and demanded the servant allow him entrance. Once Robert entered the manor, he went directly to Baron Massey's study, with Grace fast on his heels.

Robert burst into Baron Massey's study, "You will hear what I have to say! And you will tell me what happened when you spoke to King Francis about the agreement you signed!"

Baron Massey saw Grace enter behind Robert, "Grace! Leave us and close the door!" Grace did as her father asked but remained outside the door to hear what Robert had to say to her father.

Robert informed Baron Massey what happened to Elizabeth and that he just left his father, who agreed to assist in rescuing Elizabeth. He explained to Baron Massey what his father told him about the conversation he and his father had about King Francis Agreement. At hearing this, Baron Massey calmed down and agreed to tell Robert what occurred when he went to see King Francis regarding the misunderstanding and to have the agreement nullified.

Grace, as she listened at the door, gasped at what she heard. *Elizabeth was raped. Oh God, why did she not come to me? Oh, you know why, because you would have insisted she tell father, and you know how that would have gone,* she thought.

Grace was heartbroken at what happened to Elizabeth and blamed herself, more so than before. If she only did what was required of her, this would never have happened. Not wanting to hear anymore, Grace returned to her chambers, where she fell on her bed and cried.

"After speaking to Lord Davenport, I went directly to see King Francis, but instead of being allowed to see the king, I was directed to John Bonnet, to whom I explained the entire matter too. John listened, then assured me he would inform King Francis at once. If King Francis wished to speak to me, I would be summoned to meet with him and explain the entirety.

I was left with little choice. Either I spoke with John Bonnet or wait for King Francis to grant me an audience. This would take time. Time, I did not have. Either case, it appears John Bonnet never informed King Francis, even after I made it clear the information came from your father. I explained Lord Davenport was the magistrate and Lord of Cheshire, by order of King Henry the Eighth. I told him King Francis must destroy the agreement I signed, or he would face the consequences from Lord Davenport, as representative of King Henry.

I saw the horror on John Bonnet's face, of a man who feared the consequences of King Francis, if he learned of such information. I decided not to push, but I made it clear that I had no authority, and that the agreement is considered invalid…null and void.

However, John was apologetic for the misunderstanding and understood the urgency, and he would inform King Francis immediately. John Bonnet said, 'Once King Francis grants you an audience, I will send a man to bring you to him at once.' Then he said, 'Fear naught, all will be well.'

If what you say is true, then the only thing I can conclude, John never relayed the information to King Francis. Therefore, he must have somehow convinced King Francis to return to France without Elizabeth. Probably, giving some excuse for the delay, so he would be the one to escort Elizabeth to France. I say this since I heard King Francis had already left Chester to return to France, two days pasts."

Robert was horrified at what Baron Massey said. "Oh, God! Elizabeth is in more danger than I first believed! I must leave now! I must meet the men given to me by my father! We must leave at once to try and catch John Bonnet on the road. If we fail, we must be ready to sail to France immediately! There is no time to waste! If we must travel to France, we must make it soon after John Bonnet does! Then, if we can rescue Elizabeth, just after she arrives in France, we could bring her home unharmed!"

After learning what happened with Elizabeth, Baron Massey's heart softens towards his daughter. He wanted a chance to make things right and told Robert, "You go! And we will do as your father said…we will talk."

***

After King Francis's departure and before John kidnapped Elizabeth, he wanted to find a way around the main road so they could make it to Liverpool in record time. Knowing the road would be the first place Robert would look. John learned about the River Mercy when he visited a tavern in the village. He knew it would be perfect and the quickest way to Liverpool.

The man in the tavern said, "Tis the quickest route to Liverpool. Taking you straight through without dealing with the rough roads and hills. It would cut down your travel time to mere hours."

This pleased John immensely. He believed the quicker he could make it to Liverpool, thus, to the safety of French soil.

Along with King Francis's guards, John arrived at the River Mersey, where they took a boat and followed the river to Liverpool. Once in Liverpool, they would board a ship arranged by King Francis and sail safely to France.

Once we are in France, we will be safe and protected. To attempt to free Elizabeth could insight a war between France and England. That, I know will not happen. No one will assist Robert in rescuing Elizabeth, including his father, Lord Davenport, John thought, reveling in his success by fooling everyone, including King Francis.

During their journey on the River Mersey, John thoughts took him back to when Baron Massey came to see King Francis —

If I had not seen Baron Massey when he requested to see King Francis…if he had spoken to King Francis, I would have been ruined.

I explained, "My Lord, King Francis is away from Chester Castle on business." Then I told him, "My Lord, you are welcome to tell me what business you have with King Francis. As his direct council, I assure you; I will relay what you say to King Francis immediately upon his return."

I saw how Baron Massey hesitated, he didn't want to speak to me, but after reassuring him as the king's trusted counsel, his message would be delivered directly to King Francis. After Baron Massey took a few moments to consider this, reluctantly, he relayed the information he learned from Lord Davenport.

"Lord Davenport assured me that his son, no matter

*what he's done, would never lie about marrying Elizabeth.
When I learned of this, I knew I made a grave mistake in
signing the agreement you presented to me without
consulting Lord Davenport first."*

*At hearing this, I knew if King Francis heard this
information, I would have been exiled, or worse, beheaded
immediately.*

*To my relief, I managed to get rid of Baron Massey by
assuring him I would inform King Francis of the mistake,
and once an audience was granted, I would send a guard
for him to return to speak to the king. But instead, I
recommended to King Francis that he return to France
without Elizabeth Massey, how Elizabeth needed additional
time to make the necessary preparations before she could
depart. And –* as he smiled at the memory, *how he would
present Elizabeth to the king as a gift. "Your Majesty, I
know how you love pure and untouched women. Although
Elizabeth was spoiled, I will prepare her and present her to
you as if she were never touched. As pure as the day she
was born." It was not hard to convince King Francis. The
thought of Elizabeth being presented to him as such,
thrilled him immensely, and he said, "Do what you must.
But be quick, as I am anxious to get my hands on that
beauty." At this, I saw how King Francis relished at the
idea.*

*Right after King Francis left Chester Castle, I knew I
had to get to Elizabeth immediately. Although I threatened
Elizabeth that I would ride out to Watch Hill Castle five
days prior, I knew she would not voluntarily go to France.
With the men King Francis left behind, together we rode
out to find Elizabeth. When we arrived at Watch Hill
Castle, we learned from the servants that she and her
husband were out walking near the river. I knew exactly
where to find her. Therefore, the need to take her by force
was necessary.*

When I saw her in that clearing with Robert's arms

around her, I knew there was only one way to take Elizabeth, so I ordered the men, "That woman is King Francis's property, and that man who is holding her is keeping her from our king. Therefore, you must go and take her by force. Do not allow that man a chance to fight. He is a great swordsman and should not be allowed to fight." At that, the men rushed down to the clearing and snatched Elizabeth right out of Robert's arms. It pleased me to see them torn apart. Once I have her in France and protected by King Francis, there will be nothing Robert or Lord Davenport could do. Not without risking the wrath of King Henry.

After John recounted the memory, he smiled at the thought of his success and deceit.

***

The man in the tavern was right; River Mercy proved to be a smart decision. Instead of days, it took mere hours to arrive in Liverpool.

After John Bonnet and the French soldiers arrived at the Liverpool port, he ordered one of the men to see if their ship was ready. He wanted to sail for France immediately.

Once the royal guard returned and informed John the ship was waiting and ready to sail, he took Elizabeth and boarded the ship, and then once everyone was on board, he ordered the captain to prepare to set sail.

Elizabeth remained silent during their journey to Liverpool but wondered why King Francis was not with them.

"You have brought me all this way, but not once did you mention King Francis. I thought I was to return to France with King Francis? So, where is he, and why is he not here?" Elizabeth asked.

Yes, it was a risk for her to speak to John in such a way, but she needed answers and felt John Bonnet owed her those answers.

John turned towards Elizabeth, and for a few moments,

he just stared at her as he thought, *I do not owe you any answers. You are beneath me. You may think you are going to France to marry King Francis but…*John gave her a wicked smile that chilled Elizabeth to her bones…*only be in his bed…his mistress, and nothing more. Once he is done with you, I will take you for myself until I become bored with you. Then, you will be tossed out to fend for yourself.*

John was incredibly pleased with himself. Although he didn't owe Elizabeth any answers, he elected to give her one.

"My Lady, I am sorry King Francis could not be here to travel with you, but he needed to return to France on urgent business, as well as wanting to see to the preparations of your arrival personally. Therefore, he departed England for France two days prior."

As Elizabeth listened to John, she watched his behavior, and there was something in his look she did not like, with a feeling he wasn't being truthful. She wanted to rebuke his words but thought it was best to let it go.

No, I shall not confront him now. Instead, I will wait and speak to King Francis directly, she thought.

John ordered two of the royal guards to escort Elizabeth to the ship's hole where the ship's cargo was kept. King Francis guards looked at John, waited a moment, thinking he was jesting them, but he was not. John only gave them a look that said, 'best move now.' Without another thought, the guards took Elizabeth to the hole of the ship.

To John, Elizabeth was nobody who deserved no better treatment than a lowlander would receive, and this was his revenge for the efforts it took him to obtain her for King Francis.

Once the royal guards were down in the hole with Elizabeth, they noticed one corner of the hole was prepared with a bed, table, and a chair. The guards looked at each other and then at Elizabeth.

They had no idea I was to be treated this way, Elizabeth

thought.

Elizabeth wanted to ease their concerns and said, "It's fine, I will make do."

The guards bowed, then turned and left.

In the small corner of the cargo hold, Elizabeth sat on the bed until the guards disappeared to the deck above, and when she was sure she was alone, she did a quick look around at her new surroundings, then slumped forward feeling defeated. After a short time, Elizabeth laid on the bed in a fertile position and allowed her tears to fall, releasing the emotions she's been holding back since she was kidnapped.

As Elizabeth was lying on the bed crying, in what seemed to be hours, it was only a short time since they set sail when she felt ill. Elizabeth didn't understand why since she's never suffered the sickness from the motion of a ship. She sat up in bed, wanting to figure out what might be making her ill.

Was it something I ate? Shaking her head, *no, the last time I ate was before Robert and I went on our walk, which was hours ago. Could it be the stress of the journey, along with my fear?* Of course, this was plausible, until another realization hit her, *oh God, could it be?* she thought with excitement as well as being astonished at the possibility. She placed her hands on her stomach. *Is it possible, I am with child? I understood the first sign is sickness.* Then her thoughts turn to Robert, *oh Robert, what a wonderful and joyous gift from God. With everything that has happened, this child could bring great joy to all our family with the possibility of reuniting us all.*

However, this thought was crushed when Elizabeth was hit with a horrible realization that shattered her happiness.

No-no-no! Please tell me it is not so. Elizabeth looked down as she was rubbing her stomach. *If this child is not Roberts…no, this cannot be! God, please, tell me this is not so? If this child…no,* she thought.

Elizabeth's head snapped up at the horrible possibility that one horrific time when John raped her was when she became with child.

For this child, who I hope, looking down at her stomach, *will bring great joy and hope, with the possibility of reuniting our families, be John Bonnet's?* she thought.

At this thought, it was too much for Elizabeth to bear. Instead of bringing her happiness and joy, it had only increased her fears. Elizabeth placed her hands to her face, frantically rubbing it as if she could rub away her horrible thoughts.

The journey to France wasn't a long one, but with this, it would prove to be a treacherous one for Elizabeth.

With Elizabeth's growing aggravation and fear, she started fidgeting – first with her hair, then rubbing her shoulders as if suddenly cold. She wanted to find a place to hide, to conceal herself from her horrible thoughts and memories of that day, how she may have lost more than just her honor.

At this horrific thought, tears started pouring down Elizabeth's face, as her pain was too great at the possibility that the child growing inside her could be John Bonnet's. The agony of the stress was too much. She placed her hand on her neck and rubbed it roughly from front to back, hoping the pain she was producing would allow her thoughts to dissipate, but they did not.

What would Robert think? How would he feel? How could he ever understand and still love me? Could he, would he accept a child that is not his, but of a man, of the man who raped his wife, giving him a constant reminder of what happened? God, please tell me this is not so.

Robert told me that day, he would never leave me and would always love me…but this, looking down at her stomach again, with her hands lying on top, *this child within me was to be another man…no, not just any man, John Bonnet's, the man who raped me. For Robert and me* to have this child be a constant reminder of what he did will destroy everything we have with each other. But, if this child is Robert's, oh what a wonderful joy, a blessing of our love, Elizabeth thought.

The battle Elizabeth was having with herself was too much for her to bear anymore, so with her hand still on her stomach, she laid down on the bed wanting to close herself off from reality when she heard footsteps coming down the stairs.

Chapter Twenty-Five

At that moment, John Bonnet entered the cargo hold and into Elizabeth's space. He wanted to see how Elizabeth was fairing in her new surroundings, but he noticed something was wrong with her upon his approach.

"Are you unwell, child?"

Outraged, *unwell, he dares ask! Since he is the cause of my discomfort!* Elizabeth thought.

Elizabeth lashed out at John, and she held nothing back. "I am not a child! I am Lady Davenport, wife of Lord Robert Davenport," she said with pride, "Of Watch Hill Castle, Cheshire, England. Sir, you shall address me as such! Or I will ensure King Francis hears about the ill-treatment you have placed upon me! As I am sure this was not," looking around her surroundings, "What he intended for the woman he is to marry and become his Queen! If he were to learn of your mistreatment of me, he, I am sure, would be irreprehensible!" Elizabeth yelled.

Elizabeth's outburst and bravery shocked John, and for a moment, it left him speechless, but then he said, "My Lady Elizabeth," as he bowed, "Due forgive me? I meant no disrespect."

John knew once Elizabeth was with King Francis, there was nothing he could do to prevent her from speaking of her mistreatment on the ship, and he thought, *maybe I should have her moved to one of the free cabins?* Not to mention, if King Francis learned of Elizabeth's treatment, it would cause him great harm.

John shook his head. No! I shall not allow this woman to dictate to me in such a manner, he thought.

He knew there was nothing this woman could say or do that would possibly affect his relationship with King Francis. It was lust on King Francis's mind and nothing more.

At this, John took a deep breath and said, "My Lady, please forgive me. If there were any better accommodations, I would personally take you there myself. This ship is a working ship, not one of luxury. I felt this place," he said, looking around, "Would be the safest place for you. I have two of King Francis guards standing at the entrance to prevent anyone from coming down here who may want to cause you harm."

Elizabeth didn't want to say anything, but at that moment, she felt there was no choice. "No, Sir, I am not well. I believe I am suffering from the sickness caused by the movement of this ship," she said, without raising her head.

Elizabeth did not want John to see her face, afraid he would see the truth. If so, he may ask further questions she did not wish to answer.

John stared at Elizabeth for a few moments, wanting to question her further, but instead, he decided against it. He didn't believe she was being truthful but decided it was best to let it go, for now anyway.

Instead, he asked, "Shall I have the ship physician attend you?"

Elizabeth looked up at John and said, "No, Sir, I believe I will be fine with some rest."

Without further questions, John bowed and left Elizabeth to rest.

Once John was gone, Elizabeth tried to rest, but she found it was too difficult with her thoughts running away with her.

God, please tell me this is not John Bonnet's child. I could not bear to have that horrible, evil man's child, Elizabeth thought.

Elizabeth could not rest with these thoughts, so she sat up in bed in horror at the possibility that the child she may be carrying was John Bonnets. She shook her head back and forth in an attempt to free her mind from those horrible thoughts but failed. It only caused her to become dizzy and increase her illness, making her feel worse than she was. Tears ran down her face as she lay back down on the bed, trying everything she could, to not think about the possibilities of the child within her being John Bonnet.

God, please do not allow this child growing within me, be anyone other than Roberts. He is my love, my heart, and my soul. I cannot lose him. At this last thought, as Elizabeth wept, she finally fell asleep.

***

A great deal of time had passed when John decided to send one of the guards down to check on Elizabeth, and when the guard returned, he reported what he found.

"Sir, she sleeps."

John waved the soldier away and decided to check on Elizabeth himself.

As he approached Elizabeth's sleeping form, she looked so peaceful, and he didn't want to disturb her. So instead, he stood a few feet away, just watching her. He found it difficult to control his urge and wanted desperately to touch her, and he allowed his thoughts to run wild with him.

God, she is a beauty. To think, I had her before King Francis. Ah, how I will remember and hold on to that moment until I have her again. And by God, I will have her again, he thought.

John moved closer to Elizabeth, so close he could, if he chose, reach his hand out and touch her, and he wanted so desperately to touch her soft and silky hair, as he remembered how it felt the last time he touched it.

Stretching out his hand as he was just about to, he stopped himself and pulled back his hand, then immediately left before he gave into temptation.

***

Elizabeth was yanked out of her sleep from the noise of men shouting on deck. When she was fully awake, she was surprised how rested she felt and was no longer feeling sick. She again heard the men shouting as they came in rapid repetition.

"Lower the sails! Lower the anchor! Toss over the ropes!" yelled the crew.

Did I sleep through the whole voyage? How long was that? she wondered. *Is it not a day or so to sail to France?* she thought.

More shouting pulled her out of her thoughts —

"Lower the anchor!"

"I did. I slept the whole journey. Well, it probably was for the best. To endure such a hellish journey here," Elizabeth said aloud as she looked at her surroundings again, realizing she was still in the hole of the ship. "I would have gone mad."

Elizabeth heard footsteps coming from the steps leading down the hole and to where she sat on the bed. At first, she feared who it might be, but to her relief, it was the guards that led her down when she first boarded the ship.

"My Lady," the soldier said as he bowed. "I am here to escort you above, then to a cabin where you can clean up and change before we debark the ship." The guard explained as he put out the crook of his arm for Elizabeth, and she took the offered arm.

As Elizabeth approached the top of the stairs, she was temporally blinded by the bright sun, forcing her to put her hand up to shade her eyes. Once she was standing on the deck, she took a few moments to allow her eyes to adjust, and once her eyes were clear, what she saw was breathtaking. France. *It is beautiful,* she thought, seeing the docks with the hustle and bustle of the people and the sea beyond. To Elizabeth, it was beautiful, especially after being stuck in the hole of the ship.

The guard waited while Elizabeth's eyes adjusted to the sun, and once she was ready, he escorted her to the cabin.

On the way to the cabin, Elizabeth asked the guard his name. "What is your name?"

Surprised by the question, he said, "Filipe, My Lady." Then went on to explain, "John Bonnet wants to make sure you are presentable before he presents you to King Francis."

Elizabeth snorted as she looked down at herself; *thus, his fault I am a mess,* she thought, touching her gown in an attempt to shake out the dirt. *I look awful,* then shrugged her shoulders, *thus more for him than for me.* She laughed silently at the look King Francis would give her if he were to see the state she was in.

Then, she thought of the look on John Bonnet's face when King Francis inquires as to why his future Queen was a filthy mess.

Hum, I have half a mind to ignore John's wish for me to clean up and force him to present me to King Francis like this, she thought, laughing again, this time aloud.

Filipe was startled at Elizabeth's sudden laughter. "My Lady, are you…alright?" he asked.

"Forgive me, Filipe. I had to laugh at my unfortunate circumstances. If I do not, I would go mad and start crying," Elizabeth said.

Filipe smiled, then nodded in understanding. Filipe found he liked Elizabeth and felt sorry for her. He wished there were something he could do to help her, but he could not as a member of the royal guards.

When they reached the cabin, Filipe opened the door and then stood aside to allow Elizabeth to enter. When Elizabeth entered the cabin, it was very small, there was barely enough room for her, let alone the small table, chair, and bed that were connected to the side of the wall. The metal basin and pitcher were sitting on top of the table, and next to it was a bar of soap, a small cloth for washing, and a towel for drying. Elizabeth also noticed a gown, cloak, stockings, and a pair of shoes lying over the top of the chair.

Hump, well, he thought of everything it seems,

Elizabeth thought.

When John kidnapped Elizabeth, the only clothes she had were the ones she was wearing, and it was clear John prepared for this, as she noticed the trunk filled with clothes fit for a Lady, befitting the French Royal Court.

Elizabeth couldn't help it; she laughed aloud again. Filipe looked at her, understanding the reason for this outburst this time, and smiled.

"My Lady, you are to wash and dress, and once you are finished, I will take you to John Bonnet, who will then escort you off the ship and to King Francis," Filipe said.

Elizabeth was staring at the clothes, then reached out and placed her hand on the gown. It was soft and silky, "Are we in Paris then?" she asked, as Paris was the likely place for her to be presented if she were to become Queen of France.

"No, My Lady, we are in the country near Loire Valley, where King Francis has a small castle."

This surprised Elizabeth, and she wanted to ask why, but thought it was best not to know the reason and only said, "Oh."

Filipe bowed as he said, "I will wait outside the door. When you are ready, knock, and I will escort you to John Bonnet."

Elizabeth nodded in acknowledgment but did not turn to look at Filipe.

Once the door was closed, she allowed the guard she put up to fall away, letting her tears flow, with a few dripping on the gown. Elizabeth suddenly felt numb, frozen, as if she could not move, but then she took a few deep breaths to compose herself, and once she was ready, she went to the table and poured some water into the basin, then removed her dirty clothes. Next, she grabbed the cloth and bar of soap and began the tedious task of washing. Once she finished, Elizabeth slowly and carefully put on the beautiful golden silk gown, along with the stockings and shoes. Once done, she felt a little better and took a few moments to gather herself before letting Filipe know she was ready to be escorted to John Bonnet, but before she could, she heard a knock at the door.

I must have taken longer than I realized, she thought.

"Come!" she yelled. When Filipe opened the door, Elizabeth said, "I am sorry, Filipe, I did not mean to take so long. Forgive me?"

Filipe looked at Elizabeth and smiled for the first time, as he noticed how beautiful she was. Filipe bowed and said, "It is alright, My Lady. But we must go quickly. John Bonnet is waiting, and he does not like to be kept waiting."

Elizabeth looked at Filipe and laughed aloud again, then allowed him to escort her to John Bonnet.

Once Filipe delivered Elizabeth to John, he placed her arm in the crook of his, but not before he gave her a good look, and what he saw pleased him.

Yes, indeed, she shall be mine when King Francis is done with her, John thought.

"My dear, you look lovely. King Francis will be incredibly pleased when he sees you," he said as they began to walk down the ramp.

Halfway down though, Elizabeth felt fate and almost collapsed, but John caught her, and held on tight to her arm to prevent her from falling over.

With concern, he asked, "My Lady, are you still feeling unwell?"

Elizabeth did not want John to know why she believed she almost fainted, as she thought, *this is another sign that I am with child. Or…it is due to not having eaten…in, I do not know how long. It is the perfect excuse.* Elizabeth took a few moments to gather her wits before she spoke.

"I am sorry, Sir, I am…I feel I am weak since I had not eaten before you took me. I do not know how long I was asleep. I think once I have food in me, I shall be fine."

At hearing this, John motioned for one of the guards to

get Elizabeth some food.

As they waited, John watched Elizabeth intently as he questioned the truth of her words.

Yes, it was possible, as it has been almost two days since she last ate, but he felt there was something else. Then it hit him, a sudden thought he had not considered. *Could she be with child?*

John Bonnet needs this question answered, so he took Elizabeth and forced her to look at him, then asked in a soft voice, not to be heard by the others, "My Lady, are you…by chance, with child?"

Elizabeth froze at John's question, and she felt his eyes on her while he waited for her to give him an answer.

John, as he waited, was holding back joy at the possibility Elizabeth was with child.

Elizabeth did not look at John, she was afraid he would see the truth, but she knew she had to do or say something that would refute his question.

However, it was too late, and John saw the answer before she spoke. "You are with child, are you naught?" he asked in a whisper.

Elizabeth jerked her head to look at him with shock in her eyes. She was going to respond but stopped, thinking better of it. Instead, she chose to ignore John's ridiculous question and turned towards the docks, then down at the ramp, anxious to be on their way.

However, John took this silence to solidify the unspoken answer as he thought, *ah, she is. She must have discovered it on our journey here, which is why she slept the whole time.*

John decided he would not let his question go so easily, and if Elizabeth was with child, this pleased him immensely. John placed his arm around Elizabeth's shoulders as if wanting to give her support, and as he helped her down the ramp, he whispered in her ear, "How wonderful my dear, you are with child are you naught? This is glorious, so perfect for my plans," he said with glee. "Ahhh, thus, truly is a blessing from God," John said as he looked up to the sky, thanking God.

When John wrapped his arm around Elizabeth and whispered in her ear, Elizabeth could only stare straight ahead, unable to look at him, shocked and confused by his words, and wondered, *what could he mean by that? How is my being with child going to help him with his plans? Is it possible…no, it cannot be! Does he think…this child could be his? No, it is not possible!*

When John moved away to look up at the sky, Elizabeth took this moment to look at him, and what she saw, further confused her, and she tried to figure out the man who stood before her, who claimed to be a man of God.

How can this man be a man of God? I do not understand this man. He is no man of God, this, I have no doubt, she thought, and these thoughts only increased Elizabeth's fear of her current situation. *No! I cannot allow this! This is not the time to think or worry about what John Bonnet thinks.*

Elizabeth took a deep breath, then let it out slowly. She decided to save her sanity by ignoring John Bonnet, and she was feeling too ill to concern herself with him.

Before they began their long journey to Castle Saumur, John decided they would first find a tavern near the docks to allow himself, Elizabeth, and the guards to have a meal.

After Elizabeth finished her meal, she felt a great deal better, and once they were finally on their way to King Francis's castle, she wondered, *why are they taking me to King Francis's country castle instead of taking me directly to his palace in Paris?*

Elizabeth may have been young, but she was not ignorant. She knew if she were to be Queen, Paris would be the place she should have been presented and announced at court that she was to be the future Queen of France. However, Elizabeth knew those questions would have to wait until she could speak to King Francis directly.

***

As John and Elizabeth approached Castle Saumur in Main-et-Loue, night had already fallen. The only light they had was coming from the moon and stars shining bright in the sky. It allowed Elizabeth an ambiguous few of the castle, which appeared to be seated high above the village, on the edge of a hill or a cliff.

However, the closer they approached Castle Saumur's gates, Elizabeth could see it was a wonderful and beautifully constructed castle, which seemed to be surrounded by a vast land. However, what Elizabeth could not see, the castle was indeed on a cliff, high above the village that was surrounded by a large body of water – a river that ran out to sea, and the rich land surrounding the castle was ideal for growing grapes, that were used to create the finest wines in France.

Once they arrived at the castle, John Bonnet left Elizabeth in the carriage, so he could enter through the castle's main entrance, as the guards were relieved of their duties and replaced with a new set of guards, except for Filipe, who elected to stay and escort Elizabeth the rest of the way. Once they reached the side entrance, only two of the guards remained, with one of them being Filipe to escort Elizabeth to her room.

Going through the side entrance confused Elizabeth. *Why am I not going through the main castle entrance?* she thought.

Filipe assisted Elizabeth out of the carriage and guided her to a small door, and after through that door, directly to the left, they went through another door, where they found themselves at the bottom of a narrow winding staircase. Filipe went first, then Elizabeth, and the second guard followed up the rear.

Elizabeth began the treacherous climb of the stairs that seemed to go on forever, taking them to the top of the castle, to what appears to be the tower.

Why am I being taken to King Francis through the back entrance? Elizabeth thought. This confused her, not understanding what was happening. It appeared she was being hidden from the rest of the castle. *But why?*

Elizabeth knew this was not something done of a woman who was to be King Francis's Queen. At this realization, she became afraid, and began to fear the real reason she was brought to Castle Saumur. Elizabeth stopped to look at Filipe, but he refused to look at her and only motioned with his arm for her to continue, and she did as he requested.

Once they reached the tower room, Filipe opened the door and motioned for Elizabeth to enter. Upon entering the room, Elizabeth noticed it was a small plain room, nothing of what she was expecting. She expected the room to be furnished with the finest French furniture and furnishings, instead, the room had a plain, long thick wooden table, that was seated on the only lavish item in the room, a beautifully made French rug with the royal colors along with the king's royal crest situated in the center of the rug. Which is what she expected the entire room to be decorated in.

The room's only other furniture was a wooden chair resting beneath a large window overlooking the rocks and water below. To the left of the window was a large massive stone fireplace, and above the fireplace hung the king's royal crest.

As Elizabeth was looking around her surroundings, she noticed she was left alone in the room, and wondered, *why was I brought to this room…this tower? Am I a prisoner then, instead of a welcome guest of King Francis?* To Elizabeth, this seemed incredibly odd.

However, now that she was alone, it gave her time to think about the recent events and what was coming next. This had only increased her fear, making her too nervous to think of sitting down. Instead, she paced the small room as she did whenever she was scared or nervous.

***

While Elizabeth was being taken to the tower, John Bonnet was going directly to inform King Francis that his gift has arrived. John smiled, reveling in his triumph in the way he brought Elizabeth to France.

Elizabeth had to be taken to the tower so she would not be seen by the others within the castle. But, for what the king had planned for Elizabeth, at that moment, no one could know she was there, except for a few trusted servants of King Francis.

Once John Bonnet's arrival had been announced to King Francis, he entered the royal room and bowed, "Your Majesty, we have arrived. As we speak, Lady Elizabeth is being taken to the tower where she will await your arrival," he said.

King Francis looked at John, he was extremely pleased with this news, and smiled, "Good man John, you have done well. Now, let us see my newest acquisition," King Francis said, and together they headed to the tower.

***

As Elizabeth was pacing the room, she heard a noise coming from outside the door and turned just as the door opened, and she saw John Bonnet along with King Francis.

"Your Majesty," Elizabeth said, curtsying.

King Francis smile broadens as he reached his hand out to her. "Good evening, my dear Elizabeth, it is a pleasure to finally meet you," he said, taking Elizabeth's hand in his. "To see you when I first arrived in Chester…to see such beauty took my breath away. Now, to have you before me, what I saw that day was no comparison to what I see in front of me now. My dear, you are truly a great beauty. Your beauty is beyond anything I have ever seen across the lands. And my dear, I have seen a great deal," King Francis said, eyeing Elizabeth with lust in his eyes, as he pulled her hand to his mouth and kissed it lightly.

Then, when he saw the fear in Elizabeth's eyes, he quickly released her hand and said, "My dear, there is no need to fear me. Please allow me to introduce myself. I am Francis the First, the King of France," then he bowed to Elizabeth.

Elizabeth curtsied in return. Regardless of how she came to be there, she was honored to meet King Francis, and to her relief, she was amazed by how kind and polite he was. After what happened, she expected a horrible and cruel king, due to the way she was brought to France. Yet, at his kindness, she wondered if he knew of the manner in which she was treated.

"My dear, how was your journey?" King Francis asked, retaking her hand with gentleness and compassion.

Do I dare tell him what happened? Elizabeth wondered, then glanced at John Bonnet, *no, not while John is in the room. I will wait for when I am alone with King Francis to tell him,* she thought, turning her attention back to the King.

When John saw Elizabeth looked at him, he wondered, *she…this wench, will she dare tell King Francis how she was treated on our journey here.* This thought concerned John, and it caused him to worry – *if she did, what would King Francis do? Would he believe her?* The best John could do was take the risk and hope he would have the time to come up with something that would rebuke anything Elizabeth had to say. At this, John smiled.

"My dear, you must be starved from your long journey," King Francis said.

Before Elizabeth could answer, King Francis turned and called for the servants, then ordered them to bring food for Elizabeth at once. Once the servants left, he returned his attention to Elizabeth, then to the room.

"I am sorry, my dear, for the state of this room. I wanted your arrival to be in secrecy until I could present you at court. I do not want anyone to know about you, not yet. You do understand, my dear?"

Elizabeth nodded in response, "Yes, Your Majesty," she said in a whisper.

Within a short time of ordering food for Elizabeth, the food arrived, and King Francis instructed the servants to place a large variety of food on the table. Then, with Elizabeth's hand in his, he guided her to the table.

"Here, my dear, you must eat after your long journey."

"Thank you, Your Majesty, but I am afraid I am unable to eat at the moment."

Concerned, King Francis asked, "Are you unwell, my dear?"

Elizabeth was unsure what to say, and she elected to tell him of her illness during her journey to France. "Yes, Your Majesty. It seemed on our journey here; I suffered the sickness from the motion of the sea."

John watched Elizabeth closely, waiting to see if she would say anything about her treatment, and to his relief, she did not.

Ah, maybe she will not tell the king. It would be wise if she did not, John thought.

"Ah, I see, my dear. Perhaps you can eat later when your stomach has settled."

Elizabeth was grateful for King Francis's kindness and understanding. It wasn't only her sickness that prevented her from eating, but her thoughts of what her beloved Robert must be going through.

As King Francis continued to talk to Elizabeth, she wasn't listening, as her mind couldn't help but wonder what was happening to Robert. Wondering what he was going through after John kidnapped her.

Where is he? Is he already on his way here? If so, then he will talk to King Francis and make him see the truth. Then after, he will take me home. Wait, she thought with a sudden realization, *now is the time to speak to King Francis and tell him the truth.*

This was an opportunity Elizabeth could not pass up. Yes, she was scared, scared out of her wits, but this was her time, her chance to convince King Francis of his grave mistake. Elizabeth took a deep breath, and after releasing it, she pushed aside her fears. If she didn't do this now, she might never have another opportunity. She had to do whatever she could to convince King Francis of his error and the misinformed information he was given.

Elizabeth glanced at John, then said, "Your Majesty, may I have a word with you in private, please?"

Elizabeth did not want to speak in front of John; however, King Francis gave her permission to speak, but he did not dismiss John.

At this, John smiled, *ah, yes, I see I already have the king's complete trust and confidence in me*, he thought.

With King Francis refusing to dismiss John disturbed Elizabeth, but she couldn't allow this to sway her. She was determined to have her say, so she pulled back her shoulders and stood straight, standing as the lady she was, a lady born into nobility.

"Thank you, Your Majesty. This situation…in bringing me here is a horrible mistake," Elizabeth said.

King Francis did not say a word; he only lifted his eyebrow in question.

"Forgive me, Your Majesty, but I do not understand the reason I was brought to France to marry you?"

At this, King Francis turned to look at John with a questionable eye. John shrugged his shoulders and smiled, and King Francis returned the smile with understanding, then returned his attention to Elizabeth.

"To my understanding, Your Majesty, when you visited my mother and father, Baron and Baroness Massey, you were informed I was recently married to Lord and Lady Davenport's son, Lord Robert Davenport. Your Majesty, if we were to marry, knowing I am already married, would this not be a great sin in God's eyes?"

Elizabeth waited to see if King Francis had anything to say, and when he said nothing, she took a deep breath and continued.

"Forgive me, but I feel…Your Majesty, there has been a misunderstanding regarding my situation," Elizabeth said, glancing at John to see if he would stop her, but all he did was watch and listened. However, she noticed something strange.

There is a strange kind of confidence in him as if he fears nothing for King Francis to learn the truth, she thought.

King Francis took a good look at Elizabeth and what he saw was a foolish and naive girl.

"My dear, Lady Elizabeth, I am sorry for your distress. I know your love for this Robert is great. But my dear, it was discovered you and this Robert were never married. There was no record, nor a witness that could be found to prove a marriage you claim ever took place," King Francis said, taking Elizabeth's hand in his, "Have no fear my dear, I do not wrong you for what you did. You and this Robert Davenport are both very young and were desperate to prevent Robert from marrying your sister Grace. My dear, I understand. If it were me, I would have done the same thing. In marrying me," King Francis said with a smile, and from the corner of his eye, he glanced at John. "It will free you from any disgrace your unproven marriage would have brought to your family," motioning his arms out to encompass the whole of France, "My people…the people of France, need never know the truth," he said, glancing at John standing by the door looking confident.

John looked very pleased with himself that King Francis went along with his deception. Elizabeth, however, was staring at King Francis with a look of horror and shock.

King Francis looked back at Elizabeth and smiled, "When John heard you were married to Robert Davenport, with my blessing, he decided," King Francis said, glancing at John again. "He made inquiries to all the churches within and outside of Cheshire, and when he was unable to find any record nor witness to this so-called marriage you claim took place…after learning the truth, he of course informed me of this wonderful news. Because my dear," taking Elizabeth's hand in his again, "That first moment I saw you, I desired you more than I have desired any woman. And at my age, there have been many. So, I wasted no time by going directly to speak to your father, Baron Massey.

After speaking with your dear father and informed him of the truth about your marriage, I requested and was granted permission to make you my wife. You will be the next Queen of France," he said, shaking his head, "When your father learned of your deception, he was horrified and feared of the great scandal your deception would cause, along with the great disgrace that would befall them. As King of France, I ensured Baron Massey this would not happen. That once you were my wife and Queen of France, any disgrace that would have existed would immediately be vanquished.

Therefore, Baron Massey and I came to an agreement that was placed in writing, giving me you, and I as king, will assist him in obtaining their family home, Dunham Massey Castle, along with my protection and a sizable allowance. In doing this, left open for your sister Grace to marry Robert Davenport, allowing them to fulfill their original agreement with Lord Davenport. So, you see, my dear, all is well," King Francis said, grinning with satisfaction.

However, Elizabeth was horrified at what she just learned and thought, *how could father agree to such an arrangement. Oh, I know why, because they believed it to be true. Did they ever really know me, their own daughter?* Elizabeth shook her head as pain pierced her heart.

Elizabeth wasn't willing to give up, not yet. Although

she was alone, she had to find a way to make King Francis understand the truth.

"Your Majesty, please hear me. You have been terribly misinformed. I am indeed married to Robert Davenport. We were married in a church, in front of a priest, in the eyes of God. It was not in Cheshire. We traveled a great distance to a small church near Yorkshire, and we were married on Christmas Day by a Catholic priest," Elizabeth said, looking at King Francis with desperation in her eyes, pleading with him to believe her.

King Francis laughed aloud, no longer willing to continue with the charade, seeing Elizabeth as a foolish and naive innocent girl.

"My dear, you are indeed a foolish girl. No matter," waving his hand to dismiss her concerns. "I have your father's consent, and the marriage will take place as planned." He looked directly at Elizabeth, and in his firmest authoritative voice, "My dear, the matter is closed."

For the first time, Elizabeth saw in King Francis's eyes a man with evil intent. It did not matter what she said, she was his, and that was the end of it. Elizabeth stood there stunned, and King Francis was no longer showing her the kindness he first displayed, but of a man who got what he wanted no matter the cost. She saw in King Francis, the same she saw in John Bonnet, maybe worse. Elizabeth could not help but wonder how her mother and father, who she loved and adored and believed loved and adored her, could so easily turn her away – throwing her to a man such as he.

At this realization, Elizabeth felt faint, and just as she was about to collapse, King Francis caught her before she hit the floor. He called for a servant waiting outside the door to bring the only chair in the room for Elizabeth to sit on.

Once Elizabeth was seated in the chair, with concern King Francis asked, "My dear, are you alright?"

Elizabeth was in tears; she was so upset about what she just learned her father did and could not understand why no one would believe her, that she and Robert were married. She must. She must make the king see reason.

"Your Majesty, forgive me for my manors, but I must protest. I cannot and will not marry you," Elizabeth said as she raised her head high and looked directly into King Francis's eyes, which was never done. For Elizabeth, it no longer mattered. If this were to be forced upon her, she'd rather forfeit her life by speaking the truth.

"If you force me to marry you…know I will never truly be yours, not so long as Robert lives! My heart will always belong to Robert, my husband!" she said firmly. "I know that right now, he is on his way here to bring me home!" She looked at the door, then to the window, "I am sure he is out there right now trying to find a way to rescue me! You may not believe me, nor my family, but the one that matters most, is the one and only true God!" Elizabeth said, glancing at John Bonnet, then turned her attention back to King Francis. "He is the one to which you will answer to when you approach him on judgment day!" she said firmly and with confidence. "I will never be yours! To force me to marry, you will be committing a great sin in God's eyes!"

To say these things to a king such as King Francis was bold and brash and to most an immediate forfeit of one's life. So, Elizabeth watched King Francis, looking for any expressions to what he would do, but he betrayed nothing. He maintained an impassive and emotionless face, but Elizabeth didn't care. All she cared about was doing what she knew was right, by trying to get King Francis, to see and do what was right, by letting her go.

However, King Francis took no offense to what Elizabeth said. On the contrary, he ignored all her words, as ones coming from a foolish and young girl. Innocent, in the ways of the world.

After Elizabeth made her declaration, one of the royal

guards walked into the room and whispered something to
King Francis, who then turned to look at Elizabeth, then
quickly left the room with the guard. Elizabeth did not
understand what happened to cause him and John Bonnet to
leave the room in such a hurry, but she was grateful to have
time alone to think of her circumstances and what she could
do to rectify her situation.

Chapter Twenty-Six

After Robert returned to Bramhall Manor from visiting Baron Massey, he joined the men who were going to help him rescue Elizabeth.

"Are we ready to depart?" Robert asked.

"We are, My Lord," said Sir Isaac.

"Good, let us be on our way. We need to make haste to Liverpool and board my father's ship upon our arrival. There is no time to delay, and I do not want too much time between John Bonnet and us," Robert said.

"Yes, My Lord. If I may, I have a suggestion?"

"Yes, Sir Isaac, what would that be?"

"Well, I heard John Bonnet took Elizabeth down the River Mersey to Liverpool, which will cut down their time a great deal, as it would take them mere hours, then days. I recommend we go down the same route?"

"Excellent, Sir Isaac! We shall take the River Mersey as well. The quicker we get there, the better our chances will be to rescue Elizabeth. Let us be on our way."

***

Taking River Mersey was a wise decision. They arrived in Liverpool in the early morning hours, and without resting, Robert went directly to his father's ship to find the captain and have him start preparation so they could set sail for France as soon as possible.

After finding his father's ship, The Contravour, Robert found a crewman and explained who he was, then ordered the man to wake the captain, who was still asleep in his cabin, and have him brought to him at once.

For the crewman to rouse the captain from his sleep, the captain was not pleased, but he made quick haste to the deck to where Lord Robert Davenport stood waiting when he learned of the reason.

When Robert saw the captain, he said, "Captain, I am

Lord Robert Davenport, the eldest son, and heir to Lord John Davenport, who owns this ship and crew. Captain," handing him the letter, "I present you with a letter from my father, instructing you to take my men and me to France."

Captain Burtess looked at the men behind Robert and recognized them to be Lord Davenport's men, and when he looked at Sir Isaac, gave him a nod, confirming who Robert claimed to be, and thus he read the letter.

Captain Burtess,

I hereby order you to give the full use of The Contravour and the crew to my son and heir, Lord Robert Davenport. You are to treat him with the same honor and respect as you would me. You are ordered to take my son and five of my men, whom you are already acquainted with, to France, and once they have concluded their business, you will bring them back to England.

Gratefully,
Lord John Davenport,
of Bramhall Manor and Magistrate of Cheshire and Manchester.

"Lord Davenport, please allow me a few hours to make ready my ship and crew. Until then, please take your men for food and ale while you wait. Once we are ready, I will send one of my men to notify you we're ready to sail."

"Thank you, captain, we shall. It was a long and tiring journey, and we are parched with thirst and hunger," Robert said.

"I know just the place," said Sir Isaac. "Captain, you know where your man can find us."

The captain nodded in understanding, then turned to his crew and began throwing out orders to his men to prepare the ship to sail.

Robert followed Sir Isaac to a tavern that was near where their ship was docked. When the men entered the Tavern, it was full and reeked of ale, piss, and men who haven't bathed in years. They looked around for an open table and found one that was clean in the room's back corner. All the men ordered ale and whatever food was ready to be served, and once the men received their food, they ate in silence, a credit to how exhausted they were from their long journey.

While the men were eating, they caught a conversation of men talking about a man named John Bonnet who was sailing to Loire Valley, France, and the captain of the ship was looking for additional help.

At hearing this, Robert looked at Sir Isaac, and he too heard the men talking, and they knew if they hadn't heard this information, they would have sailed to Paris, going in the wrong direction. They also learned John Bonnet's ship parted just at dawn, which put them a good day ahead of them, and Robert worried they would arrive too late.

Sir Isaac explained to Robert that although John Bonnet had a good start, his father's ship was one of the fastest ships known to be built, and explained to Robert if the weather were good and the winds were strong, it would cut down the time it would usually take if they were on another ship, allowing them to arrive mere hours after John Bonnet. When Robert heard this, it gave him hope, and he was anxious to be on their way.

***

An hour later, Robert and his father's men boarded The Contravour, and shortly after, they were on their way to Loire Valley. Once The Contravour was clear from the docks, the captain ordered all sails to be at full mast, and with the wind strong, it gave the ship the speed they needed to make it to France in record time.

Once the ship was on its way, Robert took a good look around and was amazed by how grand his father's ship was. From the look of the ship, it was clear the ship was built for speed. With the sleekness of the ship and the number of sails, it spoke 'speed.' Captain Burgess had assured Robert the weather was ideal for sailing and believed they would make it to France within record time. However, although the ship was fast, for Robert, it seemed like an Eternity before they would arrive in France.

***

It was just after sunset when the Contravour arrived in France. Before the ship was fully secure, Robert and his father's men debarked the ship and wasted no time seeking information on John Bonnet ship's arrival and where their party was bound to.

"Sir Isaac, please assign a man or two to discover when John Bonnet arrived and where he was bound to. I hope this will provide us with how far ahead they are. There would be no missing him, as I am sure John Bonnet would have used King Francis royal banner," Robert ordered.

Although Robert threw out the order, it wasn't necessary, as Sir Isaac and his men knew what needed to be done but elected not to say a word and took Robert's instruction. After he finished, he looked at Sir Isaac and knew it was unnecessary but was grateful to Sir Isaac for not saying so.

"Once everyone has their information, return to the Contravour, then everyone will let us know what each of you discovered," said Sir Isaac.

***

By the time the men returned to the Contravour to relay the information they had discovered, the sun was low in the sky.

"Sir Edward, tell Robert what you told me, in what you discovered about John Bonnet and Elizabeth," said Sir Isaac.

Sir Edward bowed to Robert, "My Lord, I found a man who was aboard the ship that brought John Bonnet and

Elizabeth to France. The man said they were bound for Saumur Castle, in Main-et-Loue, which is only a few hours ride from here," said Sir Edward.

"Thank heavens! Do you know how long ago they arrived?" Robert asked.

"Yes, My Lord. They arrived early this morning and had a meal in the Tavern before starting their journey to Saumur Castle. It was heard the lady in their party was not feeling well," Sir Edward said.

To hear this worried Robert, "Sir Isaac, what would cause Elizabeth to be so weak?" Robert asked, then a realization hit him, "Forget my words, I am sure it is nothing but stress," Robert said.

Robert turned his attention to the horse's Sir Isaac had acquired. "I see you obtained horses…I did not think…thank you for thinking of it," Robert said, ashamed with his lack of experience, and was grateful to have a man like Sir Isaac and the rest of his father's men to help him. They were experienced and well-trained men, and he could not have done this without them.

Robert wanted to say a few words to the men who agreed to assist him in rescuing Elizabeth.

"I know it has been a long journey, and we still have another long journey to go. But, as you know, there is no time to rest, and I am grateful you purchased provisions for our journey," Robert said.

"As you said, we are experienced men, My Lord. There were many times we went days without rest. However, we will manage," said Sir Isaac.

"Yes, of course, forgive me," Robert said, but the men waved away his comment as if it was nothing.

"Well then, as we know, it is hours to Saumur Castle, and John Bonnet and his party have a large start. I believe this is to our benefit that he travels with Elizabeth and several of King Francis guards," Robert said, then looked to Sir Isaac for confirmation to where he was going with this, and Sir Isaac nodded in understanding. "With a large party such as his, they will be forced to take it slow. With this, if we ride hard, my hope is we will catch up to them shortly after they arrive at Saumur Castle."

At this, the men mounted their horses and with haste, they galloped away.

***

As Robert and the mercenaries approached Saumur Castle, Sir Isaac reigned in his horse and called for Robert to stop.

Robert, without a word, did as he asked.

"Forgive me, My Lord," Sir Isaac said, but before he could say another word —

Robert broke in, "Think nothing of it. You are one of my father's best men, and you have his respect, and so you have mine. This is your area of expertise, not mine. Please, do not hesitate to speak your mind."

"Thank you, My Lord. Before we approach Saumur Castle, we must have a plan," Sir Isaac said.

"Yes, you are right, Sir Isaac. What do you suggest?"

"If we ride up to Saumur Castle together, it will appear as a threat. However, if you should be the one to approach, it will not appear threatening, but that of a grieving husband seeking to retrieve his wife. While you are at the main entrance distracting the guards – there are usually two guards on duty, and we will confirm this when we meet up later. The rest of the men and I will circle the castle to assess the situation, confirm how many guards are situated around the castle, and learn the access points to know what we are dealing with.

Once we complete our assessment, I will take the men…there are Frenchmen nearby we can trust. I would like to enlist their help in case more men are needed," Sir Isaac said.

"Do you feel more men will be required?" Robert asked.

"They may not be needed, but it is best to be prepared. These Frenchmen will also know more about why King Francis would have brought Elizabeth here, than taking her to Paris. If further action is required, one with more forceful action, then the additional men will be needed. The one thing we are sure of, Saumur Castle is one of King Francis's smaller castles, which there will be only a handful of guards and servants on duty."

"Sounds like an excellent plan Sir Isaac. I am grateful to have you and the rest of the men here to help me. Shall we be off then?" Robert said, and with a nod from Sir Isaac, they were off again.

***

Once they arrived at the outer edge of Saumur Castle, Sir Isaac called, "My Lord," pulling their horses to a stop, "When you are at the gate, we will split and veer around both sides of the castle to assess the situation. After, we will ride out to gather the Frenchmen I told you of earlier," Sir Isaac said.

"Yes, of course. Shall we meet back at my father's chateau then?" Robert asked.

"Yes, My Lord. However, if anything was to go wrong, I will leave one of my men behind to watch your back," Sir Isaac said.

"Do you think it will be necessary?" Robert asked.

"My Lord, one never knows when it comes to John Bonnet. It is best to be prepared than naught," said Sir Isaac.

"Again, you are right. Forgive me, Sir Isaac, for my lack of experience," Robert said, feeling ashamed of how little experience he had.

I promise, once I have Elizabeth and we are back in England, I will work on learning all I can to be better in the future, Robert thought.

Sir Isaac waved off his concern and nodded in understanding, then left Robert and sent half his men in one direction and the rest in the other to cover every inch of the castle before meeting back up, then they would ride out to gather the Frenchmen. At the same time, Robert went directly through the front gates of Saumur Castle.

The plan was, Robert would request an audience with King Francis, and once he was inside the castle gates, he would inform the guards who he was, and why he was there, and he needed to speak to King Francis regarding urgent business that could not wait.

However, what Robert was not aware of, John Bonnet had expected him, and he informed the guards to remain alert for a man arriving, demanding to speak to the king. They were to inquire to who the man was, and if it was Robert Davenport, they were to refuse his request for entry, no matter the circumstances. The guards were further ordered, if they saw Robert, they were to order him to leave at once, and if he refused, they were to take him into custody and throw him into the dungeon.

When Robert arrived at Saumur Castle and was refused entry, he made as much commotion as he could to keep the guard's attention, allowing Sir Isaac and his men time to do what they needed to do. However, Robert was determined to force his way in, to have his voice heard by King Francis no matter what happened. Then Robert heard a voice, and he never wanted to hear it again, even though he knew it would be unavoidable.

"Ahhh, Lord Davenport, I see you made it to our lovely country," John Bonnet said.

Robert ignored John Bonnet and yelled, "I demand to see King Francis immediately!"

"My boy, I am afraid that is impossible," John said with a smirk.

No matter how hard Robert tried with the argument he made, there was no getting past the king's guards. With John Bonnet there, he threatened Robert, saying he would have Robert put to death if he did not leave at once.

However, John's threat did not affect Robert, and he ignored anything John Bonnet had to say.

"I will not leave! I need to see King Francis at once! I have proof Elizabeth and I are married! He must listen! You must listen!" Robert yelled, then turned his eyes to John, "If King Francis does not hear me out and marries Elizabeth, he will be committing a great sin! As a Catholic Clergyman, you must see that!"

Although Robert knew that John Bonnet was not a Catholic Clergyman and the true reason King Francis wanted Elizabeth, he was not ready to give that away quite yet. Instead, he'd rather allow John Bonnet to think him ignorant. Yes, he could show his hand, but now was not the time. So, Robert continued doing what he needed to do to make John Bonnet see reason.

"He must wait and allow me time to bring the priest here! The priest will have proof that Elizabeth and I are married! If King Francis refuses to grant me an audience and marries Elizabeth…what would happen when France's people find out? How do you think they will view their King? Do you think King Francis can afford to have his people revolt against him? They will no longer see a great king, but one who committed bigamy…a great sin in God's eyes! No matter what is decided today, I will bring forth the priest, and the truth will be revealed! I first wanted to give King Francis a chance to do what is right!"

John was not swayed by Robert's threats and had a secret of his own. *What would this boy think when he learns the true reason King Francis wants Elizabeth?* John thought.

"Lord Davenport, you are not well informed, are you?" John said, shaking his head to Robert's ignorance. "King Francis is already married. This marriage to Elizabeth is a ruse and nothing more. Elizabeth will soon be one of King Francis's many mistresses," he said, taking great pleasure in doing so.

John Bonnet's so-called 'revelation' was not news to Robert. Still, to hear it from John Bonnet's mouth outraged Robert. He wanted nothing more than at that very moment to kill John. He wanted to run his sword through his heart, and before Robert realized what he was doing, and without conscious thought, he lunged at John, hoping it would place him in a position that would allow him to cut his throat.

The king's guards saw what Robert intended to do, and before he could get close to John, the guards moved in and created a human wall around John that prevented Robert from touching him. Then, without a second thought, John ordered the guards to throw Robert outside the castle gates.

Although Robert was being removed, John knew he would never give up. Therefore, something drastic would need to be done. If Robert persists in seeing King Francis, John feared that eventually, the people of France would learn the truth, and this, he could not allow to happen.

Could there be a rebellion if the people learned the truth? Probably not, but John was unwilling to take the risk. He knew if it came to this, King Francis would return Elizabeth to Robert, and in doing so, destroy all he had planned. This, he could not allow.

John Bonnet yelled at Robert as the guards were carrying him away, "Leave this place, and do not return! If you do, the guards are instructed to shoot you on sight! In your death, war will erupt between our two countries! Do you want to be responsible for the death of all your countrymen?" John wanted to use the same threat he used on Elizabeth, believing Robert was just as ignorant as she was.

Robert glanced back at John, as the guards were carrying him away – *Does this man think me a fool! A brainless fool! To start a war between our two countries by attempting to rescue my wife! This man cannot be that mad!* Robert thought.

Robert was not daft to the threats of war between

France and England, threats that's been going on for years, and Robert will not give King Francis an excuse to cause King Henry to blame his father for what he is responsible for.

I am no fool! This man of God is no man of God, but an evil man with the intention to end us, Robert thought. Then, he realized the ignorance of his lack of knowledge. *I should have known King Francis was married. How can a man of his status not be? This is my fault for refusing to keep updated on what was happening with England and France. You know why it is because all your attention was on Elizabeth and nothing else. I did not care for my father or how he treated his people, so I ignored anything he had to say or wanted me to do.*

Robert's fears for Elizabeth increased, and he knew if John Bonnet was there, Elizabeth was in grave danger. He realized he could not rescue Elizabeth on his own and needed help from the men his father sent with him.

Once the guards dispatched Robert at the edge of the forest, he mounted his horse and galloped at great speed to reach his father's chateau.

Sir Raphael, the man Sir Isaac left behind, witnessed the whole event from where he was standing at the forest edge, hidden by the darkness of the night. When he saw Robert flee on his horse, he knew Robert had forgotten he was there, and he quickly mounted his horse and followed suit.

In what Sir Raphael overheard, he was sure John Bonnet had an alternative motive. What they were, he didn't know, but they needed to find out, and as soon as possible, he needed to talk to Sir Isaac and inform him what he witnessed, and together they need to decide how to act.

***

Elizabeth was too upset to concern herself about the reason King Francis and John Bonnet left, and found she was unable to remain seated, and for a moment, she looked at the table of food, suddenly ravenous, but was too upset to eat. So instead, she started pacing up and down the room, and as she was pacing, her stomach was twisting as if her insides were knotting up. She felt nervous and worried, then uncontrollably, she started rubbing her hands together. She was so nervous that she allowed her thoughts to run away with her.

What am I going to do? How can I do what King Francis has asked of me? Is it not a sin for me to marry King Francis, in knowing I am already a married woman? And how can…the thought of being with that man, or any man other than Robert? Robert, whom I love with all my heart and soul? Who I promised my life, my faithfulness, my body, and my soul to.

Elizabeth didn't know that the so-called agreement King Francis mentioned had nothing to do with her marrying him. But instead, for her to become one of the Royal Court's Ladies in waiting. In other words, another one of many of King Francis's mistresses.

As Elizabeth waited in the tower, she was so scared, horrified at what was to come. What would happen to Robert when he finally came to rescue her. In not knowing what to do, Elizabeth did the only thing she could; she began praying to God, needing his help and guidance.

God, if this is a dream, please wake me from this horrible nightmare? she thought, but she knew this was not a dream.

After almost wearing out the floor, Elizabeth decided to stand in front of the window, looked up to the sky, and sought the moon and stars. She stared, trying to penetrate the veil, seeking the heavens beyond. Then, as she was gliding her fingers across her necklace, she leaned against the window ledge and spoke to God.

God, where is Robert? Is he trying to rescue me, save me from this man, this king, and this marriage? To marry King Francis is a sin. Your sin. Has Robert already arrived in France? she thought. So many questions she did not have answers to.

Elizabeth's thoughts suddenly took her back to the moment she was pulled out of Robert's arms when the king's guards dragged her away, which caused her to shiver at the memory. So, instead, she focused on the memory of Robert's last words to her, *'I will do everything in my power to bring you home. Do not give up.'* Elizabeth kept playing Robert's last words to her over and over again, causing tears to run down her face.

While Elizabeth stood deep in thought, she was hit with a powerful feeling, one she would recognize anywhere.

It is Robert! At this, she stood straight, putting her hands on the edge of the window. *This must be why King Francis left. God, what if Robert must fight? Robert is a great swordsman, but is he good enough to defeat so many royal guards and soldiers? If not, in his attempt to rescue me, he is killed...no!* At this thought, Elizabeth started to panic. *Oh God, no! Please! If Robert is killed trying to rescue me, how will I live knowing my love, my husband is dead because he tried to save me? No! I cannot believe this will happen! I cannot!*

Elizabeth shook her head to stop herself from thinking of such a horrible thing. She could not bear to think of the possibilities, but at the same time, she could not help but wonder what might be happening to Robert at this very moment. So again, she reached out to God.

Standing at the window with both hands on the edge, Elizabeth stretched her head as if she could reach heaven and God; she began pleading to God.

God, please protect Robert, she began with tears in her eyes, *and keep him safe. Please, do not allow any harm to come to him. Please, find a way to let him know how much I love him and that I am thinking about him right now.*

Shortly after Elizabeth sent up her prayer, King Francis walked in the room with the same guard he left with, and the look she saw on King Francis's face – she did not like what it seemed to say. *God, no, tell me it is not too late,* she thought.

King Francis informed Elizabeth of grievous news, "My dear, Lady Elizabeth, Robert Davenport has arrived in France, just as you suspected. Just now, at the main gate, when the guards refused him entry, Robert attempted to fight his way through…I am sorry, my dear, in his attempts, one of my guards pierced his heart with his sword."

Elizabeth gasped, and for a moment, all she could do was stare at King Francis in utter horror and disbelief. *No, this cannot be so! It cannot!* She thought.

King Francis saw this and continued, "My Lady, he…is dead. I am sorry to have to deliver such grievous news," King Francis said, with all the care and sadness he could muster. Then in a sudden change in voice, "Now that Robert Davenport is dead, there is nothing that will prevent you from moving forward. We shall proceed with the wedding within a fourth night," he said, then turned with his guard and left the room, allowing Elizabeth time to accept what he told her and time to grieve. As King Francis left the room, he had a smile on his face, knowing there would be no wedding, nor was Robert dead.

When King Francis first walked in the room, he appeared with such kindness and sadness in delivering such grievous news, but then, to Elizabeth's horror, he took on a type of coldness. When Elizabeth saw this, she grasped her chest, feeling the pain in her heart at the loss of Robert, along with the shock of King Francis's horrible behavior. It disgusted her how cold he appeared to be after delivering such grievous news.

Being unable to say a word, Elizabeth just watched as King Francis left the room. She thought, *how can this King of France be so heartless? No, I must be mistaken…I did not hear what I heard him say? It cannot be true.*

But, for a reason she could not explain, she knew it was

true.

Elizabeth started pacing the room again, rubbing her hands, feeling nervous and scared. She again turned to God for help.

God, please tell me this is not so? Then she started crying uncontrollably, for someone to tell her that her beloved husband, who was her heart and soul, could not be what he said, that Robert was dead.

Screaming in her head as she cannot speak the words aloud, *No! No! Robert cannot be dead! He just cannot! And for King Francis to tell me in such a cold and heartless way…no! It is not true! It cannot be! To say such a thing…how can he expect me to grieve for my beloved, then right after, marry him! God…no! I will not! I cannot! He will not force me to marry him! This man, who is responsible for Robert's death! I would rather die than marry this man!*

At that thought, Elizabeth knew what she had to do. So, she went to the window and looked up to the heavens to again seek God's help. *I am sorry! But I cannot…I just cannot do this! I am sorry!* After finally finding her voice, "GOD HELP ME PLEASE!" Elizabeth screamed to the heavens.

Elizabeth was crying as she was feeling unbearable pain. *Tell me what to do?* she thought, as she was talking to God, she turned from the sky to look at the rocks and water below, and at that moment, Elizabeth knew what she had to do.

Elizabeth felt so lost, and she believed, for her, there was only one option. Only one way out, and she wondered, *can I do this?* But she hesitated, unsure if she could go through with it, but at that moment, it felt right. It was what she had to do. *But how can I?*

As she stood there contemplating what she was going to do, knowing to do such a thing would be breaking one of God's laws, not to mention the promise she made to

Robert.

But how can I live in a world where Robert is not? Robert, who was ripped from me, killed…no, murdered by the man who expects me to call him husband, she thought, then she yelled, "NO! NEVER!" to the night sky.

Elizabeth had fallen into despair, and then with a sudden jerk of her head, she remembered what she and Robert believed would happen after their death. Although their lives as Robert and Elizabeth would be over, there would be another. Another world. Another life, where they could find each other and their love, and be together once again.

Yes, Elizabeth knew if she took her life, she would not be welcomed into heaven, but if God were to show her mercy, she would be so lucky, and if God were to grant her and Robert another chance to be together in another life – *how could he not?* she thought. Elizabeth and Robert knew their love was one of the greatest and powerful loves ever to exist. *For us to have a love so powerful, how can it not last for eternity?*

Thus, it was decided. *Will God forgive me?* she thought.

To do what Elizabeth was about to do, was not one she would ever believe she would find herself in such a position, but with losing Robert, there was no life without him. In her death, they will be reunited.

Before she lost her nerve and changed her mind, Elizabeth climbed to the edge of the window. She was shaking, but she slowly eased herself to a standing position, then she looked down to the rocks and water below. Yes, she was afraid, but her pain and sorrow were great.

Elizabeth turned to look back to the room, listening to make sure no one was coming who would stop her, and once she felt secure, she turned back and looked to the sky one last time, to the moon and stars seeking heaven and God.

"God, I am so sorry for what I am about to do. I know

that doing this would be going against you and your law…a sin of the greatest kind. But I am not strong enough to live without Robert. Not after everything that's happened. In what is expected of me by King Francis —"

Elizabeth suddenly stopped as she remembered the child that she believed she was carrying. She looked down and placed her hands on her stomach, "God, if this child within me is Robert's, in doing what I am about to do, I will be killing that last part of him. But if this child is John Bonnet's, then forgive me for saying so…I will be taking with me some part of that evil man. Either way, I will be for the second time committing a great sin. To murder a child who is innocent in all of this."

At speaking these words aloud, Elizabeth hesitated at the thought of taking an innocent life with her was unbearable. To her, she could not see any other way, no matter the situation. Elizabeth knew she could not live without Robert; therefore, her decision was made.

Elizabeth again looked down to the rocks and water below. With her, the last thought was of Robert and their love and how she would see him again and soon. Her last words were a whisper, "Forgive me," then she jumped.

***

A few moments after Elizabeth jumped, a servant entered the room, and when she couldn't find Elizabeth anywhere in the room – the room was empty, and the servant could not understand how Elizabeth could have left, since there was someone at the door the whole time. The servant immediately called for the guard standing outside the door to get King Francis at once.

Moments later, King Francis entered the room, and on his heels was John Bonnet. When he entered the room, it was empty.

"Where is Lady Elizabeth?" he yelled, and without waiting for a reply, he ordered for the castle to be searched, then turned to John, "Could Robert have breached our walls and taken Elizabeth?" King Francis asked.

"Your Majesty, it is not possible. Since Robert arrived at the gate, we surrounded the castle with guards. It would have been impossible for him to get through without being seen."

At that, King Francis turned to the guard, "You, come with me!" and left the room.

However, for John Bonnet, he stayed behind while the others searched the castle for Elizabeth. He felt something was not right about the situation and believed the answers to Elizabeth's disappearance lay in the room.

John took a good look around, and there was no place for Elizabeth to hide. But, when he glanced at the window, a sudden realization hit him.

No, she could not have, he thought.

It was a horrible thought, but it would explain how Elizabeth disappeared without being seen by anyone. John quickly moved to the window and when he looked out, what he saw lying on the rocks below, was a horrific sight.

That wench! There, lying below, was Elizabeth's lifeless body.

Once John Bonnet's shock wore off, anger surged through him, furious at what he saw. *That wench! Harlot! How dare she! She has ruined all my plans!* he thought.

In his fury, John called for the guards that remained outside the door. When the guards entered the room, one was Filipe.

"Quick, we need to get down to the rocks directly below this window!" John ordered as he rushed out the door.

The two guards looked at each other, unsure what to think, but they followed John down the winding staircase with haste. Once they were out the side door, John ordered one of the guards to have a wagon brought around.

Once the guard returned with the wagon, John ordered for the wagon to be backed against the rocks, to get it as close as they could manage.

"Get her body and load it in the wagon!" When the guards went to where John was pointing, Filipe was horrified at what he saw.

No, My Lady! Tell me it is not so? Filipe thought.

But when Filipe approached the body, he could see from the clothes, it was Elizabeth, and it was confirmed when he turned the body over. Although her face was severely damaged, he could still recognize it to be Elizabeth, along with the necklace she wore.

"Did you not hear me! Take her body and place it in the wagon! Now!" John ordered.

Without question, the guards did as he instructed, but for Filipe, he wasn't sure what to do. He didn't want to do what John asked, but since he was the king's guard and John Bonnet was the king's direct counsel, there was nothing he – they could do.

After Elizabeth's body was placed in the wagon, John, after hopping on the wagon, directed the guards to a nearby cave.

The guards were confused and looked at each other, and both thought, *should we not take her back to the king?* But they did not state this, and without a word, did as they were ordered.

When they arrived at the cave entrance, John ordered the guards to carry Elizabeth's body inside, and once inside, it took them a few moments for their eyes to adjust due to it being pitched dark. Once their eyes were fully adjusted, they could see a faint light as they move deeper into the cave. When the guards looked to where the light was coming from, they saw it was a torch in the hands of John Bonnet, and they looked at each other and wondered where it came from, but the guards did not ask any questions and followed John's direction, and took Elizabeth's body and proceeded deeper into the cave.

"Stop here," John yelled at the guards. "Lay her body

there," pointing to a large stone slab a few feet from where they were standing. "Once you place her body on the stone, leave."

The guards did as they were ordered without question.

Once it was done, John ordered, "Now go! Wait outside until I call for you."

The guards did as they were ordered and waited at the mouth of the cave.

Once the guards were out of sight, John motioned for the woman who was hiding in a dark corner to come out.

This woman was no normal woman; she was a Witch. Not just any Witch, an ancient and powerful Witch who practiced the darkest of black magic, a power long forgotten. No one knows how old she was, but some believed she was older than time itself. Centuries ago, she was forced to live in this cave, away from all mankind, otherwise, she would have been burned at the stake – again.

While in solitude, she grew wild and brittle. Her hair was blacker than the darkest of nights. It hung over her face concealing the horror that lay beneath – a hideous scarred face from when the villagers try to burn her at the stake. It was too horrible to be seen.

When the Witch reveals herself, she was short in stature, wearing a long raggedy black robe, and with a snap of her fingers, a roaring fire sprang to life, illuminating the cave around them, and sitting on top of the fire was a large black cauldron.

In a scratchy and hoarse voice, "So John, what have you brought me?" she said, pointing at Elizabeth's body lying on the stone slab. "Ah, such a lovely young lady, a shame her face has been ruined. It looks like it once was a pretty face," she said, turning from the body to look at John through the cracks of her hair. "Now John, what do you want of me?" she asked, and with impatience, "Speak man, do not just stand there and gander. Be quick and tell me now, I am a very busy old woman, you know?"

John cannot stand this old woman, but he needed her help, and as he looked at this hag of a woman, he said, "I need you to place a curse on this woman —"

Before John could finish, the Witch cut him off. "A curse John," looking back at Elizabeth and pointed at her body, "She's dead. There is nothing to curse," she said, then turned her back on John, "Now be gone," waving the back of her hand as she began to walk away.

John looked at the Witch with irritation and impatience at her ridiculous questions. "Why not let me finish hag before you interrupt me," John said with irritation, raising an eye at the Witch.

"Go-go on then. What are you waiting for, hmm?" she asked, staring up at John, giving him a wicked and mockery smile. However, John could not see this due to her hair hanging over her face.

With his patience growing thin, John rolled his eyes towards the heavens and said, "I need you to curse her soul, Witch."

The Witch raised her eye in surprise to his request. "Her soul? Why would you want me to curse," pointing back at Elizabeth's body, "This poor girl's soul?" she asked, looking back at John, intrigued, "You are a wicked thing, are you not?"

Sighing, John ignored the Witch's comment and continued, "This poor girl, you say, she is no innocent! She took her own life by jumping to her death! In doing so, she's ruined all my plans! She should not be allowed peace! Nor should she be allowed to find or have love! She should never have any kind of happiness ever again! She threw her life away, therefore, giving up any say! Now, enough, hag! This needs to be done and quickly! Get on with it!"

Not deterred, the Witch stared at John, "Why curse her soul? Hmm. For vengeance, ho-hmm?"

John was growing angry with the old Witch. He had no time for her ridiculous questions and said with disdain,

"Can you do it or not, WITCH?"

"Yes–yes, of course I can. Just give me a minute to prepare the potion I need," the Witch said as she walked over to her cauldron. She tossed in some herbs, then rubbed her hand over the pot, mumbling words John could not hear. Once she was done, there was a large poof of smoke.

"It's done," she said, taking a cup and dipping it into the pot. Once it was filled with the potion, she walked over to Elizabeth's body.

John stopped her. "Wait, hag," John said, putting up his hand to stop the Witch from reaching Elizabeth's body. "Wait hag! he said again, "There is one more detail I would like you to add to the curse." The Witch just looked at John, but he ignored her leering stare. "I need you to ensure Elizabeth is always born a female and suffers this same fate, at or around the same age she suffered this night. This to be done in all her lives.

The Witch continued to stare at John, trying to pierce the man beneath the skin. "Oh, you really hate this girl do you not?" she said with mockery, then laughed, in her wicked scratchy voice.

Patience gone, John said through clenched teeth, "Just! Do! As! You! Are! told! Witch!"

Not deterred, she smiled, "All right-all right! No need to get all riled up about it," she said.

The Witch walked over to Elizabeth and poured the liquid over her body, starting from her head and ending at her toes. Once she was done, she raised her arms in the air and said a few words in a language that sounded ancient and unknown to John. The Witch evoked the curse on Elizabeth's soul before it completely departed from this world.

"It's done."

Once the curse was complete, John called for the guards to return, "Take Elizabeth's body and toss it in the river. Her body will float out to sea for the sharks to nibble on,"

John said with disgust.

The guards were shocked at John's orders, Filipe more so than the other. Both guards were Catholic, and regardless of how Elizabeth died, she did not deserve such a fate, but there was nothing they could do, so they did as they were ordered.

As the guards were preparing to lift Elizabeth from the slap, John put up his hand as he said, "Wait." John reached for Elizabeth and ripped her necklace from her neck.

John did this to present it to Robert as proof of her death, and the guards looked at John with disgust and shock, and it was not missed by John.

"She deserves no better. Now go! Be quick! We must return so I can notify King Francis of the tragedy in the loss of his new mistress," John snarled.

Again, the guards looked at John and saw something was not right about the man but did as they were told. They took Elizabeth's body to the edge of the river, where after a few swings, they were prepared to toss her in the river, instead stopped. Both men decided it was not right, and they chose to place Elizabeth's body gently and carefully in the river. Once done and as the current started carrying her out to sea, the two men crossed themselves and said a small prayer, knowing she would be food for the sharks. Felipe shivered at the thought.

***

When King Francis heard of Elizabeth's suicide, he was disappointed but felt no loss. Then, without knowing what John did, he ordered John to have Elizabeth's body returned to Robert Davenport, and John took great delight in accepting this duty. He would go himself and take pleasure in telling him of Elizabeth's death.

Chapter Twenty-Seven

It's been three days since Robert went to Saumur Castle demanding to speak to King Francis in his attempt to save Elizabeth, but failing.

When Robert left King Francis's castle, he joined up with Sir Isaac and the other men and the additional ten Frenchmen when he came across them on the road to his family chateau. Together, they continued to Chateau de Dauenport, five miles from Saumur Castle. At Chateau de Dauenport, they would eat, drink, and rest, and on the morrow, they will begin to form a plan to rescue Elizabeth.

Chateau de Dauenport was a grand estate with a vast amount of excellent hunting grounds. The chateau had six bedrooms, a large dining room, a great room, a study, a library, and a small sitting room. It wasn't a luxurious estate, but a simple one, perfect for the short number of visits the family spent at the chateau.

When Robert arrived in France, he managed to send word ahead to the servants, informing them of his expected arrival along with a large party of men by late evening or the early morning hours.

So, when the men arrived at the chateau, everything was prepared and ready for them. The cook, Josephine, who was known to the servants as Jo, prepared a grand meal, knowing when the men arrived, they would be starving.

When the men saw the food Jo prepared, they feasted well that night, as they listened to Robert recount what occurred between him and John Bonnet at Saumur Castle, which was confirmed by Sir Raphael, who Robert forgot was there. Once everyone had their fill and learned all they could, they decided any further discussion would wait until morning.

The following morning at dawn, the men gathered in the chateau's great room to discuss their plan to rescue Elizabeth. When Jo walked in the room with trays full of food, a breakfast fit for a king, the men ceased their conversation and dug into the food that consisted of eggs, bacon, ham, croissants, and many others.

It pleased Jo immensely to see the men with such vigor when she was used to cooking for only the staff, and it was good to feed a large party of healthy men.

Once the men had their fill, they returned to the matter at hand, the rescue of Elizabeth.

"When should we take the castle by force?" Robert asked. "Do we go in full assault, or do we go in quietly, stealing Elizabeth away before anyone notices?"

"We are not going to take the castle by force," said Sir Isaac. "We want this to be as quiet as possible, not to alert anyone. We do not want this to be viewed as an act of war. Once we are out of France and safe in England, there will be no way for Francis or John to try and obtain Elizabeth again.

Lord Davenport, your father, will alert King Henry to what has happened once we return," Sir Isaac explained. "We will sneak in after nightfall, when most of the castle is asleep, leaving only a few guards on duty,"

The other men nodded in agreement, and no one wanted this to be anything other than a rescue mission.

"But," Sir Isaac said, looking at Robert. "Now Robert, this will be difficult for you," placing his hand on Robert's shoulder, "We must wait a couple of days." Robert went to protest, but Sir Isaac squeezed his shoulder. "Wait and let me finish." Robert nodded, and Sir Isaac continued. "We want them to believe you have given up and returned to England. This will allow them to relax, and this is when we will make our move," Sir Isaac concluded as he looked Robert directly in the eyes.

Sir Isaac understood the pain and desperation Robert was feeling, but there was no other way around it. They had to work smart and without emotions.

Sir Isaac took Robert aside, "Raphael explained what happened when John Bonnet confronted you. You must understand, this is the best option."

At this, Robert nodded in agreement. Then after a few moments, Robert asked, "Do we even know where they are keeping her?"

"We believe Lady Elizabeth is being held in the castle's tower where King Francis takes all his women before he has his way with them. At least the ones he needs to keep secluded until they are ready to be taken to court, and there are only a few trusted servants who have access to the tower," one of the Frenchmen said.

"Do you think we can succeed? Would King Francis do anything to Elizabeth between now and the time we rescue her?" Robert asked.

"Well, that is hard to say," Jean-Claude said, turning to the other Frenchmen. "We do not think so. Of course, with the women King Francis believes to be pure, Francis likes to take his time with them because it makes them feel special and safe, but one cannot be sure."

Sir Isaac pulled out a map Lord Davenport gave him of Saumur Castle. "This map was created when King Henry planned to go to war with France. When King Henry heard this would be a place King Francis would go, in case of war if he were in danger." Sir Isaac pointed out all the necessary points to penetrate the castle and where each man would be placed based on their expertise. Once done, they finally had a rescue plan secured.

Once the rescue plan was completed and Robert was alone, he recounted what happened when he arrived at Saumur Castle. John was so casual when he told him about King Francis's reason for wanting Elizabeth. That he only wanted her to be one of his many mistresses.

To learn and understand who King Francis truly was, scared Robert more than he realized.

My love, the woman who holds my heart and soul…is in the hands of such a man, Robert thought.

Robert needed to get Elizabeth away from such a man, but there was nothing for him to do but wait. He needed the other men since he could not do this himself.

Sir Isaac is a smart man. This is his expertise. *I must wait and allow the plan to take root, Robert thought.*

With a feeling of betrayal, it tore at Robert's heart that he allowed Elizabeth to be taken by such a man was unthinkable.

***

It was the night of the rescue, and Sir Isaac, along with Sir Edward, were away to make the final preparations when Robert received a surprise visit.

One of the house servants entered the study and found Robert seated behind his father's desk.

"My Lord, there is a John Bonnet at the door. He says he is King Francis's trusted advisor and brings you a message on behalf of King Francis," the servant said as she curtsied.

John Bonnet…What could he want? Robert thought. Then with sudden hope, *perhaps he's here to tell me King Francis has granted me an audience.*

Immediately, Robert stood and agreed to see John Bonnet.

"Please show John Bonnet in."

If what I believe is true, this rescue mission may not be necessary, he thought.

When the servant showed John Bonnet to the study, Robert greeted him, "Sir, you are very welcome," and without delay, "Did King Francis agree to see me?"

John greeted Robert with the respect of a nobleman, bowing as he entered the room, as he was thinking, *ahhh, how I'm going to relish in telling him that his beloved is dead, and see that look of hope wash away from his face, and replaced with anguish. Ahhh yes, it shall be wonderful.*

"No, My Lord, I am here on another matter. I bring you news of Elizabeth," John said, seeing the hope grow in Robert's eyes. "Death." John finished with a smirk.

Robert's hope fell instantly away as his heart sank to the pit of his stomach. He watched John Bonnet closely, looking for a sign of deceit but saw none, and it shook Robert to his core at the thought of Elizabeth being dead.

When he found his voice, with shock, "Whaaat?" he said with a stutter.

John used all his strength to hold back his excitement and continued to explain what happened.

"My Lord, on the night you arrived at Saumur Castle, and after Elizabeth learned of your tragic death in your attempt to rescue her, she jumped from the tower window to the rocks below. My Lord, I am sorry to say, she took her own life," John said, carefully watching Robert's reaction.

Robert was sickened by what John said. His heart was hurting, and it felt as if John took a dagger and pierced his heart. Yet, when he looked at John, he could see the joy in his eyes, and although he tried to conceal his joy, it was apparent he was reveling in giving him such horrific news.

Robert was shocked and confused, he could not believe it was true, and when he tried to speak, all he could say was, "What?" Choking back the rising bile in his throat. He tried again, "What do you mean…she's dead?" he asked, swallowing the hard lump in his throat. "How…is that possible? How can she…she's what?" Robert asked again, wanting John to retract his words. "She…took her own life?" With his eyes wide, he was unable to believe what he was hearing was true. "No, that is not possible. She would not, she pro —"

Robert stopped. What was he going to say? He knew John was relishing from his reaction and did not want to feed into his delight.

Robert shook his head, trying to force the thought from his mind, fighting – not understanding what he just learned. Then he turned and stared at the floor, unable to look at the man who's the cause of his pain.

If what he said was true – in a whisper, "No…Oh God no…no-no-no, it cannot be. It just cannot be…it's impossible…wait?" As the realization hit him, Robert looked up at John, who could not hide the glee from his eyes. He was taking great pleasure in the satisfaction of evoking so much pain on him. The pain he was feeling pleased John. Then, realizing he'd spoken his last words aloud.

In a confused and yet angry voice, "You said she took her own life after she heard of my death! That is impossible! She would never…why in God's name would she believe me to be dead!" Robert yelled, motioning from head to toe, "As you see, I am very much alive!" Robert snarled.

Holding back his joy, John said, "My dear boy —" John sarcastically started to say before Robert stopped him.

Robert had enough of his mockery, and with closed fists and between clenched teeth, "DO! NOT! CALL! ME! BOY!" His body was tight, and he was readying himself to attack John.

However, this did not deter John. All he did was snicker at Robert for his actions and remarks. Then, he attempted to say more, but Robert quickly stopped him.

"No! You, Sir, you can clearly see I am alive! What lies did you tell Elizabeth! And what proof do you have she is even dead?" he yelled.

John smiled, *ahhh, yes, now is the time to take great pleasure in the details of her demise and what I did to such a harlot,* John thought.

"The night we arrived at Saumur Castle, she tried to make King Francis see reason by trying to explain you were married. But of course, with such a naive little girl,"

John said, smiling at the thought, "She had no true understanding of her situation, and it did not matter how hard she tried to make King Francis see reason, as her words mattered naught. She belonged to King Francis, and that was the end of it.

Elizabeth refused to marry King Francis, which I found very amusing since there was never going to be a wedding. She explained to King Francis that so long as you were out there trying to save her…to take her home, he would never have her. Then, she said that her heart would only belong to you so long as you were alive.

King Francis was interrupted by one of his guards to inform him of your arrival. He left the tower, and when he returned, he told Elizabeth you were killed in your attempt to rescue her. King Francis reasons in doing this: if she assumed you were dead, she would give up on any hope you would rescue her, allowing her to settle into her new situation.

After Francis informed her of your death, he left her alone to allow her time to accept your death and move forward with her new life as the king's mistress," he said with a smile. "When one of the servants went into the room to check on Elizabeth, she was nowhere to be found, and when the king learned Elizabeth was missing, he ordered for the castle and the grounds to be searched. Once everyone left, I remained in the room trying to learn how she escaped, and when I looked out the window wondering if somehow, she managed to climb down the tower, but instead, I saw her lifeless body lying on the rocks below. She took her own life," John said with a smile. "To the king's surprise, or shall I say disappointment, his ruse did not have the effect he wanted."

At hearing John recount what happened to Elizabeth, he felt as if he would collapse. But he stood firm and held himself together, refusing to allow John the pleasure of seeing him in such a state of distress. Instead, he carefully made his way to a chair and sat down.

As Robert sat down, he suddenly had a thought and when he snapped his head up, "Wait," Robert said, looking back at John, "How do I know what you say is the truth and not more lies to make me believe she is dead so I will give up and leave France?"

He must be lying. It cannot be true. It just cannot. This must be a dream? A horrible nightmare, one I will never wake up from, Robert thought.

Robert was so confused, he didn't want to believe Elizabeth was dead, but then, a small part of him knew it was true. There was only one way to be certain; he needed to demand proof.

"Where is her body? Do you have her body outside?" At this, Robert stood and started towards the door, wanting to see for himself. "Show me! Produce her body to me at once!" Robert demanded.

John laughed at Robert's demand. "No, her body's not outside. I ordered the guards to toss her body into the river, so it will float out to sea for the sharks to feast on," John said cheerfully, then presented Robert with Elizabeth's necklace as proof of her death.

When Robert saw the necklace, he was in a state of shock for a few moments as he stared at it. Then, with care and gentleness, he reached out and took the necklace from John's hand, as he fought to maintain control of his emotions, keeping his tears at bay, not wanting John Bonnet to see how seeing Elizabeth's necklace affected him. Yet, at the same time, he did not want to believe she was truly dead.

After retrieving Elizabeth's necklace, as he felt it between his fingers, Robert felt numb and disbelief.

Elizabeth cannot be dead. No, she cannot be dead. It's impossible. But as I look in my hands lies her necklace. The necklace I gave her that bonded our marriage. Once I put it on her neck, she swore she would never take it off, well almost never, Robert thought with a smile, as a memory surfaced of Elizabeth that made him laugh inside.

***

Elizabeth tried so hard to keep her word to Robert, as she tried to bathe and sleep with the necklace on, trying everything she could to honor her promise to him. But she quickly found it was more difficult than she believed it would be. To see this, Robert could not help but laugh at Elizabeth, of course, never in front of her. Nevertheless, it was very entertaining to watch her attempts, and he loved her all the more for trying so hard.

One day, while Robert was in the village market, he decided to buy Elizabeth a gold and ruby band, and when he arrived home, he waited until they were alone in their chambers before he presented her with it. To see the look on her face filled with surprise and joy – she loved it, as he knew she would.

"Oh, Robert, I love it! But I thought my necklace was to be what binds us together?" Elizabeth said, with concern in her voice.

Robert smiled, "But this, my love," Robert said as he slipped the ring on her finger, "You can wear without difficulty," he said, turning her to face the mirror so he could watch her admire the ring as he held her close from behind.

"When you need to bathe or sleep," Robert said with a chuckle.

Elizabeth turned around and smacked him playfully on the arm, "Oh Robert, you have been laughing at me, haven't you?" she said with jest.

"Oh, my love, only without you knowing it," Robert agreed.

Then they both burst out laughing at how she must have looked. From that day, Elizabeth wore her ring with pride, never removing it from her finger.

***

At this memory, Robert realized while he was holding Elizabeth's necklace, he did not have her ring.

"Wait, where's Elizabeth's gold and ruby ring?"

"I did not concern myself with her fingers. She may still have it on, which by now," looking up as he imagined the possibilities, "Is more than likely inside the stomach of a shark," he said with a smug response.

"How dare you!" Robert yelled, then quickly turned away, needing to control his anger as he thought, *no, this cannot be happening! She cannot be dead! But as I hold this,* looking down at the necklace in his hand, *how can it not be? It must be true. Here in my hand lies the truth.*

Robert felt shocked and disbelief in learning what happened to Elizabeth, but he still needed to be sure that what John Bonnet said was true.

"What do you mean she is dead? How can she be dead? She cannot be dead, no-no," Robert said, shaking his head in disbelief. "This cannot be…it is impossible!" Robert yelled.

Then his thoughts went back to Elizabeth's promise to him – *no, she would not…her promise to me…she would not. No matter what, she would not take her life; thus, she would be breaking her promise to me.* Then he thought, *but here in my hands lies her necklace. How can it be denied? It cannot be.* At this, Robert's shoulders slumped in the realization that it must be true.

While Robert was questioning the truth of Elizabeth's death, John took great pleasure in watching him suffer, with the pain he was feeling, as he tried to come to terms with Elizabeth's death. But then, Robert's face changed to one of anger, to great anger, then, to a man wanting vengeance. This caused John to take a step back.

Robert looked at John Bonnet; if what he said was true, he would die by his own hands to avenge Elizabeth's death.

"You, Sir, are no man of God! You are the spawn of the devil! For you, a man of God, to tell me about my beloved's death in such a heartless and cruel manner! Then, you discarded my beautiful beloved as if she were nothing! This woman, who's loved so many! Her faith in God was greater than your own! You claimed to be a Catholic Clergyman, but sir, you are not! You are a fraud! Yes, I know the truth! You have lied and deceived so many! I promise you, one day you will get your own!" he said with anger and pain, then between clenched teeth, "NOW! GET! OUT!" then he exploded, "Before I run you through!" Robert yelled at the top of his lungs, and at the same time, he drew his sword. "Now, Sir, or I will cut you in two and feed you…to the sharks!"

John had no doubts he would, from the look he saw in Robert's eyes. John knew this was no mere threat, but one Robert would follow through with, so, without a word, John Bonnet bowed to Robert, then turned and left.

Once John was gone, and Robert was finally alone, he dropped to his knees and released all the pain and sorrow he was holding back. Losing his beloved was unbearable. She who was his heart and soul, was torn from him – murdered.

They murdered her! She may have jumped, but they drove her to it! With their lies and deception! It was as good as if they pushed her themselves! God, please, tell me this is not so? How can this man of God discard Elizabeth's body in such a horrible and heartless way? Robert thought as he suffered a tremendous amount of pain and sorrow. His grief was beyond any grief he had ever know or experienced.

Robert completely lost control; unable to bear the pain anymore, he fell to his knees.

***

When Sir Isaac and Sir Edward returned to the chateau after completing their final preparation for that night's rescue, they went directly to the study to inform Robert they were ready. However, when they walked into the study, they saw Robert clumped on the floor in total anguish.

Sir Isaac and Sir Edward looked at each other with a look that wondered what happened, and immediately rushed to Robert's side.

"My Lord, are you unwell? Should we send for a doctor?" Sir Isaac asked.

On each side of Robert, Sir Isaac and Sir Edward helped him off the floor and to a chair nearby.

When Robert found his voice, he said, "No, Sir Isaac, Sir Edward, please forgive me. If you could give me a moment, I will explain what happened," Robert said, and Sir Isaac and Sir Edward nodded in understanding as they stepped back to allow Robert the time and space, he needed to gather himself together.

After getting his emotions under control, he finally said, "Sir Isaac, I…there will be no rescue tonight."

Sir Isaac and Sir Edward looked at each other, not understanding what had happened to make Robert believe this to be so.

Then together, they asked, "My Lord, why?"

Then Sir Isaac said, "We have everything in place. We —"

Robert placed his hand up, stopping Sir Isaac. "I do not know if you saw John Bonnet on your way in. I just had a visit from him," Robert said. Before Sir Isaac or Sir Edward could say another word, Robert quickly went on. "Please, before you ask any questions, allow me to finish." Both Sir Isaac and Sir Edward nodded. "At first, I thought John Bonnet had come to inform me that King Francis agreed…had granted me an audience. I thought if so, there would be no need for this evening's rescue…it was not so. His visit was to inform me…" Robert's voice cracked as he was finding it difficult to continue.

Sir Isaac and Sir Edward did not attempt to speak but waited – they wanted to give Robert the time to speak, and it was clear that what he wanted to say was not good news.

Robert took a few moments to regain his emotions before he continued. He swallowed the bile that was rising, then took a deep breath and released it. It wasn't the time for him to lose control of his emotions.

This must be said, he thought.

Although it was hard, he wanted to give Sir Isaac and Sir Edward the news about Elizabeth's death gently, but instead, not knowing how long he'd be able to control his emotions, he blurted it out instead.

"Elizabeth's dead!" He yelled, then placed his face in his hands, shaking his head, still in disbelief.

Sir Isaac and Sir Edward looked at each other, unsure what to think or believe in what Robert just said. It wasn't possible. Regardless of what they knew about King Francis and John Bonnet, Elizabeth's death was impossible. They knew it could not be. Therefore, they had many questions they needed to ask Robert to be sure what he said – what he believed to be true, was correct.

"Are you sure, My Lord?" Sir Isaac asked gently.

"Yes, I am sure," Robert said, with irritation, "There is no question, as he raised his arm to show them Elizabeth's necklace as proof of her death. Robert raised his head, "This necklace, I gave it to Elizabeth on our wedding day. For this," holding the necklace in the air, shaking it vigorously, "To be in my hand..." shaking his head, "No. There is no question she is dead. My love is dead. Taken…ripped from this world," Robert said, dropping his head, unable to look at them any longer, nor does he have any further words – feeling defeated.

"My Lord, I say this lightly, but are you sure she is dead? They could have forced Elizabeth to remove her necklace so they could present it to you as proof she is dead. Then, if you so believed, it would force you to leave France," Sir Isaac said.

"Do you not think I thought of that!" Robert hollered.

Then as suddenly as he yelled, he softened his voice. "Forgive me. I did not mean to talk to you so harshly. Sir Isaac, I understand what you say. I also believed what John said to me to be a deception. But for Elizabeth to let this go," raising the necklace to show them again, "They would have had to tear it from her dead body. Not to mention the look of satisfaction on John Bonnet's face when he told me. And…I cannot deny this, but…I also feel it in my heart. The connection we had is gone…as if she is gone from this world," Robert said, as he slumped in the chair and hung his head low.

"This is terrible news, indeed. I will inform the other men the rescue is no longer required due to the tragic event. My Lord, please allow me to say that we are grievous of this news on behalf of all the men. I know this will not be easy, but may we inquire to how…how did she —"

Robert did not let them finish. Filled with anger and pain, he jumped up – "John said she jumped from the tower window to the rocks below after hearing of my death! My death!" he shrieked.

Robert's voice broke with emotion, but he tried to be strong, not wanting the men to see him weak, so he regained control of his emotions and relayed the entirety of the events as what was told to him by John Bonnet in what happened to Elizabeth.

After hearing about the events, Sir Isaac and Sir Edward looked at each other, and without words, *we need to verify if this is true.* Then they turned back to Robert with sorrow in their hearts.

These were hard men, the hardest of all men. They had to be for them to do the things they were ordered to do by Lord Davenport. But to see Robert in his state of sorrow, they allowed the ice around their hearts to slightly melt away, allowing them to feel the pain and loss Robert was suffering. Although they would never allow it to show on their face or express such feelings aloud, it was there all the same.

Of all that Sir Isaac and Sir Edward knew about King Francis, they would never have believed him capable of such actions.

"My Lord, I do believe John Bonnet was responsible for the actions that took place," Sir Isaac said.

"I am sure it was John Bonnet as well. One day he will get his own," Robert said.

"My Lord, what can we do?" Sir Edward asked.

"Only for you to take the men and leave me alone in the chateau to allow me to grief?" Robert asked.

"But of course, My Lord. We will ask Jean-Claude if he will allow us to stay at his chateau for the night," Sir Isaac said.

It was clear Robert was using all his strength to prevent Sir Isaac and Sir Edward from seeing his true grief and anguish.

"Thank you, Sir Isaac. I will see you on the morrow then. Until then, good evening," Robert said.

"Yes, My Lord," Sir Isaac said, then with Sir Edward, they turned and left without another word, leaving Robert to his grief.

Once Sir Isaac and Sir Edward were out of the study and the door was closed, Sir Isaac turned to Sir Edward, "Edward, I need you to ride out to Saumur Castle and verify if Elizabeth is dead. I will not leave France without making sure what John Bonnet told Robert is the truth," Sir Isaac said. "If you find Elizabeth is dead, then I will need to sail to England at once. Lord Davenport will need to be notified of this information right away, and he will more than likely want to return to be with his son during his time of grief."

"Yes, Sir Isaac, I will go at once."

Both men went directly to inform the other men of the grievous news, and they were to depart the chateau to allow Robert time to grieve.

After Sir Isaac and Sir Edward left, Robert sat for a long time in the chair, struggling to accept Elizabeth was dead. To believe his love, the woman who owned his heart and soul, was dead. It was too much for him to bear. He felt his heart was being ripped from him as if trying to find that part of him that was no longer there. His wife, his whole reason for living, was torn from him, tossed out as if she were nothing. Robert lost control; he dropped to his knees and released all the pain he was holding inside.

***

After what seemed like a lifetime, Robert finally picked himself off the floor and sat in the chair at his father's desk, then looked up to seek answers from God. He needed to understand what happened.

Robert and Elizabeth found this unbelievably powerful love. A love that would stand the test of time, an eternal love, just to have it ripped from him so soon, before he was ready – no, this he did not understand.

He did not hold anything back; Robert spoke in a loud and strong voice. "God, tell me how this can be?" he asked, standing to walk over to the window, with the need to seek the night's sky, and the need to feel close to nature, to feel that connection Elizabeth had always felt when she was close to nature.

Robert opened the window and said to the night sky, "How can Elizabeth be dead? And at her own hand?" he said, shaking his head, "Taking her life, believing me dead. This woman who loved life. Who cared and helped those who were less fortunate than her. You know, you have seen her good nature. She loved those around her, including what nature had to offer. She put her heart into everything she did. She did not deserve such an ending," his voice cracked.

Robert looked down at his hands that were resting on the window seal, and after a few moments, he looked back to the night sky.

"How she must have felt, feeling so lost and alone. She must have felt trapped in the situation King Francis put her in, believing there was no one out there who would rescue her. She must have felt…it was her only way out. To free herself from such a man, she had to end her life. To her, it was her only choice. Even if it meant breaking her promise to me and one of your greatest sins. I ask you when Elizabeth comes before you for judgment that you do not judge her so harshly. That you see beyond, to the woman, she was. The woman who loved life and the life you gave this land. Judge her for her heart, which was big enough to accept all those around her."

Robert pleaded with God. His emotions were too strong, and he was unable to control what he was feeling. He did not think Elizabeth deserved hell for doing what she did.

To her, she felt trapped, and believed she had no choice to do what she felt she had to do.

From the moment Robert heard the reason Elizabeth took her life, it haunted him, and he blamed himself. *It was me! Because of me, she is dead!* Robert thought.

Robert's heart was breaking more and more with every breath he took, and he was seeing images of Elizabeth jumping to her death, and it was playing over and over again in his mind.

"Because she believed I…was dead. That I…was killed, in my attempt to rescue her," his voice cracked, as his heart was breaking, "Oh God, what she must have felt," he whispered.

Robert's chest hurt as if his heart were being ripped out, as if someone took a fist and punched a hole into his chest, grabbing hold of his heart and ripped it out. During his grief, Robert's thoughts took him to a time of the woman he knew, to the girl she was, how she grew into this beautiful woman she'd become. Then to find this powerful love, one so deep, they both never thought possible.

"God, Elizabeth was everything to me. She was my heart and soul, and now that she is gone…I feel empty. How can I ever be the same again without her? No. I will never feel complete again?" he whispered, shaking his head.

Robert felt so torn, not knowing what to do when he was suddenly filled with memories of Elizabeth, of all the wonderful times they spent together. How at first a beautiful friendship bloomed, then later, a love, one of the greatest and most powerful love to ever exist. How they believed that not even death itself could destroy the love they found. They both thought, because of their powerful love, they would be reunited again. If they made it to heaven, and upon meeting God, they would ask him to allow them to maintain their memories, and for them to be allowed the gift to remember, for when they are in their next life, they would find each other again, able to renew their love, lifetime after lifetime, for eternity.

At that moment, Robert understood why Elizabeth took her life, because she believed as he believed; in death, they would find each other again. If Elizabeth felt half of what he was feeling, then he knew and understood why she did it. To know this, how could he stay and live without her, knowing she was waiting for him, believing he was already there waiting for her.

"NO-O-O-O! I cannot do it! I cannot wait! To continue this life without Elizabeth…to live knowing she took her life because she believed me to be dead! That right now, she is up there waiting for me, because she believed I was dead! When she learns…no, I will not allow it!"

At this, Robert knew what he had to do. It was time for him to join his beloved, so they could be together once again. Robert went to his father's desk and sat down and began to write a letter to his mother and father, apologizing for what he was about to do.

Dearest Mother and Father,

It gives me great sadness to write you this letter, but I feel I must, especially after what has occurred. To what I am about to do, I owe you an explanation. You see, King Francis and John Bonnet, after kidnapping Elizabeth, told her I was killed in my attempt to rescue her. This was done to force her to mourn me and then move on with her life with King Francis. After hearing of my death, she chose to take her own life, feeling there was no one to rescue her.

In hearing of my beloved's death, I felt such pain, such sadness, and guilt. I know you never accepted our relationship, and after we were married, you turned your backs on us. My father, to have you come to my aid after what we did, meant more to me than you will ever know. Please do not be angry for my actions. For one to understand, one can only know and feel the love Elizabeth and I felt. So please, father, do not be angry with Elizabeth or me.

Mother and father, she was my love, my heart and soul. We were two souls connected, bonded as one. Our love was one you could never understand. It was the greatest love given to us by God, and with her death, I am lost. I cannot imagine living my life without her. She was everything to me. So, mother and father, I am sorry to tell you of my decision, but I feel my place is with my beloved Elizabeth in heaven if God sees fit. I will beg God for his forgiveness in taking my own life, and once I am standing before God, I will request for Elizabeth and me to be reborn together and be allowed the power of our love to guide us back to each other once again.

Please forgive me for what I am about to do. I know this will bring you great shame since it is a sin of God's to take one's life. But I sit here now, feeling such pain and sorrow, I cannot see any other way. I will soon be with my beloved Elizabeth in heaven.

Once Robert was finished writing his letter to his mother and father, he carefully folded the letter and sealed it, then placed it in the center of the desk so the servants would find it. He knelt on the floor near the fire and took his dagger out of its sheath. Then, with Elizabeth's necklace in his left hand and the dagger in his right, he said, "Elizabeth, my love, soon we will be together," and without further thought, he quickly and firmly plunged the dagger into his chest, piercing the center of his heart. Robert slid down on his right side, feeling pain for a brief moment, as he felt great sorrow with his last thought of Elizabeth, and as he took his last breath, he whispered "Elizabeth," then he was gone.

***

The next morning when Jo walked into the study expecting to find the men hard at work and with large appetites, but instead, what she saw was Robert's lifeless body lying on the floor with a dagger sticking out of his chest and a necklace clutched in his hand. Not knowing what happened, Jo screamed, calling for help.

At her scream, the entire household ran into the room, and when they saw Robert's lifeless body, they crossed themselves as they said a small prayer for his soul.

"Oh, no! By God Almighty, what has happened?" Everyone asked at once.

When Jacqueline, the head housekeeper, entered the room, she screamed, shocked, and horrified at what she saw

– Robert's lifeless body, lying on the floor with a dagger sticking out of his chest. Everyone was wondering the same thing, what happened? Did someone attack Lord Robert during the night and killed him? But there was no sign of struggle. No sign that a fight took place. There were so many questions with no answers to be given.

"Oh my, ma'dam, what has happened?" asked Maria, one of the housemaids.

"Child, can you not see?" said Jo, pointing at Robert's lifeless body. "Lord Robert is dead! Can you not see the dagger sticking out of his chest?" she said with irritation. "It looks as if someone came in the night and killed him!"

All at once, the other's asked, "But why?" Jo looked back at Robert's lifeless body, then shook her head, "Ahhh…I know naught."

One of the male servants, whose name was George, noticed the letter on the desk. He walked over to the desk to get a closer look at it and saw the letter was addressed to Lord and Lady Davenport of Bramhall Manor, England. He picked up the letter, and as he held it, he thought *maybe this contains the answers?* But he was hesitant to open it; after all, it was a letter addressed to the Lord and Lady of the chateau.

A simple servant should not read that, but if it holds the answers? he thought.

George looked around, as he saw everyone was in a panic, he knew he didn't have a choice. He was the only one who knew how to read out of all the servants, and the other men in Lord Robert's party were not in the chateau. George felt the letter in his hands contained the answers he needed, so he broke the seal and read the letter without further delay.

George did not need to read the whole letter, as the first few lines said enough.

"Everyone, you must calm down. There was no intruder!" he yelled.

"How can you say that? Look at him?" yelled one of the female servants.

"Because this letter tells me so! Now, everyone, calm yourself!" George said in a firm, authoritative voice that immediately silenced everyone.

George then instructed one of the young maids to call for a servant boy named Jon, and while George waited for Jon, he wrote a quick note urging Lord and Lady Davenport to come to France at once, on a matter of great urgency pertaining to their son.

Once Jon walked into the room, George handed him the sealed note, "Jon, go with haste and take this message of extreme urgency and send it by express to Lord and Lady Davenport in England. The address is on the letter," George instructed, then tossed him coins to cover the cost.

"We must not leave him like this," said Estella, "It's not right.

"What are we going to do?" said another one of the housemaids, showing concern for Lord Robert.

George, as the older servant took charge, "Maria, get a blanket to cover Lord Robert with! Those who are not squeamish help me carry Lord Robert's body to his bedchamber! We will place him on his bed until Lord and Lady Davenport's arrival. The rest of you get back to work!"

"What about the smell?" Maria asked, wrinkling her nose. "Will he not start to smell before they arrive?" she said with disgust.

"Do not worry child!" George scolded, "It will be taken care of!"

The servants laid Robert's body carefully on his bed, still covered with the blanket, then took a few moments to say the Lord's prayer, as everyone wondered what happened and looked to George for answers. But George gave none, as he had none to give. He felt it was best to wait to speak with Lord Davenport first. The servants loved and adored Robert. Since he was a boy, most knew him and were heartbroken to see their master in such a state.

Chapter Twenty-Eight

It was midmorning when Sir Edward and the men returned. They didn't intend to arrive so late but was delayed due to the muddy roads. When they walked into the chateau, they found it was too quiet, which caused concern, as it was usually blustering with the servants busy at work and expected – hoped to see a full spread of morning meal laid out in the dining room, that Jo would have prepared knowing they were expected.

"Something is not right here?" said Sir Edward. "It is too quiet, and it makes me nervous. I have a bad feeling. Hello there! Is anyone here?" Sir Edward called out.

A distraught Jo came at Sir Edward's call. "Thank heaven! We have been waiting for you," Joe said, curtseying to the men. "It's Milord Robert…he is —"

Joe broke off, and started crying, finding it was too difficult to say the words.

This concerned Sir Edward and the rest of the men, then they heard a male's voice that turned out to be one of the servant boys, and with difficulty, told the men what they discovered that morning.

George arrived and took over, "We carefully carried Milord to his chambers and laid him on his bed until Lord and Lady Davenport arrives," George said. "I sent a servant boy to send an express message to Lord and Lady Davenport, asking them to come quickly to France on an urgent matter regarding their son. I am afraid," with sadness, "It will be days before they arrive."

At hearing what happen, the men crossed themselves and said a small prayer for Robert's soul.

George saw the look of question on their faces and went on, "We do not know what happened, but…" he stopped and gestured for the men to move away from the other servants that gathered from hearing that the men had returned, and said in a whisper, "It was not an intruder." Then he hesitated, looking back to make sure he would not be overheard. "I am sure it was done by…Milords' own hand."

Sir Edward looked at him with a questionable eye, wondering how he knew this.

George went on to explain, "He left a letter for Lord and Lady Davenport on the desk," George said, then handed the letter to Sir Edward.

"How do you know what it says?" asked Sir Edward.

"Forgive me, Milord, but when I saw it sitting on the desk, and with everyone worried that a stranger…a killer entered the chateau in the middle of the night, I decided to open it. I only read enough to know it was done by Milord's own hand," George said.

Sir Edward nodded in understanding, then took George into Lord Davenport's study as he instructed the other men to ask Jo to prepare breakfast and feed them, then he closed the study door.

Sir Edward read the letter in full, then looked back at George. "No one, except you, read this letter?" asked Sir Edward.

George nodded, "Yes, Milord. As I said, I only read enough to know it was done by Lord Robert's own hand. I am the only one in the household who's able to read."

Sir Edward nodded in understanding, "Tell no one of what you know. Do you understand me?"

"Yes, Milord," said George.

"I will give the letter to Lord Davenport when he arrives, and I will tell him I was the one who opened the letter. Is that clear?" Sir Edward said.

"Yes, of course, Milord," George said, as he bowed, then turned to leave the room.

"Wait!" Called Sir Edward, "George, before you go,

send in the rest of my men, but not the Frenchmen."

George nodded in understanding, then left.

When the other men came into the room, Sir Edward told them what he learned, and the news shocked the men, and were concerned about how Lord Davenport would react when he learns his eldest son and heir was dead.

"How can this be? We should never have left him alone. Sir Isaac and I saw how much pain he was in," said Sir Edward.

"There was no way you could have known as grief-stricken as he was, that he would take his own life," said Sir Ralph.

"There is no one to blame here. If anyone is to blame, it is John Bonnet. The man should be quartered for what he did," said Sir James.

"Lord and Lady Davenport will be here on the morrow," said Sir Edward. "Sir Isaac left last night to inform Lord Davenport what we learned. The wind was strong and moving in the right direction, and he should have made it back to England in record time. After we learned Elizabeth was indeed dead, and by her own hand, Sir Isaac believed it was best he went personally to inform Lord and Lady Davenport of what occurred and bring them to France. But this, this is going to be a great shock to them both. I do not want to think what Lord Davenport will do in retaliation. Sir Isaac and I felt this was not a time for Robert to be alone to grieve for Elizabeth without his family by his side. For Robert to take his own life…this, we did not expect," said Sir Edward.

These hard men could not help but feel the sadness at losing not just one but two young lives.

"How do we explain this to Lord and Lady Davenport when they arrive?" Sir Edward asked with concern.

"Do we read his letter or wait for Lord Davenport?" asked Sir Marcus.

"Out of respect, we will wait for Lord Davenport," said

Sir Edward.

***

The following evening Lord and Lady Davenport arrived in France with Sir Isaac. It appeared they made it to France in record time and wasted no time in making their way to Chateau de Dauenport.

Sir Edward and the rest of Lord Davenport's mercenaries were sitting in the front room that sported an excellent view of the road. When they saw Lord and Lady Davenport and Sir Isaac, along with several of the Davenport servants rapidly approaching, the men went directly to greet them. When Lord and Lady Davenport entered the chateau, they will need to inform them of the tragic news they knew could not be put off.

When Sir Edward opened the door, he was greeted by Lord Davenport with Lady Davenport following closely behind and with Sir Isaac coming up the rear.

"Milord and milady," Sir Edward said as he bowed, "We are pleased to see you. However, I am afraid we have grievous news," Sir Edward said with a lack of emotion. "After Sir Isaac left France to inform you of what happened to Elizabeth, the other men and I stayed at Jean-Claude chateau, leaving Lord Robert alone per his request. He wanted time to grieve in private. When we returned the following morning, we were informed that Lord Robert was dead." At hearing this, Lady Davenport gasped, putting her hand over her mouth with shock. "I am afraid, Milord…it was done by his own hand."

Without saying a word, Lady Davenport was in disbelief to hear that her first-born son was dead. Lord Davenport, however, although he showed no emotion to the news, felt it deeply.

"How did this happen?" Lord Davenport asked.

"Milord, we cannot say for certain, but I believe the answers you seek are in this letter," Sir Edward said, handing the letter to Lord Davenport.

"Did either of you read this letter?" asked Lord Davenport, noticing the seal was broken.

"Yes, Milord, when we returned to the chateau, it was in an uproar. The servants feared someone had come in the night and killed Lord Robert. They were afraid the same person would return. One of the servants, who could read —"

Lord Davenport interrupted. "George?" he said.

"Yes, Milord. He saw it on the desk, and when he mentioned it to me, I decided to open the letter, to see if there were any answers to what happened. I read only enough to determine Robert took his own life," Sir Edward said.

If Lord Davenport learned George read the letter, George's chances of being put to death immediately were too high to chance. Of course, George did nothing wrong, but what he felt was necessary. However, Lord Davenport may not see it that way, and to protect what happened, he would have ordered George's death.

"When Robert's body was discovered, there was panic throughout the household, and George took charge until we returned. He had Robert's body placed in his chambers until you arrived, then sent a servant boy to send you an urgent express. I am sure you would not have received it before Sir Isaac arrived to bring you to France," Sir Edward explained.

"We did not receive the message. As soon as Sir Isaac informed us of the news, we wasted no time in leaving. God was with us, as he gave us the wind to allow Captain Burgess to sail to France in record time," Lord Davenport said.

With the letter in his hand, Lord Davenport opened it and read the letter in silence, then after a few moments, he read it aloud. Lady Davenport was horrified at what she learned and wanted to know and understand what happened. Why her son felt by taking his life was his only course of action.

From the moment they entered the chateau and heard what happened, Lady Davenport was grief-stricken when she heard of her son's death, and after hearing what Robert's letter said, she was shocked and horrified that her son felt he had no choice but to take his own life.

The pain he must have endured, Lady Davenport thought.

"What happened after you arrived in France? This letter says my son took his own life because he could not handle the way Elizabeth died. Sir Isaac and Sir Edward, tell me exactly what happened? And do not leave out any details," Lord Davenport asked.

Sir Isaac was the first to explain what happened after they arrived in France, then how Sir Isaac and Sir Edward learned what happened. Once they verified the truth of Elizabeth's death, it was decided that Sir Isaac would return to England to inform Lord Davenport of what happened. Then Sir Edward recounted what happened after they arrived at the chateau and learned of Robert's death.

When Lady Davenport heard the horrible details, she no longer had the strength to control her emotions she'd been holding back. In agony, she let out a loud sob. No matter what happened, she never stopped loving her son, and now he was dead. To Lady Davenport's surprise, Lord Davenport rushed to her side and took her in his arms to comfort her.

Lord Davenport, although a strong and emotionless man, he too, was taken back by what he heard.

"This is unbelievable! How can this be? I believed John Bonnet was not a man to be trusted, but to go as far as this, and for King Francis to be a part of it…I do not know. No matter, John Bonnet is a servant of King Francis, his actions will fall at the King's feet, and King Henry will hear of these events. Now, Isaac and Edward, take us to our son."

With Lord Davenport's arm still around Lady Davenport, together they headed to their son's chambers.

Lady Davenport was surprised at her husband's continued affection. When she thought back on their life together, there had only been a few times Lord Davenport displayed this type of kindness and affection towards her, which made her wonder, *is it possible? Does John care more for me than he displays?*

When they arrived in Robert's chamber, at Lord Davenport's command, one of the servants removed the blanket covering Robert's body to reveal their son's horrible state – the dagger still sticking out of his chest.

Lady Davenport was horrified at the sight of her son, and she immediately turned her head, unable to bear to see her son in such a state.

Horrified by what she saw, "John, we cannot leave him like this," Lady Davenport said.

Lord Davenport just stared at his son's lifeless body for a long moment before he said in a whisper, "Fool," as he shook his head. Then with sudden anger, "What a mindless young fool! To take his own life over a woman! For this love he speaks of! He has brought dishonor and disgrace to all his family!"

Pulling on her husband's arm, Lady Davenport said, "John, please. Do not speak of such a thing. He was a boy in love. Something you and I will never understand, as we never found the love our son found."

Lord Davenport ignored his wife as his anger was too great to listen to anything she had to say.

"He wants me to honor his last wish! How can I? Look, look at what he did!" Lord Davenport yelled, pointing at his son's lifeless body. "He took his own life…a sin in God's eyes! Yet, he thinks God will welcome him! Well, he will be in for a big surprise when he finds himself in purgatory instead!"

At Lord Davenport's harsh words, Lady Davenport

became uncontrollable with grief. Although it was forbidden to touch nobility unless given permission, one of the younger maids tried to comfort Lady Davenport, but she was pushed aside and scolded by Jo before she could.

Lady Davenport saw this and wanted to come to the maid's aid since the maid's intention was to help her.

"No-no, she is fine. She only wanted to help me. Please, it is alright. I will be alright," said Lady Davenport.

At this, Jo and the maid curtsied, then Jo told the maid to return to her duties. The maid nodded and left the room.

Looking at one of the male servants, Lord Davenport said, "Take him and do what he asked, but Lady Davenport and I will have no part of it!"

"John —" Lady Davenport tried to interrupt to persuade him against this action.

But Lord Davenport would not hear of it and cut her off. "Stop!" he said in a harsh, heartless voice. "He did this to himself! You and I will have no part of it! As soon as I wrap things up here, we will leave and return to England and forget this ever happened! We will tell people that Robert and Elizabeth came to a tragic death on their way to France to spend a few days with family."

Lady Davenport knew when her husband was in this state, there was no swaying him. She took one more look at her son, feeling all the love a mother could feel in losing a child in such a tragic way. Her heart broke at the loss of her son and the loss of a love he found, with the horrible way the woman he loved died.

Lady Davenport could never understand the pain her son felt. For him to believe his only way out was death by taking his own life.

We were so blind. The love Robert and Elizabeth found was so strong they believed that life was not worth living if they were to be without the other. To do the unthinkable by taking their own lives in the hopes of being reunited in heaven, Lady Davenport thought.

"Oh, my son, what have you done. I wish this were to be true, but where you will end up will not be heaven," she whispered.

Lady Davenport sent up a silent prayer; *please do not send my son to purgatory? His choice was not one of a man in his right mind, but a man blinded by grief. I know if he were in his right mind, he would never have dishonored you by taking his own life. Please see past what he did and understand his pain by granting him what he seeks from you? Please, from a mother's heart, pleading for the life of her son. Although dead here, but alive there with you,* she thought.

Then aloud, "If we only listened, this tragedy could have been avoided," Lady Davenport whispered.

Unfortunately, Lord Davenport heard what she said and turned to face his wife.

"Your son dishonored us by going behind our backs and marry Elizabeth! We had every right to be angry! We had an agreement! Have you forgotten?"

"No, of course not. But our son's feelings should have been more important than a written agreement. So why could we not have changed it? This is our fault, as well as theirs," said Lady Davenport.

Hearing Lady Davenport last words angered Lord Davenport. "No! This is not our fault!" he scolded. "Now go, and allow me to do what needs to be done here!" Ordered Lord Davenport.

Lady Davenport's heart was broken at the loss of her son, and Lord Davenport was her husband, and so, she must do what he said. But would make one request, one she would ask a servant for their help.

As she was being guided out the door, she turned to Jo, "Will you come with me?" Lady Davenport asked. "I require your service?"

Jo looked at Lady Davenport, wondering what she could want with a cook. She was no housemaid or a lady's maid but agreed. Jo followed Lady Davenport down the hall until they were out of earshot of Lord Davenport.

Jo was concerned that Lady Davenport, in her grief, had forgotten her station with the house.

"Milady, I am merely a cook. Maybe it's best I call for your housemaid. She would be better to assist you," Jo said.

"No-no. It is not the assistance I need, but only to ask a favor of you."

Jo nodded in understanding and agreed to listen and do what Lady Davenport wanted.

"You have been a part of our household for many years and have shown to be a loyal and trusted servant," Lady Davenport said.

"Yes, Milady," Jo said.

"Will you please," Lady Davenport asked, taking Jo's hands in hers, "Honor my son's last wish?"

Jo was surprised by Lady Davenport's request. However, she was also honored to be asked such a favor.

"Oh, Milady, I shall. I shall treat him as if he were one of my own sons," Jo said.

"Thank you, Josephine. It means a great deal to me to know my son will have his last wish honored." Then she proceeded to tell Josephine what Robert's last wish was. "And for your troubles, you may keep the necklace Robert was holding in his hand. It is real gold, pearls, and rubies," Lady Davenport said.

Josephine was surprised by this. It was not what she expected, nor did she think she could keep it, but she agreed anyway.

***

After completing the business Lord Davenport needed to do regarding his son, he decided to return to England that same day without delay. However, before Lord and Lady Davenport departed, Lord Davenport would speak to the servants first, and ordered all the servants to gather in the great room.

Once everyone was assembled, he began, "Most of you have been with me from before the time of Robert's birth and have shown great loyalty to my family and me. Those who are new have not had an opportunity to prove such loyalty to me, but now is your time. To prove your loyalty to my family and me, you will sign this agreement," Lord Davenport said, pointing to a document sitting on his desk. "I have here, in this agreement, that you swear your loyalty for yourself, and on behalf of your entire family, along with all future descendants. This agreement states you will never speak of what happened here regarding my son, Lord Robert Davenport, nor of his wife, Lady Elizabeth Davenport. This you promise on your life and the life of your families," Lord Davenport announced.

This of course stunned the new servants. Although they have not known or had the honor of serving Lord Davenport and his family since they became employed in his household, they heard how ruthless Lord Davenport was. That he was not one to be crossed with, and if you did, you paid with your life.

For many years, those servants who have been employed with Lord Davenport were the first to approach and sign the agreement without question. Those who could not read and write signed with an X next to their name listed in the agreement, so there could be no question about who signed it. Lord Davenport clarified that if any refused to sign the agreement, they would be immediately put to death. And if it were discovered they spoke to anyone outside the house, those they spoke with would also be put to death to ensure their secrecy.

***

Shortly after Lord and Lady Davenport left the chateau bound for England, the servants began preparations to honor Robert's last wish.

Later that day and before the sunset, the servants took

Robert's body to the river, where they learned Elizabeth's body was tossed, then placed him in a small boat filled with white and yellow daisies.

Everyone gathered around the boat holding hands, then said a small prayer for Robert and his wife, Elizabeth. When they heard what was done to her body, they were horrified and saddened at the loss of two young people.

When they completed the prayer, two male servants pushed the boat out into the lake while the others tossed more daisies on Robert's body. Once the boat reached the middle of the river, Jon, the boy servant, shot a flaming arrow into the boat, and it immediately burst into flames.

"Now, Lord Robert can be with his wife Lady Elizabeth in death, as he was with her in life," said Jaqueline.

As the servants watched the boat burn, George looked at Jo, who held the necklace in her hand. They talked about what they were going to do with the necklace, and at first, they decided to keep it. But, then with what's happened, they felt it was wrong to keep the necklace and decided there, in a silent agreement, they tossed the necklace in the river to be with Robert and Elizabeth where it rightfully belonged. They did this out of honor and respect and for the boy they loved.

***

On the ship returning to England, Lord Davenport replayed the events from the moment he learned about Robert and Elizabeth's relationship to their secret wedding, and it only fueled his already seething anger.

This is that girl's fault! She bewitched my son! She did something to lure him to her, thus, taking him away from his family! Lord Davenport thought.

Lord Davenport decided the events that led to his son's death, he concluded was the fault of Baron and Baroness Massey – the whole family.

Now, I am beginning to understand why our families went their separate ways all those years ago! Their family is evil, and their daughter a witch! They bewitched my son, and they will all be punished for it! Lord Davenport thought.

"Sir Isaac and Sir Edward, after we arrive in England, I want you to inform the men we will be riding directly to Dunham Massey to see Baron Massey! He is going to pay for the death of my son! Sir Isaac, have two of your men escort Lady Davenport back to Bramhall Manor! Once she is safe within the walls, have them gather the rest of the men and meet us at Dunham Massey!"

"Yes, My Lord," said Sir Isaac.

This decision concerned Sir Isaac. For Lord Davenport to make such a decision in the state of mind he was in, he believed was a grave mistake. Furthermore, Lord Davenport's anger was clouding his judgment at the loss of his son. To protect Lord Davenport from his own actions, he and Sir Edward formed their own plan.

"We will send two men with Lady Davenport down River Mersey, while the rest of us continue on the road with Lord Davenport. I hope by taking the longer route, it will allow Lord Davenport time to cool down; thus, reconsider his decision," said Sir Isaac.

"Yes, I agree," said Sir Edward.

But, to both of their surprise, Lord Davenport elected to take River Mersey as well, not wanting to waste any time getting back to Cheshire to confront Baron Massey.

***

Upon the Davenport's return to Cheshire, Lord Davenport did as he said, and he immediately went to see Baron Massey. One, to inform Baron Massey of Elizabeth and Robert's death. Two, to address the more serious matter.

Lord Davenport met up with the rest of his men at the edge of Dunham Massey Castle and together continued to Baron Massey's cottage.

When Lord Davenport arrived with his small party of

men at Baron Massey's cottage, ready to fight if required, he sent one of his men to knock on the door, where a housemaid greeted him.

Now at the door, Lord Davenport said, "Take me directly to see Baron Massey!"

The maid curtsied to Lord Davenport, and without delay, escorted him to Baron Massey's study, but he did not wait for the maid to announce him.

Lord Davenport said in a hostile voice, "Your daughter is dead and by her own hand! Not only your daughter but my son as well! Your daughter is to blame! She cursed my son by bewitching him! She and your family are witches!

Your daughter cast a spell on my son and forced him to fall in love with her! Then, she forced him to marry her against his will! I should have seen right through your disguise, that this was your plan all along! You and your family are in league with the devil, casting your evil black magic to get what you want! Now, I know why Davenport's and Massey's discontinued their friendship all those years ago! You and your daughter bewitched my son, and all of you will pay dearly!" Lord Davenport yelled, not giving Baron Massey a chance to say a word until he was finished.

Baron Massey was shocked at Lord Davenport's accusation, "What in God's name are you talking about! There is nothing of the sort going on here, nor are we in league with the devil! You know very well that we are a family of God! How dare you come into my home and accuse us of such!" Baron Massey yelled back, then said, "What do you mean Elizabeth is dead?"

"Because of you and your hatred of your daughter, my son is dead! You, who believed a man who claimed to be a man of God…was not! You took his words as truth! You did not even consider he could be wrong! You should have taken the time to talk to me first! In doing so, you would have learned the truth! But no, you chose to listen to this man, and now your daughter, along with my son, are dead! You, you are to blame! No matter what they did, my son would never have pretended to be married! They were truly married, and you gave your daughter to a horrible man! In doing this, you caused their deaths! You are completely to blame!"

At Lord Davenport's words and accusation, Baron Massey was stunned. He did not know what to say or how to respond. He only stood there, staring at the man, trying to understand what could have caused Lord Davenport to turn on him so quickly.

Lord Davenport watched Baron Massey's reaction as he told him what happened. His first thought was to arrest Baron Massey and his entire family on the spot, wanting nothing more than to put them to death right then and there. But instead, he decided to enforce the agreement they made all those years ago. Lord Davenport found Baron Massey at fault and in breach of the agreement.

"Baron Massey, I find you at fault and in breach of our agreement! You and your family will have seven days hence to leave Cheshire! In doing so, you are never to return! Per our agreement, I have found you at fault. Therefore, you forfeit everything you own! You will leave here with nothing but the clothes on your backs! If you, or any of your family return to Cheshire, for any reason, will be immediately put to death!"

Baron Massey tried to object but was silenced by Lord Davenport! Then after, without further words, Lord Davenport turned and left Baron Massey's cottage. His next stop was to the priest who was present the day the agreement was signed, and then to his legal counsel to have a decree drawn up.

After being threatened by Lord Davenport and given little information, the Massey's were horrified and loss of what to do. What can they do? They had no authority. Everything was dependent on Robert Davenport marrying

their daughter Grace. When that failed, they expected
something to happen, but this? They hoped, with the help
of King Francis, all would have been forgotten. Then, when
Robert spoke to Baron Massey, needing to know what
happened with his conversation with King Francis, there
was hope once again. Now, they were being forced to leave
the land they held so dear to them. Where were they to go?
What would they do?

Chapter Twenty-Nine

<u>Decree of Judgement</u>

Baron John Hamon Massey the Second, along with Baroness Elizabeth Marie Massey, Lady Grace Rachel Marie Massey, and their youngest son, Lord John Hamon Massey the Third of Dunham Massey, Cheshire England.

On the twenty-first day of the sixth month in the year of our Lord 1536, this decree is entered against Baron John Hamon Massey the Second and his entire family.

I, Lord John Davenport, magistrate of Cheshire, being the law of this land do hereby order; one, Baron John Hamon Massey the Second, one, Baroness Elizabeth Marie Massey, one, Grace Rachel Massey, and one, John Hamon Massey the Third, to be banished from this land of Cheshire and all nearby lands which are under my control. This is to be done in seven days hence after the signing of this decree. If Baron John Hamon Massey the Second and his family refuse to leave, or in after leaving return for any reason to this land, will be immediately put to death. This, due to the failure of honoring the agreement forged by Baron John Hamon Massey the Second and Lord John Davenport at the time of Robert Davenport and Grace Rachel Massey's births, in the year of our Lord 1516, to whom were to marry in their seventeenth year of life.

This agreement being broken by Baron John Hamon Massey the Second, due to one, Elizabeth Marie Massey, after she bewitched my first-born son and heir, Robert Davenport. In doing so, Baron John Hamon Massey the Second forfeits all they own: land, money, title, and power. They are ordered to leave Cheshire in seven days hence from the date of this decree, taking nothing but the clothes they wear on the day the decree is presented to them.

So ordered by,

Lord Davenport and Sir Isaac, along with his legal counsel, returned to Dunham Massey and presented Baron Massey with Lord Davenport's decree. Once Lord Davenport was gone, Baroness Massey voiced her concern.

"John, what are we going to do?" asked Baroness Massey.

"My dear, I cannot say, but we are what he says…we are at fault with the terms of our agreement!" Baron Massey yelled, then turned his anger to Elizabeth. "Elizabeth, that ungrateful girl! I curse her soul! I hope she never finds peace!"

Grace was standing outside her father's study and was horrified to learn what happened to Elizabeth and Robert. What was she going to do? It was all her fault. If she just did what her father wanted, Elizabeth would still be alive and with her right now.

"It is all my fault," she whispered.

Baroness Massey was so upset; she was in tears at what had befallen them.

"Oh, my dear, where are we to go? Who would take us in? We are ruined and disgraced!" she said in hysterics. "No one will accept us! They will be too afraid to associate themselves with the like of us!"

Baron Massey goes to his wife with the need to comfort her, but instead, he became outraged. He refused to give up everything he worked so hard for.

"Wait! It was not just Elizabeth's fault! Robert had a great deal to do with what happened! Why should we be forced to give up everything and the Davenport's nothing? We are going to stay and fight!" he yelled, with a firm finger pointing down at the floor. "We are not going to allow Lord Davenport to take what is ours! There are those who are loyal to me! I am sure, and if called upon, they will help me defend our land! I will spend the time Lord Davenport has given us to gather those loyal and prepare for battle! We will fight for our rights and our land!”

At hearing this, Baroness Massey started to panic. She was afraid, because if Baron Massey failed, they would immediately forfeit their lives.

“How can you consider doing such a thing! Do you believe you can stand up against Lord Davenport and his men! Some of his men are the hardest men England has ever seen!”

Baron Massey looked at his wife, appalled by her lack of confidence in his ability to defend what is his. *How dare she doubt my ability!* he thought.

“Shut your mouth, woman! Do not speak of what you do not know!”

Grace was still standing outside her father’s study, listening to what he was saying to her mother, and she gasped at the idea of her father fighting Lord Davenport. *This is all my fault,* she thought.

Never in Grace’s life has she heard her mother and father talk to each other in such a way. She had always seen them being affectionate and loving towards each other. To listen to them talk this way hurt her heart, again she thought, *this is my fault,* shaking her head.

Baroness Massey was horrified. She knew if her husband failed to defeat Lord Davenport, they would immediately be put to death. She had to think of her daughter Grace and their son John and make her husband see reason.

“John, let’s send Grace and John to our family in France to give them a chance at a life if we fail?” Baroness Massey pleaded with her husband.

Grace again gasped, but this time louder than she intended, and her father heard her. Baron Massey pulled open the door, and Grace was shocked when she saw her father. He was so angry. The look on his face was one she’d never seen before, of a man who was ready to kill.

"Grace! What are you doing here! Get to your chambers at once!" Baron Massey yelled.

Without a word, Grace grabbed up her gown and raced up the stairs to her chamber, then collapsed on her bed in tears.

This is all my fault! she thought, slamming her fist on her mattress.

Baron Massey slammed the door shut and returned to the conversation he was having with his wife.

"What do you mean we?" asked Baron Massey.

"My love, I am not pleased with your decision," said Baroness Massey, reaching for her husband's hand, "But I will stand with you no matter what. To ask this of our children…please, my love, we must save our children?"

At hearing his wife's words – her plea, Baron Massey calmed down and took his wife in his arms and said, "My love, I am sorry for what has befallen us. I will agree to send Grace to France, but not John. He is now of age, and he will stand with his father to protect what one day will be his."

Baroness Massey was unhappy at hearing her husband's decision, but she knew there would be no changing his mind. If she could not save both her children, she would at least save one, so she agreed to send Grace to their family in France for their daughter's protection.

Baron Massey sent an urgent message to gather those men who were still loyal to him and brave enough to go against Lord Davenport and his mercenaries. Although they were few, they were strong and willing to die for Baron Massey.

***

As magistrate, Lord Davenport held the power of law in the land, and as he approached Baron Massey's cottage with his large band of men, with the illusion as if they were hidden inside what appeared to be a dark cloud and their approach sounded like fierce thunder.

Baron Massey stood at the outline of his estate, adjacent to Dunham Massey Castle. As a member of the Massey family, he tried to get the Booth's to join in the fight. The additional men would have given support and strength against Lord Davenport and his men. However, Lord Booth refused, wanting nothing to do with the fight or Baron Massey's dispute with Lord Davenport. Thus, leaving Baron Massey with a few men who came to standby him to fight. At seeing the number of men – soldiers, not the mercenaries he expected, he knew before the fight began, he was already defeated.

To see Lord Davenport, his mercenaries, and his soldiers, they were like an army going to a battle. They were too great for Baron Massey and his men to fight. Baron Massey looked left and right to the men standing beside him and decided – knowing what the end would be; he would not allow these loyal men to lose their lives, to die for nothing. No, he would not allow it, and therefore, he laid down his sword and surrendered.

I will ask Lord Davenport to show mercy to my wife and son, as they are not to blame. It was I who wanted to fight, and I am to blame, Baron Massey thought.

Baron Massey prayed that Lord Davenport would grant him mercy, but it was not to be.

Once Lord Davenport saw Baron Massey and his men drop their swords in surrender, he ordered his men to arrest Baron Massey and place him in shackles.

Baron Massey made his plea, but Lord Davenport refused to listen. However, he did grant every man who stood with Baron Massey mercy, so long as they declare their loyalty to him, he would allow them to live and return to the safety of their homes and families. The men turned to Baron Massey, and Baron Massey nodded to the men to accept. He did not see any reason for these men to suffer his fate.

After the men who stood with Baron Massey left, Lord Davenport ordered his men to arrest his son John and to find and arrest Baroness Massey and their daughter Grace Massey.

Lord Davenport's men found and brought Baroness Massey to stand beside her husband. They informed him they could not find Grace Massey, as she was nowhere to be found in the cottage.

"Baron Massey, where is your daughter Grace?" Lord Davenport demanded.

Baron Massey refused to answer as he watched his wife and son being placed in shackles.

Lord Davenport stood and watched his men shackle the Massey's and rip away their jewelry, along with any sign of nobility from their body, leaving them with nothing but the clothes and shoes they wore. Although they were not the clothes he originally ordered for them to wear per his decree, Lord Davenport waved away this mishap and had the Massey's thrown in the caged cart. This was done because he wanted the Massey's on display for all the people to see as they rode through the village to Chester Castle, where they were to be imprisoned pending their sentencing. He ordered a few of his men to remain behind to continue searching for Grace Massey, but no matter how hard they searched, they failed to find any trace of her.

Once at Chester Castle, the Massey's were taken to the crypt at Agricola Tower, where they would wait to learn of their fate. They knew their lives were forfeited, but to how and when Lord Davenport would choose to execute them was unknown. Would it be immediate, or would he make them suffer by forcing them to wait, making them wonder when and how it would be? So, when Lord Davenport announced their execution would be a public affair, and on the following morning when the sun was high in the sky. Baron Massey was not surprised, and at the same time, relieved.

Baron Massey was placed in a cell and shackled to the wall along with his wife and son as they waited to learn how they would be executed. They cuddled together in a corner, trying to keep warm. This is when they felt how frightened their son was. He was shaking fiercely, and it had nothing to do with the cold.

"Mother, I am so scared. How can this be happening?" Little John asked.

Baroness Massey's heart ached for her son. He was too young to endure such a fate that waited them.

"Oh, my son, I am sorry you are a part of this. If there were anything we could do to save you from this fate, we would do so without question," Baroness Massey said, looking at her husband.

Baroness Massey pulled her son closer to her breast, wanting to give him all the comfort she could, at the same time trying to hold back her tears, but failed. She wanted to be strong for her son, but in their situation, it was too difficult.

While Baron Massey watched his wife and son, he could not help his thoughts: *what have I done? I allowed my anger and my honor to control my actions.* Then he placed all blame on his daughter. *Elizabeth, how could you have done this to your own family. Did we not love you? Give you everything you needed. Was it not enough to go behind our backs and get married? Now, for what you did, you have destroyed...killed us all. If I am to see you when I come before God for judgment, I will slap you before God can issue judgment on me, thus, sending me to purgatory.*

Baron Massey was angry, enraged; he was boiling with it.

***

Lord Davenport was sitting in his study, mulling over the recent events.

"How did things get to this point? Because I was a fool. A stubborn fool is how," he said while drinking strong

Scottish whisky he obtained on his last visit to Scotland.

Lord Davenport formed a hard shell around himself after what happened to his son in France. But now, it was starting to fall away. In this, he was now feeling the pain his anger concealed.

"If I just allowed Robert to marry Elizabeth…we could have changed the agreement if we both agreed.

"My love," Lady Davenport said.

Lord Davenport raised his head when he heard his wife's voice. "Mary, what are you doing up at this late hour?"

"How could I sleep after what happened. When you didn't come to our bed, I thought I would come down to check on you."

Lord Davenport jester for his wife to come to him where he sat at his desk, and she was surprised when he grabbed her around the waist and sat her on his lap.

"Mary, I may not have been the easiest man to live with, and I know I have not been an easy man to love. But know my heart aches at the loss of our first son. Robert was the man I could never be. He would have succeeded me in more ways I could not."

Mary was taken aback by her husband's confession. She was seeing a man she had not known before. She placed her hand on the side of his face and was surprised to see him lean into her touch as he closed his eyes. It made her wonder, *is it possible I mean more to him than I believed?*

As if he was reading her mind, Lord Davenport said, "Mary, although I have not shown you much affection…know, I do feel for you. After a time, you have proven to be the right woman for me, and in those times, even today, a small place in my heart has opened for you."

Lord Davenport struggled with what he was trying to say. It wasn't something he's ever spoken of, and being the hard man he was, it was difficult, nor did he think the words would form again.

"Mary, this is difficult for me. It is not easy for a man such as me to say but —"

Mary stopped him and said, "It is not necessary. You love me; is that what you want to say?" she asked with hope and joy in her heart.

Lord Davenport nodded, "I am sorry, Mary; the words are difficult for me to say. I do love you, more than you know."

It shocked Lord Davenport how easy the words slipped out of his mouth, and to Lady Davenport, it filled her heart to know the man she believed could never love, loves her.

Lady Davenport placed both her hands on her husband's face, "My love, you just did," she said and kissed him.

Lord Davenport welcomed the kiss and returned it with as much passion he could. To Lady Davenport, it was more than she ever hoped for, and at that moment, it was only the two of them. Before Lady Davenport knew it, Lord Davenport was carrying her to their bedchamber, where he truly and completely made love to her for the very first time in their lives.

***

A few hours later, feeling a type of joy Lord Davenport had never felt before, he returned to his study to contemplate what he was going to do about the Massey's and concluded —

Robert was right. What did it matter who he married, so long as it was a Massey? I was a fool! Now, I shall live knowing that I am the one, the reason why my son is dead, and the cause of the ruin of a good family, Lord Davenport thought. But then, after further thought, *maybe I should change my mind and forget what happened?*

After a few moments in silent contemplation, Lord Davenport decided, "No!" he said aloud. "Baron Massey is at fault! He should have come to me directly when he was presented with King Francis's agreement! If so, I would have told him what King Francis believed was wrong, and we both could have gone to King Francis and John Bonnet and made them see the truth! After all, he was on English soil! He would dare not do anything to a lord, one within King Henry's court while on English soil. It would have forced him to release his desire to have Elizabeth!"

Lord Davenport slammed his fist down on his desk, "No! That fool will die on the morrow, along with his wife and son! And when Grace is found, she too will be put on display and die in the same manner of her family!" Lord Davenport yelled to the rafters. "I should have executed them right on the spot!" Then he thought, "No, it is best to make a show of my power to the people! You go against me; you die! They will hang at Pentice on the morrow when the sun is high in the sky!"

***

Lady Davenport woke in the morning feeling happier than she's felt in a long time. Although her heart ached for the loss of her son, it eased some with the love she now felt for her husband. When she reached for Lord Davenport, she was disappointed to find he wasn't there, but at the same time, she was not surprised. She knew he was trying to decide what he was going to do with the Massey's, and she hoped after what she heard last night, he had reconsidered his decision and will release them.

Lady Davenport rose out of bed with a newfound glow on her face. *I should be ashamed to feel such joy when there has been such destruction and loss of life,* she thought.

Lady Davenport went to the window and looked to the sky, "Robert, my son, my heart breaks at the loss of you. But my son, something amazing happened. Something I never believed I would find. I think I understand more now of the love you had for Elizabeth. It may not be the same, but feeling what I feel for your father…I cannot help better to understand why you did what you did. No matter what, you will always hold a place in my heart until the day comes when we meet again. Oh, Robert, I love you so much, and I pray God will grant you your request in allowing you and Elizabeth to be together for eternity."

Lady Davenport turned and lit a candle, one for Robert and one for Elizabeth, then called for her maid to help her dress so that she could begin her day.

***

It was the morning of the execution, and Lord Davenport was feeling restless – fueled with anger. He could not sleep and decided in the early morning hours to ride to Chester Castle, where he will wait until it was time for the Massey's execution. He had hoped, if he rode slowly on the long road to Chester Castle, along with the cool night air, it would help clear his mind. Unfortunately, it failed, doing nothing to cool his raging anger. Instead, it continued to build – festering beyond control.

Lord Davenport was sitting in the great hall when the time arrived. "Bring forth Baron John Hamon Massey the Second, Baroness Elizabeth Marie Massey, and John Hamon Massey the Third for sentencing," Lord Davenport ordered the castle guards, who were holding the Massey's outside the doors of the great hall.

Once the Massey's were standing before Lord Davenport, he said, "I, Lord Davenport, as magistrate, the law of this land of Cheshire, do hereby sentence you," pointing to each one as he said their full name. "Baron John Hamon Massey the Second, Baroness Elizabeth Marie Massey, and John Hamon Massey the Third, and when found, Grace Rachel Marie Massey, after being found guilty shall be put to death," he paused for a few moments then said, "You will be hanged by the neck until dead. This sentence is to take place on this day when the sun is high in the sky," Lord Davenport announced.

The Massey's were shocked, even though it was

expected. Baron and Baroness Massey looked at their son – they did not want this for him.

Lord Davenport said to the guard, "Now, take them to Gloverston and prepare them for execution."

Gloverston was a place where criminals were held who were awaiting execution. It was a tower at the front of Chester Castle, near the main gate.

As the Massey's were being led out, they were horrified at what was happening, as they were still reeling from the shock, and in some ways, they were still in disbelief at what was about to happen.

Baroness Massey pulled her son close to her chest, and when she saw how frightened he was, she felt he was too young to have to endure such a fate. She felt – she needed – she had to do something to ease John from such a fate.

Baron and Baroness Massey looked at each other, and they were relieved that they sent Grace to France, where she would be safe and free to live out her life. Suddenly, in Baroness Massey's desperation to save her son, she decided to plea to Lord Davenport.

"Milord, please spare my son. He is innocent in all this?" she pleaded as tears ran down her face.

"Innocent, you say?" Lord Davenport snarled. "That, he is not! He stood with his father against me with a sword in his hand, prepared to fight!" he said. "No! He will die with you today!" he yelled, then took a moment to contemplate this decision and said, "If I were to grant him his freedom, how will I know he won't one day, when he is a man, he will not try to take his revenge on my son Edward or on me, then claim his right…no! He will die today as ordered!" It was Lord Davenport's final words on the matter.

Baroness Massey was devastated at Lord Davenport's decision. No, there was no way she could guarantee her son would not seek revenge, even if she made him promise not to. There was no saying what he would do once he was a man. Knowing this was not going to work, she proceeded to ask for another request from Lord Davenport.

"My Lord, will you allow my son something that will ease…make his passing quick?" Baroness Massey asked.

Lord Davenport took a moment to consider Baroness Massey's request. He looked at John for a long moment as he thought, *yes, he is very young. It cannot hurt to allow the boy some ease before he hangs.* So, he agreed to give the boy something to ease his passing, "You?" he called to a guard standing next to the Massey's. "Ask the physician for something to give the boy that will make his death easier," Lord Davenport ordered.

The guard nodded and bowed to Lord Davenport, then turned and led the Massey's out of the great hall.

***

The sun was just about at its highest peak in the sky when Lord Davenport addressed the people of Cheshire.

"All, here me now!" he called, and the people quickly went silent. "I, Lord Davenport, magistrate of this great land, have called all you here to bear witness," turning towards the Massey's who were standing at the edge of the gallows.

Standing near Massey's son was a guard to hold the boy still since he was swaying from the concoction the physician gave him.

"To the execution of Baron John Hamon Massey the Second, his wife, Baroness Elizabeth Marie Massey, and their son, John Hamon Massey the Third, are to be put to death, hanged until they are dead!"

At first, everyone gasped when they saw the look on Lord Davenport's face. Then, their gasp turned to an enormous roar of acceptance at his announcement. Although they were shocked at what was happening, no one understood how two families who were so close, was now, with one ending up being executed. They had no choice but to show their support to Lord Davenport, even if they disagreed with it, or they too could be facing the gallows. Whatever came between Lord Davenport and the Massey's, they knew it had to be great for it to come to this – for one to execute the other, even though they didn't know the reason, and no one would dare question Lord Davenport's decision.

At Lord Davenport's signal, the guards lined up each Massey to a noose, then placed the noose around their necks, tightening the knot. Initially, the executioner went to each noose to ensure it was done correctly, to ensure their necks broke when they dropped, thus, giving them a quick death. Once this was complete, the executioner waited for Lord Davenport's signal for him to pull the lever, which would work in rapid motion, hanging them all at once. First, Baron Massey would drop, then Baroness Massey, and right after, their son John Massey. But then, Lord Massey called the executioner over and whispered something in his ear, before he returned to his post to do another check of the nooses.

"All you here, know this, their deaths are due to the practice of witchcraft!"

The crowd gasped with shock before letting out a roar of acceptance.

"Witchcraft will not be tolerated in my land!" Lord Davenport said in a loud and firm voice. One, that was not to be questioned. "If any others are discovered practicing witchcraft, they too will suffer the same fate, if not worse!"

After Lord Davenport took a few moments to listen to the crowd roar, he raised his arm to silence them. When he dropped his arm, it was the executioner's signal to pull the lever, hanging the Massey's and ending their lives.

Lord Davenport dropped his arm, and the executioner pulled the lever, but something went wrong. Their deaths were not immediate; they hung for thirty minutes as they slowly strangled before they finally succumbed. Except for their son John, he was the lucky one. Whatever the physician gave the boy, he was dead before the executioner pulled the lever – a mercy death.

What everyone did not know, Lord Davenport had the executioner fix the nooses, wanting Baron and Baroness Massey to suffer a slow and agonizing death, as he would suffer from the loss of his son.

***

The men loyal to Baron Massey watched from a distance, remaining hidden and out of view from the crowd and Lord Davenport. They watched in horror at the horrible event that took place.

When they saw Baron and Baroness Massey and their son John were finally dead, they approach Lord Davenport and requested permission to retrieve their bodies so that they could give them a proper burial.

Lord Davenport did not care what happened to the Massey's and so agreed. However, there was a stipulation, so long as they were buried outside his lands and not on consecrated ground.

Without question, the men agreed, knowing it was fruitless to protest. So, the men went and took possession of the Massey's bodies, then took them to a place only known to them and buried their bodies in unmarked graves.

***

When Baron Massey planned to fight Lord Davenport, he informed his men that he sent his daughter Grace to France. If they failed, one of the men would write to Grace and notified her of their deaths.

After they buried the Massey's, one of the men immediately sent word to Grace, informing her of the tragic news of her family's tragic death.

***

My Dear Child,
I keep this letter as discrete as possible for yours, as well as our protection. My dear girl, I send you grievous

news. Your mother, father, and brother John were executed this day by Lord Davenport. I will leave out the details of their deaths, as there is no need for you to have the details to be your last memory of your family. It is best to remember them as the loving mother and father and adored brother they were. The reason given by Lord Davenport for their execution was accusing you and your family of practicing witchcraft. This, my child, is all I will tell you.

I am deeply sorry, my child, as we all know the true nature of their deaths. Your mother and father feared for your safety and asked that you never return to England. Lord Davenport does not know you are in France, and even as I write this letter, they search for you. If you return for any reason and are found by Lord Davenport or his men, he has ordered your death on sight. Your mother and father prayed that their family would allow you to stay and accept you as one of their own. This was their hope and last wish. I also enclosed a letter to them as well.

My child, your mother, and your father do not want you to grieve for their deaths but to take this opportunity and live a full and happy life. They have provided all that you will need. Therefore, honor them in this request.

Remember, my child, your mother and father loved you very much.

Signed,
A Friend.

After Grace read the letter, she dropped it to the floor. She was horrified and shocked at what became of her family. *No, this cannot be so. Little John? God, tell me this is not so?* she thought.

Grace was devastated. Her heart was breaking at the loss of her entire family. She was relieved when her aunt came to her and took her in her arms, allowing her to cry for the loss of her family. Her thoughts went to what Lord

Davenport accused her family of – *witchcraft? How could he accuse them of witchcraft?* she thought.

This made no sense to Grace, and at the thought, she completely lost it, and her aunt just held her and allowed her to grieve, to release all the pain she's been holding back.

Grace would do what her mother and father asked of her; she will never return to England, and do her best to make a good life in France.

When Grace finally pulled herself together, she asked her aunt and uncle if they would agree to allow her to remain with them and become a part of their family. Without hesitation, they so agreed. However, to do so, she would no longer be a Massey but take their own family name. This was done to protect and keep her safe.

Grace would honor her mother, father, brother, and her sister by living. Grace was determined to only marry for love, as she wanted what her sister found and felt. She believed this was the best way to honor her sister Elizabeth by marrying for love. If love were not found, then she'd take what her parents gave her, the trunk of everything they owned, to make a life of herself.

Grace looked over at the trunks her father sent her to France with. She hadn't opened them but now wondered what was inside. So, she went over and kneeled in front of the trunks and opened them, and was shocked at what she found – they contained all her family's riches: clothes, jewels, and money.

After the shock wore off, Grace understood the reasons why they were there. It was to prevent Lord Davenport from claiming their riches for himself. All he will receive was what was left in their cottage. Since the land was owned by the Booth's, there wasn't much left.

With her aunt and uncle's assistance, Grace found a place to hide her trunks until the day came when she would require them.

***

Grace lived a wonderful and adventurous life. Yes, after reading all those books, she finally found happiness in her own adventures. And yes, she did find love, but never forgot the love she had for her family and her dear and beloved sister Elizabeth, who she never blamed for what happened.

Because it was me, I was to blame. And for you, Elizabeth, I will love for us both, she thought, as she held her newborn daughter, whom she named Elizabeth after her sister.

***

The tragedy of losing Robert and Elizabeth was great. A whole family was destroyed, but also, a love was discovered. If Elizabeth only saw through King Francis's and John Bonnet's lies, she would have been home with her family, a reunion that would have bound their families as they always wanted. Instead, it took that one decision to create a domino effect that ended in the destruction of many that day, including John Bonnet, who ended up being exiled from his beloved France.

Epilogue

It's dark. Why is it dark? Where am I? What has happened? Elizabeth is so confused. She doesn't understand what's happened. Then she sees what appears to be a light. *Wait, what is that flash of light. What is that light? It's growing, getting bigger. What happened? Where am I?* Elizabeth tried to look around to see where she might be, but all for the light, everything else around her is dark—pitch black dark.

Why can I not see? Wait, the light, it appears to be getting brighter, and…it's white. I see someone. Elizabeth squints her eyes, trying to make out the person walking towards her. *Who is that coming, walking towards me? Is it Robert?* As the person gets closer, she can see it's not Robert. *No, it's not Robert. It's a man…he looks…he looks like the man on the holy cross.*

Although Elizabeth hoped she would meet Jesus when she died, she never believed it was possible, especially after taking her own life.

Is it possible? Could it be Jesus walking towards me? He's wearing a white robe. Elizabeth looked down at herself, *I too, am wearing a white robe.* Then she looked back up to the man approaching, she believed was Jesus walking towards her. *If it is him…Jesus, this gives me hope.* Then a realization hit her, *Robert, it must be Robert, he must be with Jesus.* Elizabeth looked around and tried to see behind the man she believed was Jesus, but she could not see Robert. There was no one else, and Elizabeth was saddened with disappointment.

When the man reached her, "Where is Robert? Is he here?" Elizabeth asked, feeling anxious to see Robert.

The man took Elizabeth's hand and said, "My dear child, no, he is not here yet, Elizabeth, but he will be soon. What have you done?" The man said with sadness.

Elizabeth looked at the man and saw the sadness on his face, along with disappointment.

Filled with shame, Elizabeth adverted her eyes; she was unable to look at him, then said, "I am sorry." Then, wondering where she was, Elizabeth turned back and looked up at the man, "Where am I?" she asked, looking around.

Elizabeth was in a place where nothing existed but her and this man. It was white, so white as if they were in a place surrounded by clouds.

The man, still holding her hand, said, "You are in a place between life and heaven. This is a place where one goes who does not belong in heaven. A place for those who need to prove themselves again."

"What do you mean?" Elizabeth asked, not understanding what was happening to her.

"I will explain more after Robert arrives."

"He's not already here?" Looking around, "He should have arrived before me," Elizabeth said, not understanding this. Then, looking back at the man, "Are you…are you who I believe you to be? Are you Lord Jesus?"

The man smiled, "Yes, my child, I am the man you know as Jesus."

Elizabeth smiled; she was honored to have the son of God greet her when she arrived.

"Do you always greet those who pass over?" she asked.

Shaking his head, "No, my child. I only appear on special cases, such as yours."

Elizabeth's attention wavered as she wondered where Robert was since he was supposed to have arrived before her.

"Where is Robert?" she asked again.

"In good time, all will be revealed. First, I must speak with you, Elizabeth. God is very angry with you. But he is more hurt than angry, because you did not allow him to help you. You gave up before you gave him time. If only you waited? It is too late now. And now, you must suffer the consequences of your decision.

My child, evil is at hand, and there is nothing I can do to help you. Since you took your own life, I am prevented from intervening. God will not allow it. This is something you must learn from and correct. With this evil…I am sorry, Elizabeth," Jesus said.

He was heartbroken that one of his cherished children hurt herself by taking her own life. One, he'd been watching and caring for since she was born. For what she did, it hurt him, and he wanted to help Elizabeth, but due to her actions, his hands were tied. No matter how much he wanted to, he could not intervene. It was up to Elizabeth and Robert; they had to prove themselves.

"What do you mean, this evil?" Elizabeth asked.

"There is someone who wants revenge on you, and because of this, this person has chosen to work with a great evil. This evil, as we speak, is working to curse your soul. I have tried, and I am unable to prevent this, since you chose to give up your life before it was your time. Because of this, God will not allow me to protect you. This is something you must learn and correct yourself," Jesus said, with sadness in his voice.

"How? What am I to do?" Elizabeth asked. Then, she saw a figure, what looked to be coming out of the clouds – it was Robert. "Robert! There's Robert! He's coming," Elizabeth said, full of joy to finally see her beloved Robert again.

Elizabeth was so happy to see Robert, and she noticed that he also was dressed in a long white robe. Then Robert and Elizabeth were standing in front of each other, and without delay, they embraced, and Jesus stood back to allow them a moment for their reunion before explaining what must happen next.

"My children," Jesus said, interrupting their reunion, needing to get Robert and Elizabeth's attention. "We must speak. Walk with me as I explain." Jesus motioned with his arm for them to follow him, and side by side, they walked together. "You both have done a great wrong in taking your own lives. God is not happy about this. As I was telling Elizabeth, evil is at hand trying to prevent you from being together. I am afraid there is nothing I can do to help," Jesus said, feeling the sadness he could not conceal from his voice. "I went to God and asked him, and he said you both made your choice; therefore, nothing can be done."

It broke his heart to see two of his children standing before him and before their time. Then to have evil working against him, and he was prevented – not allowed to stop it. This was difficult for Jesus, but he could not deny what God said. It was a choice Robert and Elizabeth made. A choice only they could correct.

Robert turned to Jesus and said, "I was going to ask God if he would allow Elizabeth and I to remember our love, and if he will allow us to find each other again. Will he not listen to my request now?" Robert asked.

"Before I explain further, there is something you both need to know. Elizabeth, Robert was not dead when you took your own life," Jesus said.

Elizabeth looked at Jesus with horror and surprise.

"He took his life only after hearing of your death."

Elizabeth placed her hand over her mouth. She was shocked at hearing this. "No. Please tell me this is not true?"

"I am sorry, Elizabeth, it is true."

Holding each other, Robert and Elizabeth could feel each other's pain, along with Elizabeth's guilt in her decision.

"Elizabeth, the child you were carrying when you took your life…" Robert looked at Elizabeth, shocked at what he just learned. But Jesus continued without stopping, "The child was Roberts."

"God no! Please tell me it is not so?" Elizabeth said in anguish, with the decision she made.

Robert and Elizabeth were holding each other tight, filled with pain and regret. They saw the mistakes they made in not trusting in God and in their love.

Jesus turned to Robert to answer his question about speaking to God. "Robert, he will not." That was all he said, then he stopped in front of a large window, that looked like swirling water. "Here we are. See this window," Jesus said, pointing at the swirling water. "You and Elizabeth will step through this window where you will be reborn. This usually does not happen so soon, but it was all I could do for you, by giving you another chance at life right away. Unfortunately, you will not be reborn together or in the same country. You will be born far apart from each other, never allowed to find each other, except…now, this is what I was granted…because of your love, and the power of it…this was a gift given to you by God. God has agreed to allow you to remember this love," Jesus said, seeing the excitement in their eyes. "Now, this is only if or when you find each other. This will not be easy. What I can do, is bestow a gift to you both. This gift is the power of sight and knowledge. It will be up to you to take this gift and use it to find each other. If your love is strong and true, your love will lead you back to each other. At the time you connect once again, the memories of this life will flow, allowing you to remember everything that happened. It will be up to you to take this gift and use it to bring you back to each other. There will be many challenges, but if you take what happens and learn from them, you will grow stronger, as will your gifts. To one day, when your love is the truest, you will once again find each other."

"If we do not find each other in this next life, will we be able to see each other again, here, before we are to be reborn again?" Robert asked.

"Robert, I cannot promise you this. But, if God permits it, then yes, you will."

Robert and Elizabeth hugged and kissed each other before being sent through the window of rebirth. Robert was first, but before he went through, he said, "Elizabeth, I love you. I will find you. I promise."

"Robert, I love you. I also promise to find you. We will find each other again," Elizabeth said as she watched Robert walk through the window of rebirth – he was gone. Then it was Elizabeth's turn. She turned to Jesus one last time before she too walked through the window of rebirth and was gone.

***

For the next four hundred plus years, Robert and Elizabeth were reborn but failed to find each other, as they were always born in different countries, as far as America. Robert at times found love and married, but he always felt he was missing something. It never fulfilled him or brought him true happiness but allowed him to exist.

For Elizabeth, she'd find love that turned to heartbreak, and almost in each life she lived, she took her own life after losing her love by jumping to her death.

The End.

Stay tuned for book two, Love Across Time, when in the twentieth – twenty-first century their story continues.

www.ingramcontent.com/pod-product-compliance
Lightning Source LLC
Chambersburg PA
CBHW060809120726
47909CB00006B/1836